NUMBER 1
FALL 2017
DEADLY PLANETS

COVER: ED VALIGURSKY
INTERIOR ILLUSTRATIONS: H.R. VAN DONGEN,
L.N. ROGNAN, JACK GAUGHAN, AND KURT RÖSCHL

EDITOR AND PUBLISHER: TOM ENGLISH
COLUMNISTS: MATT COWAN; TODD TREICHEL
PRODUCTION STAFF: HAL-9000, ROBBIE R. AND ROBOT B-9

Black Infinity #1 (Fall 2017): Special Deadly Planets Issue published by Rocket Science Books, an imprint of Dead Letter Press. Editorial contents copyright Tom English and Dead Letter Press, PO Box 134, New Kent, VA 23124-0134. All rights reserved, including the right to reproduce this book, or portions thereof, in any form including but not limited to electronic and print media, without written permission from the publisher.

Black Infinity is published quarterly by Rocket Science Books, an imprint of Dead Letter Press.

Printed in the United States of America

ISBN-13: 978-0996693677

PLEASE STAND BY

ASK THE AVERAGE PERSON what comes to mind in regards to typical science fiction fare. Some will affectionately mention seeking "out new life and new civilizations" aboard an impregnable starship with gleaming corridors, polished instrument panels, and a resident alien who's well-mannered and always washes behind his pointed ears. Others may reach further back into the history of the genre, describing a cosmos littered with inviting planets inhabited by friendly, beautiful natives who just can't wait to hook up with space travelers from earth.

These people aren't wrong. But what about the giant hairy spider that usually shows up in time to devour some hapless guy in a red shirt?

On that note, welcome to the premiere issue of *Black Infinity*—brought to you by a handful of creators who enjoy a healthy dash of horror in their science fiction, in stories and movies that emphasize the strange and unsettling. *And we are not alone!*

Indeed, alongside all those "sense of wonder" stories in which spaceflight is commonplace and 100% safe, and the galaxy is brimming with "Class M" worlds both warm and welcoming, there are countless SF novels and stories, movies and TV shows that are more *weird* than wonderful.

From its auspicious beginnings science fiction has served up both varieties, as exemplified by the works of the two fathers of the literary genre, Jules Verne and H. G. Welles. Verne took his readers on fantastic journeys: into beautiful cathedral-sized caverns, in *Journey to the Center of the Earth* (1864); and down to the fascinating ocean depths, in *Twenty Thousand Leagues Under the Sea* (1870). On these scenic trips into the unexplored and unknown, there's hardly ever anything to worry about—not from the unknown, that is.

Welles, on the other hand, tried his best to scare the socks off readers. In *The Island of Doctor Moreau* (1896) he demonstrated that science is not always your friend; in *The Time Machine* (1897) he suggested a less-than-bright future; and in *The War of the Worlds* (1898) he warned that you can't always trust your neighbors.

Fast forward to the twentieth century. Throughout the 1930s and 40s, matinee audiences were treated to self-assured space heroes such as Flash Gordon and Buck Rogers, who never failed to save the day from space armadas and diabolical death rays, to triumph over your average interplanetary despot (who looks all too human)—while winning the heart of your average alien princess (who's just as cute and sweet as the girl next door). And then *IT* happened: moviegoers seemed to mature, growing a bit more cynical, well aware that the world had changed and life was now somehow *different*.

Two bloody World Wars had proved that evil *can* prevail, at least long enough to do some serious damage; and we can't always depend on our neighbors to *immediately* do the right thing. Not to mention that, with nuclear annihilation suddenly a very possible threat, science was proving to be just as scary as it was promising.

These darker themes quickly invaded Tinsel Town and took the shine off science fiction movies. Soon what was playing out on theatre screens across the country reflected widespread feelings of uncertainty, paranoia and fear. Shortly after George Pal produced

the serious and optimistic 1950 film *Destination Moon* (based on a story by Robert A. Heinlein), creepier movie fare wormed its way into the hearts of audiences, with such iconic films as Howard Hawks' *The Thing from Another World* (1951); Ray Bradbury's *It Came from Outer Space* (1953); Nigel Kneale's *The Quatermass Xperiment* (1955); and *The Blob* (1958) with rising star Steve McQueen.

Meanwhile, over on the printed page science fiction continued to reveal its scarier side, in novels such as Richard Matheson's *I Am Legend* (1954) and *The Shrinking Man* (1956); Bradbury's story "The Foghorn" (in a 1951 issue of the popular and widely circulated mainstream magazine *The Saturday Evening Post*); and Jack Finney's classic of paranoia, *The Body Snatchers,* serialized in 1954, in *Collier's Weekly*. And of course, all these classics of spooky sci-fi were destined for the silver screen.

There are countless other examples sprinkled in the science fiction digests that proliferated throughout the decade of the 1950s. Many of these stories provided the inspiration for television shows such as *Star Trek* (which occasionally offered up a creepy episode), Rod Serling's *The Twilight Zone* and ... *The Outer Limits,* the substance of many a child's nightmares—and therefore, *fondly* remembered by those who grew up in the 60s!

What's our point? We're *not* pessimistic. We simply enjoy creepy tales that keep us on the edge of our seats by stoking a slow-burning sense of dread—especially when the stories are adorned with the traditional trappings of classic SF: strange science, weird worlds, hostile aliens, renegade robots ... and the cold vacuum of space.

These are the stories we'll feature in each issue of *Black Infinity*. We'll pay homage to the yellowed SF digests and classic sci-fi flicks of yesteryear. We'll showcase the talents of both seasoned writers and new voices. We'll work hard to entertain and do our best to look beautiful while doing so.

Above all, we'll provide an escape to other worlds and times—simpler, perhaps, but no less strange, no less intriguing, no less terrifying.

Once again, welcome to *Black Infinity*. Strap in and enjoy the ride.

Tom English
New Kent, VA

Scary Sci-fi at its best: above, Andrew Keir and James Donald extract Martian remains, in the 1967 Hammer movie Five Million Years to Earth, *AKA* Quatermass and the Pit; *left, Captain Kirk (William Shatner) comes close to being the next meal of the salt vampire, in "The Mantrap"—one of Star Trek's infrequent* SCARY *episodes. Which is sad, because* nobody *screams like the Shat! • Previous page, a typical television test pattern, a familiar sight during the 1960s for those who stayed up for late-night frights.*

Some planet in the galaxy must—by definition—be the toughest, meanest, nastiest of all. If Pyrrus wasn't it ... it was an awfully good approximation!

JASON dinALT sprawled in soft luxury on the couch, a large frosty stein held limply in one hand. His other hand rested casually on a pillow. The gun behind the pillow was within easy reach of his fingers. In his line of work he never took chances.

It was all highly suspicious. Jason didn't know a soul on this planet. Yet the card sent by service tube from the hotel desk had read: *Kerk Pyrrus would like to see Jason dinAlt.* Blunt and to the point. He signaled the desk to send the man up, then lowered his fingers a bit until they brushed the gun butt. The door slid open and his visitor stepped through.

A retired wrestler. That was Jason's first thought. Kerk Pyrrus was a gray-haired rock of a man. His body seemingly chiseled out of flat slabs of muscle. Then Jason saw the gun strapped to the inside of the other man's forearm, and he let his fingers drop casually behind the pillow.

"I'd appreciate it," Jason said, "if you'd take off your gun while you're in here." The other man stopped and scowled down at the gun as if he were seeing it for the first time.

"No, I never take it off." He seemed mildly annoyed by the suggestion.

Jason had his fingers on his own gun when he said, "I'm afraid I'll have to insist. I always feel a little uncomfortable around people who wear guns." He kept talking to distract attention while he pulled out his gun. Fast and smooth.

He could have been moving in slow motion for all the difference it made. Kerk Pyrrus stood rock still while the gun came out, while it swung in his direction. Not until the very last instant did he act. When he did, the motion wasn't visible. First his gun was in the arm holster—then it was aimed between Jason's eyes. It was an ugly, heavy weapon with a pitted front orifice that showed plenty of use.

And Jason knew if he swung his own weapon up a fraction of an inch more he would be dead. He dropped his arm carefully and Kerk flipped his own gun back in the holster with the same ease he had drawn it.

"Now," the stranger said, "if we're through playing, let's get down to business. I have a proposition for you."

Jason downed a large mouthful from the mug and bridled his temper. He was fast with a gun—his life had depended on it more than once—and this was the first time he had been outdrawn. It was the offhand, unimportant manner it had been done that irritated him.

"I'm not prepared to do business," he said acidly. "I've come to Cassylia for a vacation, get away from work."

"Let's not fool each other, dinAlt," Kerk said impatiently. "You've never worked at an honest job in your entire life. You're a professional gambler and that's why I'm here to see you."

Jason forced down his anger and threw the gun to the other end of the couch so he wouldn't be tempted to commit suicide. He *had* hoped no one knew him on Cassylia and was looking forward to a big kill at the Casino. He would worry about that later. This weight-lifter type seemed to know all the answers. Let him plot the course for a while and see where it led.

"All right, what do you want?"

Kerk dropped into a chair that creaked ominously under his weight, and dug an en-

velope out of one pocket. He flipped through it quickly and dropped a handful of gleaming Galactic Exchange notes onto the table. Jason glanced at them—then sat up suddenly.

"What are they—forgeries?" he asked, holding one up to the light.

"They're real enough," Kerk told him, "I picked them up at the bank. Exactly twenty-seven bills—or twenty-seven million credits. I want you to use them as a bankroll when you go to the Casino tonight. Gamble with them and win."

They looked real enough—and they could be checked. Jason fingered them thoughtfully while he examined the other man.

"I don't know what you have in mind," he said. "But you realize I can't make any guarantees. I gamble—but I don't always win …"

"You gamble—and you win when you want to," Kerk said grimly. "We looked into that quite carefully before I came to you."

"If you mean to say that I cheat—" Carefully, Jason grabbed his temper again and held it down. There was no future in getting annoyed.

Kerk continued in the same level voice, ignoring Jason's growing anger. "Maybe you don't call it cheating, frankly I don't care. As far as I'm concerned you could have your suit lined with aces and electromagnets in your boots. As long as you *won.* I'm not here to discuss moral points with you. I said I had a proposition.

"We have worked hard for that money— but it still isn't enough. To be precise, we need three billion credits. The only way to get that sum is by gambling—with these twenty-seven million as bankroll."

"And what do I get out of it?" Jason asked the question coolly, as if any bit of the fantastic proposition made sense.

"Everything above the three billion you can keep, that should be fair enough. You're not risking your own money, but you stand to make enough to keep you for life if you win."

"And if I lose—?"

Kerk thought for a moment, not liking

the taste of the idea. "Yes—there is the chance you might lose, I hadn't thought about that."

He reached a decision. "If you lose—well I suppose that is just a risk we will have to take. Though I think I would kill you then. The ones who died to get the twenty-seven million deserve at least that." He said it quietly, without malice, and it was more of a promise than a threat.

Stamping to his feet Jason refilled his stein and offered one to Kerk who took it with a nod of thanks. He paced back and forth, unable to sit. The whole proposition made him angry—yet at the same time had a fatal fascination. He was a gambler and this talk was like the taste of drugs to an addict.

Stopping suddenly, he realized that his mind had been made up for some time. Win or lose—live or die—how could he say no to the chance to gamble with money like that? He turned suddenly and jabbed his finger at the big man in the chair.

"I'll do it—you probably knew I would from the time you came in here. There are some terms of my own, though. I want to know who you are, and who *they* are you keep talking about. And where did the money come from. Is it stolen?"

Kerk drained his own stein and pushed it away from him.

"Stolen money? No, quite the opposite. Two years' work mining and refining ore to get it. It was mined on Pyrrus and sold here on Cassylia. You can check on that very easily. I sold it. I'm the Pyrric ambassador to this planet." He smiled at the thought. "Not that that means much, I'm ambassador to at least six other planets as well. Comes in handy when you want to do business."

Jason looked at the muscular man with his gray hair and worn, military-cut clothes, and decided not to laugh. You heard of strange things out in the frontier planets and every word could be true. He had never heard of Pyrrus either, though that didn't mean anything. There were over thirty-thousand known planets in the inhabited universe.

"I'll check on what you have told me," Jason said. "If it's true, we can do business. Call me tomorrow—"

"No," Kerk said. "The money has to be won tonight. I've already issued a check for this twenty-seven million, it will bounce as high as the Pleiades unless we deposit the money in the morning, so that's our time limit."

With each moment the whole affair became more fantastic—and more intriguing for Jason. He looked at his watch. There was still enough time to find out if Kerk was lying or not.

"All right, we'll do it tonight," he said. "Only I'll have to have one of those bills to check."

Kerk stood up to go. "Take them all, I won't be seeing you again until after you've won. I'll be at the Casino of course, but don't recognize me. It would be much better if they didn't know where your money was coming from or how much you had."

Then he was gone, after a bone-crushing handclasp that closed on Jason's hand like vise jaws. Jason was alone with the money. Fanning the bills out like a hand of cards he stared at their sepia and gold faces, trying to get the reality through his head. Twenty-seven million credits. What was to stop him from just walking out the door with them and vanishing? Nothing really, except his own sense of honor.

Kerk Pyrrus, the man with the same last name as the planet he came from, was the universe's biggest fool. Or he knew just what he was doing. From the way the interview had gone the latter seemed the better bet.

"He *knows* I would much rather gamble with the money than steal it," he said wryly.

Slipping a small gun into his waistband holster and pocketing the money he went out.

2 THE ROBOT TELLER at the bank just pinged with electronic shock when he presented one of the bills and flashed a panel that directed him to see Vice President Wain. Wain was a smooth customer who bugged his eyes and lost some of his tan when he saw the sheaf of bills.

"You ... wish to deposit these with us?" he asked while his fingers unconsciously stroked them.

"Not today," Jason said. "They were paid to me as a debt. Would you please check that they are authentic and change them? I'd like five hundred thousand credit notes."

Both of his inner chest pockets were packed tight when he left the bank. The bills were good and he felt like a walking mint. This was the first time in his entire life that carrying a large sum of money made him uncomfortable. Waving to a passing helicab he went directly to the Casino, where he knew he would be safe—for a while.

Cassylia Casino was the playspot of the nearby cluster of star systems. It was the first time Jason had seen it, though he knew its type well. He had spent most of his adult life in casinos like this on other worlds. The decor differed but they were always the same. Gambling and socialities in public— and behind the scenes all the private vice you could afford. Theoretically no-limit games, but that was true only up to a certain point. When the house was really hurt the honest games stopped being square and the big winner had to watch his step very carefully. These were the odds Jason dinAlt had played against countless times before. He was wary but not very concerned.

The dining room was almost empty and the major-domo quickly rushed to the side of the relaxed stranger in the richly cut clothes. Jason was lean and dark, looking more like the bored scion of some rich family than a professional gambler. This appearance was important and he cultivated it. The cuisine looked good and the cellar turned out to be wonderful. He had a professional talk with the sommelier while waiting for the soup, then settled down to enjoy his meal.

He ate leisurely and the large dining room was filled before he was through. Watch-ing the entertainment over a long cigar killed some more time. When he finally went to the gaming rooms they were filled and active.

Moving slowly around the room he dropped a few thousand credits. He scarcely noticed how he played, giving more attention to the feel of the games. The play all seemed honest and none of the equipment was rigged. That could be changed very quickly, he realized. Usually it wasn't necessary, house percentage was enough to assure a profit.

Once he saw Kerk out of the corner of his eye but he paid him no attention. The ambassador was losing small sums steadily at seven-and-silver and seemed to be impatient. Probably waiting for Jason to begin playing seriously. He smiled and strolled on slowly.

Jason settled on the dice table as he usually did. It was the surest way to make small winnings. *And if I feel it tonight I can clean this casino out!* That was his secret, the power that won for him steadily—and every once in a while enabled him to make a killing and move on quickly before the hired thugs came to get the money back.

The Dice reached him and he threw an eight the hard way. Betting was light and he didn't push himself, just kept away from the sevens. He made the point and passed a natural. Then he crapped out and the dice moved on.

Sitting there, making small automatic bets while the dice went around the table, he thought about the power. *Funny, after all the years of work we still don't know much about psi. They can train people a bit, and improve skills a bit—but that's all.*

He was feeling strong tonight, he knew that the money in his pocket gave him the extra lift that sometimes helped him break through. With his eyes half closed he picked up the dice—and let his mind gently caress the pattern of sunken dots. Then they shot out of his hand and he stared at a seven.

It was there.

Stronger than he had felt it in years. The

stiff weight of those million-credit notes had done it. The world all around was sharp-cut clear and the dice was completely in his control. He knew to the tenth-credit how much the other players had in their wallets and was aware of the cards in the hands of the players behind him.

Slowly, carefully, he built up the stakes.

There was no effort to the dice, they rolled and sat up like trained dogs. Jason took his time and concentrated on the psychology of the players and the stick man. It took almost two hours to build his money on the table to seven hundred thousand credits. Then he caught the stick man signaling they had a heavy winner. He waited until the hard-eyed man strolled over to watch the game, then he smiled happily, bet all his table stakes—and blew it on one roll of the dice. The house man smiled happily, the stick man relaxed—and out of the corner of his eye Jason saw Kerk turning a dark purple.

Sweating, pale, his hand trembling ever so slightly, Jason opened the front of his jacket and pulled out one of the envelopes of new bills. Breaking the seal with his finger he dropped two of them on the table.

"Could we have a no-limit game?" he asked, "I'd like to—win back some of my money."

The stick man had trouble controlling his smile now, he glanced across at the house man who nodded a quick *yes*. They had a sucker and they meant to clean him. He had been playing from his wallet all evening, now he was cracking into a sealed envelope to try for what he had lost. A thick envelope too, and probably not his money. Not that the house cared in the least. To them money had no loyalties. The play went on with the Casino in a very relaxed mood.

Which was just the way Jason wanted it. He needed to get as deep into them as he could before someone realized *they* might be on the losing end. The rough stuff would start and he wanted to put it off as long as possible. It would be hard to win smoothly then—and his *psi* power might go as quickly

as it had come. That had happened before.

He was playing against the house now, the two other players were obvious shills, and a crowd had jammed solidly around to watch. After losing and winning a bit he hit a streak of naturals and his pile of gold chips tottered higher and higher. There was nearly a billion there, he estimated roughly. The dice were still falling true, though he was soaked with sweat from the effort. Betting the entire stack of chips he reached for the dice. The stick man reached faster and hooked them away.

"House calls for new dice," he said flatly.

Jason straightened up and wiped his hands, glad of the instant's relief. This was the third time the house had changed dice to try and break his winning streak, it was their privilege. The hard-eyed Casino man opened his wallet as he had done before and drew out a pair at random. Stripping off their plastic cover he threw them the length of the table to Jason. They came up a natural seven and Jason smiled.

When he scooped them up the smile slowly faded. The dice were transparent, finely made, evenly weighted on all sides—and crooked.

The pigment on the dots of five sides of each die was some heavy metal compound, probably lead. The sixth side was a ferrous compound. They would roll true unless they hit a magnetic field—that meant the entire surface of the table could be magnetized. He could never have spotted the difference if he hadn't *looked* at the dice with his mind. But what could he do about it?

Shaking them slowly he glanced quickly around the table. There was what he needed. An ashtray with a magnet in its base to hold it to the metal edge of the table. Jason stopped shaking the dice and looked at them quizzically, then reached over and grabbed the ashtray. He dropped the base against his hand.

As he lifted the ashtray there was a concerted gasp from all sides. The dice were sticking there, upside down, box cars showing.

"Are these what you call honest dice?" he asked.

The man who had thrown out the dice reached quickly for his hip pocket. Jason was the only one who saw what happened next. He was watching that hand closely, his own fingers near his gun butt. As the man dived into his pocket a hand reached out of the crowd behind him. From its square-cut size it could have belonged to only one person. The thick thumb and index finger clamped swiftly around the house man's wrist, then they were gone. The man screamed shrilly and held up his arm, his hand dangling limp as a glove from the broken wrist bones.

With his flank well protected, Jason could go on with the game. "The old dice if you don't mind," he said quietly.

Dazedly the stick man pushed them over. Jason shook quickly and rolled. Before they hit the table he realized he couldn't control them—the transient *psi* power had gone.

End over end they turned. And faced up seven.

Counting the chips as they were pushed over to him he added up a bit under two billion credits. They would be winning that much if he left the game now—but it wasn't the three billion that Kerk needed. Well, it would have to be enough. As he reached for the chips he caught Kerk's eye across the table and the other man shook his head in a steady *no*.

"Let it ride," Jason said wearily, "one more roll."

He breathed on the dice, polished them on his cuff, and wondered how he had ever gotten into this spot. Billions riding on a pair of dice. That was as much as the annual income of some planets. The only reason there *could* be stakes like that was because the planetary government had a stake in the Casino. He shook as long as he could, reaching for the control that wasn't there—then let fly.

Everything else had stopped in the Casino and people were standing on tables and chairs to watch. There wasn't a sound from that large crowd. The dice bounced back from the board with a clatter loud in the silence and tumbled over the cloth.

A five and a one. Six. He still had to make his point. Scooping up the dice Jason talked to them, mumbled the ancient oaths that brought luck and threw again.

It took five throws before he made the six.

The crowd echoed his sigh and their voices rose quickly. He wanted to stop, take a deep breath, but he knew he couldn't. Winning the money was only part of the job—they now had to get away with it. It had to look casual. A waiter was passing with a tray of drinks. Jason stopped him and tucked a hundred-credit note in his pocket.

"Drinks are on me," he shouted while he pried the tray out of the waiter's hands. Well-wishers cleared the filled glasses away quickly and Jason piled the chips onto the tray. They more than loaded it, but Kerk appeared that moment with a second tray.

"I'll be glad to help you, sir, if you will permit me," he said.

Jason looked at him, and laughed permission. It was the first time he had a clear look at Kerk in the Casino. He was wearing loose, purple evening pajamas over what must have been a false stomach. The sleeves were long and baggy so he looked fat rather than muscular. It was a simple but effective disguise.

Carefully carrying the loaded trays, surrounded by a crowd of excited patrons, they made their way to the cashier's window. The manager himself was there, wearing a sickly grin. Even the grin faded when he counted the chips.

"Could you come back in the morning," he said, "I'm afraid we don't have that kind of money on hand."

"What's the matter," Kerk shouted, "trying to get out of paying him? You took *my* money easy enough when I lost—it works both ways!"

The onlookers, always happy to see the house lose, growled their disagreement. Jason finished the matter in a loud voice.

"I'll be reasonable, give me what cash you have and I'll take a check for the balance."

There was no way out. Under the watchful eye of the gleeful crowd the manager packed an envelope with bills and wrote a check. Jason took a quick glimpse at it, then stuffed it into an inside pocket. With the envelope under one arm he followed Kerk towards the door.

Because of the onlookers there was no trouble in the main room, but just as they reached the side entrance two men moved in, blocking the way.

"Just a moment—" one said. He never finished the sentence. Kerk walked into them without slowing and they bounced away like tenpins. Then Kerk and Jason were out of the building and walking fast.

"Into the parking lot," Kerk said. "I have a car there."

When they rounded the corner there was a car bearing down on them. Before Jason could get his gun clear of the holster Kerk was in front of him. His arm came up and his big ugly gun burst through the cloth of his sleeve and jumped into his hand. A single shot killed the driver and the car swerved and crashed. The other two men in the car died coming out of the door, their guns dropping from their hands.

After that they had no trouble. Kerk drove at top speed away from the Casino, the torn sleeve of his pajamas whipping in the breeze, giving glimpses of the big gun back in the holster.

"When you get the chance," Jason said, "you'll have to show me how that trick holster works."

"When we get the chance," Kerk answered as he dived the car into the city access tube.

3 THE BUILDING THEY STOPPED AT was one of the finer residences in Cassylia. As they had driven, Jason counted the money and separated his share. Almost sixteen million credits. It still didn't seem quite real.

When they got out in front of the building he gave Kerk the rest.

"Here's your three billion, don't think it was easy," he said.

"It could have been worse," was his only answer.

The recorded voice scratched in the speaker over the door.

"Sire Ellus has retired for the night, would you please call again in the morning. All appointments are made in advan—"

The voice broke off as Kerk pushed the door open. He did it almost effortlessly with the flat of his hand. As they went in Jason looked at the remnants of torn and twisted metal that hung in the lock and wondered again about his companion.

Strength—more than physical strength—he's like an elemental force. I have the feeling that nothing can stop him.

It made him angry—and at the same time fascinated him. He didn't want out of the deal until he found out more about Kerk and his planet. And "they" who had died for the money he gambled.

Sire Ellus was old, balding and angry, not at all used to having his rest disturbed. His complaints stopped suddenly when Kerk threw the money down on the table.

"Is the ship being loaded yet, Ellus? Here's the balance due." Ellus only fumbled the bills for a moment before he could answer Kerk's question.

"The ship—but, of course. We began loading when you gave us the deposit. You'll have to excuse my confusion, this is a little irregular. We never handle transactions of this size in cash."

"That's the way I like to do business," Kerk answered him, "I've canceled the deposit, this is the total sum. Now how about a receipt."

Ellus had made out the receipt before his senses returned. He held it tightly while he looked uncomfortably at the three billion spread out before him.

"Wait—I can't take it now, you'll have to return in the morning, to the bank. In normal business fashion," Ellus decided firmly.

Kerk reached over and gently drew the paper out of Ellus' hand.

"Thanks for the receipt," he said. "I won't be here in the morning so this will be satisfactory. And if you're worried about the money I suggest you get in touch with some of your plant guards or private police. You'll feel a lot safer."

When they left through the shattered door Ellus was frantically dialing numbers on his screen. Kerk answered Jason's next question before he could ask it.

"I imagine you would like to live to spend that money in your pocket, so I've booked two seats on an interplanetary ship," he glanced at the car clock. "It leaves in about two hours so we have plenty of time. I'm hungry, let's find a restaurant. I hope you have nothing at the hotel worth going back for. It would be a little difficult."

"Nothing worth getting killed for," Jason said. "Now where can we go to eat—there are a few questions I would like to ask you."

THEY CIRCLED CAREFULLY DOWN to the transport levels until they were sure they hadn't been followed. Kerk nosed the car into a darkened loading dock where they abandoned it.

"We can always get another car," he said, "and they probably have this one spotted. Let's walk back to the freightway, I saw a restaurant there as we came by."

Dark and looming shapes of overland freight carriers filled the parking lot. They picked their way around the man-high wheels and into the hot and noisy restaurant. The drivers and early morning workers took no notice of them as they found a booth in the back and dialed a meal.

Kerk chiseled a chunk of meat off the slab in front of him and popped it cheerfully into his mouth. "Ask your questions," he said. "I'm feeling much better already."

"What's in this ship you arranged for tonight—what kind of a cargo was I risking my neck for?"

"I thought you were risking your neck for money," Kerk said dryly. "But be assured it was in a good cause. That cargo means the survival of a world. Guns, ammunition, mines, explosives and such."

Jason choked over a mouthful of food. "Gun-running! What are you doing, financing a private war? And how can you talk about survival with a lethal cargo like that? Don't try and tell me they have a peaceful use. Who are you killing?"

Most of the big man's humor had vanished, he had that grim look Jason knew well.

"Yes, peaceful would be the right word. Because that is basically all we want. Just to live in peace. And it is not *who* are we killing—it is *what* we are killing."

Jason pushed his plate away with an angry gesture. "You're talking in riddles," he said. "What you say has no meaning."

"It has meaning enough," Kerk told him, "but only on one planet in the universe. Just how much do you know about Pyrrus?"

"Absolutely nothing."

For a moment Kerk sat wrapped in memory, scowling distantly. Then he went on.

"Mankind doesn't belong on Pyrrus—yet has been there for almost three hundred years now. The age expectancy of my people is sixteen years. Of course most adults live beyond that, but the high child mortality brings the average down.

"It is everything that a humanoid world should not be. The gravity is nearly twice Earth normal. The temperature can vary daily from arctic to tropic. The climate—well you have to experience it to believe it. Like nothing you've seen anywhere else in the galaxy."

"I'm frightened," Jason said dryly. "What do you have—methane or chlorine reactions? I've been down on planets like that—"

Kerk slammed his hand down hard on the table. The dishes bounced and the table legs creaked. "Laboratory reactions!" he growled. "They look great on a bench—but what happens when you have a world filled with those compounds? In an eye-wink of galactic time all the violence is locked up in nice, stable compounds. The atmosphere may be poisonous for an oxygen breather, but taken by itself it's as harmless as weak beer.

"There is only one setup that is pure poison as a planetary atmosphere. Plenty of H_2O, the most universal solvent you can find, plus free oxygen to work on—"

"Water and oxygen!" Jason broke in. "You mean Earth—or a planet like Cassylia here? That's preposterous."

"Not at all. Because you were born in this kind of environment you accept it as right and natural. You take it for granted that metals corrode, coastlines change, and storms interfere with communication. These are normal occurrences on oxygen-water worlds. On Pyrrus these conditions are carried to the nth degree.

"The planet has an axial tilt of almost forty-two degrees, so there is a tremendous change in temperature from season to season. This is one of the prime causes of a constantly changing icecap. The weather generated by this is spectacular to say the least."

"If that's all," Jason said, "I don't see why—"

"That's *not* all—it's barely the beginning. The open seas perform the dual destructive function of supplying water vapor to keep the weather going, and building up gigantic tides. Pyrrus' two satellites, Samas and Bessos, combine at times to pull the oceans up into thirty meter tides. And until you've seen one of these tides lap over into an active volcano you've seen nothing.

"Heavy elements are what brought us to Pyrrus—and these same elements keep the planet at a volcanic boil. There have been at least thirteen super-novas in the immediate stellar neighborhood. Heavy elements can be found on most of their planets of course—as well as completely unbreathable atmospheres. Long-term mining and exploitation can't be done by anything but a self-

sustaining colony. Which meant Pyrrus. Where the radioactive elements are locked in the planetary core, surrounded by a shell of lighter ones. While this allows for the atmosphere men need, it also provides unceasing volcanic activity as the molten plasma forces its way to the surface."

For the first time Jason was silent. Trying to imagine what life could be like on a planet constantly at war with itself.

"I've saved the best for last," Kerk said with grim humor. "Now that you have an idea of what the environment is like—think of the kind of life forms that would populate it. I doubt if there is one off-world species that would live a minute. Plants and animals on Pyrrus are *tough*. They fight the world and they fight each other. Hundreds of thousands of years of genetic weeding-out have produced things that would give even an electronic brain nightmares. Armor-plated, poisonous, claw-tipped and fanged-mouthed. That describes everything that walks, flaps or just sits and grows. Ever see a plant with teeth—that bite? I don't think you want to. You'd have to be on Pyrrus and that means you would be dead within seconds of leaving the ship. Even I'll have to take a refresher course before I'll be able to go outside the landing buildings. The unending war for survival keeps the life forms competing and changing. Death is simple, but the ways of dealing it too numerous to list."

Unhappiness rode like a weight on Kerk's broad shoulders. After long moments of thought he moved visibly to shake it off. Returning his attention to his food and mopping the gravy from his plate, he voiced part of his feelings.

"I suppose there is no logical reason why we should stay and fight this endless war. Except that Pyrrus is our home." The last piece of gravy-soaked bread vanished and he waved the empty fork at Jason.

"Be happy you're an off-worlder and will never have to see it."

"That's where you're wrong." Jason said as calmly as he could. "You see, I'm going back with you."

4 **"DON'T TALK STUPIDLY,"** Kerk said as he punched for a duplicate order of steak. "There are much simpler ways of committing suicide. Don't you realize that you're a millionaire now? With what you have in your pocket you can relax the rest of your life on the pleasure planets. Pyrrus is a death world, not a sightseeing spot for jaded tourists. I cannot permit you to return with me."

Gamblers who lose their tempers don't last long. Jason was angry now. Yet it showed only in a negative way. In the lack of expression on his face and the calmness of his voice.

"Don't tell me what I can or cannot do, Kerk Pyrrus. You're a big man with a fast gun—but that doesn't make you my boss. All you can do is stop me from going back on your ship. But I can easily afford to get there another way. And don't try to tell me I want to go to Pyrrus for sightseeing when you have no idea of my real reasons."

Jason didn't even try to explain his reasons, they were only half realized and too personal. The more he traveled, the more things looked the same to him. The old, civilized planets sank into a drab similarity. Frontier worlds all had the crude sameness of temporary camps in a forest. Not that the galactic worlds bored him. It was just that he had found their limitations—yet had never found his own. Until he met Kerk he had acknowledged no man his superior, or even his equal. This was more than egotism. It was facing facts. Now he was forced to face the fact that there was a whole world of people who might be superior to him. Jason could never rest content until he had been there and seen for himself. Even if he died in the attempt.

None of this could be told to Kerk. There were other reasons he would understand better.

"You're not thinking ahead when you prevent me from going to Pyrrus," Jason said. "I'll not mention any moral debt you

owe me for winning that money you needed. But what about the next time? If you needed that much lethal goods once, you'll probably need it again someday. Wouldn't it be better to have me on hand—old tried and true—than dreaming up some new and possibly unreliable scheme?"

Kerk chewed pensively on the second serving of steak. "That makes sense. And I must admit I hadn't thought of it before. One failing we Pyrrans have is a lack of interest in the future. Staying alive day by day is enough trouble. So we tend to face emergencies as they arrive and let the dim future take care of itself. You can come. I hope you will still be alive when we need you. As Pyrran ambassador to a lot of places I officially invite you to our planet. All expenses paid. On the condition you obey completely all our instructions regarding your personal safety."

"Conditions accepted," Jason said. And wondered why he was so cheerful about signing his own death warrant.

Kerk was shoveling his way through his third dessert when his alarm watch gave a tiny hum. He dropped his fork instantly and stood up. "Time to go," he said. "We're on schedule now." While Jason scrambled to his feet, he jammed coins into the meter until the *paid* light came on. Then they were out the door and walking fast.

Jason wasn't at all surprised when they came on a public escalator just behind the restaurant. He was beginning to realize that since leaving the Casino their every move had been carefully planned and timed. Without a doubt the alarm was out and the entire planet being searched for them. Yet so far they hadn't noticed the slightest sign of pursuit. This wasn't the first time Jason had to move just one jump ahead of the authorities—but it was the first time he had let someone else lead him by the hand while he did it. He had to smile at his own automatic agreement. He had been a loner for so many years that he found a certain inverse pleasure in following someone else.

"Hurry up," Kerk growled after a quick

glance at his watch. He set a steady, killing pace up the escalator steps. They went up five levels that way—without seeing another person—before Kerk relented and let the escalator do the work.

Jason prided himself on keeping in condition. But the sudden climb, after the sleepless night, left him panting heavily and soaked with sweat. Kerk, cool of forehead and breathing normally, didn't show the slightest sign that he had been running.

They were at the second motor level when Kerk stepped off the slowly rising steps and waved Jason after him. As they came through the exit to the street a car pulled up to the curb in front of them. Jason had enough sense not to reach for his gun. At the exact moment they reached the car the driver opened the door and stepped out. Kerk passed him a slip of paper without saying a word and slipped in behind the wheel. There was just time for Jason to jump in before the car pulled away. The entire transfer had taken less than three seconds.

There had been only a glimpse of the driver in the dim light, but Jason had recognized him. Of course he had never seen the man before, but after knowing Kerk he couldn't mistake the compact strength of a native Pyrran.

"That was the receipt from Ellus you gave him," Jason said.

"Of course. That takes care of the ship and the cargo. They'll be off-planet and safely away before the casino check is traced to Ellus. So now let's look after ourselves. I'll explain the plan in detail so there will be no slip-ups on your part. I'll go through the whole thing once and if there are any questions you'll ask them when I'm finished."

The tones of command were so automatic that Jason found himself listening in quiet obedience. Though one part of his mind wanted him to smile at the quick assumption of his incompetence.

Kerk swung the car into the steady line of traffic heading out of the city to the spaceport. He drove easily while he talked.

"There is a search on in the city, but we're well ahead of that. I'm sure the Cassylians don't want to advertise their bad sportsmanship so there won't be anything as crude as a roadblock. But the port will be crawling with every agent they have. They know once the money gets off-planet it is gone forever. When we make a break for it they will be sure we still have the goods. So there will be no trouble with the munition ship getting clear."

Jason sounded a little shocked. "You mean you're setting us up as clay pigeons to cover the take-off of the ship."

"You could put it that way. But since we have to get off-planet anyway, there is no harm in using our escape as a smokescreen. Now shut up until I've finished, like I told you. One more interruption and I dump you by the road."

Jason was sure he would. He listened intently—and quietly—as Kerk repeated word for word what he had said before, then continued.

"The official car gate will probably be wide open with the traffic through it. And a lot of the agents will be in plain clothes. We might even get onto the field without being recognized, though I doubt it. It is of no importance. We will drive through the gate and to the take-off pad. The *Pride of Darkhan*, for which we hold tickets, will be sounding its two-minute siren and unhooking the gangway. By the time we get to our seats the ship will take off."

"That's all very fine," Jason said. "But what will the guards be doing all this time?"

"Shooting at us and each other. We will take advantage of the confusion to get aboard."

This answer did nothing to settle Jason's mind, but he let it slide for the moment. "All right—say we *do* get aboard. Why don't they just prevent take-off until we have been dragged out and stood against a wall?"

Kerk spared him a contemptuous glance before he returned his eyes to the road. "I said the ship was the *Pride of Darkhan*. If you had studied this system at all, you would know what that means. Cassylia and Darkhan are sister planets and rivals in every way. It has been less than two centuries since they fought an intra-system war that almost destroyed both of them. Now they exist in an armed-to-the-teeth neutrality that neither dare violate. The moment we set foot aboard the ship we are on Darkhan territory. There is no extradition agreement between the planets. Cassylia may want us—but not badly enough to start another war."

That was all the explanation there was time for. Kerk swung the car out of the rush of traffic and onto a bridge marked *Official Cars Only*. Jason had a feeling of nakedness as they rolled under the harsh port lights towards the guarded gate ahead.

It was closed.

Another car approached the gate from the inside and Kerk slowed their car to a crawl. One of the guards talked to the driver of the car inside the port, then waved to the gate attendant. The barrier gate began to swing inwards and Kerk jammed down on the accelerator.

Everything happened at once. The turbine howled, the spinning tires screeched on the road and the car crashed open the gate. Jason had a vanishing glimpse of the open-mouthed guards, then they were skidding around the corner of a building. A few shots popped after them, but none came close.

Driving with one hand, Kerk reached under the dash and pulled out a gun that was the twin of the monster strapped to his arm. "Use this instead of your own," he said. "Rocket-propelled explosive slugs. Make a great bang. Don't bother shooting at anyone—I'll take care of that. Just stir up a little action and make them keep their distance. Like this."

He fired a single, snap-shot out the side window and passed the gun to Jason almost before the slug hit. An empty truck blew up with a roar, raining pieces on the cars around and sending their drivers fleeing in panic.

After that it was a nightmare ride through a madhouse. Kerk drove with an apparent contempt for violent death. Other cars followed them and were lost in wheel-raising turns. They careened almost the full length of the field, leaving a trail of smoking chaos.

Then the pursuit was all behind them and the only thing ahead was the slim spire of the *Pride of Darkhan*.

THE *PRIDE* WAS SURROUNDED by a strong wire fence as suited the begrudged status of her planetary origin. The gate was closed and guarded by soldiers with leveled guns, waiting for a shot at the approaching car. Kerk made no attempt to come near them. Instead he fed the last reserves of power to the car and headed for the fence. "Cover your face," he shouted.

Jason put his arms in front of his head just as they hit.

Torn metal screamed, the fence buckled, wrapped itself around the car, but did not break. Jason flew off the seat and into the padded dash. By the time Kerk had the warped door open, he realized that the ride was over. Kerk must have seen the spin of his eyeballs because he didn't talk, just pulled Jason out and threw him onto the hood of the ruined car.

"Climb over the buckled wire and make a run for the ship," he shouted.

If there was any doubt what he meant, he set Jason an example of fine roadwork. It was inconceivable that someone of his bulk could run so fast, yet he did. He moved more like a charging tank than a man. Jason shook the fog from his head and worked up some speed himself. Nevertheless, he was barely halfway to the ship when Kerk hit the gangway. It was already unhooked from the ship, but the shocked attendants stopped rolling it away as the big man bounded up the steps.

At the top he turned and fired at the soldiers who were charging through the open gate. They dropped, crawled, and returned his fire. Very few shot at Jason's running form.

The scene in front of Jason cranked over in slow motion. Kerk standing at the top of the ramp, coolly returning the fire that splashed all about. He could have found safety in an instant through the open port behind him. The only reason he stayed there was to cover Jason.

"Thanks—" Jason managed to gasp as he made the last few steps up the gangway, jumped the gap and collapsed inside the ship.

"You're perfectly welcome," Kerk said as he joined him, waving his gun to cool it off.

A grim-jawed ship's officer stood back out of range of fire from the ground and looked them both up and down. "And just what is going on here?" he growled.

Kerk tested the barrel with a wet thumb, then let the gun slide back into its holster. "We are law-abiding citizens of a different system who have committed no criminal acts. The savages of Cassylia are too barba-

rous for civilized company. Therefore we are going to Darkhan—here are our tickets—in whose sovereign territory I believe we are at this moment." This last was added for the benefit of the Cassylian officer who had just stumbled to the top of the gangway and was raising his gun.

The soldier couldn't be blamed. He saw these badly wanted criminals getting away. Aboard a Darkhan ship as well. Anger got the best of him and he brought his gun up.

"Come out of there, you scum. You're not escaping that easily. Come out slow with your hands up or I'll blast you—"

It was a frozen moment of time that stretched and stretched without breaking. The pistol covered Kerk and Jason. Neither of them attempted to reach for their own guns.

The gun twitched a bit as the ship's officer moved, then steadied back on the two men. The Darkhan spaceman hadn't gone far, just a pace across the lock. This was enough to bring him next to a red box set flush with the wall. With a single, swift gesture he flipped up the cover and poised his thumb over the button inside. When he smiled his lips peeled back to show all of his teeth. He had made up his mind, and it was the arrogance of the Cassylian officer that had been the deciding factor.

"Fire a single shot into Darkhan territory and I press this button," he shouted. "And you know what this button does—every one of your ships has them as well. Commit a hostile act against this ship and *someone* will press a button. Every control rod will be blown out of the ship's pile at that instant and half your filthy city will go up in the explosion." His smile was chiseled on his face and there was no doubt he would do what he said. "Go ahead—fire. I think I would enjoy pressing this."

The take-off siren was hooting now, the *close lock* light blinking an angry message from the bridge. Like four actors in a grim drama they faced each other an instant more.

Then the Cassylian officer, growling with unvoicable frustrated anger, turned and leaped back to the steps.

"All passengers board ship. Forty-five seconds to take-off. Clear the port." The ship's officer slammed shut the cover of the box and locked it as he talked. There was barely time to make the acceleration couches before the *Pride of Darkhan* cleared ground.

5 ONCE THE SHIP WAS IN ORBIT the captain sent for Jason and Kerk. Kerk took the floor and was completely frank about the previous night's activities. The only fact of importance he left out was Jason's background as a professional gambler. He drew a beautiful picture of two lucky strangers whom the evil forces of Cassylia wanted to deprive of their gambling profits. All this fitted perfectly the captain's preconceptions of Cassylia. In the end he congratulated his officer on the correctness of his actions and began the preparation of a long report to his government. He gave the two men his best wishes as well as the liberty of the ship.

It was a short trip. Jason barely had time to catch up on his sleep before they grounded on Darkhan. Being without luggage they were the first ones through customs. They left the shed just in time to see another ship landing in a distant pit. Kerk stopped to watch it and Jason followed his gaze. It was a gray, scarred ship. With the stubby lines of a freighter—but sporting as many guns as a cruiser.

"Yours, of course," Jason said.

Kerk nodded and started towards the ship. One of the locks opened as they came up but no one appeared. Instead a remote-release folding ladder rattled down to the ground. Kerk swarmed up it and Jason followed glumly. Somehow, he felt, this was overdoing the no-frills-and-nonsense attitude.

Jason was catching on to Pyrran ways though. The reception aboard ship for the ambassador was just what he expected. Nothing. Kerk closed the lock himself and they found couches as the take-off horn sounded. The main jets roared and acceleration smashed down on Jason.

It didn't stop. Instead it grew stronger, squeezing the air out of his lungs and the sight from his eyes. He screamed but couldn't hear his own voice through the roaring in his ears. Mercifully he blacked out.

When consciousness returned the ship was at zero-G. Jason kept his eyes closed and let the pain seep out of his body. Kerk spoke suddenly, he was standing next to the couch.

"My fault, Meta, I should have told you we had a 1-G passenger aboard. You might have eased up a bit on your usual bone-breaking take-off."

"It doesn't seem to have harmed him much—but what's he doing here?"

Jason felt mild surprise that the second voice was a girl's. But he wasn't interested enough to go to the trouble of opening his sore eyes.

"Going to Pyrrus. I tried to talk him out of it, of course, but I couldn't change his mind. It's a shame, too, I would like to have done more for him. He's the one who got the money for us."

"Oh, that's awful," the girl said. Jason wondered why it was *awful*. It didn't make sense to his groggy mind. "It would have been much better if he stayed on Darkhan," the girl continued. "He's very nice-looking. I think it's a shame he has to die."

That was too much for Jason. He pried one eye open, then the other. The voice belonged to a girl about twenty-one who was standing next to the bed, gazing down at Jason. She was beautiful.

Jason's eyes opened wider as he realized

she was *very* beautiful—with the kind of beauty never found in the civilized galaxy. The women he had known all ran to pale skin, hollow shoulders, gray faces covered with tints and dyes. They were the product of centuries of breeding weaknesses back into the race, as the advance of medicine kept alive more and more non-survival types.

This girl was the direct opposite in every way. She was the product of survival on Pyrrus. The heavy gravity that produced bulging muscles in men, brought out firm strength in straplike female muscles. She had the figure of a goddess, tanned skin and perfectly formed face. Her hair, which was cut short, circled her head like a golden crown. The only unfeminine thing about her was the gun she wore in a bulky forearm holster. When she saw Jason's eyes open she smiled at him. Her teeth were as even and as white as he had expected.

"I'm Meta, pilot of this ship. And you must be—"

"Jason dinAlt. That was a lousy take-off, Meta."

"I'm really very sorry," she laughed. "But being born on a two-G planet does make one a little immune to acceleration. I save fuel too, with the synergy curve—"

Kerk gave a noncommittal grunt. "Come along, Meta, we'll take a look at the cargo. Some of the new stuff will plug the gaps in the perimeter."

"Oh yes," she said, almost clapping her hands with happiness. "I read the specs, they're simply wonderful."

Like a schoolgirl with a new dress. Or a box of candy. That's a great attitude to have towards bombs and flame-throwers. Jason smiled wryly at the thought as he groaned off the couch. The two Pyrrans had gone and he pulled himself painfully through the door after them.

It took him a long time to find his way to the hold. The ship was big and apparently empty of crew. Jason finally found a man sleeping in one of the brightly lit cabins. He recognized him as the driver who had turned the car over to them on Cassylia. The man, who had been sleeping soundly a moment before, opened his eyes as soon as Jason drifted into the room. He was wide awake.

"How do I get to the cargo hold?" Jason asked.

The other told him, closed his eyes and went instantly back to sleep before Jason could even say thanks.

In the hold, Kerk and Meta had opened some of the crates and were chortling with joy over their lethal contents. Meta, a pressure canister in her arms, turned to Jason as he came through the door.

"Just look at this," she said. "This powder in here—why you can eat it like dirt, with less harm. Yet it is instantly deadly to all forms of vegetable life...." She stopped suddenly as she realized Jason didn't share her extreme pleasure. "I'm sorry. I forgot for a moment there that you weren't a Pyrran. So you don't really understand, do you?"

Before he could answer, the PA speaker called her name.

"Jump time," she said. "Come with me to the bridge while I do the equations. We can talk there. I know so little about any place except Pyrrus that I have a million questions to ask."

Jason followed her to the bridge where she relieved the duty officer and began taking readings for the jump-setting. She looked out of place among the machines, a sturdy but supple figure in a simple, one-piece shipsuit. Yet there was no denying the efficiency with which she went about her job.

"Meta, aren't you a little young to be the pilot of an interstellar ship?"

"Am I?" She thought for a second. "I really don't know how old pilots are supposed to be. I have been piloting for about three years now and I'm almost twenty. Is that younger than usual?"

Jason opened his mouth—then laughed. "I suppose that all depends on what planet you're from. Some places you would have trouble getting licensed. But I'll bet things are different on Pyrrus. By their standards you must rank as an old lady."

"Now you're making a joke," Meta said serenely as she fed a figure into the calculator. "I've seen old ladies on some planets. They are wrinkled and have gray hair. I don't know how old they are, I asked one but she wouldn't tell me her age. But I'm sure they must be older than anyone on Pyrrus, no one looks like that there."

"I don't mean old that way," Jason groped for the right word. "Not old—but grown-up, mature. An adult."

"Everyone is grown-up," she answered. "At least soon after they leave the wards. And they do that when they're six. My first child is grown-up, and the second one would be, too, only he's dead. So I *surely* must be."

That seemed to settle the question for her, though Jason's thoughts jumped with the alien concepts and background, inherent behind her words.

Meta punched in the last setting, and the course tape began to chunk out of the case. She turned her attention back to Jason. "I'm glad you're aboard this trip, though I am sorry you are going to Pyrrus. But we'll have lots of time to talk. There are so many things I want to find out about other planets, and why people go around acting the way they do. Not at all like home where you *know* why people are doing things all the time." She frowned over the tape for a moment, then turned her attention back to Jason. "What is your home planet like?"

One after another the usual lies he told people came to his lips, and were pushed away. Why bother lying to a girl who really didn't care if you were serf or noble? To her there were only two kinds of people in the galaxy—Pyrrans, and the rest. For the first time since he had fled from Porgorstorsaand he found himself telling someone the truth of his origin.

"My home planet? Just about the stuffiest, dullest, deadend in the universe. You can't believe the destructive decay of a planet that is mainly agrarian, caste-conscious and completely satisfied with its own boring existence. Not only is there no change—but no one *wants* change. My father was a farmer, so I should have been a farmer too—if I had listened to the advice of my betters. It was unthinkable, as well as forbidden for me to do anything else. And everything I wanted to do was against the law. I was fifteen before I learned to read—out of a book stolen from a noble school. After that there was no turning back. By the time I stowed aboard an off-world freighter at nineteen I must have broken every law on the planet. Happily. Leaving home for me was just like getting out of prison."

Meta shook her head at the thought. "I just can't imagine a place like that. But I'm sure I wouldn't like it there."

"I'm sure you wouldn't," Jason laughed. "So once I was in space, with no law-abiding talents or skills, I just wandered into one thing and another. In this age of technology I was completely out of place. Oh, I suppose I could have done well in some army, but I'm not so good at taking orders. Whenever I gambled I did well, so little by little I just drifted into it. People are the same everywhere, so I manage to make out well wherever I end up."

"I know what you mean about people being alike—but they are so *different*," she said. "I'm not being clear at all, am I? What I mean is that at home I know what people will do and why they do it at the same time. People on all the other planets do act alike, as you said, yet I have very much trouble understanding why. For instance, I like to try the local food when we set down on a planet, and if there is time I always do. There are bars and restaurants near every spaceport so I go there. And I always have trouble with the men. They want to buy me drinks, hold my hand—"

"Well, a single girl in those port joints has to expect a certain amount of interest from the men."

"Oh, I know that," she said. "What I don't understand is why they don't listen when I tell them I am not interested and to go away. They just laugh and pull up a chair, usually. But I have found that one thing works wherever I am. I tell them if they don't stop bothering me I'll break their arm."

"Does that stop them?" Jason asked.

"No, of course not. But after I break their arm they go away. And the others don't bother me either. It's a lot of fuss to go through and the food is usually awful."

Jason didn't laugh. Particularly when he realized that this girl *could* break the arm of any spaceport thug in the galaxy. She was a strange mixture of naivete and strength, unlike anyone he had ever met before. Once again he realized that he *had* to visit the planet that produced people like her and Kerk.

"Tell me about Pyrrus," he asked. "Why is it that you and Kerk assume automatically that I will drop dead as soon as I land? What is the planet like?"

All the warmth was gone from her face now. "I can't tell you. You will have to see for yourself. I know that much after visiting some of the other worlds. Pyrrus is like nothing you galaxy people have ever experienced. You won't really believe it until it is too late. Will you promise me something?"

"No," he answered. "At least not until after I hear what it is and decide."

"Don't leave the ship when we land. You *should* be safe enough aboard, and I'll be flying a cargo out within a few weeks."

"I'll promise nothing of the sort. I'll leave when I want to leave." Jason knew there was logic in her words, but his back was up at her automatic superiority.

Meta finished the jump settings without another word. There was a tension in the room that prevented them both from talking.

It was the next shipday before he saw her again, then it was completely by accident. She was in the astrogation dome when he entered, looking up at the sparkling immensity of the jump sky. For the first time he saw her off duty, wearing something other than a shipsuit. This was a loose, soft robe that accentuated her beauty.

She smiled at him. "The stars are so wonderful," she said. "Come look." Jason came close to her and with an unthinking, almost automatic movement, put his arm around her. Neither did she resent it, for she covered his hand with hers. Then they kissed and it was just the way he knew it would be.

6 AFTER THAT THEY WERE TOGETHER CONSTANTLY. When Meta was on duty he brought her meals to the bridge and they talked. Jason learned little more about her world since, by unspoken agreement, they didn't discuss it. He talked of the many planets he had visited and the people he had known. She was an appreciative listener and the time went quickly by. They enjoyed each other's company and it was a wonderful trip.

Then it ended.

There were fourteen people aboard the ship, yet Jason had never seen more than two or three at a time. There was a fixed rotation of duties that they followed in the ship's operation. When not on duty the Pyrrans minded their own business in an intense and self-sufficient manner. Only when the ship came out of jump and the PA barked *assembly* did they all get together.

Kerk was giving orders for the landing and questions were snapped back and forth. It was all technical and Jason didn't bother following it. It was the attitude of the Pyrrans that drew his attention. Their talk tended to be faster now as were their motions. They were like soldiers preparing for battle.

Their sameness struck Jason for the first time. Not that they looked alike or did the same things. It was the *way* they moved and reacted that caused the striking similarity.

They were like great, stalking cats. Walking fast, tense and ready to spring at all times, their eyes never still for an instant.

Jason tried to talk to Meta after the meeting, but she was almost a stranger. She answered in monosyllables and her eyes never met his, just brushed over them and went on. There was nothing he could really say so she moved to leave. He started to put his hand out to stop her—then thought better of it. There would be other times to talk.

Kerk was the only one who took any notice of him—and then only to order him to an acceleration couch.

Meta's landings were infinitely worse than her take-offs. At least when she landed on Pyrrus. There were sudden acceleration surges in every direction. At one point there was a free fall that seemed endless. There were loud thuds against the hull that shook the framework of the ship. It was more like a battle than a landing, and Jason wondered how much truth there was in that.

When the ship finally landed Jason didn't even know it. The constant 2 G's felt like deceleration. Only the descending moan of the ship's engines convinced him they were down. Unbuckling the straps and sitting up was an effort.

Two G's don't seem that bad—at first. Walking required the same exertion as would carrying a man of his own weight on his shoulders. When Jason lifted his arm to unlatch the door it was heavy as two arms. He shuffled slowly towards the main lock.

THEY WERE ALL THERE AHEAD of him, two of the men rolling transparent cylinders from a nearby room. From their obvious weight and the way they clanged when they bumped, Jason knew they were made of transparent metal. He couldn't conceive any possible use for them. Empty cylinders a meter in diameter, longer than a man. One end solid, the other hinged and sealed. It wasn't until Kerk spun the sealing wheel and opened one of them that their use became apparent.

"Get in," Kerk said. "When you're locked inside you'll be carried out of the ship."

"Thank you, no," Jason told him. "I have no particular desire to make a spectacular landing on your planet sealed up like a packaged sausage."

"Don't be a fool," was Kerk's snapped answer. "We're *all* going out in these tubes. We've been away too long to risk the surface without reorientation."

Jason did feel a little foolish as he saw the others getting into tubes. He picked the nearest one, slid into it feet first, and pulled the lid closed. When he tightened the wheel in the center, it squeezed down against a flexible seal. Within a minute the CO_2 content in the closed cylinder went up and an air regenerator at the bottom hummed into life.

Kerk was the last one in. He checked the seals on all the other tubes first, then jabbed the air-lock override release. As it started cycling he quickly sealed himself in the remaining cylinder. Both inner and outer locks ground slowly open and dim light filtered in through sheets of falling rain.

For Jason, the whole thing seemed an anticlimax. All this preparation for absolutely nothing. Long, impatient minutes passed before a lift truck appeared driven by a Pyrran. He loaded the cylinders onto his truck like so much dead cargo. Jason had the misfortune to be buried at the bottom of the pile so he could see absolutely nothing when they drove outside.

It wasn't until the man-carrying cylinders had been dumped in a metal-walled room, that Jason saw his first native Pyrran life.

The lift truck driver was swinging a thick outer door shut when something flew in through the entrance and struck against the far wall. Jason's eye was caught by the motion, he looked to see what it was when it dropped straight down towards his face.

Forgetful of the metal cylinder wall, he flinched away. The creature struck the transparent metal and clung to it. Jason had the perfect opportunity to examine it in every detail.

It was almost too horrible to be believable. As though it were a bearer of death stripped to the very essentials. A mouth that split the head in two, rows of teeth, serrated and pointed. Leathery, claw-tipped wings, longer claws on the limbs that tore at the metal wall.

Terror rose up in Jason as he saw that the claws were tearing gouges in the transparent metal. Wherever the creature's saliva touched the metal clouded and chipped under the assault of the teeth.

Logic said these were just scratches on the thick tube. They couldn't matter. But blind, unreasoning fear sent Jason curling away as far as he could. Shrinking inside himself, seeking escape.

Only when the flying creature began dissolving did he realize the nature of the room outside. Sprays of steaming liquid came from all sides, raining down until the cylinders were covered. After one last clash of its jaws, the Pyrran animal was washed off and carried away. The liquid drained away through the floor and a second and third shower followed.

While the solutions were being pumped away, Jason fought to bring his emotions into line. He was surprised at himself. No matter how frightful the creature had been, he couldn't understand the fear it could generate through the wall of the sealed tube. His reaction was all out of proportion to the cause. Even with the creature destroyed and washed out of sight it took all of his will power to steady his nerves and bring his breathing back to normal.

Meta walked by outside and he realized the sterilization process was finished. He opened his own tube and climbed wearily out. Meta and the others had gone by this time and only a hawk-faced stranger remained, waiting for him.

"I'm Brucco, in charge of the adaptation clinic. Kerk told me who you were. I'm sorry you're here. Now come along, I want some blood samples."

"Now I feel right at home," Jason said.

"The old Pyrran hospitality." Brucco only grunted and stamped out. Jason followed him down a bare corridor into a sterile lab.

The double gravity was tiring, a constant drag on sore muscles. While Brucco ran tests on the blood sample, Jason rested. He had almost dozed off into a painful sleep when Brucco returned with a tray of bottles and hypodermic needles.

"Amazing," he announced. "Not an antibody in your serum that would be of any use on this planet. I have a batch of antigens here that will make you sick as a beast for at least a day. Take off your shirt."

"Have you done this often?" Jason asked. "I mean juice up an outlander so he can enjoy the pleasures of your world?"

Brucco jammed in a needle that felt like it grated on the bone. "Not often at all. Last time was years ago. A half-dozen researchers from some institute, willing to pay well for the chance to study the local life forms. We didn't say no. Always need more galaxy currency."

Jason was already beginning to feel lightheaded from the shots. "How many of them lived?" he mumbled vaguely.

"One. We got him off in time. Made them pay in advance of course."

At first Jason thought the Pyrran was joking. Then he remembered they had very little interest in humor of any kind. If one-half of what Meta and Kerk had told him was true, six to one odds weren't bad at all.

There was a bed in the next room and Brucco helped him to it. Jason felt drugged and probably was. He fell into a deep sleep and into the dream.

Fear and hatred mixed in equal parts and washed over him red hot. If this was a dream, he never wanted to sleep again. If it wasn't a dream, he wanted to die. He tried to fight up against it, but only sank in more deeply. There was no beginning and no end to the fear and no way to escape.

When consciousness returned Jason could remember no detail of the nightmare. Just the fear remained. He was soaked with sweat and ached in every muscle. It must have been the massive dose of shots, he finally decided, that and the brutal gravity. That didn't take the taste of fear out of his mouth, though.

Brucco stuck his head in the door then and looked Jason up and down. "Thought you were dead," he said. "Slept the clock around. Don't move, I'll get something to pick you up."

The pickup was in the form of another needle and a glassful of evil-looking fluid. It settled his thirst, but made him painfully aware of gnawing hunger.

"Want to eat?" Brucco asked. "I'll bet you do. I've speeded up your metabolism so you'll build muscle faster. Only way you'll ever beat the gravity. Give you quite an appetite for a while though."

Brucco ate at the same time and Jason had a chance to ask some questions. "When do I get a chance to look around your fascinating planet? So far this trip has been about as interesting as a jail term."

"Relax and enjoy your food. Probably be months before you're able to go outside. If at all."

Jason felt his jaw hanging and closed it with a snap. "Could you possibly tell me why?"

"Of course. You will have to go through the same training course that our children take. It takes them six years. Of course it's their first six years of life. So you might think that you, as an adult, could learn faster. Then again they have the advantage of heredity. All I can say is you'll go outside these sealed buildings when you're ready."

Brucco had finished eating while he talked, and sat staring at Jason's bare arms with growing disgust. "The first thing we want to get you is a gun," he said. "It gives me a sick feeling to see someone without one."

Of course Brucco wore his own gun continually, even within the sealed buildings.

"Every gun is fitted to its owner and would be useless on anyone else," Brucco said. "I'll show you why." He led Jason to an armory jammed with deadly weapons. "Put your arm in this while I make the adjustments."

It was a boxlike machine with a pistol grip on the side. Jason clutched the grip and rested his elbow on a metal loop. Brucco fixed pointers that touched his arm, then copied the results from the meters. Reading the figures from his list he selected various components from bins and quickly assembled a power holster and gun. With the holster strapped to his forearm and the gun in his hand, Jason noticed for the first time they were connected by a flexible cable. The gun fitted his hand perfectly.

"This is the secret of the power holster," Brucco said, tapping the flexible cable. "It is perfectly loose while you are using the weapon. But when you want it returned to the holster—" Brucco made an adjustment and the cable became a stiff rod that whipped the gun from Jason's hand and suspended it in midair.

"Then the return." The rod-cable whirred and snapped the gun back into the holster. "The drawing action is the opposite of this, of course."

"A great gadget," Jason said, "but how *do* I draw? Do I whistle or something for the gun to pop out?"

"No, it is not sonic control," Brucco answered with a sober face. "It is much more precise than that. Here, take your left hand and grasp an imaginary gun butt. Tense your trigger finger. Do you notice the pattern of the tendons in the wrist? Sensitive actuators touch the tendons in your right wrist. They ignore all patterns except the one that says *hand ready to receive gun*. After a time the mechanism becomes completely automatic. When you want the gun—it is in your hand. When you don't—it is in the holster."

Jason made grasping motions with his right hand, crooked his index finger. There was a sudden, smashing pain against his hand and a loud roar. The gun was in his hand—half the fingers were numb—and smoke curled up from the barrel.

"Of course there are only blank charges in the gun until you learn control. Guns are *always* loaded. There is no safety. Notice the lack of a trigger guard. That enables you to bend your trigger finger a slight bit more when drawing so the gun will fire the instant it touches your hand."

It was without a doubt the most murderous weapon Jason had ever handled, as well as being the hardest to manage. Working against the muscle-burning ache of high gravity, he fought to control the devilish device. It had an infuriating way of vanishing into the holster just as he was about to pull the trigger. Even worse was the tendency to leap out before he was quite ready. The gun went to the position where his hand should be. If the fingers weren't correctly placed, they were crashed aside. Jason only stopped the practice when his entire hand was one livid bruise.

Complete mastery would come with time, but he could already understand why the Pyrrans never removed their guns. It would be like removing a part of your own body. The movement of gun from holster to hand was too fast for him to detect. It was certainly faster than the neural current that shaped the hand into the gun-holding position. For all apparent purposes it was like having a lightning bolt in your fingertip. Point the finger and *blamm*, there's the explosion.

BRUCCO HAD LEFT JASON to practice alone. When his aching hand could take no more, he stopped and headed back towards his own quarters. Turning a corner he had a quick glimpse of a familiar figure going away from him.

"Meta! Wait for a second—I want to talk to you."

She turned impatiently as he shuffled up, going as fast as he could in the doubled gravity. Everything about her seemed different from the girl he had known on the ship. Heavy boots came as high as her knees, her figure was lost in bulky coveralls of some metallic fabric. The trim waist was bulged out by a belt of canisters. Her very expression was coldly distant.

"I've missed you," he said. "I hadn't realized you were in this building." He reached for her hand but she moved it out of his reach.

"What is it you want?" she asked.

"What is it I want!" he echoed with barely concealed anger. "This is Jason, remember me? We're friends. It *is* allowed for friends to talk without 'wanting' anything."

"What happened on the ship has nothing to do with what happens on Pyrrus." She started forward impatiently as she talked. "I have finished my reconditioning and must return to work. You'll be staying here in the sealed buildings so I won't be seeing you."

"Why don't you say 'with the rest of the children'—that's what your tone implies? And don't try walking out, there are some things we have to settle first—"

Jason made the mistake of putting out his hand to stop her. He didn't really know what happened next. One instant he was standing—the next he sprawled suddenly on the floor. His shoulder was badly bruised, and Meta had vanished down the corridor.

Limping back to his own room he cursed women in general and Meta in particular. Dropping onto his rock-hard bed he tried to remember the reasons that had brought him here in the first place. And weighed them against the perpetual torture of the gravity, the fear-filled dreams it inspired, the automatic contempt of these people for any outsider. He quickly checked the growing tendency to feel sorry for himself. By Pyrran standards he *was* soft and helpless. If he wanted them to think any better of him, he would have to change a good deal.

He sank into a fatigue-drugged sleep then, that was broken only by the screaming fear of his dreams.

7 IN THE MORNING JASON AWOKE with a bad headache and the feeling he had never been to sleep. As he took some of the carefully portioned stimulants that Brucco had given him, he wondered again about the combination of factors that filled his sleep with such horror.

"Eat quickly," Brucco told him when they met in the dining room. "I can no longer spare you time for individual instruction. You will join the regular classes and take the prescribed courses. Only come to me if there is some special problem that the instructors or trainers can't handle."

The classes—as Jason should have expected—were composed of stern-faced little children. With their compact bodies and no-nonsense mannerisms they were recognizably Pyrran. But they were still children enough to consider it very funny to have an adult in their classes. Jammed behind one of the tiny desks, the red-faced Jason did not think it was much of a joke.

All resemblance to a normal school ended with the physical form of the classroom. For one thing, every child—no matter how small—packed a gun. And the courses were all involved with survival. The only possible grade in a curriculum like this was one hundred per cent and students stayed with a lesson until they mastered it perfectly. No courses were offered in the normal scholastic subjects. Presumably these were studied after the child graduated survival school and could face the world alone. Which was a logical and cold-hearted way of looking at things. In fact, logical and cold-hearted could describe any Pyrran activity.

Most of the morning was spent on the operation of one of the medikits that strapped around the waist. This was a poison analyzer that was pressed over a puncture wound. If any toxins were present, the antidote was automatically injected on the site. Simple in operation but incredibly complex in construction. Since all Pyrrans serviced their own equipment—you could then only blame yourself if it failed—they had to learn the construction and repair of all the devices. Jason did much better than the child students, though the effort exhausted him.

In the afternoon he had his first experience with a training machine. His instructor was a twelve-year-old boy, whose cold voice didn't conceal his contempt for the soft off-worlder.

"All the training machines are physical duplicates of the real surface of the planet, corrected constantly as the life forms change. The only difference between them is the varying degree of deadliness. This first machine you will use is of course the one infants are put into—"

"You're too kind," Jason murmured. "Your flattery overwhelms me." The instructor continued, taking no notice of the interruption.

"...Infants are put into as soon as they can crawl. It is real in substance, though completely deactivated."

TRAINING MACHINE WAS THE WRONG WORD, Jason realized as they entered through the thick door. This was a chunk of the outside world duplicated in an immense chamber. It took very little suspension of reality for him to forget the painted ceiling and artificial sun high above and imagine himself outdoors at last. The scene *seemed* peaceful enough. Though clouds banking on the horizon threatened a violent Pyrran storm.

"You must wander around and examine things," the instructor told Jason. "Whenever you touch something with your hand, you will be told about it. Like this—"

The boy bent over and pushed his finger against a blade of the soft grass that covered the ground. Immediately a voice barked from hidden speakers.

"Poison grass. Boots to be worn at all times."

Jason kneeled and examined the grass. The blade was tipped with a hard, shiny hook. He realized with a start that every single blade of grass was the same. The soft green lawn was a carpet of death. As he straightened up he glimpsed something under a broad-leafed plant. A crouching, scale-covered animal, whose tapered head terminated in a long spike.

"What's *that* in the bottom of my garden?" he asked. "You certainly give the babies pleasant playmates." Jason turned and realized he was talking to the air, the instructor was gone. He shrugged and petted the scaly monstrosity.

"Horndevil," the impersonal voice said from midair. "Clothing and shoes no protection. Kill it."

A sharp *crack* shattered the silence as Jason's gun went off. The horndevil fell on its side, keyed to react to the blank charge.

"Well ... I *am* learning," Jason said, and the thought pleased him. The words *kill it* had been used by Brucco while teaching him to use the gun. Their stimulus had reached an unconscious level. He was aware of wanting to shoot only after he had heard the shot. His respect for Pyrran training techniques went up.

Jason spent a thoroughly unpleasant afternoon wandering in the child's garden of horror. Death was everywhere. While all the time the disembodied voice gave him stern advice in simple language. So he could do unto, rather than being done in. He had never realized that violent death could come in so many repulsive forms. *Everything* here was deadly to man—from the smallest insect to the largest plant.

Such singleness of purpose seemed completely unnatural. Why was this planet so alien to human life? He made a mental note to ask Brucco. Meanwhile he tried to find one life form that wasn't out for his blood. He didn't succeed. After a long search he found the only thing that when touched didn't elicit deadly advice. This was a chunk of rock that projected from a meadow of poison grass. Jason sat on it with a friendly feeling and pulled his feet up. An oasis of peace. Some minutes passed while he rested his gravity-weary body.

"ROTFUNGUS—DO NOT TOUCH!"

The voice blasted at twice its normal volume and Jason leaped as if he had been shot. The gun was in his hand, nosing about for a target. Only when he bent over and looked closely at the rock where he had been sitting, did he understand. There were flaky gray patches that hadn't been there when he sat down.

"Oh you tricky devils!" he shouted at the machine. "How many kids have you frightened off that rock after they thought they had found a little peace?" He resented the snide bit of conditioning, but respected it at the same time. Pyrrans learned very early in life that there was no safety on this planet—except that which they provided for themselves.

While he was learning about Pyrrus he was gaining new insight into the Pyrrans as well.

8 DAYS TURNED INTO WEEKS in the school, cut off from the world outside. Jason almost became proud of his ability to deal death. He recognized all the animals and plants in the nursery room and had been promoted to a trainer where the beasts made sluggish charges at him. His gun picked off the attackers with dull regularity. The constant, daily classes were beginning to bore him as well.

Though the gravity still dragged at him, his muscles were making great efforts to adjust. After the daily classes he no longer collapsed immediately into bed. Only the nightmares got worse. He had finally mentioned them to Brucco, who mixed up a sleeping potion that took away most of their effect. The dreams were still there, but Jason was only vaguely aware of them upon awakening.

By the time Jason had mastered all the gadgetry that kept the Pyrrans alive, he had graduated to a most realistic trainer that was only a hair-breadth away from the real thing. The difference was just in quality. The insect poisons caused swelling and pain instead of instant death. Animals could cause bruises and tear flesh, but stopped short of ripping off limbs. You couldn't get killed in this trainer, but could certainly come very close to it.

Jason wandered through this large and rambling jungle with the rest of the five-year-olds. There was something a bit humorous, yet sad, about their unchildlike grimness. Though they still might laugh in their quarters, they realized there was no laughing outside. To them survival was linked up with social acceptance and desirability. In this way Pyrrus was a simple black-and-white society. To prove your value to yourself and your world, you only had to stay alive. This had great importance in racial survival, but had very stultifying effects on individual personality. Children were turned into like-faced killers, always on the alert to deal out death.

Some of the children graduated into the outside world and others took their places. Jason watched this process for a while before he realized that all of those from the original group he had entered with were gone. That same day he looked up the chief of the adaptation center.

"Brucco," Jason asked, "how long do you plan to keep me in this kindergarten shooting gallery?"

"You're not being 'kept' here," Brucco told him in his usual irritated tone. "You will be here until you qualify for the outside."

"Which I have a funny feeling will be never. I can now field strip and reassemble every one of your blasted gadgets in the dark. I am a dead shot with this cannon. At this present moment, if I had to, I could write a book on the Complete Flora and Fauna of Pyrrus, and How to Kill It. Perhaps I don't do as well as my six-year-old companions, but I have a hunch I do about as good a job now as I ever will. Is that true?"

Brucco squirmed with the effort to be evasive, yet didn't succeed. "I think, that is, you know you weren't born here, and—"

"Come, come," Jason said with glee, "a straight-faced old Pyrran like you shouldn't try to lie to one of the weaker races that specialize in that sort of thing. It goes without saying that I'll always be sluggish with this gravity, as well as having other inborn hand-

icaps. I admit that. We're not talking about that now. The question is—will I improve with more training, or have I reached a peak of my own *development* now?"

Brucco sweated. "With the passage of time there will be improvement of course—"

"Sly devil!" Jason waggled a finger at him. "Yes or no, now. Will I improve *now* by more training *now*?"

"No," Brucco said, and still looked troubled. Jason sized him up like a poker hand.

"Now let's think about that. I won't improve—yet I'm still stuck here. That's no accident. So you must have been ordered to keep me here. And from what I have seen of this planet, admittedly very little, I would say that Kerk ordered you to keep me here. Is that right?"

"He was only doing it for your own sake," Brucco explained, "trying to keep you alive."

"The truth is out," Jason said, "so let us now forget about it. I didn't come here to shoot robots with your offspring. So please show me the street door. Or is there a graduating ceremony first? Speeches, handing out school pins, sabers overhead—"

"Nothing like that," Brucco snapped. "I don't see how a grown man like you can talk such nonsense all the time. There is none of that, of course. Only some final work in the partial survival chamber. That is a compound that connects with the outside—really is a part of the outside—except the most violent life forms are excluded. And even some of those manage to find their way in once in a while."

"When do I go?" Jason shot the question.

"Tomorrow morning. Get a good night's sleep first. You'll need it."

THERE WAS ONE BIT of ceremony attendant with the graduation. When Jason came into his office in the morning, Brucco slid a heavy gun clip across the table.

"These are live bullets," he said. "I'm sure you'll be needing them. After this your gun will always be loaded."

They came up to a heavy air lock, the only locked door Jason had seen in the center. While Brucco unlocked it and threw the bolts, a sober-faced eight-year-old with a bandaged leg limped up.

"This is Grif," Brucco said. "He will stay with you, wherever you go, from now on."

"My personal bodyguard?" Jason asked, looking down at the stocky child who barely reached his waist.

"You might call him that." Brucco swung the door open. "Grif tangled with a sawbird, so he won't be able to do any real work for a while. You yourself admitted that you will never be able to equal a Pyrran, so you should be glad of a little protection."

"Always a kind word, that's you, Brucco," Jason said. He bent over and shook hands with the boy. Even the eight-year-olds had a bone-crushing grip.

The two of them entered the lock and Brucco swung the inner door shut behind them. As soon as it was sealed the outer door opened automatically. It was only partly open when Grif's gun blasted twice. Then they stepped out onto the surface of Pyrrus, over the smoking body of one of its animals.

Very symbolic, Jason thought. He was also bothered by the realization that he hadn't remembered to look for something coming in. Then, too, he couldn't even identify the beast from its charred remains. He glanced around, hoping he would be able to fire first himself, next time.

This was an unfulfilled hope. The few beasts that came their way were always seen first by the boy. After an hour of this, Jason was so irritated that he blasted an evil-looking thorn plant out of existence. He hoped that Grif wouldn't look too closely at it. Of course the boy did.

"That plant wasn't close. It is stupid to waste good ammunition on a plant," Grif said.

There was no real trouble during the day. Jason ended by being bored, though soaked by the frequent rainstorms. If Grif was capable of carrying on a conversation, he didn't show it. All Jason's gambits failed. The following day went the same way. On the third day, Brucco appeared and looked Jason carefully up and down.

"I don't like to say it, but I suppose you are as ready to leave now as you ever will be. Change the virus filter noseplugs every day. Always check boots for tears and metalcloth suiting for rips. Medikit supplies renewed once a week."

"And wipe my nose and wear my galoshes. Anything else?" Jason asked.

Brucco started to say something, then changed his mind. "Nothing that you shouldn't know well by now. Keep alert. And ... good luck." He followed up the words with a crushing handshake that was totally unexpected. As soon as the numbness left Jason's hand, he and Grif went out through the large entrance lock.

9 REAL AS THEY HAD BEEN, the training chambers had not prepared him for the surface of Pyrrus. There was the basic similarity of course. The feel of the poison grass underfoot and the erratic flight of a stingwing in the last instant before Grif blasted it. But these were scarcely noticeable in the crash of the elements around him.

A heavy rain was falling, more like a sheet of water than individual drops. Gusts of wind tore at it, hurling the deluge into his face. He wiped his eyes clear and could barely make out the conical forms of two volcanoes on the horizon, vomiting out clouds of smoke and flame. The reflection of this inferno was a sullen redness on the clouds that raced by in banks above them.

There was a rattle on his hard hat and something bounced off to splash to the ground. He bent over and picked up a hailstone as thick as his thumb. A sudden flurry of hail hammered painfully at his back and neck, he straightened hurriedly.

As quickly as it started the storm was over. The sun burned down, melting the hailstones and sending curls of steam up from the wet street. Jason sweated inside his armored clothing. Yet before they had gone a block it was raining again and he shook with chill.

Grif trudged steadily along, indifferent to the weather or the volcanoes that rumbled on the horizon and shook the ground beneath their feet. Jason tried to ignore his discomfort and match the boy's pace.

The walk was a depressing one. The heavy, squat buildings loomed grayly through the rain, more than half of them in ruins. They walked on a pedestrian way in the middle of the street. The occasional armored trucks went by on both sides of them. The midstreet sidewalk puzzled Jason until Grif blasted something that hurtled out of a ruined building towards them. The central location gave them some chance to see what was coming. Suddenly Jason was very tired.

"Grif, this city of yours is sure down at the heels. I hope the other ones are in better shape."

"I don't know what you mean talking about heels. But there are no other cities. Some mining camps that can't be located inside the perimeter. But no other cities."

This surprised Jason. He had always visualized the planet with more than one city. There were a *lot* of things he didn't know about Pyrrus, he realized suddenly. All of his efforts since landing had been taken up with the survival studies. There were a number of questions he wanted to ask. But ask them of somebody other than his grouchy eight-year-old bodyguard. There was one person who would be best equipped to tell him what he wanted to know.

"Do you know Kerk?" he asked the boy. "Apparently he's your ambassador to a lot of places, but his last name—"

"Sure, everybody knows Kerk. But he's busy, you shouldn't see him."

Jason shook a finger at him. "Minder of my body you may be. But minder of my soul you are not. What do you say I call the shots and you go along to shoot the monsters? OK?"

THEY TOOK SHELTER from a sudden storm of fist-sized hailstones. Then, with ill grace, Grif led the way to one of the larger, central buildings. There were more people here and some of them even glanced at Jason for a minute, before turning back to their business. Jason dragged himself up two flights of stairs before they reached a door marked COORDINATION AND SUPPLY.

"Kerk in here?" Jason asked.

"Sure," the boy told him. "He's in charge."

"Fine. Now you get a nice cold drink, or your lunch, or something, and meet me back here in a couple of hours. I imagine Kerk can do as good a job of looking after me as you can."

The boy stood doubtfully for a few seconds, then turned away. Jason wiped off some more sweat and pushed through the door.

There were a handful of people in the office beyond. None of them looked up at Jason or asked his business. Everything has a purpose on Pyrrus. If he came there—he must have had a good reason. No one would ever think to ask him what he wanted. Jason, used to the petty officialdom of a thousand worlds, waited for a few moments before he understood. There was only one other door. He shuffled over and opened it.

Kerk looked up from a desk strewed about with papers and ledgers. "I was wondering when you would show up," he said.

"A lot sooner if you hadn't prevented it," Jason told him as he dropped wearily into a chair. "It finally dawned on me that I could spend the rest of my life in your bloodthirsty nursery school if I didn't do something about it. So here I am."

"Ready to return to the 'civilized' worlds, now that you've seen enough of Pyrrus?"

"I am not," Jason said. "And I'm getting very tired of everyone telling me to leave. I'm beginning to think that you and the rest of the Pyrrans are trying to hide something."

Kerk smiled at the thought. "What could we have to hide? I doubt if any planet has as simple and one-directional an existence as ours."

"If that's true, then you certainly wouldn't mind answering a few direct questions about Pyrrus?"

Kerk started to protest, then laughed. "Well done. I should know better by now than to argue with you. What do you want to know?"

Jason tried to find a comfortable position on the hard chair, then gave up. "What's the population of your planet?" he asked.

For a second Kerk hesitated, then said, "Roughly thirty thousand. That is not very much for a planet that has been settled this long, but the reason for that is obvious."

"All right, population thirty thousand," Jason said. "Now how about surface control of your planet. I was surprised to find out that this city within its protective wall—the perimeter—is the only one on the planet. Let's not consider the mining camps, since they are obviously just extensions of the city. Would you say then, that you people control more or less of the planet's surface than you did in the past?"

Kerk picked up a length of steel pipe from the desk, that he used as a paperweight, and toyed with it as he thought. The thick steel bent like rubber at his touch, as he concentrated on his answer.

"That's hard to say offhand. There must be records of that sort of thing, though I wouldn't know where to find them. It depends on so many factors—"

"Let's forget that for now then," Jason said. "I have another question that's really more relevant. Wouldn't you say that the population of Pyrrus is declining steadily, year after year?"

There was a sharp *twang* as the steel snapped in Kerk's fingers, the pieces dropping to the floor. He stood, over Jason, his hands extended towards the smaller man, his face flushed and angry.

"Don't ever say that," he roared. "Don't let me ever hear you say that again!"

Jason sat as quietly as he could, talking slowly and picking out each word with care. His life hung in the balance.

"Don't get angry, Kerk. I meant no harm. I'm on your side, remember? I can talk to you because you've seen much more of the universe than the Pyrrans who have never left the planet. You are used to discussing things. You know that words are just symbols. We can talk and know you don't have to lose your temper over mere words—"

Kerk slowly lowered his arms and stepped away. Then he turned and poured himself a glass of water from a bottle on the desk. He kept his back turned to Jason while he drank.

Very little of the sweat that Jason wiped from his sopping face was caused by the heat in the room.

"I'm ... sorry I lost my temper," Kerk said, dropping heavily into his chair. "Doesn't usually happen. Been working hard lately, must have got my temper on edge." He made no mention of what Jason had said.

"Happens to all of us," Jason told him. "I won't begin to describe the condition my nerves were in when I hit this planet. I'm finally forced to admit that everything you said about Pyrrus is true. It is the most deadly spot in the system. And only native-born Pyrrans could possibly survive here. I can manage to fumble along a bit after my training, but I know I would never stand a chance on my own. You probably know I have an eight-year-old as a bodyguard. Gives a good idea of my real status here."

Anger suppressed, Kerk was back in control of himself now. His eyes narrowed in thought. "Surprises me to hear you say that. Never thought I would hear you admit that anyone could be better than you at anything. Isn't that why you came here? To prove that you were as good as any native-born Pyrran?"

"Score one for your side," Jason admitted. "I didn't think it showed that much. And I'm glad to see your mind isn't as muscle-bound as your body. Yes, I'll admit that was probably my main reason for coming, that and curiosity."

Kerk was following his own train of thoughts, and puzzled where they were leading him. "You came here to prove that you were as good as any native-born Pyrran. Yet now you admit that any eight-year-old can outdraw you. That just doesn't stack up with what I know about you. If you give with one hand, you must be taking back with the other. In what way do you still feel your natural superiority?"

Jason thought a long time before answering.

"I'll tell you," he finally said. "But don't snap my neck for it. I'm gambling that your civilized mind can control your reflexes. Because I have to talk about things that are strictly taboo on Pyrrus.

"In your people's eyes I'm a weakling because I come from off-world. Realize though, that this is also my strength. I can see things that are hidden from you by long association. You know, the old business of not being able to see the forest for the trees in the way." Kerk nodded agreement and Jason went on.

"To continue the analogy further, I landed from an airship, and at first all I *could* see was the forest. To me certain facts are obvious. I think that you people know them too, only you keep your thoughts carefully repressed. They are hidden thoughts that are completely taboo. I am going to say one of them out loud now and hope you can control yourself well enough to not kill me."

Kerk's great hands tightened on the arms of his chair, the only sign that he had heard. Jason talked quietly, as smoothly and easily as a lancet probing into a brain.

"Human beings are losing the war on Pyrrus. There is no chance they can win. They could leave for another planet, but that wouldn't be victory. Yet, if they stay and continue this war, they only prolong a particularly bloody form of racial suicide. With each generation the population drops. Until eventually the planet will win."

One arm of Kerk's plastic and steel chair tore loose under the crushing grasp of his fingers. He didn't notice it. The rest of his body was rock-still and his eyes fixed on Jason.

Looking away from the fractured chair,

Jason sought for the right words.

"This is not a real war, but a disastrous treating of symptoms. Like cutting off cancerous fingers one by one. The only result can be ultimate death. None of you seem to realize that. All you see are the trees. It has never occurred to you that you could treat the *causes* of this war and end it forever."

Kerk dropped the arm of the chair clattering to the floor. He sat up, astonished. "What the devil do you mean? You sound like a grubber."

Jason didn't ask what a grubber was—but he filed the name.

"Call me a Pyrran by adoption. I want this planet to survive as much as you do. I think this war can be ended by finding the *causes*—and changing them, whatever they are."

"You're talking nonsense," Kerk said. "This is just an alien world that must be battled. The causes are self-obvious facts of existence."

"No, they're not," Jason insisted. "Consider for a second. When you are away for any length of time from this planet, you must take a refresher course. To see how things have changed for the worse while you were gone. Well, that's a linear progression. If things get worse when you extend into the future, then they have to get better if you extend into the past. It is also good theory—though I don't know if the facts will bear me out—to say that if you extend it far enough into the past you will reach a time when mankind and Pyrrus were not at war with each other."

Kerk was beyond speech now, only capable of sitting and listening while Jason drove home the blows of inescapable logic.

"There is evidence to support this theory. Even you will admit that I, if I am no match for Pyrran life, am surely well versed in it. And all Pyrran flora and fauna I've seen have one thing in common. They're not functional. *None* of their immense armory of weapons is used against each other. Their toxins don't seem to operate against Pyrran life. They are good only for dispensing death to Homo sapiens. And *that* is a physical impossibility. In the three hundred years that men have been on this planet, the life forms couldn't have naturally adapted in this manner."

"But they *have* done it!" Kerk bellowed.

"You are so right," Jason told him calmly. "And if they have done it there must be some agency at work. Operating how—I have no idea. But something has caused the life on Pyrrus to declare war, and I'd like to find out what that something is. What was the dominant life form here when your ancestors landed?"

"I'm sure I wouldn't know," Kerk said. "You're not suggesting, are you, that there are sentient beings on Pyrrus other than those of human descent? Creatures who are organizing the planet to battle us?"

"I'm not suggesting it—you are. That means you're getting the idea. I have no idea what caused this change, but I would sure like to find out. Then see if it can be changed back. Nothing promised, of course. You'll agree, though, that it is worth investigating."

FIST SMACKING INTO HIS PALM, his heavy footsteps shaking the building, Kerk paced back and forth the length of the room. He was at war with himself. New ideas fought old beliefs. It was so sudden—and so hard not to believe.

Without asking permission Jason helped himself to some chilled water from the bottle, and sank back into the chair, exhausted. Something whizzed in through the open window, tearing a hole in the protective screen. Kerk blasted it without changing stride, without even knowing he had done it.

The decision didn't take long. Geared to swift activity, the big Pyrran found it impossible not to decide quickly. The pacing stopped and a finger stabbed at Jason.

"I don't say you have convinced me, but I find it impossible to find a ready answer to your arguments. So until I do, we will have to operate as if they are true. Now what do you plan to do, what *can* you do?"

Jason ticked the points off on his fingers. "One, I'll need a place to live and work that is well protected. So instead of spending my energies on just remaining alive I can devote some study to this project. Two, I want someone to help me—and act as a bodyguard at the same time. And someone, please, with a little more scope of interest than my present watchdog. I would suggest Meta for the job."

"Meta?" Kerk was surprised. "She is a space pilot and defense-screen operator, what good could she possibly be on a project like this?"

"The most good possible. She has had experience on other worlds and can shift her point of view—at least a bit. And she must know as much about this planet as any other educated adult and can answer any questions I ask." Jason smiled. "In addition to which she is an attractive girl, whose company I enjoy."

Kerk grunted. "I was wondering if you would get around to mentioning that last reason. The others make sense though, so I'm not going to argue. I'll round up a replacement for her and have Meta sent here. There are plenty of sealed buildings you can use."

After talking to one of the assistants from the outer office, Kerk made some calls on the screen. The correct orders were quickly issued. Jason watched it all with interest.

"Pardon me for asking," he finally said. "But are you the dictator of this planet? You just snap your fingers and they all jump."

"I suppose it looks that way," Kerk admitted. "But that is just an illusion. No one is in complete charge on Pyrrus, neither is there anything resembling a democratic system. After all, our total population is about the size of an army division. Everyone does the job they are best qualified for. Various activities are separated into departments with the most qualified person in charge. I run Coordination and Supply, which is about the loosest category. We fill in the gaps between departments and handle procuring from off-planet."

Meta came in then and talked to Kerk. She completely ignored Jason's presence. "I was relieved and sent here," she said. "What is it? Change in flight schedule?"

"You might call it that," Kerk said. "As of now you are dismissed from all your old assignments and assigned to a new department: Investigation and Research. That tired-looking fellow there is your department head."

"A sense of humor," Jason said. "The only native-born one on Pyrrus. Congratulations, there's hope for the planet yet."

Meta glanced back and forth between them. "I don't understand. I can't believe it. I mean a new department—why?"

"I'm sorry," Kerk said. "I didn't mean to be cruel. I thought perhaps you might feel more at ease. What I said was true. Jason has a way—or may have a way—to be of immense value to Pyrrus. Will you help him?"

Meta had her composure back. And a little anger. "Do I have to? Is that an order? You know I have work to do. I'm sure you will realize it is more important than something a person from *off-planet* might imagine. He can't really understand—"

"Yes. It's an order." The snap was back in Kerk's voice. Meta flushed at the tone.

"Perhaps I can explain," Jason broke in. "After all the whole thing is my idea. But first I would like your co-operation. Will you take the clip out of your gun and give it to Kerk?"

Meta looked frightened, but Kerk nodded in solemn agreement. "Just for a few minutes, Meta. I have my gun so you will be safe here. I think I know what Jason has in mind, and from personal experience I'm afraid he is right."

Reluctantly Meta passed over the clip and cleared the charge in the gun's chamber. Only then did Jason explain.

"I have a theory about life on Pyrrus, and I'm afraid I'll have to shatter some illusions when I explain. To begin with, the fact must be admitted that your people are slowly losing the war here and will eventually be destroyed—"

Before he was half through the sentence, Meta's gun was directed between his eyes and she was wildly snapping the trigger. There was only hatred and revulsion in her expression. Kerk took her by the shoulders and sat her in his chair, before anything worse happened. It took a while before she could calm down enough to listen to Jason's words. It is not easy to have the carefully built-up falsehoods of a lifetime shattered. Only the fact that she had seen something of other worlds enabled her to listen at all.

The light of unreason was still in her eyes when he had finished, telling her the things he and Kerk had discussed. She sat tensely, pushed forward against Kerk's hands, as if they were the only things that stopped her from leaping at Jason.

"Maybe that is too much to assimilate at one sitting," Jason said. "So let's put it in simpler terms. I believe we can find a reason for this unrelenting hatred of humans. Perhaps we don't smell right. Maybe I'll find an essence of crushed Pyrran bugs that will render us immune when we rub it in. I don't know yet. But whatever the results, we *must* make the investigation. Kerk agrees with me on that."

Meta looked at Kerk and he nodded agreement. Her shoulders slumped in sudden defeat. She whispered the words.

"I ... can't say I agree, or even understand all that you said. But I'll help you. If Kerk thinks that it is the right thing."

"I do," he said. "Now, do you want the clip back for your gun? Not planning to take any more shots at Jason?"

"That was foolish of me," she said coldly while she reloaded the gun. "I don't need a gun. If I had to kill him, I could do it with my bare hands."

"I love you, too," Jason smiled at her. "Are you ready to go now?"

"Of course." She brushed a fluffy curl of hair into place. "First we'll find a place where you can stay. I'll take care of that. After that the work of the new department is up to you."

10

THERE WERE EMPTY ROOMS in one of the computer buildings. These were completely sealed to keep stray animal life out of the delicate machinery. While Meta checked a bed-roll out of stores, Jason painfully dragged a desk, table and chairs in from a nearby empty office. When she returned with a pneumatic bed he instantly dropped on it with a grateful sigh. Her lip curled a bit at his obvious weakness.

"Get used to the sight," he said. "I intend to do as much of my work as I can, while maintaining a horizontal position. You will be my strong right arm. And right now, Right Arm, I wish you could scare me up something to eat. I also intend to do most of my eating in the previously mentioned prone condition."

Snorting with disgust, Meta stamped out. While she was gone, Jason chewed the end of a stylus thoughtfully, then made some careful notes.

After they had finished the almost-tasteless meal he began the search.

"Meta, where can I find historical records of Pyrrus?"

"I've never heard of any ... I really don't know."

"But there has to be something—somewhere," he insisted. "Even if your present-day culture devotes all of its time and energies to survival, you can be sure it wasn't always that way. All the time it was developing, people were keeping records, making notes. Now where do we look? Do you have a library here?"

"Of course," she said. "We have an excellent technical library. But I'm sure there wouldn't be any of *that* sort of thing there."

Trying not to groan, Jason stood up. "Let me be the judge of that. Just lead the way."

OPERATION OF THE LIBRARY was completely automatic. A projected index gave the call number for any text that had to be consulted. The tape was delivered to the charge desk thirty seconds after the number had been punched. Returned tapes were dropped through a hopper and refiled automatically. The mechanism worked smoothly.

"Wonderful," Jason said, pushing away from the index. "A tribute to technological ingenuity. Only it contains nothing of any value to us. Just reams of textbooks."

"What *else* should be in a library?" Meta sounded sincerely puzzled.

Jason started to explain, then changed his mind. "Later we will go into that," he said. "Much later. Now we have to find a lead. Is it possible that there are any tapes—or even printed books—that aren't filed through this machine?"

"It seems unlikely, but we could ask Poli. He lives here somewhere and is in charge of the library—filing new books and tending the machinery."

The single door into the rear of the building was locked, and no amount of pounding could rouse the caretaker.

"If he's alive, this should do it," Jason said. He pressed the out-of-order button on the control panel. It had the desired affect. Within five minutes the door opened and Poli dragged himself through it.

Death usually came swiftly on Pyrrus. If wounds slowed a man down, the ever-ready forces of destruction quickly finished the job. Poli was the exception to this rule. Whatever had attacked him originally had done an efficient job. Most of the lower part of his face was gone. His left arm was curled and useless. The damage to his body and legs had left him with the bare capability to stumble from one spot to the next.

Yet he still had one good arm as well as his eyesight. He could work in the library and relieve a fully fit man. How long he had been dragging the useless husk of a body around the building, no one knew. In spite of the pain that filled his red-rimmed, moist eyes, he had stayed alive. Growing old, older than any other Pyrran as far as Jason had seen. He tottered forward and turned off the alarm that had called him.

When Jason started to explain the old man took no notice. Only after the librarian had rummaged a hearing aid out of his clothes, did Jason realize he was deaf as well. Jason explained again what he searched for. Poli nodded and printed his answer on a tablet.

there are many old books—in the store-rooms below

Most of the building was taken up by the robot filing and sorting apparatus. They moved slowly through the banks of machinery, following the crippled librarian to a barred door in the rear. He pointed to it. While Jason and Meta fought to open the age-incrusted bars, he wrote another note on his tablet.

not opened for many years, rats

Jason's and Meta's guns appeared reflexively in their hands as they read the message. Jason finished opening the door by himself. The two native Pyrrans stood facing the opening gap. It was well they did. Jason could never have handled what came through that door.

He didn't even open it for himself. Their sounds at the door must have attracted all the vermin in the lower part of the building. Jason had thrown the last bolt and started to pull on the handle—when the door was *pushed* open from the other side.

OPEN THE GATEWAY TO HELL and see what comes out. Meta and Poli stood shoulder to shoulder firing into the mass of loathsomeness that boiled through the door. Jason jumped to one side and picked off the occasional animal that came his way. The destruction seemed to go on forever.

Long minutes passed before the last clawed beast made its death rush. Meta and Poli waited expectantly for more, they were happily excited by this chance to deal destruction. Jason felt a little sick after the silent ferocious attack. A ferocity that the Pyrrans reflected. He saw a scratch on Meta's face where one of the beasts had caught her. She seemed oblivious to it.

Pulling out his medikit, Jason circled the piled bodies. Something stirred in their midst and a crashing shot ploughed into it. Then he reached the girl and pushed the analyzer probes against the scratch. The machine clicked and Meta jumped as the antitoxin needle stabbed down. She realized for the first time what Jason was doing.

"Thank you," she said.

Poli had a powerful battery lamp and, by unspoken agreement, Jason carried it. Crippled though he was, the old man was still a Pyrran when it came to handling a gun. They slowly made their way down the refuse-laden stairs.

"What a stench," Jason grimaced.

At the foot of the stairs they looked around. There *had* been books and records there at one time. They had been systematically chewed, eaten and destroyed for decades.

"I like the care you take with your old books," Jason said disgustedly.

"They could have been of no importance," Meta said coolly, "or they would be filed correctly in the library upstairs."

Jason wandered gloomily through the rooms. Nothing remained of any value. Fragments and scraps of writing and printing. Never enough in one spot to bother collecting. With the toe of one armored boot, he kicked angrily at a pile of debris, ready to give up the search. There was a glint of rusty metal under the dirt.

"Hold this!" He gave the light to Meta and

began scratching aside the rubble. A flat metal box with a dial lock built into it, was revealed.

"Why that's a log box!" Meta said, surprised.

"That's what I thought," Jason said.

11 RESEALING THE CELLAR, they carried the box back to Jason's new office. Only after spraying with decontaminant, did they examine it closely. Meta picked out engraved letters on the lid.

"S. T. POLLUX VICTORY—that must be the name of the spacer this log came from. But I don't recognize the class, or whatever it is the initials *S. T.* stand for."

"Stellar Transport," Jason told her, as he tried the lock mechanism. "I've heard of them but I've never seen one. They were built during the last wave of galactic expansion. Really nothing more than gigantic metal containers, put together in space. After they were loaded with people, machinery and supplies, they would be towed to whatever planetary system had been chosen. These same tugs and one-shot rockets would brake the S. T.'s in for a landing. Then leave them there. The hull was a ready source of metal and the colonists could start right in building their new world. And they were *big*. All of them held at least fifty thousand people ..."

Only after he said it, did he realize the significance of his words. Meta's deadly stare drove it home. There were now less people on Pyrrus than had been in the original settlement.

And human population, without rigid birth controls, usually increased geometrically. Jason dinAlt suddenly remembered Meta's itchy trigger finger.

"But we can't be sure how many people were aboard this one," he said hurriedly. "Or

even if this is the log of the ship that settled Pyrrus. Can you find something to pry this open with? The lock is corroded into a single lump."

Meta took her anger out on the box. Her fingers managed to force a gap between lid and bottom. She wrenched at it. Rusty metal screeched and tore. The lid came off in her hands and a heavy book thudded to the table.

The cover legend destroyed all doubt.

LOG OF S. T. POLLUX VICTORY. OUTWARD BOUND—SETANI TO PYRRUS. 55,000 SETTLERS ABOARD.

Meta couldn't argue now. She stood behind Jason with tight-clenched fists and read over his shoulder as he turned the brittle, yellowed pages. He quickly skipped through the opening part that covered the sailing preparations and trip out. Only when he had reached the actual landing did he start reading slowly. The impact of the ancient words leaped out at him.

"Here it is," Jason shouted. "Proof positive that we're on the right trail. Even *you* will have to admit that. Read it, right here."

...Second day since the tugs left, we are completely on our own now. The settlers still haven't grown used to this planet, though we have orientation talks every night. As well as the morale agents who I have working twenty hours a day. I suppose I really can't blame the people, they all lived in the underways of Setani and I doubt if they saw the sun once a year. This planet has weather with a vengeance, worse than anything I've seen on a hundred other planets. Was I wrong during the original planning stages not to insist on settlers from one of the agrarian worlds? People who could handle

the outdoors.

These citified Setanians are afraid to go out in the rain. But of course they have adapted completely to their native 1.5 gravity so the two gee here doesn't bother them much. That was the factor that decided us. Anyway—too late now to do anything about it. Or about the unending cycle of rain, snow, hail, hurricanes and such. Answer will be to start the mines going, sell the metals and build completely enclosed cities.

The only thing on this forsaken planet that isn't actually against us are the animals. A few large predators at first, but the guards made short work of them. The rest of the wild life leaves us alone. Glad of that! They have been fighting for existence so long that I have never seen a more deadly looking collection. Even the little rodents no bigger than a man's hand are armored like tanks....

"I don't believe a word of it," Meta broke in. "That can't be Pyrrus he's writing about...." Her words died away as Jason wordlessly pointed to the title on the cover.

He continued scanning the pages, flipping them quickly. A sentence caught his eye and he stopped. Jamming his finger against the place, he read aloud.

"'...And troubles keep piling up. First Har Palo with his theory that the vulcanism is so close to the surface that the ground keeps warm and the crops grow so well. Even if he is right—what can we do? We must be self-dependent if we intend to survive. And now this other thing. It seems that the forest fire drove a lot of new species our way. Animals, insects and even birds have attacked the people. (Note for Har: check if possible seasonal migration might explain attacks.)

"'There have been fourteen deaths from wounds and poisoning. We'll have to enforce the rules for insect lotion at all times. And I suppose build some kind of perimeter defense to keep the larger beasts out of the camp.'

"This is a beginning," Jason said. "At least now we are aware of the real nature of the battle we're engaged in. It doesn't make Pyrrus any easier to handle, or make the life forms less dangerous, to know that they were once better disposed towards mankind. All this does is point the way. Something took the peaceful life forms, shook them up, and turned this planet into one big death-trap for mankind. That *something* is what I want to uncover."

12 FURTHER READING OF THE LOG produced no new evidence. There was a good deal more information about the early animal and plant life and how deadly they were, as well as the first defenses against them. Interesting historically, but of no use whatsoever in countering the menace. The captain apparently never thought that life forms were altering on Pyrrus, believing instead that dangerous beasts were being discovered. He never lived to change his mind. The last entry in the log, less than two months after the first attack, was very brief. And in a different handwriting.

Captain Kurkowski died today, of poisoning following an insect bite. His death is greatly mourned.

The "why" of the planetary revulsion had yet to be uncovered.

"Kerk must see this book," Jason said. "He should have some idea of the progress being made. Can we get transportation—or do we walk to city hall?"

"Walk, of course," Meta said.

"Then you bring the book. At two G's I find it very hard to be a gentleman and carry the packages."

They had just entered Kerk's outer office when a shrill screaming burst out of the phone-screen. It took Jason a moment to realize that it was a mechanical signal, not a human voice.

"What is it?" he asked.

Kerk burst through the door and headed for the street entrance. Everyone else in the office was going the same way. Meta looked confused, leaning towards the door, then looking back at Jason.

"What does it mean? Can't you tell me?" He shook her arm.

"Sector alarm. A major breakthrough of some kind at the perimeter. Everyone but other perimeter guards has to answer."

"Well, go then," he said. "Don't worry about me. I'll be all right."

His words acted like a trigger release. Meta's gun was in her hand and she was gone before he had finished speaking. Jason sat down wearily in the deserted office.

The unnatural silence in the building began to get on his nerves. He shifted his chair over to the phone-screen and switched it on to *receive*. The screen exploded with color and sound. At first Jason could make no sense of it at all. Just a confused jumble of faces and voices. It was a multi-channel set designed for military use. A number of images were carried on the screen at one time, rows of heads or hazy backgrounds where the user had left the field of view. Many of the heads were talking at the same time and the babble of their voices made no sense whatsoever.

After examining the controls and making a few experiments, Jason began to understand the operation. Though all stations were on the screen at all times, their audio channels could be controlled. In that way two, three or more stations could be hooked together in a link-up. They would be in round-robin communication with each other, yet never out of contact with the other stations.

Identification between voice and sound was automatic. Whenever one of the pictured images spoke, the image would glow red. By trial and error Jason brought in the audio for the stations he wanted and tried to follow the course of the attack.

Very quickly he realized this was something out of the ordinary. In some way, no one made it clear, a section of the perimeter had been broken through and emergency defenses had to be thrown up to encapsulate it. Kerk seemed to be in charge, at least he was the only one with an override transmit-

ter. He used it for general commands. The many, tiny images faded and his face appeared on top of them, filling the entire screen.

"All perimeter stations send twenty-five per cent of your complement to Area Twelve."

The small images reappeared and the babble increased, red lights flickering from face to face.

"...Abandon the first floor, acid bombs can't reach."

"If we hold we'll be cut off, but salient is past us on the west flank. Request support."

"DON'T, MERVV... IT'S USELESS!"

"...And the napalm tanks are almost gone. Orders?"

"The truck is still there, get it to the supply warehouse, you'll find replacements...."

OUT OF THE WELTER OF TALK, only the last two fragments made any sense. Jason had noticed the signs below when he came in. The first two floors of the building below him were jammed with military supplies. This was his chance to get into the act.

Just sitting and watching was frustrating. Particularly when it was a desperate emergency. He didn't overvalue his worth, but he was sure there was always room for another gun.

By the time he had dragged himself down to the street level a turbo-truck had slammed to a stop in front of the loading platform. Two Pyrrans were rolling out drums of napalm with reckless disregard for their own safety. Jason didn't dare enter that maelstrom of rolling metal. He found he could be of use tugging the heavy drums into position on the truck while the others rolled them up. They accepted his aid without acknowledgment.

It was exhausting, sweaty work, hauling the leaden drums into place against the heavy gravity. After a minute Jason worked by touch through a red haze of hammering blood. He realized the job was done only when the truck suddenly leaped forward and he was thrown to the floor. He lay there, his chest heaving. As the driver hurled the heavy vehicle along, all Jason could do was bounce around in the bottom. He could see well enough, but was still gasping for breath when they braked at the fighting zone.

To Jason, it was a scene of incredible confusion. Guns firing, flames, men and women running on all sides. The napalm drums were unloaded without his help and the truck vanished for more. Jason leaned against a wall of a half-destroyed building and tried to get his bearings. It was impossible. There seemed to be a great number of small animals: he killed two that attacked him. Other than that he couldn't determine the nature of the battle.

A Pyrran, tan face white with pain and exertion, stumbled up. His right arm, wet with raw flesh and dripping blood, hung limply at his side. It was covered with freshly applied surgical foam. He held his gun in his left hand, a stump of control cable dangling from it. Jason thought the man was looking for medical aid. He couldn't have been more wrong.

Clenching the gun in his teeth, the Pyrran clutched a barrel of napalm with his good hand and hurled it over on its side. Then, with the gun once more in his hand, he began to roll the drum along the ground with his feet. It was slow, cumbersome work, but he was still in the fight.

Jason pushed through the hurrying crowd and bent over the drum. "Let me do it," he said. "You can cover us both with your gun."

The man wiped the sweat from his eyes with the back of his arm and blinked at Jason. He seemed to recognize him. When he smiled it was a grimace of pain, empty of humor. "Do that. I can still shoot. Two half men—maybe we equal one whole." Jason was laboring too hard to even notice the insult.

AN EXPLOSION HAD BLASTED a raw pit in the street ahead. Two people were at the bottom, digging it even deeper with shovels. The whole thing seemed meaningless. Just as

Jason and the wounded man rolled up the drum the diggers leaped out of the excavation and began shooting down into its depths. One of them turned, a young girl, barely in her teens.

"Praise Perimeter!" she breathed. "They found the napalm. One of the new horrors is breaking through towards Thirteen, we just found it." Even as she talked she swiveled the drum around, kicked the easy-off plug, and began dumping the gelid contents into the hole. When half of it had gurgled down, she kicked the drum itself in. Her companion pulled a flare from his belt, lit it, and threw it after the drum.

"Back quick. They don't like heat," he said.

This was putting it very mildly. The napalm caught, tongues of flame and roiling, greasy smoke climbed up to the sky. Under Jason's feet the earth shifted and moved. *Something* black and long stirred in the heart of the flame, then arched up into the sky over their heads. In the midst of the searing heat it still moved with alien, jolting motions. It was immense, at least two meters thick and with no indication of its length. The flames didn't stop it at all, just annoyed it.

Jason had some idea of the thing's length as the street cracked and buckled for fifty meters on each side of the pit. Great loops of the creature began to emerge from the ground. He fired his gun, as did the others. Not that it seemed to have any effect. More and more people were appearing, armed with a variety of weapons. Flame-throwers and grenades seemed to be the most effective.

"Clear the area ... we're going to saturate it. Fall back."

The voice was so loud it jarred Jason's ear. He turned and recognized Kerk, who had arrived with truckloads of equipment. He had a power speaker on his back, the mike hung in front of his lips. His amplified voice brought an instant reaction from the crowd. They began to move.

There was still doubt in Jason's mind

what to do. Clear the area? But what area? He started towards Kerk, before he realized that the rest of the Pyrrans were going in the opposite direction. Even under two gravities they *moved*.

Jason had a naked feeling of being alone on the stage. He was in the center of the street, and the others had vanished. No one remained. Except the wounded man Jason had helped. He stumbled towards Jason, waving his good arm. Jason couldn't understand what he said. Kerk was shouting orders again from one of the trucks. They had started to move too. The urgency struck home and Jason started to run.

It was too late. On all sides the earth was buckling, cracking, as more loops of the underground thing forced its way into the light. Safety lay ahead. Only in front of it rose an arch of dirt-encrusted gray.

THERE ARE SECONDS OF TIME that seem to last an eternity. A moment of subjective time that is grabbed and stretched to an infinite distance. This was one of those moments. Jason stood, frozen. Even the smoke in the sky hung unmoving. The high-standing loop of alien life was before him, every detail piercingly clear.

Thick as a man, ribbed and gray as old bark. Tendrils projected from all parts of it, pallid and twisting lengths that writhed slowly with snakelike life. Shaped like a plant, yet with the motions of an animal. And cracking, splitting. This was the worst.

Seams and openings appeared. Splintering, gaping mouths that vomited out a horde of pallid animals. Jason heard their shriekings, shrill yet remote. He saw the needlelike teeth that lined their jaws.

The paralysis of the unknown held him there. He should have died. Kerk was thundering at him through the power speaker, others were firing into the attacking creature. Jason knew nothing.

Then he was shot forward, pushed by a rock-hard shoulder. The wounded man was still there, trying to get Jason clear. Gun clenched in his jaws he dragged Jason along with his good arm. Towards the creature. The others stopped firing. They saw his plan and it was a good one.

A loop of the thing arched into the air, leaving an opening between its body and the ground. The wounded Pyrran planted his feet and tightened his muscles. One-handed, with a single thrust, he picked Jason off the ground and sent him hurtling under the living arch. Moving tendrils brushed fire along his face, then he was through, rolling over and over on the ground. The wounded Pyrran leaped after him.

It was too late. There had been a chance for one person to get out. The Pyrran could have done it easily—instead he had pushed Jason first. The thing was aware of movement when Jason brushed its tendrils. It dropped and caught the wounded man under its weight. He vanished from sight as the tendrils wrapped around him and the animals swarmed over. His trigger must have pulled back to full automatic because the gun kept firing a long time after he should have been dead.

Jason crawled. Some of the fanged animals ran towards him, but were shot. He knew nothing about this. Then rude hands grabbed him up and pulled him forward. He slammed into the side of a truck and Kerk's face was in front of his, flushed and angry. One of the giant fists closed on the front of Jason's clothes and he was lifted off his feet, shaken like a limp bag of rags. He offered no protest and could not have even if Kerk had killed him.

When he was thrown to the ground, someone picked him up and slid him into the back of the truck. He did not lose consciousness as the truck bounced away, yet he could not move. In a moment the fatigue would go away and he would sit up. That was all he was, just a little tired. Even as he thought this he passed out.

13 "JUST LIKE OLD TIMES," Jason said when Brucco came into the room with a tray of food. Without a word Brucco served Jason and the wounded men in the other beds, then left. "Thanks," Jason called after his retreating back.

A joke, a twist of a grin, like it always was. Sure. But even as he grinned and his lips shaped a joke, Jason felt them like a veneer on the outside. Something plastered on with a life of its own. Inside he was numb and immovable. His body was stiff as his eyes still watched that arch of alien flesh descend and smother the one-armed Pyrran with its million burning fingers.

He could feel himself under the arch. After all, hadn't the wounded man taken his place? He finished the meal without realizing that he ate.

Ever since that morning, when he had recovered consciousness, it had been like this. He knew that he should have died out there in that battle-torn street. *His* life

should have been snuffed out, for making the mistake of thinking that he could actually help the battling Pyrrans. Instead of being underfoot and in the way. If it hadn't been for Jason, the man with the wounded arm would have been brought here to the safety of the reorientation buildings. He knew he was lying in the bed that belonged to that man.

The man who had given his life for Jason's. The man whose name he didn't even know.

There were drugs in the food and they made him sleep. The medicated pads soaked the pain and rawness out of the burns where the tentacles had seared his face. When he awoke the second time, his touch with reality had been restored.

A man had died so he could live. Jason faced the fact. He couldn't restore that life, no matter how much he wanted to. What he could do was make the man's death worthwhile. If it can be said that any death was worthwhile ... He forced his thoughts from that track.

Jason knew what he had to do. His work was even more important now. If he could solve the riddle of this deadly world, he could repay in part the debt he owed.

Sitting up made his head spin and he held to the edge of the bed until it slowed down. The others in the room ignored him as he slowly and painfully dragged on his clothes. Brucco came in, saw what he was doing, and left again without a word.

Dressing took a long time, but it was finally done. When Jason finally left the room he found Kerk waiting for him.

"Kerk ... I want to tell you...."

"Tell me *nothing!*" The thunder of Kerk's voice bounced back from the ceiling and walls. "I'm telling *you.* I'll tell you once and that will be the end of it. You're not wanted on Pyrrus, Jason dinAlt, neither you nor your precious off-world schemes are wanted here. I let you convince me once with your twisted tongue. Helped you at the expense of more important work. I should have known what the result of your 'logic' would be. Now I've seen. Welf died so you could live. He was twice the man you will ever be."

"Welf? Was that his name?" Jason asked stumblingly. "I didn't know—"

"You didn't even know." Kerk's lips pulled back from his teeth in a grimace of disgust. "You didn't even know his name— yet he died that you might continue your miserable existence." Kerk spat, as if the words gave a vile flavor to his speech, and stamped towards the exit lock. Almost as an afterthought he turned back to Jason.

"You'll stay here in the sealed buildings until the ship returns in two weeks. Then you will leave this planet and never come back. If you do, I'll kill you instantly. With pleasure." He started through the lock.

"Wait," Jason shouted. "You can't decide like that. You haven't even seen the evidence I've uncovered. Ask Meta—" The lock thumped shut and Kerk was gone.

The whole thing was just too stupid. Anger began to replace the futile despair of a moment before. He was being treated like an irresponsible child, the importance of his discovery of the log completely ignored.

Jason turned and saw for the first time that Brucco was standing there. "Did you hear that?" Jason asked him.

"Yes. And I quite agree. You can consider yourself lucky."

"Lucky!" Jason was the angry one now. "Lucky to be treated like a moronic child, with contempt for everything I do—"

"I said lucky," Brucco snapped. "Welf was Kerk's only surviving son. Kerk had high hopes for him, was training him to take his place eventually." He turned to leave but Jason called after him.

"Wait. I'm sorry about Welf. I can't be any sorrier knowing that he was Kerk's son. But at least it explains why Kerk is so quick to throw me out—as well as the evidence I have uncovered. The log of the ship—"

"I know, I've seen it," Brucco said. "Meta brought it in. Very interesting historical document."

"That's all you can see it as—an historical document? The significance of the planetary change escapes you?"

"It doesn't escape me," Brucco answered briefly, "but I cannot see that it has any relevancy today. The past is unchangeable and we must fight in the present. That is enough to occupy all our energies."

Jason felt too exhausted to argue the point any more. He ran into the same stone wall with all the Pyrrans. Theirs was a logic of the moment. The past and the future unchangeable, unknowable—and uninteresting. "How is the perimeter battle going?" he asked, wanting to change the subject.

"Finished. Or in the last stages at least," Brucco was almost enthusiastic as he showed Jason some stereos of the attackers. He did not notice Jason's repressed shudder.

"This was one of the most serious breakthroughs in years, but we caught it in time. I hate to think what would have happened if they hadn't been detected for a few weeks more."

"What are those things?" Jason asked. "Giant snakes of some kind?"

"Don't be absurd," Brucco snorted. He tapped the stereo with his thumbnail. "Roots. That's all. Greatly modified, but still roots. They came in under the perimeter barrier, much deeper than anything we've had before. Not a real threat in themselves as they have very little mobility. Die soon after being cut. The danger came from their being used as access tunnels. They're bored through and through with animal runs, and two or three species of beasts live in a sort of symbiosis inside.

"Now we know what they are we can watch for them. The danger was they could have completely undermined the perimeter and come in from all sides at once. Not much we could have done then."

THE EDGE OF DESTRUCTION. Living on the lip of a volcano. The Pyrrans took satisfaction from any day that passed without total annihilation. There seemed no way to change their attitude. Jason let the conversation die there. He picked up the log of the *Pollux Victory* from Brucco's quarters and carried it back to his room. The wounded Pyrrans there ignored him as he dropped onto the bed and opened the book to the first page.

For two days he did not leave his quarters. The wounded men were soon gone and he had the room to himself. Page by page he went through the log, until he knew every detail of the settlement of Pyrrus. His notes and cross-references piled up. He made an accurate map of the original settlement, superimposed over a modern one. They didn't match at all.

It was a dead end. With one map held over the other, what he had suspected was painfully clear. The descriptions of terrain and physical features in the log were accurate enough. The city had obviously been moved since the first landing. Whatever records had been kept would be in the library—and he had exhausted that source. Anything else would have been left behind and long since destroyed.

Rain lashed against the thick window above his head, lit suddenly by a flare of lightning. The unseen volcanoes were active again, vibrating the floor with their rumblings deep in the earth.

The shadow of defeat pressed heavily down on Jason. Rounding his shoulders and darkening, even more, the overcast day.

14

JASON SPENT ONE DEPRESSED DAY lying on his bunk counting rivets, forcing himself to accept defeat. Kerk's order that he was not to leave the sealed building tied his hands completely. He felt himself close to the answer—but he was never going to get it.

One day of defeat was all he could take. Kerk's attitude was completely emotional, untempered by the slightest touch of logic. This fact kept driving home until Jason could no longer ignore it. Emotional reasoning was something he had learned to mistrust early in life. He couldn't agree with

Kerk in the slightest—which meant he had to utilize the ten remaining days to solve the problem. If it meant disobeying Kerk, it would still have to be done.

He grabbed up his noteplate with a new enthusiasm. His first sources of information had been used up, but there must be others. Chewing the scriber and needling his brain, he slowly built up a list of other possibilities. Any idea, no matter how wild, was put down. When the plate was filled he wiped the long shots and impossibles—such as consulting off-world historical records. This was a Pyrran problem, and had to be settled on this planet or not at all.

The list worked down to two probables. Either old records, notebooks or diaries that individual Pyrrans might have in their possession, or verbal histories that had been passed down the generations by word of mouth. The first choice seemed to be the most probable and he acted on it at once. After a careful check of his medikit and gun he went to see Brucco.

"What's new and deadly in the world since I left?" he asked.

Brucco glared at him. "You can't go out, Kerk has forbidden it."

"Did he put you in charge of guarding me to see if I obeyed?" Jason's voice was quiet and cold.

Brucco rubbed his jaw and frowned in thought. Finally he just shrugged. "No, I'm not guarding you—nor do I want the job. As far as I know this is between you and Kerk and it can stay that way. Leave whenever you want. And get yourself killed quietly some place so there will be an end to the trouble you cause once and for all."

"I love you, too," Jason said. "Now brief me on the wildlife."

The only new mutation that routine precautions wouldn't take care of was a slate-colored lizard that spit a fast nerve poison with deadly accuracy. Death took place in seconds if the saliva touched any bare skin. The lizards had to be looked out for, and shot before they came within range. An hour of lizard-blasting in a training chamber made him proficient in the exact procedure.

JASON LEFT THE SEALED BUILDINGS QUIETLY and no one saw him go. He followed the map to the nearest barracks, shuffling tiredly through the dusty streets. It was a hot, quiet afternoon, broken only by rumblings from the distance, and the occasional crack of his gun.

It was cool inside the thick-walled barracks buildings, and he collapsed onto a bench until the sweat dried and his heart stopped pounding. Then he went to the nearest recreation room to start his search.

Before it began it was finished. None of the Pyrrans kept old artifacts of any kind and thought the whole idea was very funny. After the twentieth negative answer Jason was ready to admit defeat in this line of investigation. There was as much chance of meeting a Pyrran with old documents as finding a bundle of grandfather's letters in a soldier's kit bag.

This left a single possibility—verbal histories. Again Jason questioned with the same lack of results. The fun had worn off the game for the Pyrrans and they were beginning to growl. Jason stopped while he was still in one piece. The commissary served him a meal that tasted like plastic paste and wood pulp. He ate it quickly, then sat brooding over the empty tray, hating to admit to another dead end. Who could supply him with answers? All the people he had talked to were so young. They had no interest or patience for story-telling. That was an old folks' hobby—and there were no oldsters on Pyrrus.

With one exception that he knew of, the librarian, Poli. It was a possibility. A man who worked with records and books might have an interest in some of the older ones. He might even remember reading volumes now destroyed. A very slim lead indeed, but one that had to be pursued.

Walking to the library almost killed Jason. The torrential rains made the footing bad, and in the dim light it was hard to see what was coming. A snapper came in close enough to take out a chunk of flesh before he could blast it. The antitoxin made him dizzy and he lost some blood before he could get the wound dressed. He reached the library, exhausted and angry.

Poli was working on the guts of one of the catalogue machines. He didn't stop until Jason had tapped him on the shoulder. Switching on his hearing aid, the Pyrran stood quietly, crippled and bent, waiting for Jason to talk.

"Have you any old papers or letters that you have kept for your personal use?"

A shake of the head, *no*.

"What about stories—you know, about great things that have happened in the past, that someone might have told you when you were young?" Negative.

Results negative. Every question was answered by a shake of Poli's head, and very soon the old man grew irritated and pointed to the work he hadn't finished.

"Yes, I know you have work to do," Jason said. "But this is important." Poli shook his head an angry *no* and reached to turn off his hearing aid. Jason groped for a question that might get a more positive answer. There was something tugging at his mind, a word he had heard and made a note of, to be investigated later. Something that Kerk had said....

"That's it!" It was right there—on the tip of his tongue. "Just a second, Poli, just one more question. What is a 'grubber'? Have you ever seen one or know what they do, or where they can be found—"

The words were cut off as Poli whirled and lashed the back of his good arm into Jason's face. Though the man was aged and crippled, the blow almost fractured Jason's jaw, sending him sliding across the floor. Through a daze he saw Poli hobbling towards him, making thick bubbling noises in his ruined throat; what remained of his face twisted and working with anger.

This was no time for diplomacy. Moving as fast as he could, with the high-G, foot-slapping shuffle, Jason headed for the sealed door. He was no match for any Pyrran in hand-to-hand combat, young and small or old and crippled. The door thunked open, as he went through, and barely closed in Poli's face.

Outside the rain had turned to snow and Jason trudged wearily through the slush, rubbing his sore jaw and turning over the only fact he had. *Grubber* was a key—but to what? And who did he dare ask for more information? Kerk was the man he had talked to best, but not any more. That left only Meta as a possible source. He wanted to see her at once, but sudden exhaustion swept through him. It took all of his strength to stumble back to the school buildings.

IN THE MORNING HE ATE and left early. There was only a week left. It was impossible to hurry and he cursed as he dragged his double-weight body to the assignment center. Meta was on night perimeter duty and should be back to her quarters soon. He shuffled over there and was lying on her bunk when she came in.

"Get out," she said in a flat voice. "Or do I throw you out?"

"Patience, please," he said as he sat up. "Just resting here until you came back. I have a single question, and if you will answer it for me I'll go and stop bothering you."

"What is it?" she asked, tapping her foot with impatience. But there was also a touch of curiosity in her voice. Jason thought carefully before he spoke.

"Now *please*, don't shoot me. You know I'm an off-worlder with a big mouth, and you have heard me say some awful things without taking a shot at me. Now I have another one. Will you please show your superiority to the other people of the galaxy by holding your temper and not reducing me to component atoms?"

His only answer was a tap of the foot, so he took a deep breath and plunged in.

"What is a 'grubber'?"

For a long moment she was quiet, unmoving. Then she curled her lips back in disgust. "You find the most repulsive topics."

"That may be so," he said, "but it still doesn't answer my question."

"It's ... well, the sort of thing people just don't talk about."

"I do," he assured her.

"Well, I *don't!* It's the most disgusting thing in the world, and that's all I'm going to say. Talk to Krannon, but not to me." She had him by the arm while she talked and he was half dragged to the hall. The door slammed behind him and he muttered "*lady wrestler*" under his breath. His anger ebbed away as he realized that she had given him a clue in spite of herself. Next step, find out who or what Krannon was.

Assignment center listed a man named Krannon, and gave his shift number and work location. It was close by and Jason walked there. A large, cubical, and windowless building, with the single word *food* next to each of the sealed entrances. The small entrance he went through was a series of automatic chambers that cycled him through ultrasonics, ultraviolet, antibio spray, rotating brushes and three final rinses. He was finally admitted, damper but much cleaner to the central area. Men and robots were stacking crates and he asked one of the men for Krannon. The man looked him up and down coldly and spat on his shoes before answering.

Krannon worked in a large storage bay by himself. He was a stocky man in patched coveralls whose only expression was one of intense gloom. When Jason came in he stopped hauling bales and sat down on the nearest one. The lines of unhappiness were cut into his face and seemed to grow deeper while Jason explained what he was after. All the talk of ancient history on Pyrrus bored him as well and he yawned openly. When Jason finished he yawned again and didn't even bother to answer him.

Jason waited a moment, then asked again. "I said do you have any old books, papers, records or that sort of thing?"

"You sure picked the right guy to bother, off-worlder," was his only answer. "After talking to me you're going to have nothing but trouble."

"Why is that?" Jason asked.

"Why?" For the first time he was animated with something besides grief. "I'll tell you why! I made one mistake, just one, and I get a life sentence. For life—how would you like that? Just me alone, being by myself all the time. Even taking orders from the grubbers."

Jason controlled himself, keeping the elation out of his voice. "Grubbers? What are grubbers?"

The enormity of the question stopped Krannon, it seemed impossible that there could be a man alive who had never heard of grubbers. Happiness lifted some of the gloom from his face as he realized that he had a captive audience who would listen to his troubles.

"Grubbers are traitors—that's what they are. Traitors to the human race and they ought to be wiped out. Living in the jungle. The things they do with the animals—"

"You mean they're people ... Pyrrans like yourself?" Jason broke in.

"Not like *me*, mister. Don't make that mistake again if you want to go on living. Maybe I dozed off on guard once so I got stuck with this job. That doesn't mean I like it or like them. They stink, really stink, and if it wasn't for the food we get from them they'd all be dead tomorrow. That's the kind of killing job I could really put my heart into."

"If they supply you with food, you must give them something in return?"

"Trade goods, beads, knives, the usual things. Supply sends them over in cartons and I take care of the delivery."

"How?" Jason asked.

"By armored truck to the delivery site. Then I go back later to pick up the food they've left in exchange."

"Can I go with you on the next delivery?"

Krannon frowned over the idea for a minute. "Yeah, I suppose it's all right if you're stupid enough to come. You can help me load. They're between harvests now, so the next trip won't be for eight days—"

"But that's after the ship leaves—it'll be too late. Can't you go earlier?"

"Don't tell me your troubles, mister," Krannon grumbled, climbing to his feet. "That's when I go and the date's not changing for you."

Jason realized he had got as much out of the man as was possible for one session. He started for the door, then turned.

"One thing," he asked. "Just what do these savages—the grubbers—look like?"

"How do I know," Krannon snapped. "I trade with them, I don't make love to them. If I ever saw one, I'd shoot him down on the spot." He flexed his fingers and his gun jumped in and out of his hand as he said it. Jason quietly let himself out.

Lying on his bunk, resting his gravity-weary body, he searched for a way to get Krannon to change the delivery date. His millions of credits were worthless on this world without currency. If the man couldn't be convinced, he had to be bribed. With what? Jason's eyes touched the locker where his off-world clothing still hung, and he had an idea.

It was morning before he could return to the food warehouse—and one day closer to his deadline. Krannon didn't bother to look up from his work when Jason came in.

"Do you want this?" Jason asked, handing the outcast a flat gold case inset with a single large diamond. Krannon grunted and turned it over in his hands.

"A toy," he said. "What is it good for?"

"Well, when you press this button you get a light." A flame appeared through a hole in the top. Krannon started to hand it back.

"What do I need a little fire for? Here, keep it."

"Wait a second," Jason said, "that's not all it does. When you press the jewel in the center one of these comes out." A black pellet the size of his fingernail dropped into his palm. "A grenade, made of solid ulranite. Just squeeze it hard and throw. Three seconds later it explodes with enough force to blast open this building."

This time Krannon almost smiled as he reached for the case. Destructive and death-dealing weapons are like candy to a Pyrran. While he looked at it Jason made his offer.

"The case and bombs are yours if you move the date of your next delivery up to tomorrow—and let me go with you."

"Be here at 0500," Krannon said. "We leave early."

15 THE TRUCK RUMBLED UP to the perimeter gate and stopped. Krannon waved to the guards through the front window, then closed a metal shield over it. When the gates swung open the truck—really a giant armored tank—ground slowly forward. There was a second gate beyond the first, that did not open until the interior one was closed. Jason looked through the second-driver's periscope as the outer gate lifted. Automatic flame-throwers flared through the opening, cutting off only when the truck reached them. A scorched area ringed the gate, beyond that the jungle began. Unconsciously Jason shrank back in his seat.

All the plants and animals he had seen only specimens of, existed here in profusion. Thorn-ringed branches and vines laced themselves into a solid mat, through which the wild life swarmed. A fury of sound hurled at them, thuds and scratchings rang on the armor. Krannon laughed and closed the switch that electrified the outer grid. The scratchings died away as the beasts completed the circuit to the grounded hull.

It was slow-speed, low-gear work tearing through the jungle. Krannon had his face buried in the periscope mask and silently fought the controls. With each mile the going seemed to get better, until he finally swung up the periscope and opened the window armor. The jungle was still thick and deadly, but nothing like the area immediately around the perimeter. It appeared as if most of the lethal powers of Pyrrus were concentrated in the single area around the settle-ment. Why? Jason asked himself. Why this intense and planetary hatred?

The motors died and Krannon stood up, stretching. "We're here," he said. "Let's unload."

There was bare rock around the truck, a rounded hillock that projected from the jungle, too smooth and steep for vegetation to get a hold. Krannon opened the cargo hatches and they pushed out the boxes and crates. When they finished Jason slumped down, exhausted, onto the pile.

"Get back in, we're leaving," Krannon said.

"You are, I'm staying right here."

Krannon looked at him coldly. "Get in the truck or I'll kill you. No one stays out here. For one thing you couldn't live an hour alone. But worse than that the grubbers would get you. Kill you at once, of course, but that's not important. But you have equipment that we can't allow into their hands. You want to see a grubber with a gun?"

While the Pyrran talked, Jason's thoughts had rushed ahead. He hoped that Krannon was as thick of head as he was fast of reflex.

Jason looked at the trees, let his gaze move up through the thick branches. Though Krannon was still talking, he was automatically aware of Jason's attention. When Jason's eyes widened and his gun jumped into his hand, Krannon's own gun appeared and he turned in the same direction.

"There—in the top!" Jason shouted, and fired into the tangle of branches. Krannon fired, too. As soon as he did, Jason hurled himself backwards, curled into a ball, rolling down the inclined rock. The shots had covered the sounds of his movements, and before Krannon could turn back the gravity had dragged him down the rock into the thick foliage. Crashing branches slapped at him, but slowed his fall. When he stopped moving he was lost in the tangle. Krannon's shots came too late to hit him.

Lying there, tired and bruised, Jason

heard the Pyrran cursing him out. He stamped around on the rock, fired a few shots, but knew better than to enter the trees. Finally he gave up and went back to the truck. The motor gunned into life and the treads clanked and scraped down the rock and back into the jungle. There were muted rumblings and crashes that slowly died away.

Then Jason was alone.

UP UNTIL THAT INSTANT he hadn't realized quite how alone he would be. Surrounded by nothing but death, the truck already vanished from sight. He had to force down an overwhelming desire to run after it. What was done was done.

This was a long chance to take, but it was the only way to contact the grubbers. They were savages, but still they had come from human stock. And they hadn't sunk so low as to stop the barter with the civilized Pyrrans. He had to contact them, befriend them. Find out how they had managed to live safely on this madhouse world.

If there had been another way to lick the problem, he would have taken it; he didn't relish the role of martyred hero. But Kerk and his deadline had forced his hand. The contact had to be made fast and this was the only way.

There was no telling where the savages were, or how soon they would arrive. If the woods weren't too lethal he could hide there, pick his time to approach them. If they found him among the supplies, they might skewer him on the spot with a typical Pyrran reflex.

Walking warily he approached the line of trees. Something moved on a branch, but vanished as he came near. None of the plants near a thick-trunked tree looked poisonous, so he slipped behind it. There was nothing deadly in sight and it surprised him. He let his body relax a bit, leaning against the rough bark.

Something soft and choking fell over his head, his body was seized in a steel grip. The more he struggled the tighter it held him until the blood thundered in his ears and his lungs screamed for air.

Only when he grew limp did the pressure let up. His first panic ebbed a little when he realized that it wasn't an animal that attacked him. He knew nothing about the grubbers, but they were human so he still had a chance.

His arms and legs were tied, the power holster ripped from his arm. He felt strangely naked without it. The powerful hands grabbed him again and he was hurled into the air, to fall face down across something warm and soft. Fear pressed in again, it was a large animal of some kind. And all Pyrran animals were deadly.

When the animal moved off, carrying him, panic was replaced by a feeling of mounting elation. The grubbers had managed to work out a truce of some kind with at least one form of animal life. He had to find out how. If he could get that secret—and get it back to the city—it would justify all his work and pain. It might even justify Welf's death if the age-old war could be slowed or stopped.

Jason's tightly bound limbs hurt terribly at first, but grew numb with the circulation shut off. The jolting ride continued endlessly, he had no way of measuring the time. A rainfall soaked him, then he felt his clothes steaming as the sun came out.

The ride was finally over. He was pulled from the animal's back and dumped down. His arms dropped free as someone loosed the bindings. The returning circulation soaked him in pain as he lay there, struggling to move. When his hands finally obeyed him he lifted them to his face and stripped away the covering, a sack of thick fur. Light blinded him as he sucked in breath after breath of clean air.

Blinking against the glare, he looked around. He was lying on a floor of crude planking, the setting sun shining into his eyes through the doorless entrance of the building. There was a ploughed field outside, stretching down the curve of hill to the edge of the jungle. It was too dark to see much inside the hut.

Something blocked the light of the doorway, a tall animallike figure. On second look Jason realized it was a man with long hair and thick beard. He was dressed in furs, even his legs were wrapped in fur leggings. His eyes were fixed on his captive, while one hand fondled an ax that hung from his waist.

"Who're you? What y'want?" the bearded man asked suddenly.

Jason picked his words slowly, wondering if this savage shared the same hair-trigger temper as the city dwellers.

"My name is Jason. I come in peace. I want to be your friend ..."

"Lies!" the man grunted, and pulled the ax from his belt. "Junkman tricks. I saw y'hide. Wait to kill me. Kill you first." He tested the edge of the blade with a horny thumb, then raised it.

"Wait!" Jason said desperately. "You don't understand."

The ax swung down.

"I'm from off-world and—"

A solid thunk shook him as the ax buried itself in the wood next to his head. At the last instant the man had twitched it aside. He grabbed the front of Jason's clothes and pulled him up until their faces touched.

"S'true?" he shouted. "Y'from off-world?" His hand opened and Jason dropped back before he could answer. The savage jumped over him, towards the dim rear of the hut.

"Rhes must know of this," he said as he fumbled with something on the wall. Light sprang out.

All Jason could do was stare. The hairy, fur-covered savage was operating a communicator. The calloused, dirt-encrusted fingers deftly snapped open the circuits, dialed a number.

16 **IT MADE NO SENSE.** Jason tried to reconcile the modern machine with the barbarian and couldn't. Who was he calling? The existence of one communicator meant there was at least another. Was Rhes a person or a thing?

With a mental effort he grabbed hold of his thoughts and braked them to a stop. There was something new here, factors he hadn't counted on. He kept reassuring himself there was an explanation for everything, once you had your facts straight.

Jason closed his eyes, shutting out the glaring rays of the sun where it cut through the tree tops, and reconsidered his facts. They separated evenly into two classes; those he had observed for himself, and those he had learned from the city dwellers. This last class of "facts" he would hold, to see if they fitted with what he learned. There was a good chance that most, or all, of them would prove false.

"Get up," the voice jarred into his thoughts. "We're leaving."

His legs were still numb and hardly usable. The bearded man snorted in disgust and hauled him to his feet, propping him against the outer wall. Jason clutched the knobby bark of the logs when he was left alone. He looked around, soaking up impressions.

It was the first time he had been on a farm since he had run away from home. A different world with a different ecology, but the similarity was apparent enough to him. A new-sown field stretched down the hill in front of the shack. Ploughed by a good farmer. Even, well cast furrows that followed the contour of the slope. Another, larger log building was next to this one, probably a barn.

There was a snuffling sound behind him and Jason turned quickly—and froze. His hand called for the missing gun and his finger tightened down on a trigger that wasn't there.

It had come out of the jungle and padded up quietly behind him. It had six thick legs with clawed feet that dug into the ground. The two-meter long body was covered with matted yellow and black fur, all except the skull and shoulders. These were covered with overlapping horny plates. Jason could see all this because the beast was that close.

He waited to die.

The mouth opened, a froglike division of the hairless skull, revealing double rows of jagged teeth.

"Here, Fido," the bearded man said, coming up behind Jason and snapping his fingers at the same time. The thing bounded forward, brushing past the dazed Jason, and rubbed his head against the man's leg. "Nice doggy," the man said, his fingers scratching under the edge of the carapace where it joined the flesh.

The bearded man had brought two of the riding animals out of the barn, saddled and bridled. Jason barely noticed the details of smooth skin and long legs as he swung up on one. His feet were quickly lashed to the stirrups. When they started the skull-headed beast followed them.

"Nice doggy!" Jason said, and for no reason started to laugh. The bearded man turned and scowled at him until he was quiet.

BY THE TIME THEY ENTERED THE JUNGLE it was dark. It was impossible to see under the thick foliage, and they used no lights. The animals seemed to know the way. There were scraping noises and shrill calls from the jungle around them, but it didn't bother Jason too much. Perhaps the automatic manner in which the other man undertook the journey reassured him. Or the presence of the "dog" that he felt rather than saw. The trip was a long one, but not too uncomfortable.

The regular motion of the animal and his fatigue overcame Jason and he dozed into a fitful sleep, waking with a start each time he slumped forward. In the end he slept sitting up in the saddle. Hours passed this way, until he opened his eyes and saw a square of light before them. The trip was over.

His legs were stiff and galled with saddle sores. After his feet were untied getting down was an effort, and he almost fell. A door opened and Jason went in. It took his eyes some moments to get used to the light, until he could make out the form of a man on the bed before him.

"Come over here and sit down." The voice was full and strong, accustomed to command. The body was that of an invalid. A blanket covered him to the waist, above that the flesh was sickly white, spotted with red nodules, and hung loosely over the bones. There seemed to be nothing left of the man except skin and skeleton.

"Not very nice," the man on the bed said, "but I've grown used to it." His tone changed abruptly. "Naxa said you were from off-world. Is that true?"

Jason nodded yes, and his answer stirred the living skeleton to life. The head lifted from the pillow and the red-rimmed eyes sought his with a desperate intensity.

"My name is Rhes and I'm a … grubber. Will you help me?"

Jason wondered at the intensity of Rhes' question, all out of proportion to the simple content of its meaning. Yet he could see no reason to give anything other than the first and obvious answer that sprang to his lips.

"Of course I'll help you, in whatever way I can. As long as it involves no injury to anyone else. What do you want?"

The sick man's head had fallen back limply, exhausted, as Jason talked. But the fire still burned in the eyes.

"Feel assured … I want to injure no others," Rhes said. "Quite the opposite. As you see I am suffering from a disease that our remedies will not stop. Within a few more days I will be dead. Now I have seen ... the city people ... using a device, they press it over a wound or an animal bite. Do you have one of these machines?"

"That sounds like a description of the medikit." Jason touched the button at his waist that dropped the medikit into his hand. "I have mine here. It analyzes and treats most ..."

"Would you use it on me?" Rhes broke in, his voice suddenly urgent.

"I'm sorry," Jason said. "I should have realized." He stepped forward and pressed the machine over one of the inflamed areas on Rhes' chest. The operation light came on and the thin shaft of the analyzer probe slid down. When it withdrew the device hummed, then clicked three times as three separate hypodermic needles lanced into the skin. Then the light went out.

"Is that all?" Rhes asked, as he watched Jason stow the medikit back in his belt.

Jason nodded, then looked up and noticed the wet marks of tears on the sick man's face. Rhes became aware at the same time and brushed at them angrily.

"When a man is sick," he growled, "the body and all its senses become traitor. I don't think I have cried since I was a child—but you must realize it's not myself I'm crying for. It's the untold thousands of my people who have died for lack of that little device you treat so casually."

"Surely you have medicines, doctors of your own?"

"Herb doctors and witch doctors," Rhes said, consigning them all to oblivion with a chop of his hand. "The few hard-working and honest men are hampered by the fact that the faith healers can usually cure better than their strongest potion."

The talking had tired Rhes. He stopped suddenly and closed his eyes. On his chest, the inflamed areas were already losing their angry color as the injections took affect. Jason glanced around the room, looking for clues to the mystery of these people.

FLOOR AND WALLS were made of wood lengths fitted together, free of paint or decoration. They looked simple and crude, fit only for the savages he had expected to meet. Or were they crude? The wood had a sweeping, flamelike grain. When he bent close he saw that wax had been rubbed over the wood to bring out this pattern. Was this the act of savages—or of artistic men seeking to make the most of simple materials? The final effect was far superior to the drab paint and riveted steel rooms of the city-dwelling Pyrrans. Wasn't it true that both ends of the artistic scale were dominated by simplicity? The untutored aborigine made a simple expression of a clear idea, and created beauty. At the other extreme, the sophisticated critic rejected over-elaboration and decoration and sought the truthful clarity of uncluttered art. At which end of the scale was he looking now?

These men were savages, he had been told that. They dressed in furs and spoke a slurred and broken language, at least Naxa did. Rhes admitted he preferred faith healers to doctors. But, if all this were true, where did the communicator fit into the picture? Or the glowing ceiling that illuminated the room with a soft light?

Rhes opened his eyes and stared at Jason, as if seeing him for the first time. "Who are you?" he asked. "And what are you doing here?"

There was a cold menace in his words and Jason understood why. The city Pyrrans hated the "grubbers" and, without a doubt, the feeling was mutual. Naxa's ax had proved that. Naxa had entered silently while they talked, and stood with his fingers touching the haft of this same ax. Jason knew his life was still in jeopardy, until he gave an answer that satisfied these men.

He couldn't tell the truth. If they once suspected he was spying among them to aid the city people, it would be the end. Nevertheless, he had to be free to talk about the survival problem.

The answer hit him as soon as he had stated the problem. All this had only taken an instant to consider, as he turned back to face the invalid, and he answered at once. Trying to keep his voice normal and unconcerned.

"I'm Jason dinAlt, an ecologist, so you see I have the best reasons in the universe for visiting this planet—"

"What is an ecologist?" Rhes broke in. There was nothing in his voice to indicate whether he meant the question seriously, or as a trap. All traces of the ease of their earlier conversation were gone, his voice had the deadliness of a stingwing's poison. Jason chose his words carefully.

"Simply stated, it is that branch of biology that considers the relations between organisms and their environment. How climatic and other factors affect the life forms, and how the life forms in turn affect each other and the environment." That much Jason knew was true—but he really knew very little more about the subject so he moved on quickly.

"I heard reports of this planet, and finally came here to study it firsthand. I did what work I could in the shelter of the city, but it wasn't enough. The people there think I'm crazy, but they finally agreed to let me make a trip out here."

"What arrangements have been made for your return?" Naxa snapped.

"None," Jason told him. "They seemed quite sure that I would be killed instantly and had no hope of me coming back. In fact, they refused to let me go and I had to break away."

This answer seemed to satisfy Rhes and his face cracked into a mirthless smile. "They would think that, those junkmen. Can't move a meter outside their own walls without an armor-plated machine as big as a barn. What did they tell you about us?"

Again Jason knew a lot depended on his answer. This time he thought carefully before speaking.

"Well ... perhaps I'll get that ax in the back of my neck for saying this ... but I have to be honest. You must know what they think. They told me you were filthy and ignorant savages who smelled. And you ... well, had curious customs you practiced with the animals. In exchange for food, they traded you beads and knives...."

Both Pyrrans broke into a convulsion of laughter at this. Rhes stopped soon, from weakness, but Naxa laughed himself into a coughing fit and had to splash water over his head from a gourd jug.

"That I believe well enough," Rhes said, "it sounds like the stupidity they would talk. Those people know nothing of the world they live in. I hope the rest of what you said is true, but even if it is not, you are welcome here. You are from off-world, that I know. No junkman would have lifted a finger to save my life. You are the first off-worlder my people have ever known and for that you are doubly welcome. We will help you in any way we can. My arm is your arm."

These last words had a ritual sound to them, and when Jason repeated them, Naxa nodded at the correctness of this. At the same time, Jason felt that they were more than empty ritual. Interdependence meant survival on Pyrrus, and he knew that these people stood together to the death against the mortal dangers around them. He hoped the ritual would include him in that protective sphere.

"That is enough for tonight," Rhes said. "The spotted sickness had weakened me, and your medicine has turned me to jelly. You will stay here, Jason. There is a blanket, but no bed at least for now."

Enthusiasm had carried Jason this far, making him forget the two-gee exertions of the long day. Now fatigue hit him a physical blow. He had dim memories of refusing food and rolling in the blanket on the floor. After that, oblivion.

17

EVERY SQUARE INCH OF HIS BODY ached where the doubled gravity had pressed his flesh to the unyielding wood of the floor. His eyes were gummy and his mouth was filled with an indescribable taste that came off in chunks. Sitting up was an effort and he had to stifle a groan as his joints cracked.

"Good day, Jason," Rhes called from the bed. "If I didn't believe in medicine so strongly, I would be tempted to say there is a miracle in your machine that has cured me overnight."

There was no doubt that he was on the mend. The inflamed patches had vanished and the burning light was gone from his eyes. He sat, propped up on the bed, watching the morning sun melt the night's hailstorm into the fields.

"There's meat in the cabinet there," he said, "and either water or visk to drink."

The visk proved to be a distilled beverage of extraordinary potency that instantly cleared the fog from Jason's brain, though it did leave a slight ringing in his ears. And the meat was a tenderly smoked joint, the best food he had tasted since leaving Darkhan. Taken together they restored his faith in life and the future. He lowered his glass with a relaxed sigh and looked around.

With the pressures of immediate survival and exhaustion removed, his thoughts returned automatically to his problem. What were these people really like—and how had they managed to survive in the deadly wilderness? In the city he had been told they were savages. Yet there was a carefully tended and repaired communicator on the wall. And by the door a crossbow—that fired machined metal bolts, he could see the tool marks still visible on their shanks. The one thing he needed was more information. He could start by getting rid of some of his misinformation.

"Rhes, you laughed when I told you what the city people said, about trading you trinkets for food. What do they really trade you?"

"Anything within certain limits," Rhes said. "Small manufactured items, such as electronic components for our communicators. Rustless alloys we can't make in our forges, cutting tools, atomic electric converters that produce power from any radioactive element. Things like that. Within reason they'll trade anything we ask that isn't on the forbidden list. They need the food badly."

"And the items on the forbidden list?"

"Weapons, of course, or anything that might be made into a powerful weapon. They know we make gunpowder so we can't get anything like large castings or seamless tubing we could make into heavy gun barrels. We drill our own rifle barrels by hand, though the crossbow is quiet and faster in the jungle. Then they don't like us to know very much, so the only reading matter that gets to us are tech maintenance manuals, empty of basic theory.

"The last banned category you know about—medicine. This is the one thing I cannot understand, that makes me burn with hatred with every death they might have prevented."

"I know their reasons," Jason said.

"Then tell me, because I can think of none."

"Survival—it's just that simple. I doubt if you realize it, but they have a decreasing population. It is just a matter of years before they will be gone. Whereas your people at least must have a stable—if not slightly growing population—to have existed without their mechanical protections. So in the city they hate you and are jealous of you at the same time. If they gave you medicine and you prospered, you would be winning the battle they have lost. I imagine they tolerate you as a necessary evil, to supply them with food, otherwise they wish you were all dead."

"It makes sense," Rhes growled, slamming his fist against the bed. "The kind of twisted logic you expect from junkmen. They use us to feed them, give us the absolute minimum in return, and at the same time cut us off from the knowledge that will get us out of this hand to mouth existence. Worse, far worse, they cut us off from the stars and the rest of mankind." The hatred on his face was so strong that Jason unconsciously drew back.

"Do you think we are savages here, Jason? We act and look like animals because we have to fight for existence on an animal level. Yet we know about the stars. In that chest over there, sealed in metal, are over thirty books, all we have. Fiction most of them, with some history and general science thrown in. Enough to keep alive the stories of the settlement here and the rest of the universe outside. We see the ships land in the city and we know that up there are worlds we can only dream about and never see. Do you wonder that we hate these beasts that call themselves men, and would destroy them in an instant if we could? They are right to keep weapons from us—for sure as the sun rises in the morning we would kill them to a man if we were able, and take over the things they have withheld from us."

IT WAS A HARSH CONDEMNATION, but essentially a truthful one. At least from the point of view of the outsiders. Jason didn't try to explain to the angry man that the city Pyrrans looked on their attitude as being the only possible and logical one. "How did this battle between your two groups ever come about?" he asked.

"I don't know," Rhes said, "I've thought about it many times, but there are no records of that period. We do know that we are all descended from colonists who arrived at the same time. Somewhere, at some time, the two groups separated. Perhaps it was a war, I've read about them in the books. I have a partial theory, though I can't prove it, that it was the location of the city."

"Location—I don't understand."

"Well, you know the junkmen, and you've seen where their city is. They managed to put it right in the middle of the most savage spot on this planet. You know they don't care about any living thing except themselves, shoot and kill is their only logic. So they wouldn't consider where to build their city, and managed to build it in the stupidest spot imaginable. I'm sure my ancestors saw how foolish this was and tried to tell them so. That would be reason enough for a war, wouldn't it?"

"It might have been—if that's really what happened," Jason said. "But I think you have the problem turned backwards. It's a war between native Pyrran life and humans, each fighting to destroy the other. The life forms change continually, seeking that final destruction of the invader."

"Your theory is even wilder than mine," Rhes said. "That's not true at all. I admit that life isn't too easy on this planet ... if what I have read in the books about other planets is true ... but it doesn't change. You have to be fast on your feet and keep your eyes open for anything bigger than you, but you can survive. Anyway, it doesn't really matter why. The junkmen always look for trouble and I'm happy to see that they have enough."

Jason didn't try to press the point. The effort of forcing Rhes to change his basic attitudes wasn't worth it—even if possible. He hadn't succeeded in convincing anyone in the city of the lethal mutations even when they could observe all the facts. Rhes could still supply information though.

"I suppose it's not important who started the battle," Jason said for the other man's benefit, not meaning a word of it, "but you'll have to agree that the city people are permanently at war with all the local life. Your people, though, have managed to befriend at least two species that I have seen. Do you have any idea how this was done?"

"Naxa will be here in a minute," Rhes said, pointing to the door, "as soon as he's taken care of the animals. Ask him. He's the best talker we have."

"Talker?" Jason asked. "I had the opposite idea about him. He didn't talk much, and what he did say was, well ... a little hard to understand at times."

"Not that kind of talking." Rhes broke in impatiently. "The talkers look after the animals. They train the dogs and doryms, and the better ones like Naxa are always trying to work with other beasts. They dress crudely, but they have to. I've heard them say that the animals don't like chemicals, metal or tanned leather, so they wear untanned furs for the most part. But don't let the dirt fool you, it has nothing to do with his intelligence."

"Doryms? Are those your carrying beasts —the kind we rode coming here?"

Rhes nodded. "Doryms are more than pack animals, they're really a little bit of everything. The large males pull the ploughs and other machines, while the younger animals are used for meat. If you want to know more, ask Naxa, you'll find him in the barn."

"I'd like to do that," Jason said, standing up. "Only I feel undressed without my gun—"

"Take it, by all means, it's in that chest by the door. Only watch out what you shoot around here."

NAXA WAS IN THE REAR OF THE BARN, filing down one of the spadelike toenails of a dorym. It was a strange scene. The fur-dressed man with the great beast—and the contrast of a beryllium-copper file and electroluminescent plates lighting the work.

The dorym opened its nostrils and pulled away when Jason entered; Naxa patted its neck and talked softly until it quieted and stood still, shivering slightly.

Something stirred in Jason's mind, with the feeling of a long unused muscle being stressed. A hauntingly familiar sensation.

"Good morning," Jason said. Naxa grunted something and went back to his filing. Watching him for a few minutes, Jason tried to analyze this new feeling. It itched and slipped aside when he reached for it, escaping him. Whatever it was, it had started when Naxa had talked to the dorym.

"Could you call one of the dogs in here, Naxa? I'd like to see one closer up."

Without raising his head from his work, Naxa gave a low whistle. Jason was sure it couldn't have been heard outside of the barn. Yet within a minute one of the Pyrran dogs slipped quietly in. The talker rubbed the beast's head, mumbling to it, while the animal looked intently into his eyes.

The dog became restless when Naxa turned back to work on the dorym. It prowled around the barn, sniffing, then moved quickly towards the open door. Jason called it back.

At least he meant to call it. At the last moment he said nothing. Nothing aloud. On sudden impulse he kept his mouth closed— only he called the dog with his mind. Thinking the words *come here*, directing the impulse at the animal with all the force and direction he had ever used to manipulate dice. As he did it he realized it had been a long time since he had even considered using his psi powers.

The dog stopped and turned back towards him.

It hesitated, looking at Naxa, then walked over to Jason.

Seen this closely the beast was a nightmare hound. The hairless protective plates, tiny red-rimmed eyes, and countless, saliva-dripping teeth did little to inspire confidence. Yet Jason felt no fear. There was a rapport between man and animal that was understood. Without conscious thought he reached out and scratched the dog along the back, where he knew it itched.

"Didn't know y're a talker," Naxa said. As he watched them, there was friendship in his voice for the first time.

"I didn't know either—until just now," Jason said. He looked into the eyes of the animal before him, scratched the ridged and ugly back, and began to understand.

The talkers must have well developed psi facilities, that was obvious now. There is no barrier of race or alien form when two creatures share each other's emotions. Empathy first, so there would be no hatred or fear. After that direct communication. The talkers might have been the ones who first broke through the barrier of hatred on Pyrrus and learned to live with the native life. Others could have followed their example—this might explain how the community of "grubbers" had been formed.

Now that he was concentrating on it, Jason was aware of the soft flow of thoughts

around him. The consciousness of the dorym was matched by other like patterns from the rear of the barn. He knew without going outside that more of the big beasts were in the field back there.

"This is all new to me," Jason said. "Have you ever thought about it, Naxa? What does it feel like to be a talker? I mean, do you *know* why it is you can get the animals to obey you while other people have no luck at all?"

Thinking of this sort troubled Naxa. He ran his fingers through his thick hair and scowled as he answered. "Nev'r thought about it. Just do it. Just get t'know the beast real good, then y'can guess what they're going t'do. That's all."

It was obvious that Naxa had never thought about the origin of his ability to control the animals. And if he hadn't—probably no one else had. They had no reason to. They simply accepted the powers of talkers as one of the facts of life.

Ideas slipped towards each other in his

mind, like the pieces of a puzzle joining together. He had told Kerk that the native life of Pyrrus had joined in battle against mankind, he didn't know why. Well—he still didn't know why, but he was getting an idea of the "how."

"About how far are we from the city?" Jason asked. "Do you have an idea how long it would take us to get there by dorym?"

"Half a day there—half back. Why? Y'want to go?"

"I don't want to get into the city, not yet. But I would like to get close to it," Jason told him.

"See what Rhes say," was Naxa's answer.

RHES GRANTED INSTANT PERMISSION without asking any questions. They saddled up and left at once, in order to complete the round trip before dark.

They had been traveling less than an hour before Jason knew they were going in the direction of the city. With each minute the feeling grew stronger. Naxa was aware of it too, stirring in the saddle with unvoiced feelings. They had to keep touching and reassuring their mounts which were growing skittish and restless.

"This is far enough," Jason said. Naxa gratefully pulled to a stop.

The wordless thought beat through Jason's mind, filling it. He could feel it on all sides—only much stronger ahead of them in the direction of the unseen city. Naxa and the doryms reacted in the same way, restlessly uncomfortable, not knowing the cause.

One thing was obvious now. The Pyrran animals were sensitive to psi radiation—probably the plants and lower life forms as well. Perhaps they communicated by it, since they obeyed the men who had a strong control of it. And in this area was a wash of psi radiation such as he had never experienced before. Though his personal talents specialized in psychokinesis—the mental control of inanimate matter—he was still sensitive to most mental phenomena. Watching a sports event he had many times felt the unanimous accord of many minds expressing the same thought. What he felt now was like that.

Only terribly different. A crowd exulted at some success on the field, or groaned at a failure. The feeling fluxed and changed as the game progressed. Here the wash of thought was unending, strong and frightening. It didn't translate into words very well. It was part hatred, part fear—and all destruction.

"KILL THE ENEMY" was as close as Jason could express it. But it was more than that. An unending river of mental outrage and death.

"Let's go back now," he said, suddenly battered and sickened by the feelings he had let wash through him. As they started the return trip he began to understand many things.

His sudden unspeakable fear when the Pyrran animal had attacked him that first day on the planet. And his recurrent nightmares that had never completely ceased, even with drugs. Both of these were his reaction to the hatred directed at the city. Though for some reason he hadn't felt it directly up to now, enough had reached through to him to get a strong emotional reaction.

Rhes was asleep when they got back and Jason couldn't talk to him until morning. In spite of his fatigue from the trip, he stayed awake late into the night, going over in his mind the discoveries of the day. Could he tell Rhes what he had found out? Not very well. If he did that, he would have to explain the importance of his discovery and what he meant to use it for. Nothing that aided the city dwellers would appeal to Rhes in the slightest. Best to say nothing until the entire affair was over.

18 AFTER BREAKFAST HE TOLD RHES that he wanted to return to the city.

"Then you have seen enough of our barbarian world, and wish to go back to your friends. To help them wipe us out perhaps?"

Rhes said it lightly, but there was a touch of cold malice behind his words.

"I hope you don't really think that," Jason told him. "You must realize that the opposite is true. I would like to see this civil war ended and your people getting all the benefits of science and medicine that have been withheld. I'll do everything I can to bring that about."

"They'll never change," Rhes said gloomily, "so don't waste your time. But there is one thing you must do, for your protection and ours. Don't admit, or even hint, that you've talked to any grubbers!"

"Why not?"

"Why not! Suffering death are you that simple! They will do anything to see that we don't rise too high, and would much prefer to see us all dead. Do you think they would hesitate to kill you if they as much as suspected you had contacted us? They realize—even if you don't—that you can singlehandedly alter the entire pattern of power on this planet. The ordinary junkman may think of us as being only one step above the animals, but the leaders don't. They know what we need and what we want. They could probably guess just what it is I am going to ask you.

"Help us, Jason dinAlt. Get back among those human pigs and lie. Say you never talked to us, that you hid in the forest and we attacked you and you had to shoot to save yourself. We'll supply some recent corpses to make that part of your story sound good. Make them believe you, and even after you think you have them convinced keep on acting the part because they will be watching you. Then tell them you have finished your work and are ready to leave. Get safely off Pyrrus, to another planet, and I promise you anything in the universe. Whatever you want you shall have. Power, money—*anything*.

"This is a rich planet. The junkmen mine and sell the metal, but we could do it much better. Bring a spaceship back here and land anywhere on this continent. We have no cities, but our people have farms everywhere, they will find you. We will then have commerce, trade—on our own. This is what we all want and we will work hard for it. And *you* will have done it. Whatever you want we will give. That is a promise and we do not break our promises."

The intensity and magnitude of what he described rocked Jason. He knew that Rhes spoke the truth and the entire resources of the planet would be his, if he did as asked. For one second he was tempted, savoring the thought of what it would be like. Then came realization that it would be a half answer, and a poor one at that. If these people had the strength they wanted, their first act  would be the attempted destruction of the city men. The result would be bloody civil war that would probably destroy them both. Rhes' answer was a good one—but only half an answer.

Jason had to find a better solution. One that would stop *all* the fighting on this planet and allow the two groups of humans to live in peace.

"I will do nothing to injure your people, Rhes—and everything in my power to aid them," Jason said.

This half answer satisfied Rhes, who could see only one interpretation of it. He spent the rest of the morning on the communicator, arranging for the food supplies that were being brought to the trading site.

"The supplies are ready and we have sent the signal," he said. "The truck will be there tomorrow and you will be waiting for it. Everything is arranged as I told you. You'll leave now with Naxa. You must reach the meeting spot before the trucks."

19

"TRUCKS ALMOST HERE. Y'know what to do?" Naxa asked.

Jason nodded, and looked again at the dead man. Some beast had torn his arm off and he had bled to death. The severed arm had been tied into the shirt sleeve, so from a distance it looked normal. Seen close up this limp arm, plus the white skin and shocked expression on the face, gave Jason an unhappy sensation. He liked to see his corpses safely buried. However he could understand its importance today.

"Here they're. Wait until his back's turned," Naxa whispered.

The armored truck had three powered trailers in tow this time. The train ground up the rock slope and whined to a stop. Krannon climbed out of the cab and looked care-

fully around before opening up the trailers. He had a lift robot along to help him with the loading.

"Now!" Naxa hissed.

Jason burst into the clearing, running, shouting Krannon's name. There was a crackling behind him as two of the hidden men hurled the corpse through the foliage after him. He turned and fired without stopping, setting the thing afire in midair.

There was the crack of another gun as Krannon fired, his shot jarred the twice-dead corpse before it hit the ground. Then he was lying prone, firing into the trees behind the running Jason.

Just as Jason reached the truck there was a whirring in the air and hot pain ripped into his back, throwing him to the ground. He looked around as Krannon dragged him through the door, and saw the metal shaft of a crossbow bolt sticking out of his shoulder.

"Lucky," the Pyrran said. "An inch lower would have got your heart. I warned you about those grubbers. You're lucky to get off with only this." He lay next to the door and snapped shots into the now quiet wood.

Taking out the bolt hurt much more than it had going in. Jason cursed the pain as Krannon put on a dressing, and admired the singleness of purpose of the people who had shot him. They had risked his life to make his escape look real. And also risked the chance that he might turn against them after being shot. They did a job completely and thoroughly and he cursed them for their efficiency.

Krannon climbed warily out of the truck, after Jason was bandaged. Finishing the loading quickly, he started the train of trailers back towards the city. Jason had an anti-pain shot and dozed off as soon as they started.

WHILE HE SLEPT, Krannon must have radioed ahead, because Kerk was waiting when they arrived. As soon as the truck entered the perimeter he threw open the door and dragged Jason out. The bandage pulled and Jason felt the wound tear open. He ground his teeth together; Kerk would not have the satisfaction of hearing him cry out.

"I told you to stay in the buildings until the ship left. Why did you leave? Why did you go outside? You talked to the grubbers—didn't you?" With each question he shook Jason again.

"I didn't talk to—anyone." Jason managed to get the words out. "They tried to take me, I shot two—hid out until the trucks came back."

"Got another one then," Krannon said. "I saw it. Good shooting. Think I got some, too. Let him go Kerk, they shot him in the back before he could reach the truck."

That's enough explanations, Jason thought to himself. Don't overdo it. Let him make up his mind later. Now's the time to change the subject. There's one thing that will get his mind off the grubbers.

"I've been fighting your war for you Kerk, while you stayed safely inside the perimeter." Jason leaned back against the side of the truck as the other loosened his grip. "I've found out what your battle with this planet is really about—and how you can win it. Now let me sit down and I'll tell you."

More Pyrrans had come up while they talked. None of them moved now. Like Kerk, they stood frozen, looking at Jason. When Kerk talked, he spoke for all of them.

"What do you mean?"

"Just what I said. Pyrrus is fighting you—actively and consciously. Get far enough out from this city and you can feel the waves of hatred that are directed at it. No, that's wrong—you can't because you've grown up with it. But I can, and so could anyone else with any sort of psi sensitivity. There is a message of war being beamed against you constantly. The life forms of this planet are psi-sensitive, and respond to that order. They attack and change and mutate for your destruction. And they'll keep on doing so until you are all dead. Unless you can stop the war."

"How?" Kerk snapped the word and every face echoed the question.

"By finding whoever or whatever is sending that message. The life forms that attack you have no reasoning intelligence. They are being ordered to do so. I think I know how to find the source of these orders. After that it will be a matter of getting across a message, asking for a truce and an eventual end to all hostilities."

A dead silence followed his words as the Pyrrans tried to comprehend the ideas. Kerk moved first, waving them all away.

"Go back to your work. This is my responsibility and I'll take care of it. As soon as I find out what truth there is here—if any—I'll make a complete report." The people drifted away silently, looking back as they went.

 "FROM THE BEGINNING NOW," Kerk said. "And leave out nothing."

"There is very little more that I can add to the physical facts. I saw the animals, understood the message. I even experimented with some of them and they reacted to my mental commands. What I must do now is track down the source of the orders that keep this war going.

"I'll tell you something that I have never told anyone else. I'm not only lucky at gambling. I have enough psi ability to alter probability in my favor. It's an erratic ability that I have tried to improve for obvious reasons. During the past ten years I managed to study at all of the centers that do psi research. Compared to other fields of knowledge it is amazing how little they know. Basic psi talents can be improved by practice, and some machines have been devised that act as psionic amplifiers. One of these, used correctly, is a very good directional indicator."

"You want to build this machine?" Kerk asked.

"Exactly. Build it and take it outside the city in the ship. Any signal strong enough to keep this centuries-old battle going should be strong enough to track down. I'll follow it, contact the creatures who are sending it, and try to find out why they are doing it. I assume you'll go along with any reasonable plan that will end this war?"

"Anything reasonable," Kerk said coldly. "How long will it take you to build this machine?"

"Just a few days if you have all the parts here," Jason told him.

"Then do it. I'm canceling the flight that's leaving now and I'll keep the ship here, ready to go. When the machine is built I want you to track the signal and report back to me."

"Agreed," Jason said, standing up. "As soon as I have this hole in my back looked at I'll draw up a list of things needed."

A grim, unsmiling man named Skop was assigned to Jason as a combination guide and guard. He took his job very seriously, and it didn't take Jason long to realize that he was a prisoner-at-large. Kerk had accepted his story, but that was no guarantee that he believed it. At a single word from him, the guard could turn executioner.

The chill thought hit Jason that undoubtedly this was what would happen. Whether Kerk accepted the story or not—he couldn't afford to take a chance. As long as there was the slightest possibility Jason had contacted the grubbers, he could not be allowed to leave the planet alive. The woods people were being simple if they thought a plan this obvious might succeed. Or had they just gambled on the very long chance it might work? *They* certainly had nothing to lose by it.

Only half of Jason's mind was occupied with the work as he drew up a list of materials he would need for the psionic direction finder. His thoughts plodded in tight circles, searching for a way out that didn't exist. He was too deeply involved now to just leave. Kerk would see to that. Unless he could find a way to end the war and settle the grubber question he was marooned on Pyrrus for life. A very short life.

When the list was ready he called Supply. With a few substitutions, everything he might possibly need was in stock, and would be sent over. Skop sank into an apparent doze in his chair and Jason, his head propped against the pull of gravity by one arm, began a working sketch of his machine.

Jason looked up suddenly, aware of the silence. He could hear machinery in the building and voices in the hall outside. What kind of silence then—?

Mental silence. He had been so preoccupied since his return to the city that he hadn't noticed the complete lack of any kind of psi sensation. The constant wash of animal reactions was missing, as was the vague tactile awareness of his PK. With sudden realization he remembered that it was always this way inside the city.

He tried to listen with his mind—and stopped almost before he began. There was a constant press of thought about him that he was made aware of when he reached out. It was like being in a vessel far beneath the ocean, with your hand on the door that held back the frightening pressure. Touching the door, without opening it, you could feel the stresses, the power pushing in and waiting to crush you. It was this way with the psi pressure on the city. The unvoiced hate-filled screams of Pyrrus would instantly destroy any mind that received them. Some function of his brain acted as a psi-circuit breaker, shutting off awareness before his mind could be blasted. There was just enough leak-through to keep him aware of the pressure—and supply the raw materials for his constant nightmares.

There was only one fringe benefit. The lack of thought pressure made it easier for him to concentrate. In spite of his fatigue the diagram developed swiftly.

META ARRIVED LATE THAT AFTERNOON, bringing the parts he had ordered. She slid the long box onto the workbench, started to speak, but changed her mind and said nothing. Jason looked up at her and smiled.

"Confused?" he asked.

"I don't know what you mean," she said, "I'm not confused. Just annoyed. The regular trip has been canceled and our supply schedule will be thrown off for months to come. And instead of piloting or perimeter assignment all I can do is stand around and wait for you. Then take some silly flight following your directions. Do you wonder that I'm annoyed?"

Jason carefully set the parts out on the chassis before he spoke. "As I said, you're confused. I can point out how you're confused—which will make you even more confused. A temptation that I frankly find hard to resist."

She looked across the bench at him, frowning. One finger unconsciously curling and uncurling a short lock of hair. Jason liked her this way. As a Pyrran operating at full blast she had as much personality as a gear in a machine. Once out of that pattern she reminded him more of the girl he had known on that first flight to Pyrrus. He wondered if it was possible to really get across to her what he meant.

"I'm not being insulting when I say 'confused,' Meta. With your background you couldn't be any other way. You have an insular personality. Admittedly, Pyrrus is an unusual island with a lot of high-power problems that you are an expert at solving. That doesn't make it any less of an island. When you face a cosmopolitan problem you are confused. Or even worse, when your island problems are put into a bigger context. That's like playing your own game, only having the rules change constantly as you go along."

"You're talking nonsense," she snapped at him. "Pyrrus isn't an island and battling for survival is definitely not a game."

"I'm sorry," he smiled. "I was using a figure of speech, and a badly chosen one at that. Let's put the problem on more concrete terms. Take an example. Suppose I were to tell you that over there, hanging from the doorframe, was a stingwing—"

Meta's gun was pointing at the door before he finished the last word. There was a crash as the guard's chair went over. He had jumped from a half-doze to full alertness in an instant, his gun also searching the doorframe.

"That was just an example," Jason said. "There's really nothing there." The guard's gun vanished and he scowled a look of contempt at Jason, as he righted the chair and dropped into it.

"You both have proved yourself capable of handling a Pyrran problem." Jason continued. "But what if I said that there is a thing hanging from the doorframe that *looks* like a stingwing, but is really a kind of large insect that spins a fine silk that can be used to weave clothes?"

The guard glared from under his thick eyebrows at the empty doorframe, his gun whined part way out, then snapped back into the holster. He growled something inaudible at Jason, then stamped into the outer room, slamming the door behind him. Meta frowned in concentration and looked puzzled.

"It couldn't be anything except a stingwing," she finally said. "Nothing else could possibly look like that. And even if it didn't spin silk, it would bite if you got near, so you would have to kill it." She smiled with satisfaction at the indestructible logic of her answer.

"Wrong again," Jason said. "I just described the mimic-spinner that lives on Stover's Planet. It imitates the most violent forms of life there, does such a good job that it has no need for other defenses. It'll sit quietly on your hand and spin for you by the yard. If I dropped a shipload of them here on Pyrrus, you never could be sure when to shoot, could you?"

"But they are not here now," Meta insisted.

"Yet they could be quite easily. And if they were, all the rules of your game would change. Getting the idea now? There are some fixed laws and rules in the galaxy—but they're not the ones you live by. Your rule is war unending with the local life. I want to step outside your rule book and end that war. Wouldn't you like that? Wouldn't you like an existence that was more than just an endless battle for survival? A life with a chance for happiness, love, music, art—all the enjoyable things you have never had the time for."

All the Pyrran sternness was gone from her face as she listened to what he said, letting herself follow these alien concepts. He had put his hand out automatically as he talked, and had taken hers. It was warm and her pulse fast to his touch.

Meta suddenly became conscious of his hand and snapped hers away, rising to her feet at the same time. As she started blindly towards the door, Jason's voice snapped after her.

"The guard, Skop, ran out because he didn't want to lose his precious two-value logic. It's all he has. But you've seen other parts of the galaxy, Meta, you know there is

a lot more to life than kill-and-be-killed on Pyrrus. You feel it is true, even if you won't admit it."

She turned and ran out the door.

Jason looked after her, his hand scraping the bristle on his chin thoughtfully. "Meta, I have the faint hope that the woman is winning over the Pyrran. I think that I saw—perhaps for the first time in the history of this bloody war-torn city—a tear in one of its citizen's eyes."

21 DROP THAT EQUIPMENT and Kerk will undoubtedly pull both your arms off," Jason said. "He's over there now, looking as sorry as possible that I ever talked him into this."

Skop cursed under the bulky mass of the psi detector, passing it up to Meta who waited in the open port of the spaceship. Jason supervised the loading, and blasted all the local life that came to investigate. Horndevils were thick this morning and he shot four of them. He was last aboard and closed the lock behind him.

"Where are you going to install it?" Meta asked.

"You tell me," Jason said. "I need a spot for the antenna where there will be no dense metal in front of the bowl to interfere with the signal. Thin plastic will do, or if worst comes to worst I can mount it outside the hull with a remote drive."

"You may have to," she said. "The hull is an unbroken unit, we do all viewing by screen and instruments. I don't think ... wait ... there is one place that might do."

She led the way to a bulge in the hull that marked one of the lifeboats. They went in through the always-open lock, Skop struggling after them with the apparatus.

"These lifeboats are half buried in the ship," Meta explained. "They have transparent front ports covered by friction shields that withdraw automatically when the boat is launched."

"Can we pull back the shields now?"

"I think so," she said. She traced the

launching circuits to a junction box and opened the lid. When she closed the shield relay manually, the heavy plates slipped back into the hull. There was a clear view, since most of the viewport projected beyond the parent ship.

"Perfect," Jason said. "I'll set up here. Now how do I talk to you in the ship?"

"Right here," she said. "There's a pre-tuned setting on this communicator. Don't touch anything else—and particularly not this switch." She pointed to a large pull-handle set square into the center of the control board. "Emergency launching. Two seconds after that is pulled the lifeboat is shot free. And it so happens this boat has no fuel."

"Hands off for sure," Jason said. "Now have Husky there run me in a line with ship's power and I'll get this stuff set up."

The detector was simple, though the tuning had to be precise. A dish-shaped antenna pulled in the signal for the delicately balanced detector. There was a sharp fall-off on both sides of the input so direction could be precisely determined. The resulting signal was fed to an amplifier stage. Unlike the electronic components of the first stage, this one was drawn in symbols on white paper. Carefully glued-on input and output leads ran to it.

When everything was ready and clamped into place, Jason nodded to Meta's image on the screen. "Take her up—and easy please. None of your nine-G specials. Go into a slow circle around the perimeter, until I tell you differently."

Under steady power the ship lifted and grabbed for altitude, then eased into its circular course. They made five circuits of the city before Jason shook his head.

"The thing seems to be working fine, but we're getting too much noise from all the local life. Get thirty kilometers out from the city and start a new circuit."

THE RESULTS WERE BETTER THIS TIME. A powerful signal came from the direction of the city,

confined to less than a degree of arc. With the antenna fixed at a right angle to the direction of the ship's flight, the signal was fairly constant. Meta rotated the ship on its main axis, until Jason's lifeboat was directly below.

"Going fine now," he said. "Just hold your controls as they are and keep the nose from drifting."

After making a careful mark on the setting circle, Jason turned the receiving antenna through one hundred eighty degrees of arc. As the ship kept to its circle, he made a slow collecting sweep of any signals beamed at the city. They were halfway around before he got a new signal.

It was there all right, narrow but strong. Just to be sure he let the ship complete two more sweeps, and he noted the direction on the gyro-compass each time. They coincided. The third time around he called to Meta.

"Get ready for a full right turn, or whatever you call it. I think I have our bearing. Get ready—*now*."

It was a slow turn and Jason never lost the signal. A few times it wavered, but he brought it back on. When the compass settled down Meta pushed on more power.

They set their course towards the native Pyrrans.

An hour's flight at close to top atmospheric speed brought no change. Meta complained, but Jason kept her on course. The signal never varied and was slowly picking up strength. They crossed the chain of volcanoes that marked the continental limits, the ship bucking in the fierce thermals. Once the shore was behind and they were over water, Skop joined Meta in grumbling. He kept his turret spinning, but there was very little to shoot at this far from land.

When the islands came over the horizon the signal began to dip.

"Slow now," Jason called. "Those islands ahead look like our source!"

A continent had been here once, floating on Pyrrus' liquid core. Pressures changed, land masses shifted, and the continent had sunk beneath the ocean. All that was left now of the teeming life of that land mass was confined to a chain of islands, once the mountain peaks of the highest range of mountains. These islands, whose sheer, sides rose straight from the water, held the last inhabitants of the lost continent. The weeded-out descendants, of the victors of uncountable violent contests. Here lived the oldest native Pyrrans.

"Come in lower," Jason signaled. "Towards that large peak. The signals seem to originate there."

They swooped low over the mountain, but nothing was visible other than the trees and sun-blasted rock.

The pain almost took Jason's head off. A blast of hatred that drove through the amplifier and into his skull. He tore off the phones, and clutched his skull between his hands. Through watering eyes he saw the black cloud of flying beasts hurtle up from the trees below. He had a single glimpse of the hillside beyond, before Meta blasted power to the engines and the ship leaped away.

"We've found them!" Her fierce exultation faded as she saw Jason through the communicator. "Are you all right? What happened?"

"Feel ... burned out ... I've felt a psi blast before, but nothing like that! I had a glimpse of an opening, looked like a cave mouth, just before the blast hit. Seemed to come from there."

"Lie down," Meta said. "I'll get you back as fast as I can. I'm calling ahead to Kerk, he has to know what happened."

A GROUP OF MEN WERE WAITING in the landing station when they came down. They stormed out as soon as the ship touched, shielding their faces from the still-hot tubes. Kerk burst in as soon as the port was cracked, peering around until he spotted Jason stretched out on an acceleration couch.

"Is it true?" he barked. "You've traced the alien criminals who started this war?"

"Slow, man, slow," Jason said. "I've traced the source of the psi message that keeps your war going. I've found no evidence as to who started this war, and certainly wouldn't go so far as to call them criminals—"

"I'm tired of your word-play," Kerk broke in. "You've found these creatures and their location has been marked."

"On the chart," Meta said, "I could fly there blindfolded."

"Fine, fine," Kerk said, rubbing his hands together so hard they could hear the harsh rasp of the callouses. "It takes a real effort to grasp the idea that, after all these centuries, the war might be coming to an end. But it's possible now. Instead of simply killing off these self-renewing legions of the damned that attack us, we can get to the leaders. Search them out, carry the war to them for a change—and blast their stain from the face of this planet!"

"Nothing of the sort!" Jason said, sitting up with an effort. "Nothing doing! Since I came to this planet I have been knocked around, and risked my life ten times over. Do you think I have done this just to satisfy your blood-thirsty ambitions? It's peace I'm after—not destruction. You promised to contact these creatures, attempt to negotiate with them. Aren't you a man of honor who keeps his word?"

"I'll ignore the insult—though I'd have killed you for it at any other time," Kerk said. "You've been of great service to our people, we are not ashamed to acknowledge an honest debt. At the same time—do not accuse me of breaking promises that I never made. I recall my exact words. I promised to go along with any reasonable plan that would end this war. That is just what I intend to do. Your plan to negotiate a peace is not reasonable. Therefore we are going to destroy the enemy."

"Think first," Jason called after Kerk, who had turned to leave. "What is wrong with trying negotiation or an armistice? Then, if that fails, you can try your way."

The compartment was getting crowded as

other Pyrrans pushed in. Kerk, almost to the door, turned back to face Jason.

"I'll tell you what's wrong with armistice," he said. "It's a coward's way out, that's what it is. It's all right for you to suggest it, you're from off-world and don't know any better. But do you honestly think I could entertain such a defeatist notion for one instant? When I speak, I speak not only for myself, but for all of us here. We don't mind fighting, and we know how to do it. We know that if this war was over we could build a better world here. At the same time, if we have the choice of continued war or a cowardly peace—*we vote for war*. This war will only be over when the enemy is utterly destroyed!"

The listening Pyrrans shouted in agreement, and when Kerk pushed out through the crowd some of them patted his shoulder as he went by. Jason slumped back on the couch, worn out by his exertions and exhausted by the attempt to win the violent Pyrrans over to a peaceful point of view.

When he looked up they were gone—all except Meta. She had the same look of blood-thirsty elation as the others, but it drained away when she glanced at him.

"What about it, Meta?" he asked bitterly. "No doubts? Do you think that destruction is the only way to end this war?"

"I don't know," she said. "I can't be sure. For the first time in my life I find myself with more than one answer to the same question."

"Congratulations," he said. "It's a sign of growing up."

22 JASON STOOD TO ONE SIDE and watched the deadly cargo being loaded into the hold of the ship. The Pyrrans were in good humor as they stowed away riot guns, grenades and gas bombs. When the back-pack atom bomb was put aboard one of them broke into a marching song, and the others picked it up. Maybe they were happy, but the approaching carnage only filled Jason with an intense gloom. He felt that somehow he was a traitor to life. Perhaps the

life form he had found needed destroying—and perhaps it didn't. Without making the slightest attempt at conciliation, destruction would be plain murder.

Kerk came out of the operations building and the starter pumps could be heard whining inside the ship. They would leave within minutes. Jason forced himself into a foot-dragging rush and met Kerk halfway to the ship.

"I'm coming with you, Kerk. You owe me at least that much for finding them."

Kerk hesitated, not liking the idea. "This is an operational mission," he said. "No room for observers, and the extra weight— And it's too late to stop us Jason, you know that."

"You Pyrrans are the worst liars in the universe," Jason said. "We both know that ship can lift ten times the amount it's carrying today. Now ... do you let me come, or forbid me without reason at all?"

"Get aboard," Kerk said. "But keep out of the way or you'll get trampled."

This time, with a definite destination ahead, the flight was much faster. Meta took the ship into the stratosphere, in a high ballistic arc that ended at the islands. Kerk was in the co-pilot's seat, Jason sat behind them where he could watch the screens. The landing party, twenty-five volunteers, were in the hold below with the weapons. All the screens in the ship were switched to the forward viewer. They watched the green island appear and swell, then vanish behind the flames of the braking rockets. Jockeying the ship carefully, Meta brought it down on a flat shelf near the cave mouth.

Jason was ready this time for the blast of mental hatred—but it still hurt. The gunners laughed and killed gleefully as every animal on the island closed in on the ship. They were slaughtered by the thousands, and still more came.

"Do you have to do this?" Jason asked. "It's murder—carnage, just butchering those beasts like that."

"Self-defense," Kerk said. "They attack us and they get killed. What could be simpler?

Now shut up, or I'll throw you out there with them."

It was a half an hour before the gunfire slackened. Animals still attacked them, but the mass assaults seemed to be over. Kerk spoke into the intercom.

"Landing party away—and watch your step. They know we're here and will make it as hot as they can. Take the bomb into that cave and see how far back it runs. We can always blast them from the air, but it'll do no good if they're dug into solid rock. Keep your screen open, leave the bomb and pull back at once if I tell you to. Now move."

The men swarmed down the ladders and formed into open battle formation. They were soon under attack, but the beasts were picked off before they could get close. It didn't take long for the man at point to reach the cave. He had his pickup trained in front of him, and the watchers in the ship followed the advance.

"Big cave," Kerk grunted. "Slants back and down. What I was afraid of. Bomb dropped on that would just close it up. With no guarantee that anything sealed in it, couldn't eventually get out. We'll have to see how far down it goes."

There was enough heat in the cave now to use the infra-red filters. The rock walls stood out harshly black and white as the advance continued.

"No signs of life since entering the cave," the officer reported. "Gnawed bones at the entrance and some bat droppings. It looks like a natural cave—so far."

Step by step the advance continued, slowing as it went. Insensitive as the Pyrrans were to psi pressure, even they were aware of the blast of hatred being continuously leveled at them. Jason, back in the ship, had a headache that slowly grew worse instead of better.

"*Watch out!*" Kerk shouted, staring at the screen with horror.

The cave was filled from wall to wall with pallid, eyeless animals. They poured from tiny side passages and seemed to literally emerge from the ground. Their front ranks dissolved in flame, but more kept pressing in. On the screen the watchers in the ship saw the cave spin dizzily as the operator fell. Pale bodies washed up and concealed the lens.

"Close ranks—flame-throwers and gas!" Kerk bellowed into the mike.

Less than half of the men were alive after that first attack. The survivors, protected by the flame-throwers, set off the gas grenades. Their sealed battle armor protected them while the section of cave filled with gas. Someone dug through the bodies of their attackers and found the pickup.

"Leave the bomb there and withdraw," Kerk ordered. "We've had enough losses already."

A different man stared out of the screen. The officer was dead. "Sorry, sir," he said, "but it will be just as easy to push ahead as back as long as the gas grenades hold out. We're too close now to pull back."

"That's an order," Kerk shouted, but the man was gone from the screen and the advance continued.

Jason's fingers hurt where he had them clamped to the chair arm. He pulled them loose and massaged them. On the screen the black and white cave flowed steadily towards them. Minute after minute went by this way. Each time the animals attacked again, a few more gas grenades were used up.

"Something ahead—looks different," the panting voice cracked from the speaker. The narrow cave slowly opened out into a gigantic chamber, so large the roof and far walls were lost in the distance.

"What are those?" Kerk asked. "Get a searchlight over to the right there."

The picture on the screen was fuzzy and hard to see now, dimmed by the layers of rock in-between. Details couldn't be made out clearly, but it was obvious this was something unusual.

"Never saw ... anything quite like them before," the speaker said. "Look like big plants of some kind, ten meters tall at least—yet they're moving. Those branches, tentacles or whatever they are, keep pointing towards us and I get the darkest feeling in my head ..."

"Blast one, see what happens," Kerk said.

The gun fired and at the same instant an intensified wave of mental hatred rolled over the men, dropping them to the ground. They rolled in pain, blacked out and unable to think or fight the underground beasts that poured over them in renewed attack.

In the ship, far above, Jason felt the shock to his mind and wondered how the men below could have lived through it. The others in the control room had been hit by it as well. Kerk pounded on the frame of the screen and shouted to the unhearing men below.

"Pull back, come back...."

It was too late. The men only stirred slightly as the victorious Pyrran animals washed over them, clawing for the joints in their armor. Only one man moved, standing up and beating the creatures away with his bare hands. He stumbled a few feet and bent over the writhing mass below him. With a heave of his shoulders he pulled another man up. The man was dead but his shoulder pack was still strapped to his back. Bloody fingers fumbled at the pack, then both men were washed back under the wave of death.

"That was the bomb!" Kerk shouted to Meta. "If he didn't change the setting, it's still on ten-second minimum. Get out of here!"

Jason had just time to fall back on the acceleration couch before the rockets blasted. The pressure leaned on him and kept mounting. Vision blacked out but he didn't lose consciousness. Air screamed across the hull, then the sound stopped as they left the atmosphere behind.

Just as Meta cut the power a glare of white light burst from the screens. They turned black instantly as the hull pickups burned out. She switched filters into place, then pressed the button that rotated new pickups into position.

Far below, in the boiling sea, a climbing cloud of mushroom-shaped flame filled the spot where the island had been seconds before. The three of them looked at it, silently and unmoving. Kerk recovered first.

"Head for home, Meta, and get operations on the screen. Twenty-five men dead, but they did their job. They knocked out those beasts—whatever they were—and ended the war. I can't think of a better way for a man to die."

Meta set the orbit, then called operations.

"Trouble getting through," she said. "I have a robot landing beam response, but no one is answering the call."

A man appeared on the empty screen. He was beaded with sweat and had a harried look in his eyes. "Kerk," he said, "is that you? Get the ship back here at once. We need her firepower at the perimeter. All blazes broke loose a minute ago, a general attack from every side, worse than I've ever seen."

"What do you mean?" Kerk stammered in unbelief. "The war is over—we blasted them, destroyed their headquarters completely."

"The war is going like it never has gone before," the other snapped back. "I don't know what you did, but it stirred up the stewpot of hell here. Now stop talking and get the ship back!"

Kerk turned slowly to face Jason, his face pulled back in a look of raw animal savagery.

"You—! You did it! I should have killed you the first time I saw you. I wanted to, now I know I was right. You've been like a plague since you came here, sowing death in every direction. I knew you were wrong, yet I let your twisted words convince me. And look what has happened. First you killed Welf. Then you murdered those men in the cave. Now this attack on the perimeter—all who die there, you will have killed!"

Kerk advanced on Jason, step by slow step, hatred twisting his features. Jason backed away until he could retreat no further, his shoulders against the chart case. Kerk's hand lashed out, not a fighting blow, but an open slap. Though Jason rolled with it, it still battered him and stretched him full length on the floor. His arm was against the chart case, his fingers near the sealed tubes that held the jump matrices.

Jason seized one of the heavy tubes with both hands and pulled it out. He swung it with all his strength into Kerk's face. It broke the skin on his cheekbone and forehead and blood ran from the cuts. But it didn't slow or stop the big man in the slightest. His smile held no mercy as he reached down and dragged Jason to his feet.

"Fight back," he said, "I will have that much more pleasure as I kill you." He drew back the granite fist that would tear Jason's head from his shoulders.

"Go ahead," Jason said, and stopped struggling. "Kill me. You can do it easily. Only don't call it justice. Welf died to save me. But the men on the island died because of your stupidity. I wanted peace and you wanted war. Now you have it. Kill me to soothe your conscience, because the truth is something you can't face up to."

With a bellow of rage Kerk drove the piledriver fist down.

Meta grabbed the arm in both her hands and hung on, pulling it aside before the blow could land. The three of them fell together, half crushing Jason.

"Don't do it," she screamed. "Jason didn't want those men to go down there. That was your idea. You can't kill him for that!"

Kerk, exploding with rage, was past hearing. He turned his attention to Meta, tearing her from him. She was a woman and her supple strength was meager compared to his great muscles. But she was a Pyrran woman and she did what no off-worlder could. She slowed him for a moment, stopped the fury of his attack until he could rip her hands loose and throw her aside. It didn't take him long to do this, but it was just time enough for Jason to get to the door.

JASON STUMBLED THROUGH, and jammed shut the lock behind him. A split second after he had driven the bolt home Kerk's weight plunged into the door. The metal screamed and bent, giving way. One hinge was torn loose and the other held only by a shred of metal. It would go down on the next blow.

Jason wasn't waiting for that. He hadn't stayed to see if the door would stop the raging Pyrran. No door on the ship could stop him. Fast as possible, Jason went down the gangway. There was no safety on the ship, which meant he had to get off it. The lifeboat deck was just ahead.

Ever since first seeing them, he had given a lot of thought to the lifeboats. Though he hadn't looked ahead to this situation, he knew a time might come when he would need transportation of his own. The lifeboats had seemed to be the best bet, except that Meta had told him they had no fuel. She had been right in one thing—the boat he had been in had empty tanks, he had checked. There were five other boats, though, that he hadn't examined. He had wondered about the idea of useless lifeboats and come to what he hoped was a correct conclusion.

This spaceship was the only one the Pyrrans had. Meta had told him once that they always had planned to buy another ship, but never did. Some other necessary war expense managed to come up first. One ship was really enough for their uses. The only difficulty lay in the fact they had to keep that ship in operation or the Pyrran city was dead. Without supplies they would be wiped out in a few months. Therefore the ship's crew couldn't conceive of abandoning their ship. No matter what kind of trouble she got into, they couldn't leave her. When the ship died, so did their world.

With this kind of thinking, there was no need to keep the lifeboats fueled. Not all of them, at least. Though it stood to reason at least one of them held fuel for short flights that would have been wasteful for the parent ship. At this point Jason's chain of logic grew weak. Too many "ifs." *If* they used the lifeboats at all, one of them should be fueled. *If* they did, it would be fueled now. And *if* it were fueled—which one of the six would it be? Jason had no time to go looking. He had to be right the first time.

His reasoning had supplied him with an answer, the last of a long line of suppositions. If a boat were fueled, it should be the one nearest to the control cabin. The one he was diving towards now. His life depended on this string of guesses.

Behind him the door went down with a crash. Kerk bellowed and leaped. Jason hurled himself through the lifeboat port with the nearest thing to a run he could manage under the doubled gravity. With both hands he grabbed the emergency launching handle and pulled down.

An alarm bell rang and the port slammed shut, literally in Kerk's face. Only his Pyrran reflexes saved him from being smashed by it.

Solid-fuel launchers exploded and blasted the lifeboat clear of the parent ship. Their brief acceleration slammed Jason to the deck, then he floated as the boat went into free fall. The main drive rockets didn't fire.

In that moment Jason learned what it was like to know he was dead. Without fuel the boat would drop into the jungle below, falling like a rock and blasting apart when it hit. There was no way out.

Then the rockets caught, roared, and he dropped to the deck, bruising his nose. He sat up, rubbing it and grinning. There was fuel in the tanks—the delay in starting had only been part of the launching cycle, giving the lifeboat time to fall clear of the ship. Now to get it under control. He pulled himself into the pilot's seat.

The altimeter had fed information to the autopilot, leveling the boat off parallel to the ground. Like all lifeboat controls these were childishly simple, designed to be used by novices in an emergency. The autopilot could not be

shut off, it rode along with the manual controls, tempering foolish piloting. Jason hauled the control wheel into a tight turn and the autopilot gentled it to a soft curve.

Through the port he could see the big ship blaring fire in a much tighter turn. Jason didn't know who was flying it or what they had in mind—he took no chances. Jamming the wheel forward into a dive he cursed as they eased into a gentle drop. The larger ship had no such restrictions. It changed course with a violent maneuver and dived on him. The forward turret fired and an explosion at the stern rocked the little boat. This either knocked out the autopilot or shocked it into submission. The slow drop turned into a power dive and the jungle billowed up.

Jason pulled the wheel back and there was just time to get his arms in front of his face before they hit.

Thundering rockets and cracking trees ended in a great splash. Silence followed and the smoke drifted away. High above, the spaceship circled hesitantly. Dropping a bit as if wanting to go down and investigate. Then rising again as the urgent message for aid came from the city. Loyalty won and she turned and spewed fire towards home.

23

TREE BRANCHES HAD BROKEN the lifeboat's fall, the bow rockets had burned out in emergency blast, and the swamp had cushioned the landing a bit. It was still a crash. The battered cylinder sank slowly into the stagnant water and thin mud

of the swamp. The bow was well under before Jason managed to kick open the emergency hatch in the waist.

There was no way of knowing how long it would take for the boat to go under, and Jason was in no condition to ponder the situation. Concussed and bloody, he had just enough drive left to get himself out. Wading and falling he made his way to firmer land, sitting down heavily as soon as he found something that would support him.

Behind him the lifeboat burbled and sank under the water. Bubbles of trapped air kept rising for a while, then stopped. The water stilled and, except for the broken branches and trees, there was no sign that a ship had ever come this way.

Insects whined across the swamp, and the only sound that broke the quiet of the woods beyond was the cruel scream of an animal pulling down its dinner. When that had echoed away in tiny waves of sound everything was silent.

Jason pulled himself out of the half trance with an effort. His body felt like it had been through a meat grinder, and it was almost impossible to think with the fog in his head. After minutes of deliberation he figured out that the medikit was what he needed. The easy-off snap was very difficult and the button release didn't work. He finally twisted his arm around until it was under the orifice and pressed the entire unit down. It buzzed industriously, though he couldn't feel the needles, he guessed it had worked. His sight spun dizzily for a while then cleared. Pain-killers went to work and he slowly came out of the dark cloud that had enveloped his brain since the crash.

Reason returned and loneliness rode along with it. He was without food, friendless, surrounded by the hostile forces of an alien planet. There was a rising panic that started deep inside of him, that took concentrated effort to hold down.

"Think, Jason, don't emote," he said it aloud to reassure himself, but was instantly sorry, because his voice sounded weak in the emptiness, with a ragged edge of hysteria to it. Something caught in his throat and he coughed to clear it, spitting out blood. Looking at the red stain he was suddenly angry. Hating this deadly planet and the incredible stupidity of the people who lived on it. Cursing out loud was better and his voice didn't sound as weak now. He ended up shouting and shaking his fist at nothing in particular, but it helped. The anger washed away the fear and brought him back to reality.

Sitting on the ground felt good now. The sun was warm and when he leaned back he could almost forget the unending burden of doubled gravity. Anger had carried away fear, rest erased fatigue. From somewhere in the back of his mind there popped up the old platitude. *Where there's life, there's hope.* He grimaced at the triteness of the words, at the same time realizing that a basic truth lurked there.

Count his assets. Well battered, but still alive. None of the bruises seemed very important, and no bones were broken. His gun was still working, it dipped in and out of the power holster as he thought about it. Pyrrans made rugged equipment. The medikit was operating as well. If he kept his senses, managed to walk in a fairly straight line and could live off the land, there was a fair chance he might make it back to the city. What kind of a reception would be waiting for him there was a different matter altogether. He would find that out after he arrived. Getting there had first priority.

On the debit side there stood the planet Pyrrus. Strength-sapping gravity, murderous weather, and violent animals. Could he survive? As if to add emphasis to his thoughts, the sky darkened over and rain hissed into the forest, marching towards him. Jason scrambled to his feet and took a bearing before the rain closed down visibility. A jagged chain of mountains stood dimly on the horizon, he remembered crossing them on the flight out. They would do as a first goal. After he had reached them, he would worry about the next leg of the journey.

Leaves and dirt flew before the wind in quick gusts, then the rain washed over him. Soaked, chilled, already bone-tired, he pitted the tottering strength of his legs against the planet of death.

When nightfall came it was still raining. There was no way of being sure of the direction, and no point in going on. If that wasn't enough, Jason was on the ragged edge of exhaustion. It was going to be a wet night. All the trees were thick-boled and slippery, he couldn't have climbed them on a one-G world. The sheltered spots that he investigated, under fallen trees and beneath thick bushes, were just as wet as the rest of the forest. In the end he curled up on the leeward side of a tree, and fell asleep, shivering, with the water dripping off him.

The rain stopped around midnight and the temperature fell sharply. Jason woke sluggishly from a dream in which he was being frozen to death, to find it was almost true. Fine snow was sifting through the trees, powdering the ground and drifting against him. The cold bit into his flesh, and when he sneezed it hurt his chest. His aching and numb body only wanted rest, but the spark of reason that remained in him, forced him to his feet. If he lay down now, he would die. Holding one hand against the tree so he wouldn't fall, he began to trudge around it. Step after shuffling step, around and around, until the terrible cold eased a bit and he could stop shivering. Fatigue crawled up him like a muffling, gray blanket. He kept on walking, half the time with his eyes closed. Opening them only when he fell and had to climb painfully to his feet again.

The sun burned away the snow clouds at dawn. Jason leaned against his tree and blinked up at the sky with sore eyes. The ground was white in all directions, except around the tree where his stumbling feet had churned a circle of black mud. His back against the smooth trunk, Jason sank slowly down to the ground, letting the sun soak into him.

Exhaustion had him light-headed, and his lips were cracked from thirst. Almost continuous coughing tore at his chest with fingers of fire. Though the sun was still low it was hot already, burning his skin dry. Dry and hot.

It wasn't right. This thought kept nagging at his brain until he admitted it. Turned it over and over and looked at it from all sides. What wasn't right? The way he felt.

Pneumonia. He had all the symptoms.

His dry lips cracked and blood moistened them when he smiled. He had avoided all the animal perils of Pyrrus, all the big carnivores and poisonous reptiles, only to be laid low by the smallest beast of them all. Well, he had the remedy for this one, too. Rolling up his sleeve with shaking fingers, he pressed the mouth of the medikit to his bare arm. It clicked and began to drone an angry whine. That meant something, he knew, but he just couldn't remember what. Holding it up he saw that one of the hypodermics was projecting halfway from its socket. Of course. It was empty of whatever antibiotic the analyzer had called for. It needed refilling.

Jason hurled the thing away with a curse, and it splashed into a pool and was gone. End of medicine, end of medikit, end of Jason dinAlt. Single-handed battler against the perils of deathworld. Strong-hearted stranger who could do as well as the natives. It had taken him all of one day on his own to get his death warrant signed.

A choking growl echoed behind him. He turned, dropped and fired in the same motion. It was all over before his conscious mind was aware it had happened. Pyrran training had conditioned his reflexes on the pre-cortical level. Jason gaped at the ugly beast dying not a meter from him and realized he had been trained well.

His first reaction was unhappiness that he had killed one of the grubber dogs. When he looked closer he realized this animal was slightly different in markings, size and temper. Though most of its forequarters were blown away, blood pumping out in dying spurts, it kept trying to reach Jason. Before the eyes glazed with death it had struggled its way almost to his feet.

It wasn't quite a grubber dog, though chances were it was a wild relative. Bearing the same relation as dog to wolf. He wondered if there were any other resemblances between wolves and this dead beast. Did they hunt in packs, too?

As soon as the thought hit him he looked up—not a moment too soon. The great forms were drifting through the trees, closing in on him. When he shot two, the others snarled with rage and sank back into the forest. They didn't leave. Instead of being frightened by the deaths they grew even more enraged.

Jason sat with his back to the tree and waited until they came close before he picked them off. With each shot and dying scream the outraged survivors howled the louder. Some of them fought when they met, venting their rage. One stood on his hind legs and raked great strips of bark from a tree. Jason aimed a shot at it, but he was too far away to hit.

There were advantages to having a fever, he realized. Logically he knew he would live only to sunset, or until his gun was empty. Yet the fact didn't bother him greatly. Nothing really mattered. He slumped, relaxed completely, only raising his arm to fire, then letting it drop again. Every few minutes he had to move to look in back of the tree, and kill any of them that were stalking him in the blind spot. He wished dimly that he were leaning against a smaller tree, but it wasn't worth the effort to go to one.

Sometime in the afternoon he fired his last shot. It killed an animal he had allowed to get close. He had noticed he was missing the longer shots. The beast snarled and dropped, the others that were close pulled back and howled in sympathy. One of them exposed himself and Jason pulled the trigger.

There was only a slight click. He tried again, in case it was just a misfire, but there was still only the click. The gun was empty, as was the spare clip pouch at his belt. There were vague memories of reloading, though he couldn't remember how many times he had done it.

This, then, was the end. They had all been right, Pyrrus was a match for him. Though they shouldn't talk. It would kill them all in the end, too. Pyrrans never died in bed. Old Pyrrans never died, they just got *et*.

Now that he didn't have to force himself to stay alert and hold the gun, the fever took hold. He wanted to sleep and he knew it would be a long sleep. His eyes were almost closed as he watched the wary carnivores slip closer to him. The first one crept close enough to spring, he could see the muscles tensing in its leg.

It leaped. Whirling in midair and falling before it reached him. Blood ran from its gaping mouth and the short shaft of metal projected from the side of his head.

The two men walked out of the brush and looked down at him. Their mere presence seemed to have been enough for the carnivores, because they all vanished.

Grubbers. He had been in such a hurry to reach the city that he had forgotten about the grubbers. It was good that they were here and Jason was very glad they had come. He couldn't talk very well, so he smiled to thank them. But this hurt his lips too much so he went to sleep.

24 FOR A STRANGE LENGTH OF TIME after that, there were only hazy patches of memory that impressed themselves on Jason. A sense of movement and large beasts around him. Walls, woodsmoke, the murmur of voices. None of it meant very much and he was too tired to care. It was easier and much better just to let go.

"About time," Rhes said. "A couple more days lying there like that and we would have buried you, even if you were still breathing."

Jason blinked at him, trying to focus the face that swam above him. He finally recognized Rhes, and wanted to answer him. But talking only brought on a spell of body-wracking coughing. Someone held a cup to his lips and sweet fluid trickled down his throat. He rested, then tried again.

"How long have I been here?" The voice was thin and sounded far away. Jason had trouble recognizing it for his own.

"Eight days. And why didn't you listen when I talked to you?" Rhes said.

"You should have stayed near the ship when you crashed. Didn't you remember what I said about coming down anywhere on this continent? No matter, too late to worry about that. Next time listen to what I say. Our people moved fast and reached the site of the wreck before dark. They found the broken trees and the spot where the ship had sunk, and at first thought whoever had been in it had drowned. Then one of the dogs found your trail, but lost it again in the swamps during the night. They had a fine time with the mud and the snow and didn't have any luck at all in finding the spoor again. By the next afternoon they were ready to send for more help when they heard your firing. Just made it, from what I hear. Lucky one of them was a talker and could tell the wild dogs to clear out. Would have had to kill them all otherwise, and that's not healthy."

"Thanks for saving my neck," Jason said. "That was closer than I like to come. What happened after? I was sure I was done for, I remember that much. Diagnosed all the symptoms of pneumonia. Guaranteed fatal in my condition without treatment. Looks like you were wrong when you said most of your remedies were useless—they seemed to work well on me."

His voice died off as Rhes shook his head in a slow *no*, lines of worry sharp-cut into his face. Jason looked around and saw Naxa and another man. They had the same deeply

unhappy expressions as Rhes.

"What is it?" Jason asked, feeling the trouble. "If your remedies didn't work—what did? Not my medikit. That was empty. I remember losing it or throwing it away."

"You were dying," Rhes said slowly. "We couldn't cure you. Only a junkman medicine machine could do that. We got one from the driver of the food truck."

"But how?" Jason asked, dazed. "You told me the city forbids you medicine. He couldn't give you his own medikit. Not unless he was—"

Rhes nodded and finished the sentence. "Dead. Of course he was dead. I killed him myself, with a great deal of pleasure."

This hit Jason hard. He sagged against the pillows and thought of all those who had died since he had come to Pyrrus. The men who had died to save him, died so he could live, died because of his ideas. It was a burden of guilt that he couldn't bear to think about. Would it stop with Krannon—or would the city people try to avenge his death?

"Don't you realize what that means!" he gasped out the words. "Krannon's death will turn the city against you. There'll be no more supplies. They'll attack you when they can, kill your people—"

"Of course we know that!" Rhes leaned forward, his voice hoarse and intense. "It wasn't an easy decision to come to. We have always had a trading agreement with the junkmen. The trading trucks were inviolate. This was our last and only link to the galaxy outside and eventual hope of contacting them."

"Yet you broke that link to save me—why?"

"Only you can answer that question completely. There was a great attack on the city and we saw their walls broken, they had to be moved back at one place. At the same time the spaceship was over the ocean, dropping bombs of some kind—the flash was reported. Then the ship returned and *you* left it in a smaller ship. They fired at you but didn't kill you. The little ship wasn't destroyed either, we are starting to raise it now. What does it all mean? We had no way of telling. We only knew it was something vitally important. You were alive, but would obviously die before you could talk. The small ship might be repaired to fly, perhaps that was your plan and that is why you stole it for us. We *couldn't* let you die, not even if it meant all-out war with the city. The situation was explained to all of our people who could be reached by screen and they voted to save you. I killed the junkman for his medicine, then rode two doryms to death to get here in time.

"Now tell us—what does it mean? What is your plan? How will it help us?"

Guilt leaned on Jason and stifled his mouth. A fragment of an ancient legend cut across his mind, about the Jonah who wrecked the spacer so all in it died, yet he lived. Was that he? Had he wrecked a world? Could he dare admit to these people that he had taken the lifeboat only to save his own life?

The three Pyrrans leaned forward, waiting for his words. Jason closed his eyes so he wouldn't see their faces. What could he tell them? If he admitted the truth they would undoubtedly kill him on the spot, considering it only justice. He wasn't fearful for his own life any more, but if he died the other deaths would all have been in vain. And there still was a way to end this planetary war. All the facts were available now, it was just a matter of putting them together. If only he wasn't so tired, he could see the solution. It was right there, lurking around a corner in his brain, waiting to be dragged out.

Whatever he did, he couldn't admit the truth now. If he died all hope died. He had to lie to gain time, then find the true solution as soon as he was able. That was all he could do.

"You were right," Jason said haltingly. "The small ship has an interstellar drive in it. Perhaps it can still be saved. Even if it

can't there is another way. I can't explain now, but I will tell you when I am rested. Don't worry. The fight is almost over."

They laughed and pounded each other on the back. When they came to shake his hand as well, he closed his eyes and made believe he was asleep. It is very hard to be a hypocrite if you aren't trained for it.

Rhes woke him early the next morning. "Do you feel well enough to travel?" he asked.

"Depends what you mean by travel," Jason told him. "If you mean under my own power, I doubt if I could get as far as that door."

"You'll be carried," Rhes broke in. "We have a litter swung between two doryms. Not too comfortable, but you'll get there. But only if you think you are well enough to move. We called all the people within riding distance and they are beginning to gather. By this afternoon we will have enough men and doryms to pull the ship out of the swamp."

"I'll come," Jason said, pushing himself to a sitting position. The effort exhausted him, bringing a wave of nausea. Only by leaning his full weight against the wall could he keep from falling back. He sat, propped there, until he heard shouts and the stamping of heavy feet outside, and they came to carry him out.

The trip drained away his small store of energy, and he fell into an exhausted sleep. When he opened his eyes the doryms were standing knee deep in the swamp and the salvage operation had begun. Ropes vanished out of sight in the water while lines of struggling animals and men hauled at them. The beasts bellowed, the men cursed as they slipped and fell. All of the Pyrrans tugging on the lines weren't male, women were there as well. Shorter on the average than the men, they were just as brawny. Their clothing was varied and many-colored, the first touch of decoration Jason had seen on this planet.

Getting the ship up was a heart-breaking job. The mud sucked at it and underwater roots caught on the vanes. Divers plunged time and again into the brown water to cut them free. Progress was incredibly slow, but the work never stopped. Jason's brain was working even slower. The ship would be hauled up eventually—what would he do then? He had to have a new plan by that time, but thinking was impossible work. His thoughts corkscrewed and he had to fight down the rising feeling of panic.

The sun was low when the ship's nose finally appeared above the water. A ragged cheer broke out at first sight of that battered cone of metal and they went ahead with new energy.

Jason was the first one who noticed the dorym weaving towards them. The dogs saw it, of course, and ran out and sniffed. The rider shouted to the dogs and kicked angrily at the sides of his mount. Even at this distance Jason could see the beast's heaving sides and yellow foam-flecked hide. It was barely able to stagger now and the man jumped down, running ahead on foot. He was shouting something as he ran that couldn't be heard above the noise.

There was a single moment when the sounds slacked a bit and the running man's voice could be heard. He was calling the same word over and over again. It sounded like *wait*, but Jason couldn't be sure. Others had heard him though, and the result was instantaneous. They stopped, unmoving, where they were. Many of those holding the ropes let go of them. Only the quick action of the anchor men kept the ship from sliding back under, dragging the harnessed doryms with it. A wave of silence washed across the swamp in the wake of the running man's shouts. They could be heard clearly now.

"Quake! Quake on the way! South—only safe way is south!"

One by one the ropes dropped back into the water and the Pyrrans turned to wade to solid land. Before they were well started Rhes' voice cracked out.

"Stay at work! Get the ship up, it's our only hope now. I'll talk to Hananas, find out how much time we have."

These solitary people were unused to orders. They stopped and milled about, reason fighting with the urgent desire to run. One by one they stepped back to the ropes as they worked out the sense of Rhes' words. As soon as it was clear the work would continue he turned away.

"What is it? What's happening?" Jason called to him as he ran by.

"It's Hananas," Rhes said, stopping by the litter, waiting for the newcomer to reach him. "He's a quakeman. They know when quakes are coming, before they happen."

Hananas ran up, panting and tired. He was a short man, built like a barrel on stubby legs, a great white beard covering his neck and the top of his chest. Another time Jason might have laughed at his incongruous waddle, but not now. There was a charged difference in the air since the little man had arrived.

"Why didn't ... you have somebody near a plate? I called all over this area without an answer. Finally ... had to come myself—"

"How much time do we have?" Rhes cut in. "We have to get that ship up before we pull out."

"Time! Who knows about time!" the graybeard cursed. "Get out or you're dead."

"Calm down, Han," Rhes said in a quieter voice, taking the oldster's arms in both his hands. "You know what we're doing here—and how much depends on getting the ship up. Now how does it feel? This going to be a fast one or a slow one?"

"Fast. Faster than anything I felt in a long time. She's starting far away though, if you had a plate here I bet Mach or someone else up near the firelands would be reporting new eruptions. It's on the way and, if we don't get out soon, we're not getting out t'all."

There was a burble of water as the ship was hauled out a bit farther. No one talked now and there was a fierce urgency in their movements. Jason still wasn't sure exactly what had happened.

"Don't shoot me for a foreigner," he said,

"but just what is wrong? Are you expecting earthquakes here, are you sure?"

"Sure!" Hananas screeched. "Of course I'm sure. If I wasn't sure I wouldn't be a quakeman. It's on the way."

"There's no doubt of that," Rhes added. "I don't know how you can tell on your planet when quakes or vulcanism are going to start, machines maybe. We have nothing like that. But quakemen, like Hananas here, always know about them before they happen. If the word can be passed fast enough, we get away. The quake is coming all right, the only thing in doubt is how much time we have."

The work went on and there was a good chance they would die long before it was finished. All for nothing. The only way Jason could get them to stop would be to admit the ship was useless. He would be killed then and the grubber chances would die with him. He chewed his lip as the sun set and the work continued by torchlight.

Hananas paced around, grumbling under his breath, halting only to glance at the northern horizon. The people felt his restlessness and transmitted it to the animals. Dogfights broke out and the doryms pulled reluctantly at their harnesses. With each passing second their chances grew slimmer and Jason searched desperately for a way out of the trap of his own constructing.

"Look—" someone said, and they all turned. The sky to the north was lit with a red light. There was a rumble in the ground that was felt more than heard. The surface of the water blurred, then broke into patterns of tiny waves. Jason turned away from the light, looking at the water and the ship. It was higher now, the top of the stern exposed. There was a gaping hole here, blasted through the metal by the spaceship's guns.

"Rhes," he called, his words jammed together in the rush to get them out. "Look at the ship, at the hole blasted in her stern. I landed on the rockets and didn't know how badly she was hit. But the guns hit the star drive!"

Rhes gaped at him unbelievingly as he went on. Improvising, playing by ear, trying to manufacture lies that rang of the truth.

"I watched them install the drive—it's an auxiliary to the other engines. It was bolted to the hull right there. It's gone now, blown up. The boat will never leave this planet, much less go to another star."

He couldn't look Rhes in the eyes after that. He sank back into the furs that had been propped behind him, feeling the weakness even more. Rhes was silent and Jason couldn't tell if his story had been believed. Only when the Pyrran bent and slashed the nearest rope did he know he had won.

The word passed from man to man and the ropes were cut silently. Behind them the ship they had labored so hard over, sank back into the water. None of them watched. Each was locked in his own world of thought as they formed up to leave. As soon as the doryms were saddled and packed they started out, Hananas leading the way. Within minutes they were all moving, a single file that vanished into the darkness.

Jason's litter had to be left behind, it would have been smashed to pieces in the night march. Rhes pulled him up into the saddle before him, locking his body into place with a steel-hard arm. The trek continued.

When they left the swamp they changed directions sharply. A little later Jason knew why, when the southern sky exploded. Flames lit the scene brightly, ashes sifted down and hot lumps of rock crashed into the trees. They steamed when they hit, and if it hadn't been for the earlier rain they would have been faced with a forest fire as well.

Something large loomed up next to the line of march, and when they crossed an open space Jason looked at it in the reflected light from the sky.

"Rhes—" he choked, pointing.

Rhes looked at the great beast moving next to them, shaggy body and twisted horns as high as their shoulders, then looked away. He wasn't frightened or apparently interested. Jason looked around then and began to understand.

All of the fleeing animals made no sound, that's why he hadn't noticed them before. But on both sides dark forms ran between the trees. Some he recognized, most of them he didn't. For a few minutes a pack of wild dogs ran near them, even mingling with the domesticated dogs. No notice was taken. Flying things flapped overhead. Under the greater threat of the volcanoes all other battles were forgotten. Life respected life. A herd of fat, piglike beasts with curling tusks, blundered through the line. The doryms slowed, picking their steps carefully so they wouldn't step on them. Smaller animals sometimes clung to the backs of the bigger ones, riding untouched a while, before they leaped off.

Pounded mercilessly by the saddle, Jason fell wearily into a light sleep. It was shot through with dreams of the rushing animals, hurrying on forever in silence. With his eyes open or shut he saw the same endless stream of beasts.

It all meant something, and he frowned as he tried to think what. Animals running, Pyrran animals.

He sat bolt upright suddenly, wide awake, staring down in comprehension.

"What is it?" Rhes asked.

"Go on," Jason said. "Get us out of this, and get us out safely. I told you the lifeboat wasn't the only answer. I know how your people can get what they want—end the war now. There *is* a way, and I know how it can be done."

25 THERE WERE FEW COHERENT MEMORIES OF THE RIDE. Some things stood out sharply like the spaceship-sized lump of burning scoria that had plunged into a lake near them, showering the line with hot drops of water. But mostly it was just a seemingly endless ride, with Jason still too weak to care much about it. By dawn the danger area was behind them and the march had slowed to a walk. The animals had vanished as the quake was left behind, going

their own ways, still in silent armistice.

The peace of mutually shared danger was over, Jason found that out when they stopped to rest and eat. He and Rhes went to sit on the soft grass, near a fallen tree. A wild dog had arrived there first. It lay under the log, muscles tensed, the ruddy morning light striking a red glint from its eyes. Rhes faced it, not three meters away, without moving a muscle. He made no attempt to reach one of his weapons or to call for help. Jason stood still as well, hoping the Pyrran knew what he was doing.

With no warning at all the dog sprang straight at them. Jason fell backwards as Rhes pushed him aside. The Pyrran dropped at the same time—only now his hand held the long knife, yanked from the sheath strapped to his thigh. With unseen speed the knife came up, the dog twisted in midair, trying to bite it. Instead it sank in behind the dog's forelegs, the beast's own weight tearing a deadly gaping wound the length of its body. It was still alive when it hit the ground, but Rhes was astraddle it, pulling back the bony-plated head to cut the soft throat underneath.

The Pyrran carefully cleaned his knife on the dead animal's fur, then returned it to the sheath. "They're usually no trouble," he said quietly, "but it was excited. Probably lost the rest of the pack in the quake." His actions were the direct opposite of the city Pyrrans. He had not looked for trouble nor started the fight. Instead he had avoided it as long as he could. But when the beast charged it had been neatly and efficiently dispatched. Now, instead of gloating over his victory, he seemed troubled over an unnecessary death.

It made sense. Everything on Pyrrus made sense. Now he knew how the deadly planetary battle had started—and he knew how it could be ended. All the deaths had *not* been in vain. Each one had helped him along the road a little more towards the final destination. There was just one final thing to be done.

Rhes was watching him now, and he

knew they shared the same thoughts. "Explain yourself," Rhes said. "What did you mean when you said we could wipe out the junkmen and get our freedom?"

Jason didn't bother to correct the misquote, it was best they consider him a hundred per cent on their side.

"Get the others together and I'll tell you. I particularly want to see Naxa and any other talkers who are here."

They gathered quickly when the word was passed. All of them knew that the junkman had been killed to save this offworlder, that their hope of salvation lay with him. Jason looked at the crowd of faces turned towards him and reached for the right words to tell them what had to be done. It didn't help to know that many of them would be killed doing it.

"The small star ship can't be used," he said. "You all saw that it was ruined beyond repair. But that was the easy way out. The hard way is still left. Though some of you may die, in the long run it will be the best solution.

"We are going to invade the city, break through the perimeter. I know how it can be done...."

A mutter of sound spread across the crowd. Some of them looked excited, happy with the thought of killing their hereditary enemies. Others stared at Jason as if he were mad. A few were dazed at the magnitude of the thought, this carrying of the battle to the stronghold of the heavily armed enemy. They quieted when Jason raised his hand.

"I know it sounds impossible," he said. "But let me explain. Something must be done—and now is the time to do it. The situation can only get worse from now on. The city Pyrr ... the junkmen can get along without your food, their concentrates taste awful but they sustain life. But they are going to turn against you in every way they can. No more metals for your tools or replacements for your electronic equipment. Their hatred will probably make them seek out your farms and destroy them from the ship. All of this won't be comfortable—and there will be worse to come. In the city they are losing their war against this planet. Each year there are less of them, and some day they will all be dead. Knowing how they feel I am sure they will destroy their ship first, and the entire planet as well, if that is possible."

"How can we stop them?" someone called out.

"By hitting *now*," Jason answered. "I know all the details of the city and I know how the defenses are set up. Their perimeter is designed to protect them from animal life, but we could break through it if we were really determined."

"What good would that do?" Rhes snapped. "We crack the perimeter and they draw back—then counter-attack in force. How can we stand against their weapons?"

"We won't have to. Their spaceport touches the perimeter, and I know the exact spot where the ship stands. That is the place where we will break through. There is no formal guard on the ship and only a few people in the area. We will capture the ship. Whether we can fly it or not is unimportant. Who controls the ship controls Pyrrus. Once there we threaten to destroy it if they don't meet our terms. They have the choice of mass suicide or co-operation. I hope they have the brains to co-operate."

His words shocked them into silence for an instant, then they surged into a wave of sound. There was no agreement, just excitement, and Rhes finally brought them to order.

"Quiet!" he shouted. "Wait until Jason finishes before you decide. We still haven't heard how this proposed invasion is to be accomplished."

"The plan I have depends on the talkers." Jason said. "Is Naxa there?" He waited until the fur-wrapped man had pushed to the front. "I want to know more about the talkers, Naxa. I know you can speak to doryms and the dogs here—but what about the wild animals? Can you make them do what you want?"

"They're animals ... course we can talk t'them. Th'more talkers, th'more power. Make 'em do just what we want."

"Then the attack will work," Jason said excitedly. "Could you get your talkers all on one side of the city—the opposite side from the spaceport—and stir the animals up? Make them attack the perimeter?"

"Could we!" Naxa shouted, carried away by the idea. "We'd bring in animals from all over, start th'biggest attack they ev'r saw!"

"Then that's it. Your talkers will launch the attack on the far side of the perimeter. If you keep out of sight, the guards will have no idea that it is anything more than an animal attack. I've seen how they work. As an attack mounts they call for reserves inside the city and drain men away from the other parts of the perimeter. At the height of the battle, when they have all their forces committed across the city, I'll lead the attack that will break through and capture the ship. That's the plan and it's going to work."

Jason sat down then, half fell down, drained of strength. He lay and listened as the debate went back and forth, Rhes ordering it and keeping it going. Difficulties were raised and eliminated. No one could find a basic fault with the plan. There were plenty of flaws in it, things that might go wrong, but Jason didn't mention them. These people wanted his idea to work and they were going to make it work.

It finally broke up and they moved away. Rhes came over to Jason.

"The basics are settled," he said. "All here are in agreement. They are spreading the word by messenger to all the talkers. The talkers are the heart of the attack, and the more we have, the better it will go off. We don't dare use the screens to call them, there is a good chance that the junkmen can intercept our messages. It will take five days before we are ready to go ahead."

"I'll need all of that time if I'm to be any good," Jason said. "Now let's get some rest."

26 "IT'S A STRANGE FEELING," Jason said. "I've never really seen the perimeter from this side before. Ugly is about the only word for it."

He lay on his stomach next to Rhes, looking through a screen of leaves, downhill towards the perimeter. They were both wrapped in heavy furs, in spite of the midday heat, with thick leggings and leather gauntlets to protect their hands. The gravity and the heat were already making Jason dizzy, but he forced himself to ignore this.

Ahead, on the far side of a burnt corridor, stood the perimeter. A high wall, of varying height and texture, seemingly made of everything in the world. It was impossible to tell what it had originally been constructed of. Generations of attackers had bruised, broken, and undermined it. Repairs had been quickly made, patches thrust roughly into place and fixed there. Crude masonry crumbled and gave way to a rat's nest of woven timbers. This overlapped a length of pitted metal, large plates riveted together. Even this metal had been eaten through and bursting sandbags spilled out of a jagged hole. Over the surface of the wall detector wires and charged cables looped and hung. At odd intervals automatic flame-throwers thrust their nozzles over the wall above and swept the base of the wall clear of any life that might have come close.

"Those flame things can cause us trouble," Rhes said. "That one covers the area where you want to break in."

"It'll be no problem," Jason assured him. "It may look like it is firing a random pattern, but it's really not. It varies a simple sweep just enough to fool an animal, but was never meant to keep men out. Look for yourself. It fires at regularly repeated two, four, three and one minute intervals."

They crawled back to the hollow where Naxa and the others waited for them. There were only thirty men in the party. What they had to do could only be done with a fast, light force. Their strongest weapon was surprise. Once that was gone their other weapons wouldn't hold out for seconds against the city guns. Everyone looked uncomfortable in the fur and leather wrappings, and some of the men had loosened them to cool off.

"Wrap up," Jason ordered. "None of you have been this close to the perimeter before and you don't understand how deadly it is here. Naxa is keeping the larger animals away and you all can handle the smaller ones. That isn't the danger. Every thorn is poisoned, and even the blades of grass carry a deadly sting. Watch out for insects of any kind and once we start moving breathe only through the wet cloths."

"He's right," Naxa snorted. "N'ver been closer'n this m'self. Death, death up by that wall. Do like 'e says."

They could only wait then, honing down already needle-sharp crossbow bolts, and glancing up at the slowly moving sun. Only Naxa didn't share the unrest. He sat, eyes unfocused, feeling the movement of animal life in the jungle around them.

"On the way," he said. "Biggest thing I 'ver heard. Not a beast 'tween here and the mountains, ain't howlin' 'is lungs out, runnin' towards the city."

Jason was aware of part of it. A tension in the air and a wave of intensified anger and hatred. It would work, he knew, if they could only keep the attack confined to a small area. The talkers had seemed sure of it. They had stalked out quietly that morning, a thin line of ragged men, moving out in a mental sweep that would round up the Pyrran life and send it charging against the city.

"They hit!" Naxa said suddenly.

The men were on their feet now, staring in the direction of the city. Jason had felt the twist as the attack had been driven home, and knew that this was it. There was the sound of shots and a heavy booming far away. Thin streamers of smoke began to blow above the treetops.

"Let's get into position," Rhes said.

Around them the jungle howled with an echo of hatred. The half-sentient plants writhed and the air was thick with small flying things. Naxa sweated and mumbled as he turned back the animals that crashed towards them. By the time they reached the last screen of foliage before the burned-out area, they had lost four men. One had been stung by an insect, Jason got the medikit to him in time, but he was so sick he had to turn back. The other three were bitten or scratched and treatment came too late. Their swollen, twisted bodies were left behind on the trail.

"Dam' beasts hurt m'head," Naxa muttered. "When we go in?"

"Not yet," Rhes said. "We wait for the signal."

One of the men carried the radio. He sat it down carefully, then threw the aerial over a branch. The set was shielded so no radiation leaked out to give them away. It was turned on, but only a hiss of atmospheric static came from the speaker.

"We could have timed it—" Rhes said.

"No we couldn't," Jason told him. "Not accurately. We want to hit that wall at the height of the attack, when our chances are best. Even if they hear the message it won't mean a thing to them inside. And a few minutes later it won't matter."

The sound from the speaker changed. A voice spoke a short sentence, then cut off.

"Bring me three barrels of flour."

"Let's go," Rhes urged as he started forward.

"Wait," Jason said, taking him by the arm. "I'm timing the flame-thrower. It's due in ... *there*!" A blast of fire sprayed the ground, then turned off. "We have four minutes to the next one—we hit the long period!"

They ran, stumbling in the soft ashes, tripping over charred bones and rusted metal. Two men grabbed Jason under the arm and half-carried him across the ground. It hadn't been planned that way, but it saved precious seconds. They dropped him against the wall and he fumbled out the bombs he had made. The charges from Krannon's gun, taken when he was killed, had been hooked together with a firing circuit. All the moves had been rehearsed carefully and they went smoothly now.

Jason had picked the metal wall as being the best spot to break in. It offered the most resistance to the native life, so the chances were it wouldn't be reinforced with sandbags or fill, the way other parts of the wall were. If he was wrong, they were all dead.

The first men had slapped their wads of sticky congealed sap against the wall. Jason pressed the charges into them and they stuck, a roughly rectangular pattern as high as a man. While he did this the detonating wire was run out to its length and the raiders pressed back against the base of the wall. Jason stumbled through the ashes to the detonator, fell on it and pressed the switch at the same time.

Behind him a thundering bang shook the wall and red flame burst out. Rhes was the first one there, pulling at the twisted and smoking metal with his gloved hands. Others grabbed on and bent the jagged pieces aside. The hole was filled with smoke and nothing was visible through it. Jason dived into the opening, rolled on a heap of rubble and smacked into something solid. When he blinked the smoke from his eyes he looked around him.

He was inside the city.

The others poured through now, picking him up as they charged in so he wouldn't be trampled underfoot. Someone spotted the spaceship and they ran that way.

A man ran around the corner of a building towards them. His Pyrran reflexes sent him springing into the safety of a doorway the same moment he saw the invaders. But they were Pyrrans, too. The man slumped slowly back onto the street, three metal bolts sticking out of his body. They ran on without

stopping, running between the low storehouses. The ship stood ahead.

Someone had reached it ahead of them, they could see the outer hatch slowly grinding shut. A hail of bolts from the bows crashed into it with no effect.

"Keep going!" Jason shouted. "Get next to the hull before he reaches the guns."

This time three men didn't make it. The rest of them were under the belly of the ship when every gun let go at once. Most of them were aimed away from the ship, still the scream of shells and electric discharges was ear-shattering. The three men still in the open dissolved under the fire. Whoever was inside the ship had hit all the gun trips at once, both to knock out the attackers and summon aid. He would be on the screen now, calling for help. Their time was running out.

Jason reached up and tried to open the hatch, while the others watched. It was locked from the inside. One of the men brushed him aside and pulled at the inset handle. It broke off in his hand but the hatch remained closed.

The big guns had stopped now and they could hear again.

"Did anyone get the gun from that dead man?" he asked. "It would blow this thing open."

"No," Rhes said, "we didn't stop."

Before the words were out of his mouth two men were running back towards the buildings, angling away from each other. The ship's guns roared again, a string of explosions cut across one man. Before they could change direction and find the other man he had reached the buildings.

He returned quickly, darting into the open to throw the gun to them. Before he could dive back to safety the shells caught him.

Jason grabbed up the gun as it skidded

almost to his feet. They heard the sound of wide-open truck turbines screaming towards them as he blasted the lock. The mechanism sighed and the hatch sagged open. They were all through the air lock before the first truck appeared. Naxa stayed behind with the gun, to hold the lock until they could take the control room.

Everyone climbed faster than Jason, once he had pointed them the way, so the battle was over when he got there. The single city Pyrran looked like a pin-cushion. One of the techs had found the gun controls and was shooting wildly, the sheer quantity of his fire driving the trucks back.

"Someone get on the radio and tell the talkers to call the attack off," Jason said. He found the communications screen and snapped it on. Kerk's wide-eyed face stared at him from the screen.

"*You!*" Kerk said, breathing the word like a curse.

"Yes, it's me," Jason answered. He talked without looking up, while his hands were busy at the control board. "Listen to me, Kerk—and don't doubt anything I say. I may not know how to fly one of these ships, but I do know how to blow them up. Do you hear that sound?" He flipped over a switch and the faraway whine of a pump droned faintly. "That's the main fuel pump. If I let it run—which I won't right now—it could quickly fill the drive chamber with raw fuel. Pour in so much that it would run out of the stern tubes. Then what do you think would happen to your one and only spacer if I pressed the firing button? I'm not asking you what would happen to me, since you don't care—but you need this ship the way you need life itself."

There was only silence in the cabin now, the men who had won the ship turned to face him. Kerk's voice grated loudly through the room.

"What do you want, Jason—what are you trying to do? Why did you lead those animals in here...?" His voice cracked and broke as anger choked him and spilled over.

"Watch your tongue, Kerk," Jason said with soft menace. "These *men* you are talking about are the only ones on Pyrrus who have a spaceship. If you want them to share it with you, you had better learn to talk nicely. Now come over here at once—and bring Brucco and Meta." Jason looked at the older man's florid and swollen face and felt a measure of sympathy. "Don't look so unhappy, it's not the end of the world. In fact, it might be the beginning of one. And another thing, leave this channel open when you go. Have it hooked into every screen in the city so everyone can see what happens here. Make sure it's taped too, for replay."

Kerk started to say something, but changed his mind before he did. He left the screen, but the set stayed alive. Carrying the scene in the control room to the entire city.

27 THE FIGHT WAS OVER. It had ended so quickly the fact hadn't really sunk in yet. Rhes rubbed his hand against the gleaming metal of the control console, letting the reality of touch convince him. The other men milled about, looking out through the viewscreens or soaking in the mechanical strangeness of the room.

Jason was physically exhausted, but he couldn't let it show. He opened the pilot's medbox and dug through it until he found the stimulants. Three of the little gold pills washed the fatigue from his body, and he could think clearly again.

"Listen to me," he shouted. "The fight's not over yet. They'll try anything to take this ship back and we have to be ready. I want one of the techs to go over these boards until he finds the lock controls. Make sure all the air locks and ports are sealed. Send men to check them if necessary. Turn on all the screens to scan in every direction, so no one can get near the ship. We'll need a guard in the engine room, my control could be cut if they broke in there. And there had better be a room-by-room search of the ship, in case someone else is locked in with us."

The men had something to do now and

felt relieved. Rhes split them up into groups and set them to work. Jason stayed at the controls, his hand next to the pump switch. The battle wasn't over yet.

"There's a truck coming," Rhes called, "going slow."

"Should I blast it?" the man at the gun controls asked.

"Hold your fire," Jason said, "until we can see who it is. If it's the people I sent for, let them through."

As the truck came on slowly, the gunner tracked it with his sights. There was a driver and three passengers. Jason waited until he was positive who they were.

"Those are the ones," he said. "Stop them at the lock, Rhes, make them come in one at a time. Take their guns as they enter, then strip them of *all* their equipment. There is no way of telling what could be a concealed weapon. Be especially careful of Brucco—he's the thin one with a face like an ax edge—make sure you strip him clean. He's a specialist in weapons and survival. And bring the driver too, we don't want him reporting back about the broken air lock or the state of our guns."

Waiting was hard. His hand stayed next to the pump switch, even though he knew he could never use it. Just as long as the others thought he would.

There were stampings and muttered curses in the corridor; the prisoners were pushed in. Jason had one look at their deadly expressions and clenched fists before he called to Rhes.

"Keep them against the wall and watch them. Bowmen keep your weapons up." He looked at the people who had once been his friends and who now swam in hatred for him. Meta, Kerk, Brucco. The driver was Skop, the man Kerk had once appointed to guard him. He looked ready to explode now that the roles had been reversed.

"Pay close attention," Jason said, "because your lives depend upon it. Keep your backs to the wall and don't attempt to come any closer to me than you are now. If you do,

you will be shot instantly. If we were alone, any one of you could undoubtedly reach me before I threw this switch. But we're not. You have Pyrran reflexes and muscles—but so do the bowmen. Don't gamble. Because it won't be a gamble. It will be suicide. I'm telling you this for your own protection. So we can talk peacefully without one of you losing his temper and suddenly getting shot. *There is no way out of this.* You are going to be forced to listen to everything I say. You can't escape or kill me. The war is over."

"And we lost—and all because of you ... you *traitor!*" Meta snarled.

"Wrong on both counts," Jason said blandly. "I'm not a traitor because I owe my allegiance to all men on this planet, both inside the perimeter and out. I never pretended differently. As to losing—why you haven't lost anything. In fact you've won. Won your war against this planet, if you will only hear me out." He turned to Rhes, who was frowning in angry puzzlement. "Of course your people have won also, Rhes. No more war with the city, you'll get medicine, off-planet contact—everything you want."

"Pardon me for being cynical," Rhes said, "but you're promising the best of all possible worlds for everyone. That will be a little hard to deliver when our interests are opposed so."

"You strike through to the heart of the matter," Jason said. "Thank you. This mess will be settled by seeing that everyone's interests are not opposed. Peace between the city and farms, with an end to the useless war you have been fighting. Peace between mankind and the Pyrran life forms—because that particular war is at the bottom of all your troubles."

"The man's mad," Kerk said.

"Perhaps. You'll judge that after you hear me out. I'm going to tell you the history of this planet, because that is where both the trouble and the solution lie.

"When the settlers landed on Pyrrus three hundred years ago they missed the one important thing about this planet, the factor that makes it different from any other planet in the galaxy. They can't be blamed for the oversight, they had enough other things to worry about. The gravity was about the only thing familiar to them, the rest of the environment was a shocking change from the climate-controlled industrial world they had left. Storms, vulcanism, floods, earthquakes—it was enough to drive them insane, and I'm sure many of them did go mad. The animal and insect life was a constant annoyance, nothing at all like the few harmless and protected species they had known. I'm sure they never realized that the Pyrran life was telepathic as well—"

"That again!" Brucco snapped. "True or not, it is of no importance. I was tempted to agree with your theory of psionic-controlled attack on us, but the deadly fiasco you staged proved that theory wrong."

"I agree," Jason answered. "I was completely mistaken when I thought some outside agency directed the attack on the city with psionic control. It seemed a logical theory at the time and the evidence pointed that way. The expedition to the island *was* a deadly fiasco—only don't forget that attack was the direct opposite of what I wanted to have done. If I had gone into the cave myself none of the deaths would have been necessary. I think it would have been discovered that the plant creatures were nothing more than an advanced life form with unusual psi ability. They simply resonated strongly to the psionic attack on the city. I had the idea backwards thinking they instigated the battle. We'll never know the truth, though, because they are destroyed. But their deaths did prove one thing. It allows us to find the real culprits, the creatures who are leading, directing and inspiring the war against the city."

"*Who?*" Kerk breathed the question, rather than spoke it.

"Why *you*, of course," Jason told him. "Not you alone, but all of your people in the city. Perhaps you don't like this war. However you are responsible for it, and keep it going."

Jason had to force back a smile as he looked at their dumfounded expressions. He had to prove his point quickly, before even his allies began to think him insane.

"Here is how it works. I said Pyrran life was telepathic—and I meant all life. Every single insect, plant and animal. At one time in this planet's violent history these psionic mutations proved to be survival types. They existed when other species died, and in the end I'm sure they co-operated in wiping out the last survivors of the non-psi strains. Co-operation is the key word here. Because while they still competed against each other under normal conditions, they worked together against anything that threatened them as a whole. When a natural upheaval or a tidal wave threatened them, they fled from it in harmony.

"You can see a milder form of this same behavior on any planet that is subject to forest fires. But here, mutual survival was carried to an extreme because of the violent conditions. Perhaps some of the life forms even developed precognition like the human quakemen. With this advance warning the larger beasts fled. The smaller ones developed seeds, or burrs or eggs, that could be carried to safety by the wind or in the animals' fur, thus insuring racial survival. I know this is true, because I watched it myself when we were escaping a quake."

"Admitted—all your points admitted," Brucco shouted. "But what does it have to do with *us*? So all the animals run away together, what does that have to do with the war?"

"They do more than run away together," Jason told him. "They work together against any natural disaster that threatens them all. Some day I'm sure, ecologists will go into raptures over the complex adjustments that occur here in the advent of blizzards, floods, fires and other disasters. There is only one reaction we really care about now, though. That's the one directed towards the city people. Don't you realize yet—they treat you all as another natural disaster!

"We'll never know exactly how it came about, though there is a clue in that diary I found, dating from the first days on this planet. It said that a forest fire seemed to have driven new species towards the settlers. Those weren't new beasts at all—just old ones with new attitudes. Can't you just imagine how those protected, over-civilized settlers acted when faced with a forest fire? They panicked of course. If the settlers were in the path of the fire, the animals must have rushed right through their camp. Their reaction would undoubtedly have been to shoot the fleeing creatures down.

"When they did that they classified themselves as a natural disaster. Disasters take any form. Bipeds with guns could easily be included in the category. The Pyrran animals attacked, were shot, and the war began. The survivors kept attacking and informed all the life forms what the fight was about. The radioactivity of this planet must cause plenty of mutations—and the favorable, survival mutation was now one that was deadly to man. I'll hazard a guess that the psi function even instigates mutations, some of the deadlier types are just too one-sided to have come about naturally in a brief three hundred years.

"The settlers, of course, fought back, and kept their status as a natural disaster intact. Through the centuries they improved their killing methods, not that it did the slightest good, as you know. You city people, their descendants, are heirs to this heritage of hatred. You fight and are slowly being defeated. How can you possibly win against the biologic reserves of a planet that can recreate itself each time to meet any new attack?"

Silence followed Jason's words. Kerk and Meta stood white-faced as the impact of the disclosure sunk in. Brucco mumbled and checked points off on his fingers, searching for weak spots in the chain of reason. The fourth city Pyrran, Skop, ignored all these foolish words that he couldn't understand—or want to understand—and would have killed Jason in an instant if there had been the slightest chance of success.

It was Rhes who broke the silence. His quick mind had taken in the factors and sorted them out. "There's one thing wrong," he said. "What about us? We live on the surface of Pyrrus without perimeters or guns. Why aren't we attacked as well? We're human, descended from the same people as the junkmen."

"You're not attacked," Jason told him, "because you don't identify yourself as a natural disaster. Animals can live on the slopes of a dormant volcano, fighting and dying in natural competition. But they'll flee together when the volcano erupts. That eruption is what makes the mountain a natural disaster. In the case of human beings, it is their thoughts that identify them as life form or disaster. Mountain or volcano. In the city everyone radiates suspicion and death. They enjoy killing, thinking about killing, and planning for killing. This is natural selection, too, you realize. These are the survival traits that work best in the city. Outside the city men think differently. If they are threatened individually, they fight, as will any other creature. Under more general survival threats they co-operate completely with the rules for universal survival that the city people break."

"How did it begin—this separation, I mean, between the two groups?" Rhes asked.

"We'll probably never know," Jason said. "I think your people must have originally been farmers, or psionic sensitives who were not with the others during some natural disaster. They would, of course, act correctly by Pyrran standards, and survive. This would cause a difference of opinion with the city people who saw killing as the answer. It's obvious, whatever the reason, that two separate communities were established early, and soon separated except for the limited amount of barter that benefited both."

"I still can't believe it," Kerk mumbled. "It makes a terrible kind of truth, every step of the way, but I still find it hard to accept.

There *must* be another explanation."

Jason shook his head slowly. "None. This is the only one that works. We've eliminated the other ones, remember? I can't blame you for finding it hard to believe, since it is in direct opposition to everything you've understood to be true in the past. It's like altering a natural law. As if I gave you proof that gravity didn't really exist, that it was a force altogether different from the immutable one we know, one you could get around when you understood how. You'd want more proof than words. Probably want to see someone walking on air."

"Which isn't such a bad idea at that," he added, turning to Naxa. "Do you hear any animals around the ship now? Not the ones you're used to, but the mutated, violent kind that live only to attack the city."

"Place's crawling with 'em," Naxa said, "just lookin' for somethin' t'kill."

"Could you capture one?" Jason asked. "Without getting yourself killed, I mean."

Naxa snorted contempt as he turned to leave. "Beast's not born yet, that'll hurt me."

They stood quietly, each one wrapped tightly around by his own thoughts, while they waited for Naxa to return. Jason had nothing more to say. He would do one more thing to try and convince them of the facts, after that it would be up to each of them to reach a conclusion.

The talker returned quickly with a sting-wing, tied by one leg to a length of leather. It flapped and shrieked as he carried it in.

"In the middle of the room, away from everybody," Jason told him. "Can you get that beast to sit on

something and not flap around?"

"My hand good enough?" he asked, flipping the creature up so it clung to the back of his gauntlet. "That's how I caught it."

"Does anyone doubt that this is a real stingwing?" Jason asked. "I want to make sure you all believe there is no trickery here."

"The thing is real," Brucco said. "I can smell the poison in the wing-claws from here." He pointed to the dark marks on the leather where the liquid had dripped. "If that eats through the gloves, he's a dead man."

"Then we agree it's real," Jason said. "Real and deadly, and the only test of the theory will be if you people from the city can approach it like Naxa here."

They drew back automatically when he said it. Because they knew that stingwing was synonymous with death. Past, present and future. You don't change a natural law. Meta spoke for all of them.

"We ... can't. This man lives in the jungle, like an animal himself. Somehow he's learned to get near them. But you can't expect us to."

Jason spoke quickly, before the talker could react to the insult. "Of course I expect you to. That's the whole idea. If you don't hate the beast and expect it to attack you—why it won't. Think of it as a creature from a different planet, something harmless."

"I can't," she said. "It's a *stingwing!*"

As they talked Brucco stepped forward, his eyes fixed steadily on the creature perched on the glove. Jason signaled the bowmen to hold their fire. Brucco stopped at a safe distance and kept looking steadily at the stingwing. It rustled its leathery wings uneasily and hissed. A drop of poison formed at the tip of each great poison claw on its wings. The control room was filled with a deadly silence.

Slowly he raised his hand. Carefully putting it out, over the animal. The hand dropped a little, rubbed the stingwing's head once, then fell back to his side. The animal did nothing except stir slightly under the touch.

There was a concerted sigh, as those who had been unknowingly holding their breath breathed again.

"How did you do it?" Meta asked in a hushed voice.

"Hm-m-m, what?" Brucco said, apparently snapping out of a daze. "Oh, touching the thing. Simple, really. I just pretended it was one of the training aids I use, a realistic and harmless duplicate. I kept my mind on that single thought and it worked." He looked down at his hand, then back to the stingwing. His voice quieter now, as if he spoke from a distance. "It's not a training aid you know. It's real. Deadly. The off-worlder is right. He's right about everything he said."

With Brucco's success as an example, Kerk came close to the animal. He walked stiffly, as if on the way to his execution, and runnels of sweat poured down his rigid face. But he believed and kept his thoughts directed away from the stingwing and he could touch it unharmed.

Meta tried but couldn't fight down the horror it raised when she came close. "I am trying," she said, "and I do believe you now—but I just can't do it."

Skop screamed when they all looked at him, shouted it was all a trick, and had to be clubbed unconscious when he attacked the bowmen.

Understanding had come to Pyrrus.

28 "WHAT DO WE DO NOW?" Meta asked. Her voice was troubled, questioning. She voiced the thoughts of all the Pyrrans in the room, and the thousands who watched in their screens.

"What will we do?" They turned to Jason, waiting for an answer. For the moment their differences were forgotten. The people from the city were staring expectantly at him, as were the crossbowmen with half-lowered weapons. This stranger had confused and changed the old world they had known, and presented them with a newer and stranger one, with alien problems.

"Hold on," he said, raising his hand. "I'm no doctor of social ills. I'm not going to try and cure this planet full of muscle-bound sharpshooters. I've just squeezed through up to now, and by the law of averages I should be ten times dead."

"Even if all you say is true, Jason," Meta said, "you are still the only person who can help us. What will the future be like?"

Suddenly weary, Jason slumped into the pilot's chair. He glanced around at the circle of people. They seemed sincere. None of them even appeared to have noticed that he no longer had his hand on the pump switch. For the moment at least, the war between city and farm was forgotten.

"I'll give you my conclusions," Jason said, twisting in the chair, trying to find a comfortable position for his aching bones. "I've been doing a lot of thinking the last day or two, searching for the answer. The very first thing I realized, was that the perfect and logical solution wouldn't do at all. I'm afraid the old ideal of the lion lying down with the lamb doesn't work out in practice. About all it does is make a fast lunch for the lion. Ideally, now that you all know the real causes of your trouble, you should tear down the perimeter and have the city and forest people mingle in brotherly love. Makes just as pretty a picture as the one of lion and lamb. And would undoubtedly have the same result. Someone would remember how really filthy the grubbers are, or how stupid junkmen can be, and there would be a fresh corpse cooling. The fight would spread and the victors would be eaten by the wildlife that swarmed over the undefended perimeter. No, the answer isn't that easy."

As the Pyrrans listened to him they realized where they were, and glanced around uneasily. The guards raised their crossbows again, and the prisoners stepped back to the wall and looked surly.

"See what I mean?" Jason asked. "Didn't take long did it?" They all looked a little sheepish at their unthinking reactions.

"If we're going to find a decent plan for the future, we'll have to take inertia into consideration. Mental inertia for one. Just because you know a thing is true in theory, doesn't make it true in fact. The barbaric religions of primitive worlds hold not a germ of scientific fact, though they claim to explain all. Yet if one of these savages has all the logical ground for his beliefs taken away—he doesn't stop believing. He then calls his mistaken beliefs 'faith' because he knows they are right. And he knows they are right because he has faith. This is an unbreakable circle of false logic that can't be touched. In reality, it is plain mental inertia. A case of thinking 'what always was' will also 'always be.' And not wanting to blast the thinking patterns out of the old rut.

"Mental inertia alone is not going to cause trouble—there is cultural inertia, too. Some of you in this room believe my conclusions and would like to change. But will all your people change? The unthinking ones, the habit-ridden, reflex-formed people who *know* what is now, will always be. They'll act like a drag on whatever plans you make, whatever attempts you undertake to progress with the new knowledge you have."

"Then it's useless—there's no hope for our world?" Rhes asked.

"I didn't say that," Jason answered. "I merely mean that your troubles won't end by throwing some kind of mental switch. I see three courses open for the future, and the chances are that all three will be going on at the same time.

"First—and best—will be the rejoining of city and farm Pyrrans into the single human group they came from. Each is incomplete now, and has something the other one needs. In the city here you have science and contact with the rest of the galaxy. You also have a deadly war. Out there in the jungle, your first cousins live at peace with the world, but lack medicine and the other benefits of scientific knowledge, as well as any kind of cultural contact with the rest of mankind. You'll both have to join together and benefit from the exchange. At the same time you'll have to forget the superstitious hatred you have of each other. This will only be done outside of the city, away from the war. Every one of you who is capable should go out voluntarily, bringing some fraction of the knowledge that needs sharing. You won't be harmed if you go in good faith. And you will learn how to live *with* this planet, rather than against it. Eventually you'll have civilized communities that won't be either 'grubber' or 'junkman.' They'll be Pyrran."

"But what about our city here?" Kerk asked.

"It'll stay right here—and probably won't change in the slightest. In the beginning you'll need your perimeter and defenses to stay alive, while the people are leaving. And after that it will keep going because there are going to be any number of people here who you won't convince. They'll stay and fight and eventually die. Perhaps you will be able to do a better job in educating their children. What the eventual end of the city will be, I have no idea."

They were silent as they thought about the future. On the floor Skop groaned but did not move. "Those are two ways," Meta said. "What is the third?"

"The third possibility is my own pet scheme," Jason smiled. "And I hope I can find enough people to go along with me. I'm going to take my money and spend it all on outfitting the best and most modern spacer, with every weapon and piece of scientific equipment I can get my hands on. Then I'm going to ask for Pyrran volunteers to go with me."

"What in the world for?" Meta frowned.

"Not for charity, I expect to make my investment back, and more. You see, after these past few months, I can't possibly return to my old occupation. Not only do I have enough money now to make it a waste of time, but I think it would be an unending bore. One thing about Pyrrus—if you live—is that it spoils you for the quieter places.

So I'd like to take this ship that I mentioned and go into the business of opening up new worlds. There are thousands of planets where men would like to settle, only getting a foothold on them is too rough or rugged for the usual settlers. Can you imagine a planet a Pyrran couldn't lick after the training you've had here? And enjoy doing it?

"There would be more than pleasure involved, though. In the city your lives have been geared for continual deadly warfare. Now you're faced with the choice of a fairly peaceful future, or staying in the city to fight an unnecessary and foolish war. I offer the third alternative of the occupation you know best, that would let you accomplish something constructive at the same time.

"Those are the choices. Whatever you decide is up to each of you personally."

Before anyone could answer, livid pain circled Jason's throat. Skop had regained consciousness and surged up from the floor. He pulled Jason from the chair with a single motion, holding him by the neck, throttling him.

"Kerk! Meta!" Skop shouted hoarsely. "Grab guns! Open the locks—our people'll be here, kill the grubbers and their lies!"

Jason tore at the fingers that were choking the life out of him, but it was like pulling at bent steel bars. He couldn't talk and the blood hammered in his ears.

Meta hurtled forward like an uncoiled spring and the crossbows twanged. One bolt caught her in the leg, the other transfixed her upper arm. But she had been shot as she jumped and her inertia carried her across the room, to her fellow Pyrran and the dying off-worlder.

She raised her good arm and chopped down with the edge of her hand.

It caught Skop a hard blow on the biceps and his arm jumped spasmodically, his hand leaping from Jason's throat.

"What are you doing?" he shouted in strange terror to the wounded girl who fell against him. He pushed her away, still clutching Jason with his other hand. She

didn't answer. Instead she chopped again, hard and true, the edge of her hand catching Skop across the windpipe, crushing it. He dropped Jason and fell to the floor, retching and gasping.

Jason watched the end through a haze, barely conscious.

Skop struggled to his feet, turned pain-filled eyes to his friends.

"You're wrong," Kerk said. "Don't do it."

The sound the wounded man made was more animal than human. When he dived towards the guns on the far side of the room the crossbows twanged like harps of death.

When Brucco went over to help Meta no one interfered. Jason gasped air back into his lungs, breathing in life. The watching glass eye of the viewer carried the scene to everyone in the city.

"Thanks, Meta ... for understanding ... as well as helping." Jason had to force the words out.

"Skop was wrong and you were right, Jason," she said. Her voice broke for a second as Brucco snapped off the feathered end of the steel bolt with his fingers, and pulled the shaft out of her arm. "I can't stay in the city, only people who feel as Skop did will be able to do that. And I'm afraid I can't go into the forest—you saw what luck I had with the stingwing. If it's all right I'd like to come with you. I'd like to very much."

It hurt when he talked, so Jason could only smile, but she knew what he meant.

Kerk looked down in unhappiness at the body of the dead man. "He was wrong—but I know how he felt. I can't leave the city, not yet. Someone will have to keep things in hand while the changes are taking place. Your ship is a good idea, Jason, you'll have no shortage of volunteers. Though I doubt if you'll get Brucco to go with you."

"Of course not," Brucco snapped, not looking up from the compression bandage he was tying. "There's enough to do right here on Pyrrus. The animal life, quite a study to be made, probably have every ecologist in the galaxy visiting here."

Kerk walked slowly to the screen overlooking the city. No one attempted to stop him. He looked out at the buildings, the smoke still curling up from the perimeter, and the limitless sweep of green jungle beyond.

"You've changed it all, Jason," he said. "We can't see it now, but Pyrrus will never be the way it was before you came. For better or worse."

"Better," Jason croaked, and rubbed his aching throat. "Now get together and end this war so people will really believe it."

Rhes turned and after an instant's hesitation, extended his hand to Kerk. The gray-haired Pyrran felt the same repugnance himself about touching a grubber.

They shook hands then, because they were both strong men.

👽 👽 👽

Deathworld *first appeared when the novel was serialized in the January, February, and March 1960 issues of* Astounding Science Fiction.

———

Author Harry Harrison began his professional life as a comic book artist, working with industry legend Wally Wood. In the early 1950's he illustrated science fiction stories for publisher Bill Gaines' famed and frequently-reprinted EC Comics Weird Science *and* Weird Fantasy. *Soon afterward, Harrison traded his T-square for a typewriter, and went on to produce numerous well-received SF tales, including "The Stainless Steel Rat" series, two Death-world sequels, and the ecological novel* Make Room! Make Room!, *the basis for the 1973 movie* Soylent Green, *starring Charlton Heston and Edward G. Robinson.*

It was a dangerous planet—swallowing up men with no apparent menace to fight against. It was up to Allison and his computer to discover ...

THE INVISIBLE ENEMY

by JERRY SOHL

FOR AN HOUR they had been circling the spot at 25,000 feet while technicians weighed and measured the planet and electronic fingers probed where no eye could see.

And for an hour Harley Allison had sat in the computer room accepting the information and recording it on magnetic tapes and readying them for insertion into the machine, knowing already what the answer would be and

resenting what the commander was trying to do.

It was quiet in the ship except for the occasional twitter of a speaker that recited bits of information which Allison dutifully recorded. It was a relief from the past few days of alarm bells and alerts and flashing lights and the drone of the commander's voice over the intercom, even as that had been a relief from the lethargy and mindlessness that comes with covering enormous stellar distances, for it was wonderful to see faces awaken to interest in things when the star drive went off and to become aware of a changing direction and the lessening velocity. Then had eyes turned from books and letters and other faces to the growing pinpoints of the Hyades on the scanners.

Then had Allison punched the key that had released the ship from computer control and gave it to manual, and in the ensuing lull the men of the *Nesbitt* were read the official orders by Commander William Warrick. Then they sat down to controls unmanned for so long, to seek out the star among the hundreds in the system, then its fourth planet and, a few hours ago, the small space ship that lay on its side on the desert surface of the planet.

THERE WAS LAUGHTER and the scrape of feet in the hall, and Allison looked up to see Wendell Hallom enter the computer room, followed by several others.

"Well, looks like the rumors were right," Hallom said, eyes squinting up at the live screen above the control panel. The slowly rotating picture showed the half-buried space ship and the four pillars of the force field about it tilted at ridiculous angles. "I suppose you knew all about this, Allison."

"I didn't know any more than you, except we were headed for the Hyades," Allison said. "I just work here, too, you know."

"I wish I was home," Tony Lazzari said, rolling his eyes. "I don't like the looks of that yellow sand. I don't know why I ever joined this man's army."

"It was either join or go to jail," Gordon Bacon said.

"I ought to punch you right in the nose." Lazzari moved toward Bacon who thumbed his nose at him. "In fact, I got a good mind to turn it inside out."

Allison put a big hand on his shoulder, pulled him back. "Not in here you don't. I got enough troubles. That's all I'd need."

"Yeah," Hallom said. "Relax, kid. Save your strength. You're going to need it. See that pretty ship up there with nobody on it?"

"You and the commander," Bacon said. "Why's he got it in for you, Allison?"

"I wouldn't know," Allison said smiling thinly. "I've got a wonderful personality, don't you think?"

Hallom grunted. "Allison's in the Computer Corps, ain't he? The commander thinks that's just like being a passenger along for the ride. And he don't like it."

"That's what happens when you get an old line skipper and try to help him out with a guy with a gadget," Bacon observed.

"It wouldn't be so bad," Homer Petry said at the door, "if it had been tried before."

"Mr. Allison," a speaker blared.

"All right, you guys," Allison said. "Clear out." He depressed a toggle. "Yes, Lieutenant?"

"You have everything now, Allison. Might as well run it through."

"The commander can't think of anything else?"

There was a cough. "The commander's standing right here. Shall I ask him?"

"I'll run this right through, Lieutenant."

COMMANDER WILLIAM WARRICK was a fine figure of a man: tall, militant, greying, hatchet-nosed. He was a man who hewed so close to the line that he let little humanity get between, a man who would be perpetually young, for even at fifty there was an absence of paunch, though his eyes held a look of a man who had many things to remember.

He stood for a while at one end of the control room without saying anything, his never-absent map pointer in his right hand, the end of it slapping the open palm of his left hand. His cold eyes surveyed the men who stood crowded shoulder-to-shoulder facing him.

"Men," he said, and his deep voice was resonant in the room, "take a good look at the screen up there." And the eyes of nearly fifty men shifted to the giant screen beside and above him.

"That's the *Esther*." The ship was on gyro, circling the spot, and the screen showed a rotation ship on the sand.

"We'll be going down soon and we'll get a better look. But I want you to look at her now because you might be looking at the *Nesbitt* if you're not careful."

The commander turned to look at the ship himself before going on.

"The *Esther* is a smaller ship. It had a complement of only eight men. Remember the tense there. *Had.* They disappeared just as the men in the two ships before them did, each carrying eight men—the *Mordite* and the *Halcyon*. All three ships were sent to look for Traveen Abbott and Lew Gesell, two explorers for the Federation who had to their credit successful landings on more than ninety worlds. They were cautious, experienced and wise. Yet this planet swallowed them up as it did the men of the three ships that followed."

Commander Warrick paused and looked at them severely. "We're fifty men and I think we have a better chance than an eight-man crew, not just because there are more of us but because we have the advantage of knowing we're against something really deadly. In case you haven't deduced our mission, it is simply to find out what it is and destroy it."

The insignia on the commander's collar and sleeve glittered in the light from the ever-changing screen as the ship circled the site of the *Esther*.

"This is a war ship. We are armed with the latest weapons. And—" his eyes caught Allison's "—we even have a man from the Computer Corps with us, if that can be counted as an advantage."

Allison who stood at the rear of the room behind the assembled soldier-technicians, reddened. "The tapes got us here. Commander."

"We could have made it without them," the commander said without ire. "But we're here with or without tape. But just because we are we're not rushing down there. We know the atmosphere is breathable, the gravity is close to Earth's and there are no unusually dangerous bacteria. All this came from the *Esther* prior to the ... incident, whatever it was. But we checked again just to make sure. The gravity is nine-tenths that of Earth's, there is a day of twenty-four and a half hours, temperature and humidity tropical at this parallel, the atmosphere slightly less rich in oxygen, though not harmfully so—God only knows how a desert planet like this can have any oxygen at all with so little vegetation and no evident animal life. There is no dangerous radiation from the surface or from the sun. Mr. Allison has run the assembled data through his machine—would

you care to tell the men what the machine had to say, Allison?"

Allison cleared his throat and wondered what the commander was driving at. "The planet could sustain life, if that's what you mean, Commander."

"But what did the machine say about the inhabitants, Mr. Allison?"

"There wasn't enough data for an assumption."

"Thank you. You men can get some idea of how the Computer Corps helps out in situations like this."

"That's hardly fair. Commander," Allison protested. "With more data—"

"We'll try to furnish you with armfuls of data." The commander smiled broadly. "Perhaps we might let you collect a little data yourself."

There was laughter at this. "So much for the Computer Corps. We could go down now, but we're circling for eighteen more hours for observation. Then we're going down. Slowly."

THE SHIP CAME OUT OF THE DEEP BLUE SKY in the early morning, and the commander was a man of his word. The *Nesbitt* moved down slowly, beginning at sunup and ending in the sand within a few hundred feet of the *Esther* in an hour.

"You'd think," Lazzari said as the men filed back into the control room for another briefing, "that the commander has an idea he can talk this thing to death."

"I'd rather be talked to death by the commander than by you," Hallom said. "He has a pleasanter voice."

"I just don't like it, all that sand down there and nothing else."

"We passed over a few green places," Allison corrected. "A few rocky places, too. It's not all sand."

"But why do we have to go down in the middle of it?" Lazzari insisted. "That's where the other ships went down. Whatever it is attacked them on the sand."

"If it was up to me, I'd say *let the thing be*, whatever it is. Live and let live. That's my motto."

"You're just lazy," said Petry, the thin-faced oldster from Chicago. "If we was pickin' apples you'd be askin' why. If you had your way you'd spend the rest of your life in a bunk."

"Lazy, hell!" Lazzari snorted. "I just don't think we should go poking our nose in where somebody's going to bite it off."

"That's not all they'll bite off, Buster," said Gar Caldwell, a radar and sonics man from Tennessee.

Wang Lee, force field expert, raised his thin oriental eyebrows and said, "It is obvious we know more than our commander. We know, for example, *it* bites. It follows then that it has teeth. We ought to report that to the commander."

The commander strode into the room, map pointer under his arm, bearing erect, shoulders back, head high. Someone called attention and every man stiffened but Allison, who leaned against the door. Commander Warrick surveyed them coldly for a moment before putting them at ease.

"We're dividing into five teams," he said. "Four in the field and the command team here. The rosters will be read shortly and duplicate equipment issued. The lieutenants know the plans and they'll explain them to you. Each unit will have a g-car, force field screen, television and radio for constant communication with the command team. There will be a blaster for each man, nuclear bombardment equipment for the weapons man, and so on."

He put his hands on his hips and eyed them all severely. "It's going to be no picnic. It's hot as hell out there. A hundred degrees in the daytime and no shade. It's eighty at night and the humidity's high. But I want you to find out what it is before it finds out what *you* are. I don't want any missing men. The Federation's lost three small ships and twenty-four men already. And Mr. Allison—"

Allison jerked from the wall at the unexpected calling of his name.

"Yes, Commander?"

"You understand this is an emergency situation?"

"Well, yes. Commander."

The commander smiled slyly and Allison could read something other than humor behind his eyes.

"Then you must be aware that, under Federation regulations governing ships in space, the commander exercises unusual privileges regarding his crew and civilians who may be aboard."

"I haven't read the regulation, Commander, but I'll take your word for it that it exists."

"Thank you, Mr. Allison." The lip curled ever so slightly. "I'd be glad to read it to you in my quarters immediately after this meeting, except there isn't time. For your information, in an emergency situation, though you are merely attached to the ship in an advisory capacity, you come under the jurisdiction of the ship's commander. Since we're short of men. I'm afraid I'll have to make use of you."

Allison balled two big, brown hands and put them behind his back. They had told him at Computer Corps School he might meet men like Commander Warrick—men who did not yet trust the maze of computer equipment that only a few months ago had been made mandatory on all ships of the *Nesbitt* class. It was natural that men who had fought through campaigns with the old logistics and slide-rule tactics were not going to feel immediately at home with computers and the men that went with them. It wasn't easy trusting the courses of their ships or questions of attack and defense to magnetized tape.

"I understand. Commander," Allison said. "I'll be glad to help out in whatever way you think best."

"Good of you, I'm sure." The Commander turned to one of the lieutenants near him. "Lieutenant Cheevers, break out a blaster for Mr. Allison, He may need it."

WHEN THE GREAT PORT WAS OPENED, the roasting air that rushed in blasted the faces of the men loading the treadwagons. Allison, the unaccustomed weight of the blaster making him conscious of it, went with several of them down the ramp to look out at the yellow sand.

Viewing it from the surface was different from looking at it through a scanner from above. He squinted his eyes as he followed the expanse to the horizon and found there were tiny carpets of vegetation here and there, a few larger grass islands, a wooded area on a rise far away on the right, mountains in the distance on the left. And above it all was a deep blue sky with a blazing white sun. The air had a burned smell.

A tall lieutenant—Cork Rogers who would lead the first contingent—moved down the ramp into the broiling sun and gingerly stepped into the sand. He sank into it up to his ankles. He came back up, shaking his head. "Even the sand's hot."

Allison bent down, the sun feeling like a hot iron on his back, bent over and picked up a handful of sand. It was yellower than Earth sand and he was surprised to find it had very little weight. It was more like sawdust, yet it was granular. He looked at several tiny grains closely, saw that they were hollow. They were easily crushed.

"Why was I born?" Lazzari asked no one in particular, his arms loaded with electrical equipment for the wagon. "And since I was, how come I ever got in this lousy outfit?"

"Better save your breath," Allison said, coming up the ramp and wiping his hands on his trousers.

"Yeah, I know. I'm going to need it." He stuck his nose up and sniffed. "They call that air!"

In a few minutes, the first treadwagon loaded with its equipment and men purred down the ramp on its tracks and into the sand. It waited there, its eye-tube already revolving slowly high on its mast above the weapons bridge. The soldier on the bridge was at ready, his tinted visor pulled down. He was actually in the small g-car which could be catapulted at an instant's notice.

Not much later there were four treadwagons in the sand and the commander came down the ramp, a faint breeze tugging at his sleeves and collar.

He took the salute of each of the officers in turn—Lieutenant Cork Rogers of Unit North, Lieutenant Vicky Noromak of Unit East, Lieutenant Glen Foster of Unit West and Lieutenant Carl Quartz of Unit South. They raised the green and gold of the Federation flag as he and the command team stood at attention behind him.

Then the commander's hand whipped down and immediately the purrs of the wagons became almost deafening as they veered from one another and started off through the sand, moving gracefully over the rises, churning powder wakes and leaving dusty clouds.

IT WAS QUIET AND COOL in the control room. Commander Warrick watched the four television panels as they showed the terrain in panorama from out-positions a mile in each direction from the ship. On all of them there were these same things: the endless, drifting yellow sand with its frequent carpets of grass, the space ship a mile away, the distant mountain, the green area to the right.

Bacon sat at the controls for the panels, Petry at his side. Once every fifteen seconds a radio message was received from one of the treadwagon units: "Unit West reporting nothing at 12:18:15." The reports droned out over the speaker system with monotonous regularity. Petry checked off the quarter minutes and the units reporting.

Because he had nothing better to do, Allison had been sitting in the control room for four hours and all he had seen were the television panels and all he had heard were the reports—except when Lieutenant Cheevers and three other men returned from an inspection of the *Esther.*

"Pile not taken, eh?" The commander pursed his lips and ran a forefinger along his jaw. "Anything above median level would have taken the pile. I can't see it being ignored."

The lieutenant shook his head. "The *Esther* was relatively new. That would have made her pile pretty valuable."

"I can't figure out why the eight men on the *Esther* couldn't handle the situation. They had the *Mordite* and the *Halcyon* as object lessons. They must have been taken by surprise. No sign of a struggle, eh, Cheevers?"

"None, sir. We went over everything from stem to stern. Force field was still working, though it had fallen out of line. We turned it off."

"No blood stains? No hair? No bones?"

"No, sir."

"That's odd, don't you think? Where could they have gone?" The commander sighed. "I expect we'll know soon enough. As it is, unless something is done, the *Esther* will sink farther into this sand until she's sunk out of sight with the other two ships." He frowned. "Lieutenant, how would you like to assume command of the *Esther* on our return? It must still be in working order if the pile is there. I'll give you a crew."

"We're not through here yet, sir." Cheevers grinned. "But I'd like it."

"Look good on your service records, eh, Corvin?" The commander then saw Allison sitting at the rear of the room watching the panels. "What do you make of all this, Allison?"

"I hardly know what to think, Commander."

"Why don't you run a tape on it?"

"I wish I could, but with what little we know so far it wouldn't do any good."

"Come, now, Allison, surely a good man like you—you're a computer man, remember?—surely you could do something. I've heard of the wonders of those little machines. I'll bet you could run that through the machine and it will tell us exactly what we want to know."

"There's not enough data. I'd just get an ID—Insufficient Data—response as I did before."

"It's too bad, Allison, that the computer people haven't considered that angle of it—that someone has to get the data to feed the machine, that the Federation must still rely on guts and horse sense and the average soldier-technician. I'll begin thinking computers are a good thing when they can go out and get their own data."

THAT HAD BEEN TWO HOURS AGO. Two hours for Allison to cool off in. Two hours to convince himself it had been best not to answer the commander. And now they all sat, stony-faced and quiet, watching the never-ending sweep of the eye-tubes that never showed anything different except the changing shadows as the planet's only sun moved across the sky. Yellow sand and carpets of green, the ship, the mountain, the wooded area....

It was the same on the next four-hour watch. The eye-tubes turned and the watchers in the ship watched and saw nothing new, and radio reports droned on every fifteen seconds until the men in the room were scarcely conscious of them.

And the sun went down.

Two moons, smaller than Earth's single moon, rode high in the sky, but they didn't help as much, infrared beams from the treadwagons rendered the panel pictures as plain as day. And there was nothing new.

The commander ordered the units moved a mile farther away the second day. When the action was completed, the waiting started all over again.

It would not be fair to say *nothing* was new. There was one thing—tension. Nerves that had been held ready for action began demanding it. And with the ache of taut nerves came impatience and an over-exercising of the imagination. The quiet, heat, humidity and monotony of nothing the second day and night erupted in a blast from Unit East early on the morning of the third day. The nuclear weapons man in the g-car had fired at something he saw moving out on the sand.

At the site Technician Gar Caldwell reported by radio while Lieutenant Noromak and another man went through the temporarily damped force field to investigate. There was nothing at the target but some badly burned and fused sand.

Things went back to normal again.

Time dragged through the third day and night, and the hot breezes and high humidity and the waiting grated already raw nerves.

On the morning of the fourth day Homer Petry, who had been checking off the radio reports as they came in, suddenly announced: "No radio report from Unit West at 8:14:45!"

Instantly all eyes went to the Unit West panel. The screen showed a revolving panorama of shimmering yellow sand and blue sky.

Lieutenant Cheevers opened the switch. "Unit West! Calling Unit West!"

No answer.

"What the hell's the matter with you. Unit West!"

The commander yelled, "Never mind. Lieutenant! Get two men and shoot over there. I'll alert the other units."

Lieutenant Cheevers picked up Allison, who happened to be in the control room at the time, and Hallom, and in a matter of moments the port dropped open and with the lieutenant at the controls and the two men digging their feet in the side stirrups and their hands clasping the rings for this purpose on either side, the small g-car soared out into the sweltering air and screamed toward Unit West.

The terrain rushed by below them as the car picked up still more speed and Allison, not daring to move his head too far from the protective streamlining lest it get caught in the hot airstream, saw the grass-dotted, sunbaked sand blur by.

Then the speed slackened and, raising his head, he saw the treadwagon and the four force-field pillars they were approaching.

But he saw no men.

The lieutenant put the car in a tight turn and landed it near the wagon. The three grabbed their weapons, jumped from the car and ran with difficulty through the sand to the site.

The force field blocked them.

"What the hell!" Cheevers kicked at the inflexible, impenetrable shield and swore some more.

The treadwagon was there in the middle of the square formed by the force field posts, and there was no one in it. The eye-tube was still rotating slowly and noiselessly, weapons on the bridge beneath still pointed menacingly at the empty desert, the g-car was still in its place, and the Federation flag fluttered in the slight breeze.

But there was nothing living inside the square. The sand was oddly smooth in many places where there should have been footprints and Allison wondered if the slight breeze had already started its work of moving the sand to obliterate them.

There were no bodies, no blood, no signs of a struggle.

Since they couldn't get through the barrier, they went back to the g-car and went over it, landing inside the invisible enclosure, still alert for any emergency.

But nothing attacked because there was nothing there. Only the sand, the empty treadwagons, the weapons, the stores.

"Poor Quartz," Cheevers said.

"What, sir?" Hallom asked.

"Lieutenant Quartz. I knew him better than any of the others."

He picked up a handful of sand and threw it angrily at the wagon's treads.

Allison saw it hit, watched it fall, then noticed the tread prints were obliterated inside the big square. But as he looked out across the waste to the ship he noticed the tread prints there were quite clear.

He shivered in the hot sun.

The lieutenant reported by the wagon's radio, and after they had collected and packed all the gear, Allison and Hallom drove the treadwagons back to the ship.

"I TELL YOU IT'S IMPOSSIBLE!" The commander's eyes were red-rimmed and bloodshot and he ran sweating hands through wisps of uncombed grey hair. "There must have been *something!*"

"But there wasn't, sir," Cheevers said with anguish. "And nothing was overlooked, believe me."

"But how can that be?" The commander raised his arms angrily, let them fall. "And how will it look in the record? Ten men gone. Just like that." He snapped his fingers. "The Federation won't like it—especially since it is exactly what happened to the others. If only there had been a fight! If there were a chance for reprisal! But this—" he waved an arm to include the whole planet. "It's maddening!"

It was night before the commander could contain himself enough to talk rationally about what had happened and to think creatively of possible action.

"I'm not blaming you, Lieutenant Cheevers, or anybody," he said slouched in his desk chair and idly eying the three remaining television screens that revealed an endless, turning desert scene. "I have only myself to blame for what happened." He grunted. "I only wish I knew what happened." He turned to Cheevers, Allison and Hallom, who sat on the other side of the desk. "I've done nothing but think about this thing all day. I don't know what to tell those fellows out there, how they can protect themselves from this. I've examined the facts from every angle, but I always end up where I started." He stared at Cheevers. "Let's hear your idea again, Cheevers."

"It's like I say, sir. The attack could have come from the air."

"Carried away like eagles, eh? You've still got that idea?"

"The sand was smooth, Commander. That would support the idea of wings of birds setting the air in motion so the sand would cover up the footprints."

The commander bit his lower lip, drummed on the desk with his fingers and stared hard at Cheevers. "It *is* possible. Barely possible. But it still doesn't explain why we see no birds, why we saw no birds

on the other viewers during the incident, why the other teams saw no birds in flight. We've asked. Remember? Nobody has seen a living thing. Where then are we going to get enough birds to carry off ten men? And how does this happen with no bloodshed? Surely *one* of our men could have got off one shot, could have wounded one bird."

"The birds could have been invisible, sir," Hallom said hesitantly.

"Invisible birds!" The commander glared. Then he shrugged. "Hell, I suppose anything is possible."

"That's what Allison's machine says."

"I ran the stuff through the computer," Allison said.

"I forgot there was such a thing ... So that's what came out, eh?"

"Not exactly. Commander." Allison withdrew a roll of facsimile tape. "I sent through what we had. There are quite a few possibilities." He unrolled a little of it. "The men could still exist at the site, though rendered invisible—"

"Nuts!" the commander said. "How the hell—!"

"The data," Allison went on calmly, "was pretty weird itself and the machine lists only the possibilities, taking into consideration everything no matter how absurd. Other possibilities are that we are victims of hypnosis and that we are to see only what *they*—whoever *they* are—want us to see; that the men were surprised and spirited away by something invisible, which would mean none of the other units would have seen or reported it; or that the men themselves would not have seen the—let's say 'invisible birds'; that the men sank into the sand somehow by some change in the composition of the ground itself, or were taken there by something, that there was a change in time or space—"

"That's enough," the commander snapped. He rose, eyes blazing. "I can see we're going to get nothing worthwhile from the Computer Corps. 'Change in Time' hell! I want a straight answer, not a bunch of fancies or something straight from a fairy tale. The only thing you've said so far I'd put any stock in is the idea of the birds.

And the lieutenant had that idea first. But as far as their being invisible is concerned, I hardly think that's likely."

"But if it had been just birds," Allison said, putting away the roll of tape, "there would have been resistance, and blood would have been spilled somewhere."

Commander Warrick snorted. "If there'd been a fight we'd have seen some evidence of it. It was too quick for a fight, that's all. And I'm warning the other units of birds and of attack without warning."

As a result, the three remaining units altered the mechanism of their eye-tubes to include a sweep of the sky after each 360-degree pan of the horizon.

THE FOURTH NIGHT PASSED and the blazing sun burst forth the morning of the fifth day with the situation unchanged except that anxiety and tension were more in evidence among the men than ever before. The commander ordered sedatives for all men coming off watches so they could sleep.

The fifth night passed without incident.

It was nearly noon on the sixth day when Wang Lee, who was with Lieutenant Glenn Foster's Unit West, reported that one of the men had gone out of his head. The commander said he'd send over a couple men to get him in a g-car. But before Petry and Hollam left, Lee was on the radio again.

"It's Prince, the man I told you about," he said. "Maybe you can see him in the screen. He's got his blaster out and insists we turn off the force field."

The television screen showed the sky in a long sweep past the sun, down to the sand and around, sweeping past the figure of a man, obviously Prince, as it panned the horizon.

"Lieutenant Foster's got a blaster on him," Lee went on.

"Damn it!" Sweat popped out on the commander's forehead as he looked at the screen. "Not enough trouble without that." He turned to Cheevers. "Tell Foster to blast him before he endangers the whole outfit."

But the words were not swift enough. The screen went black and the speaker emitted a harsh click.

IT WAS LATE AFTERNOON when the treadwagon from Unit West purred to a stop beside the wagon from Unit South and Petry and Bacon stepped out of it.

"There she is," Cheevers told the commander, at his side on the ramp. "Prince blasted her but didn't put her out of commission. Only the radio—you can see the mast has been snapped off. No telling how many men he got in that blast before...."

"And now they're all gone. Twenty men." The commander stared dumbly at the wagon and his shoulders slouched a little now. He looked from the wagon to the horizon and followed it along toward the sun, shading his squinting red eyes. "What is it out there, Cheevers? What are we up against?"

"I wish I knew, sir."

They walked down the ramp to the sand and waded through it out to the treadwagon. They examined it from all sides.

"Not a goddam bloodstain anywhere," the commander said, wiping his neck with his handkerchief. "If Prince really blasted the men there ought to be stains and hair and remains and stench and—well, something."

"Did Rogers or Noromak report anything while I was gone?"

"Nothing. Not a damned thing ... Scene look the same as before?"

"Just like before. Smooth sand inside the force field and no traces, though we did find Prince's blaster. At least I think it's his. Found it half-buried in the sand where he was supposed to be standing. We can check his serial number on it."

"Twenty men!" the commander breathed. He stared at the smooth sweep of sand again. "Twenty men swallowed up by nothing again." He looked up at the cloudless sky. "No birds, no life, no nothing. Yet something big enough to...." He shook his fist at the nothingness. "Why don't you show yourself, whoever you are—whatever you are? Why do you sneak and steal men?"

"Easy, Commander," Cheevers said, alarmed at the commander's red face, wide eyes and rising voice.

The commander relaxed, turned to the lieutenant with a wry face. "You'll have a command someday, Corvin. Then you'll know how it is."

"I think I know, sir," be said quietly.

"You only think you know. Come on, let's go in and get a drink. I need one. I've got to send in another report."

IF IT HAD BEEN UP TO ALLISON, he would have called in the two remaining units—Unit East, Lieutenant Noromak's outfit, and Unit North, Lieutenant Rogers' group—because in the face of what had twice proved so undetectable and unpredictable, there was no sense in throwing good men after those who had already gone. He could not bear to think of how the men felt who manned the remaining outposts. Sitting ducks.

But it was not up to him. He could only run the computer and advise. And even his advice need not be heeded by the commanding officer, whose will and determination to discover the planet's threat had become something more to pity than admire because he was willing to sacrifice the remaining two units rather than withdraw and consider some other method of attack.

Allison saw a man who no longer looked like a soldier, a man in soiled uniform, unshaven, an irritable man who had spurned eating and sleeping and had come to taking his nourishment from the bottle, a man who now barked his orders in a raucous voice, a man who could stand no sudden noises and, above all, could not tolerate any questions of his decisions. And so he became a lonely man because no one wanted to be near him, and he was left alone to stare with fascination at the two remaining TV panels and listen to the half-minute reports ... and take a drink once in a while.

Allison was no different from the others. He did not want to face the commander. But he did not want to join the muttering soldiers in crew quarters either. So he kept to the computer room and, for something to do, spliced the tapes he had made from flight technician's information for their homeward flight. It took him more than three hours and when he was finished he put the reels in the flight compartment and, for what he thought surely must have been the hundredth time, took out the tapes he had already made on conditions and factors involved in the current emergency. He rearranged them and fed them into the machine again, then tapped out on the keys a request for a single factor that might emerge and prove helpful.

He watched the last of the tape whip into the machine, heard the gentle hum, the click of relays and watched the current indicators in the three different stages of the machine, knew that, inside, memory circuits were giving information, exchanging data, that other devices were examining results, probing for other related information, extracting useful bits, adding this to the stream, to be rejected or passed, depending upon whether it fitted the conditions.

At last the delivery section was energized, the soft ding of the response bell and the lighted green bar preceded a moment when the answer facsimile tape whirred out; and even as he looked at it he knew, by its length, that it was as evasive and generalized as the information he had asked it to examine.

He had left the door to the computer room open and through it suddenly came the sound of hoarse voices. He jumped to his feet and ran out and down the hall to the control room.

The two television panels showed nothing new, but there was an excited radio voice that he recognized as Lieutenant Rogers'.

"He's violent, Commander, and there's nothing we can do," the lieutenant was saying. "He keeps running and trying to break through the force field—oh, my God!"

"What is it?" the commander cried, getting to his feet.

"He's got his blaster out and he's saying something."

The commander rushed to the microphone and tore it from Cheevers's hands. "Don't force him to shoot and don't you shoot. Lieutenant. Remember what happened to Unit West."

"But he's coming up to the wagon now—"

"Don't lose your head, Rogers! Try to knock him out—*but don't use your blaster!*"

"He's entering the wagon now, Commander."

There was a moment's silence.

"He's getting into the g-car, Commander! We can't let him do that!"

"Knock him out!"

"I think we've got him—they're tangling—several men—he's knocked one away—he's got the damned thing going!"

There was a sound of clinking metal, a rasp and scrape and the obvious roar of the little g-car.

"He got away in it! Maybe you can pick it up on the screen...."

The TV screen moved slowly across the sky and swept by a g-car that loomed large on it.

"Let him go," the commander said. "We'll send you another. Anybody get hurt?"

"Yes, sir. One of the men got a bad cut. They're still working on him on the sand. Got knocked off the wagon and fell into the sand. I saw his head was pretty bloody a moment ago before the men gathered around him and ... *my God! No! No!*"

"What!"

"*They're coming out of the ground—*"

"*What?*"

There were audible hisses and clanks and screams and ... and suddenly it was quiet.

"Lieutenant! Lieutenant Rogers!" The commander's face was white. "Answer me, Lieutenant, do you hear? Answer me! You—you can't do this to me!"

But the radio was quiet.

But above, the television screen showed a panorama of endless desert illuminated by infrared and as it swept by one spot Allison caught sight of the horrified face of Tony Lazzari as the g-car soared by.

ALLISON PUSHED THE SHOVEL deep into the sand, lifted as much of it as he could get in it, deposited it on the conveyor. There were ten of them digging in the soft yellow sand in the early morning sun, sweat rolling off their backs and chins—not because the sand was heavy or that the work was hard but because the day was already unbearably hot—digging a hole that couldn't be dug. The sand kept slipping into the very place they were digging. They had only made a shallow depression two or three feet deep at the most and more than twenty feet wide.

They had found nothing.

Commander Warrick, who stood in the g-car atop Unit North's treadwagon, with Lieutenant Noromak and Lieutenant Cheevers at his side, had first ordered Unit East to return to the ship, which Allison considered the smartest thing he had done in the past five days. Then a group of ten, mostly men who had not been in the field, were dispatched in Unit South's old wagon, with the officers in the g-car accompanying them, to Unit North.

There was no sign of a struggle, just the smooth sand around the wagon, the force field still intact and functioning.

Then the ten men had started digging....

"All right," the commander called from the wagon. "Everybody out. We'll blast."

They got out of the hole and on the other side of the wagon while the commander ordered Cheevers to aim at the depression.

The shot was deafening, but when the clouds of sand had settled, the depression was still there with a coating of fused sand covering it.

Later, when the group returned to the ship, three g-car parties were sent out to look for Lazzari. They found him unconscious in the sun in his g-car in the sand. They brought him back to the ship where he was revived.

"What did you see?" the commander asked when Lazzari regained consciousness.

Lazzari just stared.

Allison had seen men like this before. "Commander," he said, "this man's in a catatonic state. He'd better be watched because he can have periods of violence."

The commander glared. "You go punch your goddamn computer, Mr. Allison. I'll handle Lazzari."

And as the commander questioned the man, Lazzari suddenly started to cry, then jerked and, wild-eyed, leaped for the commander.

They put Lazzari in a small room.

Allison could have told the commander that was a mistake, too, but he didn't dare.

And, as the commander was planning his next moves against the planet's peril, Lazzari dashed his head against a bulkhead, fractured his skull, and died.

THE FUNERAL FOR LAZZARI, the commander said, was to be a military one—as military as was possible on a planet revolving around a remote star in the far Hyades. Since rites were not possible for the twenty-nine others of the *Nesbitt* who had vanished, the commander said Lazzari's would make up for the rest.

Then for the first time in a week men had something else to think about besides the nature of things on the planet of the yellow sand that had done away with two explorers, the crews of three ships and twenty-nine Federation soldier-technicians who had come to do battle.

New uniforms were issued, each man showered and shaved. Lieutenant Cheevers read up on the burial service, Gordon Bacon practiced *Taps* on his bugle, Homer Petry gathered some desert flowers in a g-car, and Wendell Hallom washed and prepared Lazzari for the final rites which were to be held within a few hundred feet of the ship.

Though Allison complied with the directives, he felt uneasy about a funeral on the sand. He spent the hour before the afternoon services in the computer room, running tapes through the machine again, seeking the factor responsible for what had occurred.

He reasoned that persons on the sand were safe as long as the onslaught of the *things* out of the ground was not triggered by some action of men in the parties.

He did not know what the Unit South provocation had been—the radio signals had just stopped. He did know the assault on Unit West occurred after Prince's blast at the men on the treadwagon (though the blast in the sand at Unit North had brought nothing to the surface—if one were to believe Lieutenant Roger's final words about *things* coming out of the ground).

And the attack at Unit North was fomented by Lazzari's taking off in the g-car and throwing those battling him to the sand.

Allison went so far as to cut new tapes for each incident, adding every possible detail he could think of. Then he inserted these into the machine and tapped out a question of the advisability of men further exposing themselves by holding a burial service for Lazzari in the sand.

In a few moments the response *whirred* out.

He caught his breath because the message was so short. Printed on the facsimile tape were these words:

Not advised.

Heartened by the brevity of the message and the absence of all the *ifs*, *ands*, and *buts* of previous responses, he tapped out another question: Was there danger to life?

Agonizing minutes. Then:

Yes.

Whose life?

All.

Do you know the factor responsible for the deaths?

Yes.

He cursed himself for not realizing the machine knew the factor and wished he had asked for it instead. With his heart tripping like a jackhammer, Allison tapped out: What is the triggering factor?

When the answer came he found it ridiculously simple and wondered why no one had thought of it before. He stood staring at the tape for a long time knowing there could now be no funeral for Tony Lazzari.

He left the computer room, found the commander talking to Lieutenant Cheevers in the control room. Commander Warrick seemed something of his old self, attired in a natty tropical, clean shaven and with a military bearing and a freshness about him that had been missing for days.

"Commander," Allison said. "I don't mean to interrupt, but—we can't have the funeral."

The commander turned to him with a look full of suspicion. Then he said, "Allison, this is the one and only trip you will ever make with me. When we get back it will be either you or me who gets off this ship for the last time. If you want to run a ship you have to go to another school besides the one for Computer Corps men."

"I've known how you feel, Commander," Allison said, "and—"

"The General Staff ought to know that you can't mix army and civilian. I shall make it a point to register my feelings on the matter when we return."

"You can tell them what you wish, Commander, but it so happens that I've found out the factor responsible for all the attacks."

"And it so happens," the commander said icily, "that the lieutenant and I are reviewing the burial rites. A strict military burial has certain formalities which cannot be overlooked, though I don't expect you to understand that. There is too little time to go into any of, your fancy theories now."

"This is no theory, Commander. It's a certainty."

"Did your computer have anything to do with it?"

"It had everything to do with it. I'd been feeding the tapes for days—"

"While we're on the subject, Allison, we're not using computer tapes for our home journey. We're going the whole way manually. I'm awaiting orders now to move off this God-forsaken world, in case you want to know. I'm recommending it as out-of-bounds for all ships of the Federation. And I'm also recommending that computer units be removed from the *Nesbitt* and from all other ships."

"You'll never leave this planet if you have the funeral," Allison said heatedly. "It will be death for all of us."

"Is that so?" The commander smiled thinly. "Courtesy of your computer, no doubt. Or is it that you're afraid to go out on the sand again?"

"I'm not afraid of the sand, Commander. I'll go out any time. But it's the others I'm thinking of. I won't go out to see Lazzari buried because of the blood on his head and neither should anyone else. You see, the missing factor—the thing that caused all the attacks—is blood."

"Blood?" The commander laughed, looked at Cheevers, who was not laughing, then back at Allison. "Sure you feel all right?"

"The blood on Lazzari, Commander. It will trigger another attack."

"What about the blood that's in us, Allison? That should have prevented us from stepping out to the sand without being attacked in the first place. Your reasoning—or rather your computer's reasoning—is ridiculous."

"It's *fresh* blood. Blood spilled on the sand."

"It seems to me you've got blood on the brain. Lazzari was a friend of yours, wasn't he, Allison?"

"That has nothing to do with it."

The commander looked at him hard and long, then turned to the lieutenant. "Cheevers, Allison doesn't feel very well. I think he'd better be locked up in the computer room until after the funeral."

Allison was stunned. "Commander—!"

"Will you please take him away at once,

Lieutenant? I've heard all I want from him."

Sick at heart, Allison watched the commander walk out of the control room.

"You coming along, Allison?" Cheevers asked.

Allison looked at the lieutenant. "Do you know what will happen if you go out there?" But there was no sympathy or understanding in the eyes of the officer. He turned and walked down the hall to the computer room and went in.

"It doesn't make any difference what I think," Cheevers said, his hand on the knob of the door, his face not unkind. "You're not in the service. I *am*. I have to do what the commander says. Someday I may have a command of my own. Then I'll have a right to my own opinion."

"You'll never have a command of your own ... after today."

"Think so?" It seemed to Allison that the lieutenant sighed a little. "Goodbye, Allison."

It was an odd way to put it. Allison saw the door close and click shut. Then he heard the lieutenant walk away. It was quiet.

ANGUISH IN EVERY FIBER, Allison clicked on the small screen above the computer, turned a knurled knob until he saw the area of the intended burial. He hated to look at what he was going to see. The eye of the wide, shallow grave stared at him from the viewplate.

In a few minutes he saw Bacon, carrying a Federation flag, move slowly into view, followed by six men with blasters at raise, then Hallom and his bugle. Lieutenant Cheevers and his book, the stretcher bearing Lazzari with three pallbearers on either side, and the rest of the men in double ranks, the officers leading them.

Go ahead Commander. Have your military field day because it's one thing you know how to do well. It's men like you who need a computer....

The procession approached the depression, Bacon moving to one side, the firing party at the far side of the shallow. Lieutenant Cheevers at the near end, making room for the pallbearers who moved into the depression and deposited their load there. The others moved to either side of the slope in single file.

Make it slick, Commander. By the numbers, straight and strong, because it's the last thing you'll ever do....

The men suddenly stiffened to attention, uncovering and holding their dress hats over their left breasts.

Bacon removed the Federation flag from its staff, draped it neatly over Lazzari. Cheevers then moved to the front and conducted the services, which lasted for several minutes.

This is the end, Commander....

Allison could see Commander Warrick facing the firing party, saw the blast volleys. But he was more interested in Lazzari. Two soldiers were shoveling the loose sand over him. Hallom raised his bugle to his lips.

Then *they* came.

Large, heavy, white porpoise-like creatures they were, swimming up out of the sand as if it were water, and snatching men in their powerful jaws, rending and tearing—clothes and all—as they rose in a fury of attacks that whipped up sand to nearly hide the scene.

There were twenty or more, and then more than a hundred rising and sinking and snapping and slashing, sun glistening on their shiny sides, flippers working furiously to stay atop the sand.

This, then, was the sea and these were the fish in it, fish normally disinterested in ordinary sweating men and machines and treadwagons, but hungry for men's blood or anything smeared with it—so hungry that a drop of it on the sand must have been a signal conducted to the depths to attract them all.

And when the men were gone there were still fish-like creatures burrowing into the sand, moving through it swiftly, half in and out like sharks, seeking every last vestige of—*blood*.

Then, as suddenly as they had come, the

things were gone.

Then there was nothing but smooth sand where before it had been covered by twenty men with bowed heads ... except one spot which maximum magnification showed to be a bugle half-buried in the sand.

ALLISON DID NOT KNOW how long he sat there looking at the screen, but it must have been an hour, because when he finally moved he could only do so with effort.

He alone had survived out of fifty men, and *he*—the computer man. He was struck with the wonder of it.

He rose to leave the room. He needed a drink.

Only then did he remember that Cheevers had locked him in.

He tried the door.

It opened!

Cheevers *had* believed him, then. Somehow, this made the whole thing more tragic ... there might have been others who would have believed, too, if the commander had not stood in the way....

The first thing Allison did was close the great port. Then he hunted until he found the bottle he was looking for. He took it to the computer room with him, opened the flight compartment, withdrew the tapes, set them in their proper slots and started them on their way.

Only when he heard the ship tremble alive did he take a drink ... a long drink.

There would have to be other bottles after this one. There had to be. It was going to be a long, lonely ride home.

And there was much to forget.

👽 👽 👽

Jerry Sohl's "The Invisible Enemy" first appeared in the September 1955 issue of Imaginative Tales. *In 1964, Sohl streamlined the story for the pioneering MGM television series* The Outer Limits. *Although the production is hindered by a limited budget and the primitive special effects of its day, the episode nonetheless has much to recommend it. Byron Haskins, best remembered for his direction of producer George Pal's classic* The War of the Worlds, *brought a somber eeriness to the proceedings; and Adam West, two years before starring in the campy ABC series* Batman, *delivers a subdued and believable performance as Major Merritt, leader of an expedition sent to Mars to uncover the unexplained disappearances of two earlier manned missions.*

Jerry Sohl was no stranger to science fiction on film. His credits include Rod Serling's The Twilight Zone *(uncredited), the original* Star Trek, *and* The Invaders. *Sohl also adapted H.P. Lovecraft's "The Colour Out of Space" as the sensationally titled 1965 movie* Die, Monster, Die!

Matt Cowan's **Threat Watch**

YOU MAY NOW ACCESS THE FILES. THESE FILES CONTAIN DATA MODULES COMPILED FROM EVIDENCE PRESENTED IN MOVIES AND TELEVISION. EACH MODULE FOCUSES ON A SPECIFIC THREAT: INSIDIOUS ALIENS, COSMIC ASSASSINS, SCIENTIFIC ABOMINATIONS, MURDEROUS COMPUTERS AND ... **DEADLY PLANETS.**

ACCESSING ... ACCESSING.... OPENING MODULE 1:

DEADLY PLANETS

Space exploration is an inherently dangerous endeavor. The chosen vessel of transportation must be capable of projecting its compliment of life forms through the vacuum of space at breakneck speeds while providing them with adequate oxygen, temperature, gravity, water, nourishment and medication; while avoiding contact with asteroids, comets, debris, black holes, or other unfriendly travelers, among other potentialities in order to make landfall. This issue we examine what can happen when the chosen destination proves inhospitable to new arrivals, by examining four such instances from classic films. So, don your space suit (No, not the red one!) and let's explore some of the deadliest planets in the universe.

ALTAIR IV
FORBIDDEN PLANET (Metro-Goldwyn-Mayer Corp, 1956)

Spacecraft: C-57D
Life Forms: Dr. Morbius, his daughter Altaira, Robbie the Robot, The Krell
Deadliest Menance: An invisible, unstoppable force, impervious to damage
Reason to Go: The planet is beautiful, and home to extraordinary scientific achievements
Reason Not to Go: Everyone besides the Morbius family who've landed on its surface have been destroyed
Necessities For Survival: The ability to uncover the secrets behind the aggressive, invisible force on the planet

Planetary Threat Level: 7.5 out of 10
Favorite Scene: The crew of C-57D unleashing all their firepower against the alien force attacking them

Synopsis: When United Planets ship C-57D arrives at the Earth-like planet Altair IV to check on colonists sent there 20 years previous, they are warned to stay away by the only surviving member of that group, Dr. Morbius, who claims he can't guarantee their safety. Ignoring his warning, they set down anyway and are taken to the doctor's impressive residence by his affable, mechanical servant, Robbie the Robot, who happens to be a bad ass: Robbie can speak an incredible array of languages; lift more than five tons; replicate virtually anything after analyzing it; and is equipped with a built-in disintegration ray. Despite his awesome capabilities, his programming prevents him from harming any living person.

Dr. Morbius explains to Captain John Adams *(played by a young Leslie Nielsen)* that

an invisible force tore his fellow colonists to pieces, then vaporized their ship when the survivors tried to use it to flee. In the end, only the doctor, his wife, and his daughter Altaira remained alive. He believes it was their love for the place that protected them. (Unfortunately, Morbius' wife later died of natural causes.) When the crew meets Altaira, the officers are instantly taken with her beauty, leading to some not-so-subtle, competitive flirting.

Added to Dr. Morbius' miraculous survival is the question of how he managed to single-handedly create such extraordinary inventions, far beyond the combined capabilities of the rest of the colonists *(as evidenced by both his high-tech residence and robotic servant)*. When Captain Adam's crew begins to be attacked by an alien force, they must figure out what it is and how to defeat it. Could it really be the blood-thirsty ghosts of Altair IV's extinct former inhabitants The Krell?

My Take:
This film stands the test of time for many reasons, not the least of which are its beautiful landscapes. It was the first movie ever set entirely on another planet and was nominated for an Academy Award for Best Visual Effects. The fact that it was a huge influence on Gene Roddenberry's *Star Trek* is noticeable in everything from its teleportation effects to the crew's laser pistols. I was riveted watching as the crew of the C-57D encounter the wonders of Altair IV while seeking out the ancient secrets it hides. Don't let its age hold you back. This seminal classic still has much to offer modern viewers.   ***Movie Rating:* 8 out of 10**

AURA
PLANET OF THE VAMPIRES (American International Pictures, 1965)

Spacecraft: The *Argos* and the *Galliott*
Known Life Forms: A host of formless psychic beings
Deadliest Menace: The spirits inhabiting the planet
Reason to Go: To answer a distress signal
Reason Not to Go: The parasitic nature of entities existing there
Necessities For Survival: An incredibly strong force of will
Planetary Threat Level: 7 out of 10
Favorite Scene: Exploring the alien space craft, complete with giant skeletons

Synopsis: On an expedition into deep space, two large vessels, the *Argos* and the *Galliott*, go to investigate a distress call they receive. In the process, both ships are forced to crash on the nearby, fog enshrouded planet of Aura. The crew of the *Argos* are instantly overtaken by a mad rage which drives them to attack each other.

Once they regain control of themselves, they discover the damage to their ship is severe enough to ground them until repairs can be made.

When an away team finds the *Galliott*, they discover everyone onboard was violently killed by their fellow crew mates. Following a quick trip back to gather some tools, they return to find the corpses have vanished. Leaving there, they stumble upon a derelict ship that contains the skeletal remains of an enormous alien race. Things go from bad to worse when their deceased crew mates return, bringing a nightmarish proposition with them.

My Take: This film is rumored to have helped inspire Ridley Scott's iconic 1979 movie *Alien*. While the costumes are decidedly odd, they help lend the movie its own distinctive style. The exploration of the alien ship was my favorite part, particularly when the astronauts accidentally seal themselves inside and are forced to try and decipher a way to escape. Any movie containing giant skeletons automatically receives positive marks in my book.

Movie Rating: 6 out of 10

MORGANTHUS
GALAXY OF TERROR (New World Pictures, 1981)

Spacecraft: The *Quest*
Known Life Forms:
Still to be determined
Deadliest menace:
Massively strong tentacles that appear out of nowhere to rend people apart
Reason to Go:
Despite the storms it experiences, the planet has breathable air and apparently Earth-like gravity
Reason Not to Go:
To avoid being horribly murdered

Necessities For Survival: The ability to keep your wits about you under any circumstances
Planetary Threat Level: 8 out of 10
Favorite Scene: When the crystal star throwing crewman Quuhod is attacked by his own severed arm

Synopsis: The crew of the starship *Quest* travel to the planet Morganthus on a mission to rescue survivors of a ship that recently crashed there. Unfortunately, they are also forced to crash on its surface. After going to search for survivors, they discover a vast pyramid-shaped edifice which they go to investigate, only to find themselves beset by various horrifying creatures lurking in the mists. One by one the crew encounters a towering slime-drenched maggot, a maniacal doppelgänger, bloodthirsty severed appendages, malformed huge-headed aliens, and more. With the power and variety of abominations facing these spacefarers, will any of them survive?

My Take: Produced by legendary B-filmmaker Roger Corman, this 1981 attempt to capitalize on the success of *Alien* is rather a mixed bag. The casting is definitely a plus, offering up Robert Englund *(Freddy Krueger from the Nightmare On Elm Street movies)*, Sid Haig *(House of*

1,000 Corpses), Ray Walston *(My Favorite Martian)*, and Erin Moran *(Happy Days)* to portray the stalwart crew of the *Quest*. There's an obvious attempt to endow each of them with some defining nuance, just not enough for us to really invest in them. We have Captain Trantor *(Grace Zabriskie)* who's still dealing with the psychological effects of a past tragedy; Alluma *(Erin Moran)* who possesses some psychic abilities; Quuhod *(Sid Haig)* who's armed with a batch of unique crystalline throwing stars as his preferred weapon; and Kore *(Ray Walston)*, the ship's cook who's always willing to assist his allies. The film's special effects were overseen by James Cameron *(Avatar)* and generally do an effective job throughout. I found many of the ideas put forth intriguing, even if they didn't always materialize to their fullest extent. I'll warn you there's a tastelessly exploitive sex scene which lent the film some early notoriety but really leaves a black mark on the project in my opinion. If you can ignore that and aren't looking for a deep plot, it has enough positives to make it a fun watch. *Rating:* **7 out of 10**

MARS
THE LAST DAYS ON MARS (Magnolia Pictures, 2013)

Spacecraft: The *Aurora*
Known Life Forms: Bacteria capable of animating the dead
Deadliest Menace: Organisms which have become infected by the virus
Reason to Go: To advance science by studying the planet
Reason Not to Go: Because the only life to be found there will transform you into a murderous zombie
Necessities For Survival: Astronaut suit, oxygen, rations, and the wherewithal to leave Martian bacteria well enough alone
Planetary Threat Level: 6 out of 10
Favorite Scene: When the mutated Marko Petrović first returns to the base

Synopsis: Nineteen hours from returning home to Earth, following the conclusion of their six month assignment to Mars, the eight person crew of Tantalus Base find their evacuation suddenly jeopardized. The trouble arises after crewman Marko Petrović makes an excuse to take a rover out one last time because he secretly believes he's found evidence of life, for which he doesn't want to share credit. Unfortunately, a huge rift abruptly splits the ground to engulf him. Not long afterward, he and another crew mate who lingered around the crevasse return as hideously blighted, fast moving corpses bent on savagely murdering everyone else. It isn't long before more of the crew begin adding to their ranks as the bacteria that transformed the first two infect them as well.

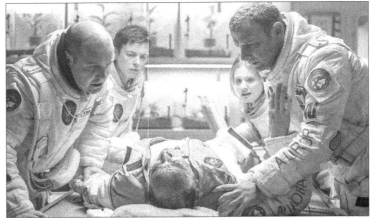

My Take: Boiled down to its basics, this film is essentially zombies versus astronauts on the surface of Mars. These zombies are effectively creepy looking, and the fact that they can move fast makes them scarier to me than your traditional slow lurching munchers. I also liked that they weren't completely mindless either. They certainly can't be reasoned with, but they are capable of utilizing tools, if only for their lethality, and since they don't immediately forget everything from their former lives, they're capable of thinking through basic maneuvers. I did feel the movie began to falter following the initial zombie attack. Things carry on with astronauts fleeing through space station corridors, some making ruthless choices along the way while trying to work out the cause of these transformations. Even so, the story momentum lags. Perhaps this is because the survivors are able to avoid their undead colleagues for a prolonged stretch in the middle, or it could be that some of the characters came off a bit flat to me. Ultimately, *The Last Days of Mars* can't compare with *Alien* or *The Thing*, but it still has enough going for it to keep you entertained when you're craving that late night zombie fix. ***Movie Rating:*** **6 out of 10**

Newcomers to a perilous planet may scoff at the dangers—
until they experience ...

THE WILD NIGHT

by Lynn M. Cochrane

FROST SPARKLED ON THE BRANCHES OF THE TREES, turning the lights of the settlement into myriads of tiny jewels. Sonya watched them, worried. The jewels moved and twinkled as the branches were tossed in the rising wind. It was cold. Sonya curled and uncurled her toes inside her boots, trying to keep her feet warm. The fleece lining didn't seem to be working, despite the boots being new. The cold seeped up from the ground through them. She banged her mittened hands against her upper arms in a vain attempt to keep warm—and immediately cursed herself for the noise, silently mouthing the obscenities. It was far too dark to be seen but human sounds were easy to pick out against the wind noises—for anyone native born.

That was what they were relying on, of course. Mr. Costello was a newcomer, neither native born nor on planet long enough to have acquired the skill. He didn't have the knowledge of the variations of human life dictated by the planet itself, either. He'd made that plain during the afternoon.

Sonya could pick out human sounds as easily as if the wind noises didn't exist. She heard the gravel stirring rhythmically as Tom walked up the path on her left. She heard a twig snap as a boot trod on it on her right. Probably Mark. It was too far away to be Jenny. Sonya moved forward with them, closer to the new school house. Mr. Costello had been warned.

"STORM FORCE TEN FORECAST," whispered Mark, sitting down. "Dad says I'm to go straight home tonight and prepare, just in case." He pulled a face.

Sonya, settling herself into her chair for afternoon school, read his expression as one of irritation and boredom. The wind was always blowing. It could reach storm force ten very easily. Once or even twice a week

wasn't unusual but by the fourth time, everyone was getting annoyed.

"Force eight, check. Force nine, double check. Force ten, cross check," she muttered, quoting the wind lore. "Force eleven's Wild."

"That's what's forecast on the infotext," whispered Tom, turning onto a clean page in his math book. "They're reckoning on eleven gusting twelve. It'll be his first Wild night, if they're right." He indicated the teacher with a toss of his head.

"You, boy! Silence!" Mr. Costello shouted across the room from where he was just starting to work with a group of younger pupils. "You should know how to behave in school by now. See me at the end of the day."

"But, Sir, we were discussing the weather forecast," said Mark.

"Enough! I'll see all of that group at the end of the day! You're here to learn, not discuss future possibilities!"

Sonya swapped glances with Tom and Mark and looked apologetically at Jenny, Simon and Wayne. The six of them formed the oldest group in the school. If there was ever any trouble, they were the ones who got blamed. Mr. Costello didn't expect any problems with them. No one did.

It had been the same for as long as Sonya could remember. As the oldest of the children in the new mining colony, they had always been expected to behave as little adults. The only concession to their age was the provision of a school. Until ten weeks or so before, even that had only been one class taught by the wife of the mining manager with the occasional help of any pregnant or nursing mothers who had been excused from their normal duties. Now, with an influx of new pupils into the nursery, Mr. Costello had been taken on. The old, easy rules had gone with the youngest pupils, left in the old school house. New rules applied here, stricter and less easy to tolerate. Mr. Costello expected silence and hard work. He had difficulty getting either. It wasn't that they deliberately defied him. It was just that they hadn't yet acquired the necessary new habits.

School dragged. That wasn't unusual, of course, but with the new rules and new teacher had come new subjects and a longer day. There was even work to be done every evening. Sonya found it interesting but she knew that Tom and Mark were much less happy about it. There was little enough time for recreation. Tom and Mark both had a series of chores when they got home and minimal personal satisfaction from them. Any forecast of force eight or above simply doubled their work.

Mr. Costello finally started to dismiss his pupils, youngest first. Sonya watched out of the corner of her eye while working on a comprehension exercise. Once all the younger children had gone, it seemed that he found little jobs to do for far longer than was necessary. When the room was finally tidy, he came across and sat down on the spare chair at their table.

"To say that I am disappointed with you is being far too mild," he said. "You are well aware of the rules. The only exception to the rule of silence is when you are helping each other. Why do you think the rules don't apply to you?"

"Sorry, Sir," said Tom, echoed by Mark.

"The rules do apply to us, sir," said Sonya, "but we were passing on vital information. We've been taught to pass on the weather forecast whenever we have an update."

"That is hardly vital information in a math lesson."

"No, Sir," said Sonya, realizing that nothing except experience was going to make Mr. Costello understand the strange weather patterns of his new home.

"It's almost law, here, to pass on the weather forecast," said Tom. "It can be the difference between life and death. If you're caught out when the weather goes Wild, you're lucky if you only end up dead."

"Explain yourself, boy!"

Sonya caught the note of warning in Mr. Costello's voice and bit her bottom lip. She tried to attract Tom's attention to warn him off, although she knew it was a futile exercise. Tom always went ahead with what he intended to do.

"Why do you think so many of the first wave of settlers are either badly maimed or dead?" he asked. "They didn't know about not being caught out when the weather goes Wild. My Dad had to shoot his best friend after a Wild night. If it gets really Wild, even these domes can be ripped up. Some whole families have had to be shot and it's quite common for part of a crop to be lost. The protection covers will have to be put on all the fields tonight and taken off tomorrow morning and there might well be other things that will need to be cleared up."

"Enough!"

Sonya winced at the sharp sound in Mr. Costello's voice.

"I will not be spoken to like that! The whole group will do an extra comprehension tonight for talking in class without due reason and you will also write me an apology."

"You've been warned, Sir," said Tom. "It may well be a Wild night and if it is, there will be damage by tomorrow morning. Most of us will be late, if we're in at all, but that won't matter because you'll be expected to help clear up as well. Everyone helps after a Wild night. Even mining is halted until everything is cleared."

They left the school house rapidly, before Mr. Costello could decide on further suitable punishment.

SONYA WALKED HOME through pelting rain. A bad sign. She looked into the fields either side, trying to spot the tell-tale rapid growth of anchor-roots on the glow-gourd plants. She couldn't be certain. Not everyone grew them, although each family had a smallholding and was not only expected to be largely self-sufficient but also to grow enough of the local crops for there to be trade off-planet. The ore was valuable, of course—valuable enough for the colony to have been set up—but the easily grown native plants of one planet were often great luxuries somewhere else; luxuries that people paid well for. Working the land was done by everyone who could walk. Even young children could learn to weed between the glow-gourd plants, and those unable to walk due to injury could pack produce.

Sonya was lucky. She had her own small field of glow-gourds that was her responsibility alone. She grew a slightly rarer variety and had had some successful harvests. Her parents grew the more common type and her two younger brothers were currently specializing in day-leaf. It wasn't as valuable as glow-gourds but its slightly smoky spicy flavor made it a useful seasoning. As with the glow-gourds, it was gaining in popularity off-planet. Only the daily harvesting it needed stopped more people from growing it, now. Most other families worked as a unit, with the older children doing much of the daily work after school and the parents only helping out when it was necessary, but Sonya's parents had chosen to make each person responsible for part of the family's income. Sonya quite enjoyed looking after her field and voluntarily checked her brothers' when high winds were forecast.

Sonya worked in her field until the light started to fail. By then, she had a large basket of harvested glow-gourds and a pile of dead leaves and stems that she buried in the corner of the field to make compost for the next harvest. She pulled the protection covers over her field, winching the segmented dome into place underneath the rigid one that kept the temperature up far enough to grow and harvest plants outside their normal short season. Then she helped with her brothers' covers and checked those of her parents' fields. After that, she went round checking the baffles that broke up the wind and helped to protect the low domes of their smallholding and living quarters.

There was a message for her on the infotext when she finally got in.

Lesson at the new school house, 21:00, if it's not Wild by then.

IT HADN'T QUITE MATERIALIZED YET, Sonya thought, as she crept forward. The wind was only force ten, or thereabouts, and the sky was still cloudy—low grey-brown cumulus little more than twice her height overhead because of the shallow atmosphere. They were safe enough for their prank.

They were about to race forward and hammer on the dome of the school house, mimicking the sounds of a Wild night, when the first rent in the clouds appeared. Blue brilliance flared briefly. Sonya fell to the ground, hiding her eyes. Around her, she could hear her classmates throwing themselves down. The prank looked suddenly much more dangerous.

The next flare was orange—and answered almost at once by a vivid green that hurt even through the thick protective clothes. Sonya lay still, trying to hide, well aware that only the insane were out in Wild weather—the time when nature went berserk; when aurora could be fatal, swept into stinging rays by force eleven or twelve winds. After a Wild night, plants could walk and people could have roots.

👁 👁 👁

Lynn M. Cochrane lives in the outskirts of Birmingham, UK. She has been writing most of her life and has produced four collections of poems. She has had several short stories published in anthologies. She is currently working on a novel set in the time when the Mesolithic gave way to the Neolithic. She is a mother and a grandmother and taught Geography in Birmingham for many years. She is a member of Cannon Hill Writers' Group, leading writing workshops from time to time, and is currently editor of their showcase anthology, Salvo *and their sampler pamphlets* Grapeshot.

For man the most hospitable planet is earth. But the cradle of human life holds deadly perils, as well—and dark secrets which for untold millennia were kept ...

ON ICE
by Simon Strantzas

THE BEARDED FRENCHMAN landed the plane on a narrow sheet of ice as expertly as anyone could. It wasn't smooth, and the four passengers were utterly silent as the hull shuddered and echoed and threatened to split along its riveted seams. Wendell closed his eyes so tight he saw stars, and clung to what was around him to keep from being thrown from his seat. When the plane finally slid to a stop, part of him wanted to leap up and hug not only the ground but the men around him. He didn't, because when he finally opened his eyelids the first thing he saw was the thuggish Dogan's disgusted smirk, and it quickly extinguished any lingering elation. Isaacs, for all his faults, was not so inhibited. Instead, he had his hands pressed together in supplication and whispered furiously under his breath. It caught Dogan's eye, and the look he and Wendell shared might have been the first time they had agreed on anything.

"The oil companies have already done a survey of Melville Island, so there shouldn't be too many surprises ahead," Dr. Hanson said. "However, their priority has never been fossils—except, of course, the liquid kind—and it's unlikely they saw much while speeding across the ice on ATVs, doing damage to the strata. So we have ample exploring to do. We'll hike inland for a day and set up base camp. From there, we'll radiate our dig outward."

Gauthier unloaded the plane two bags at a time, and his four passengers moved the gear to the side. They packed light—only the most essential tools and equipment—so the hike would be manageable, but seeing the bags spread across the encrusted surface, Wendell wondered if he were up to the task. It took too long to load everything on his narrow shoulders, and when he was done he suspected the pack weighed more than thirty pounds. Dr. Hanson looked invigorated by his own burden, his face a smiling crimson flush. Isaacs was the opposite, however, and visibly uncomfortable. Wendell hoped the goggle-eyed boy wouldn't be a liability in the days ahead.

They walked across the frigid snow, and nearly an hour went by before Dr. Hanson turned and looked at the breathless entourage behind him.

"So, Wendell," he called out, barely containing his anticipation and glee. "Have you noticed anything peculiar so far?"

Wendell glanced at both Dogan and Isaacs, but neither showed any interest in Wendell's answer. Even Dr. Hanson seemed more concerned in hearing himself speak.

"For all the research the oil companies did here, it looks as though they made a major error in classifying the rock formations. It doesn't really surprise me—you said they weren't here looking for rocks. Still, they thought all these formations were the result of normal tectonic shifts—that these were normal terrestrial rocks."

There was a pause.

"And that's not the case?"

"No, these are aquatic rocks. The entire island is full of them."

"And how do you account for so many aquatic rocks on an island, Wendell?"

"Lowering water levels, increased volcanic activity. The normal shifts of planetary mass. It's unusual for something so large to be pushed up from the ocean, but the Arctic island clusters have always had some unique attributes."

Dr. Hanson nodded sagely before catching his breath to speak. Wendell noticed that the dribble from Hanson's nose was opaque as it slowly froze.

"These islands have always had a sense of mystery about them. The Inuit don't come here, which is strange enough, but they have a name for these clusters: *alornerk*. It means 'the deep land.' I don't know where that term comes from, but some claim it has survived from the days when the island was still submerged."

"That would mean either Melville Island only surfaced sometime in the last ten thousand years, or—"

"Or there was intelligent life in the Arctic two hundred million years before it showed up anywhere else on the planet."

"But that's impossible!" Dogan interrupted, startling Wendell. He looked just as confused. Dr. Hanson merely laughed excitedly.

"Yes, it's the worst kind of lazy science, isn't it? I wouldn't put too much stock in it."

THEY FELL BACK into a single line quickly: Dr. Hanson leading the way, then Dogan, Wendell, Isaacs, and finally the pilot, Gauthier. Wendell made a concerted effort to keep close to the front so he might hear anything Dogan and Dr. Hanson discussed, but the sound of their footsteps on the snow had a deafening and delirious effect—at times he hallucinated more sounds than could be possible. The constant crunch made him lightheaded, a problem exacerbated by the cold that worked at his temples.

But it was Isaacs who suffered the worst. Periodically, Wendell checked to see how far behind his fellow student had fallen, and to ensure he hadn't vanished altogether. Yet Isaacs was always there, only a few feet back, fidgeting and scanning the landscape. Gauthier likely kept him in place. The two made quite a sight, and Wendell was amused by how little Gauthier did to conceal his contempt. Isaacs was a frightened rabbit in a cage. Gauthier, the snarling wolf beyond the lock.

"This feels wrong," Isaacs whined, and Wendell did his best to pretend he hadn't heard him. It did not dissuade Isaacs from continuing. "You can't tell me this feels right to you guys. You can't tell me you guys don't feel everything closing in."

Wendell glanced back. It was reassuring to see that even an expensive jacket couldn't prevent Isaacs from being ravaged by the weather—his eyes bulged, his color was pale.

"Isaacs, look around. There's not a wall or anything in sight. Nothing to box you in. The idea you feel confined—"

"I feel it, too."

Nothing about Gauthier's face betrayed that he'd spoken. Nevertheless, Wendell slowed to close the distance between them. Isaacs did the same, eyes wide and eager.

"What are you talking about?"

"Don't you feel it?" Isaacs asked. "I feel it all over my body. I don't like being here alone."

"You aren't alone. There are five of us, plus a plane. And Gauthier has a satellite phone, just in case. The only thing boxing you in is all your protection. You're practically surrounded."

"Then why are we so alone? Where are all the animals?"

"They were probably on the shore. Gauthier, we saw some birds or something when we flew over, right?"

The pilot shook his head slowly. It spooked Wendell nearly as much as Isaacs had.

"Well, I'm sure there are animals around. They're probably hiding from us because they're afraid."

"I don't have a good feeling about this, Wendell," Isaacs said. "I don't have a good feeling about this at all. We should get back on the plane and go."

"Wait, did Dogan put you guys up to this?"

The look of surprise did not seem genuine, though it was hard to be certain. Wendell wanted to press further, but he heard Dr. Hanson's voice.

"Wendell! Isaacs! Come, you must see this!"

Wendell turned to the men before him. They looked confused.

When the three reached Dr. Hanson and the visibly uncomfortable Dogan, Wendell didn't immediately understand what the concern was. Before them lay ice, just as it lay everywhere. Dr. Hanson smiled, but it held no warmth. It was thin and quivering and echoed his uneasy eyes.

"Do you see it? Right there. On the ground. Where my foot is."

There was only ice. Wendell kneeled to get a better look, but a pair of iron hands grabbed him and yanked him back to his feet. He stumbled as Gauthier set him down.

"Don't," was all the pilot said.

"Are you really that much of an idiot?" Dogan asked, and Wendell felt once again the butt of some foul trick. Had it not been for Dr. Hanson's distinct lack of humor, Wendell might have stormed off into the snow. Instead, he tamped his irritation and looked again.

He wasn't certain how long it took, but slowly what the rest had seen resolved. Isaacs, too, spotted it before Wendell, serenading them with a litany of "oh, no," repeated over and over. Dr. Hanson tried to help by asking everyone to back away, while Wendell wondered why no one simply told him what he was missing.

Then he realized it wasn't him who was missing something but someone else, because trapped beneath the sheet of ice was what could only be a severed human finger.

The flesh was pale, verging on white, and beneath the clouded surface it was barely visible. Wendell inspected the hands of the party to be sure it hadn't come from any of them.

"I don't like this. I don't like this at all."

"It's not going to leap out and grab you, Isaacs. Get a grip on yourself."

"But where did it come from? Dr. Hanson, could it have come from Dr. Lansing's party? You said they were here for a few days. Why else would they have left after finding only those three small ichthyosaur bones?"

"I asked Dr. Lansing that very question, Wendell. He simply responded by asking me how many bones beyond three I thought would be necessary to collect to prove his point. Five? Ten? Fifty? He said all he felt necessary were three to prove ichthyosaurs travelled this far north. I'll grant you: that makes little sense, but that's Dr. Lansing for you. Even he, however, wouldn't be foolish enough to waste time poring over this discovery. More than likely, it was due to some accident involving the oil men here before us. There's nothing we can do for the fellow that lost it, and we have more important discoveries to dig up, discoveries beside which this will ultimately pale. Let's march on. We still have a journey ahead of us."

Dr. Hanson resumed walking, Dogan trotting after him. Isaacs looked as though he was going to be sick, but before he could Gauthier shoved him.

"Keep moving. Standing too long in the open like this isn't a good idea. You never know what's watching."

Wendell looked around, but all he saw were hills of ice in every direction. If anything was watching, he had no idea where it might be hiding.

WENDELL COULDN'T STOP THINKING about the finger as they continued on. Maybe it was the sound of their footsteps, or the dark beneath his parka's hood, but he felt increasingly isolated from the group, and as they travelled he became further ensnared in thought. He'd never seen a severed body part before, and though it barely looked real beneath the ice, it still made him uncomfortable. Someone had come to Melville Island and not only lost a finger but decided to leave without it. How was that possible? Wendell shivered and tried to get his mind on other less morbid things. Like water.

Water is the world's greatest sculptor. It is patient, careful, persistent, and over countless years it is capable of carving the largest canyons out of the hardest rock. Who knew how long it took to carve the shapes that surrounded the five of them as they walked? It was like a bizarre art gallery, full of strange smooth sculptures that few had ever seen. Wendell reached into his pocket and fished out his digital camera. As he snapped numerous photos, he realized he was the only one doing so. Dr. Hanson barely slowed his pace to acknowledge the formations, and the sight of the towering rocks left Isaacs further terrorized.

"Do you have to take pictures? Can't we just keep going?"

"Dr. Hanson said to document everything."

"Then why didn't you take one of that finger?"

It was a fair point. Why hadn't he taken that photograph?

"It's not really part of the history of Melville Island, or the life that was here, is it?"

Isaacs shrugged, then spun around like an animal suddenly aware of a predator. Wendell stepped back.

"What is it?"

Isaacs took a deep breath, then exhaled slowly.

"Nothing. I guess."

He wanted to say more, but despite Wendell's prodding Isaacs remained quiet.

They trudged along the ice, keeping their heads down as they followed Dr. Hanson. He had studied the maps for months and was certain that their best bet was to set up base camp about twenty-five miles in. From that point, they could radiate their survey outward and see what they might discover.

Wendell wondered, though, if it wouldn't have been better to remain nearer the shoreline where remnants of a water-dwelling dinosaur might be more evident. He kept his opinion private, not wanting to contradict a man capable of ending his career before it started. Which was why Wendell was both surprised and irritated when Dogan posed the same question. And even more so when he heard Dr. Hanson's response.

"Good question, Dogan. I like that you're thinking. It shows a real spark your fellow team could learn from. However, in this case you haven't thought things through. Don't forget that during the Mesozoic Era we're most interested in the Earth had yet to fully cool. Melville Island was more tropical than it is now. The greatest concentration of vertebrates will likely be farther inland. It shouldn't take us more than a few more hours to get there."

The thought of travelling a few more hours made Wendell's body ache. The cold had already seeped through his insulated boots and the two layers of socks he wore inside them.

"Maybe we could stop and rest for a second? I don't know how much longer I can carry this gear." As Wendell spoke the words, his pack's weight doubled in tacit agreement.

"I suppose it couldn't hurt," Dr. Hanson said, and Wendell wasted no time slipping the burden off his shoulders. Immediately relieved, he then sat on the snow to give his tired feet a rest. Dr. Hanson, Isaacs, and Dogan all followed his lead. Only Gauthier remained standing, one hand on his belt, the other in his frozen beard. He looked across the horizon while the others used the moment to eat protein bars and contemplate what had led them to their seats at the top of the world.

It had been days, and overfamiliarity combined with sheer exhaustion was enough to keep them quiet. No one spoke or glanced another's way. They simply kept their heads down and tried to recuperate before the next leg of the journey. Dr. Hanson's eyes were wide as he plotted their next steps. Isaacs experienced jitters, which continued to multiply as the group remained stationary. Dogan, however, was the opposite. With eyes closed and arms wrapped around his legs, he appeared to have fallen asleep. Until Gauthier delivered a swift kick to his ribs.

"What was—?"

The pilot shushed him quickly. Dogan, to Wendell's astonishment, complied.

"Did any of you see that?"

They all turned. Around them was the vast icy expanse, wind pushing clouds over the snow-encrusted tundra, eddies dancing across the rough terrain. But Wendell saw nothing different from what he'd already witnessed. A glance at the other men revealed the same confusion. Wendell looked at the towering Gauthier, waiting for the answer to the question before them, but the pilot was silent. He merely continued to stare. Isaacs could not bear it.

"What? What do you see?"

"Shut up," Gauthier hissed, and Isaacs cowered, his breathing uneven. Dr. Hanson flashed an expression that was buried so quickly Wendell didn't have time to process it.

Gauthier raised his arm and pointed away from where they had been walking, off into the distant vastness that flanked them.

"I think something's been tracking us."

"What do you mean?"

"I mean I've been watching while you four were stumbling along, and I saw something—a shadow—keeping pace with us. It's been there ever since we left the runway."

"Where is it?"

"There. Do you see it? In the distance. It's not moving now. Just a shadow. Watching us."

Wendell squinted, but still saw nothing.

"It's likely a polar bear," Dr. Hanson said. "I've been warned they come to the island, looking for seal. No doubt he knows we're here."

"Should we be worried?" Isaacs asked.

"It's not going to come after us," Dogan said. Dr. Hanson was more hesitant.

"Well, I don't know if I'd go that far. But there's enough of us that it should keep its distance."

That failed to reassure Wendell. And if he wasn't reassured, then Isaacs—

"So you're saying a polar bear is following us, and we shouldn't be worried? Nothing to worry about at all?"

"It's okay, Isaacs. You'll be okay. Gauthier, tell them not to worry."

"Don't worry. It's moving now. It looks too small to be a polar bear anyway. Probably just a pack of wolves."

It wasn't long before they were moving again.

THEY SUCCESSFULLY MADE IT to the camp site without further report of being trailed. The lack did nothing to calm Isaac's nerves, but Dogan reverted to his old ways, insinuating himself between Dr. Hanson and Wendell any time they might have had a moment to speak. It was infuriating.

The five of them had been awake and travelling for well over twenty hours, and as far as Wendell could tell the sun had not moved an inch. The clouds, however, were not so bound, and he suspected their speed had as much to do with Hanson's decision to camp down as did the coordinates Dr. Lansing had provided him. The last thing Wendell wanted to do when they finally stopped walking was set up the tent, but Gauthier helped them all find the motivation through the promotion of fear.

"The way this wind is breaking? There are storms brewing ahead, somewhere beyond the ridges. The weather here is unpredictable. If we don't get cover and fast, we might not be around long enough for you four to start digging up bones. Get ready for what's coming."

"But what *is* coming?" Dogan asked. Gauthier laughed.

"A storm, man. A storm."

In the time it took to tell them, thick smoke-like clouds had rolled across the clear sky, casting a long shadow across the top of the world. Somehow, from somewhere, the men found the energy to erect their shelter, and Wendell silently admitted it felt good to have Dogan as an ally for once.

The storm arrived as the last peg was hammered in place. The five of them huddled beneath the tarpaulin tent, one of the tall water-carved rocks acting as both anchor and partial shield from the winds. Inside the enclosed space their heat quickly escalated, but Gauthier warned them to keep their coats on in case the wind wrenched the tent from the ground.

Strangely, Isaacs was the most at peace during the ordeal. While Dogan and Wendell held down the edges of the tent, their knuckles white, Isaacs had his eyelids closed and head tilted back to rest on his shoulders. He sat cross-legged, his body moving with the slightest sway. Wendell thought he also heard him humming, but convinced himself it was only the wind bending around the sheltering rocks.

They stayed hunkered for hours, wind howling outside, pulling at the thin barrier of canvas standing between them. The sound of it rippling back and forth was a terrifying thunder, and even after hours enduring it, the noise did not become any less so. Each clap was an icy knife in Wendell's spine, and as he shook under the tremendous stress he used every ounce of will he had within him to maintain his rationality and tamp down his fear. Deep breaths, slow, long, continued until the knot inside his chest slackened. It was only when he felt he could look again at his fellow captives without screaming that he dared. Isaacs remained blissfully distant, his mind cracked and he was simply gone from

it to another place. Gauthier and Dr. Hanson spoke among themselves, planning and debating the next course of action, all at a volume that was drowned by the howls and ripples. Only Dogan noticed Wendell, and the scowl across his face suggested that whatever truce the circumstances had negotiated for them was fleeting at best. He stared directly at Wendell with a stubbly, twisted face and did not bother to look away when Wendell caught him, as though he wore his disgust with pride. Wendell took a breath to speak and tasted the most noxious air. Dogan shook his twisted face, but it was no use; the fetid odor filled their lungs. Wendell covered his nose and mouth with his gloved hand. Whatever it was, it was sickly and bitter and smelled not unlike dead fish.

Outside there was a long sorrowful howl that sounded so near their shelter that Wendell prayed desperately it was only the wind echoing between the stones.

SLEEP DID WONDERS for Wendell's demeanor, and when he emerged from the battered shelter a few hours later he stepped into a

world canopied by a cloudless sky punctuated at the horizon by a single glowing orb. Gauthier was already awake, and Wendell found him prepping their equipment, beads of moisture frozen in his unkempt beard. He did not look pleased. Something was wrong.

It was only once outside the tent Wendell noticed it—something in the post-storm air, some excess of electricity, or maybe a remnant of the foul odor that stained his clothes. Whatever it was, it was troubling.

Dr. Hanson emerged a few minutes afterward with an eagerness to meet the glaciers head-on.

"You're up early. Good man! Why don't you hand me one of those coffees?"

Isaacs, too, joined them, and when the thick-set Dogan finally emerged from the tent, the look on his face upon seeing the rest of the team gathered made Wendell certain any ground gained the night before had been lost. Dogan was the same man he'd always been, and Wendell did his best to deal with it. He was frankly too tired to keep caring.

"After we've made our breakfast," Dr. Hanson said, blind to the turmoil of the students around him, "let's start our search for some ichthyosaur fossils. Right now, we are most concerned with locating those."

"Dr. Hanson?" Isaacs said.

"We should start at those ridges." Dogan pointed into the distance opposite, where a slightly elevated ring circled the land. "Water would have receded soonest from those areas, leaving the earliest and most complete fossils for us to find."

"Good thinking, Dogan. I applaud that."

"Dr. Hanson?" Isaacs repeated.

Dogan may have gotten the Doctor's attention, but Wendell was not going to be outdone.

"Maybe, Dr. Hanson, we should use a grid pattern closer to where Dr. Lansing and his students made their discovery? I mean, it makes sense to me to start with a known quantity and radiate from there."

Dogan shot Wendell a look, and Dr. Hanson laughed at them. "Both good ideas, men, but don't worry. I already have a plan. You see, based on my expectations, the fossil—"

"Dr. Hanson?"

Hanson sighed.

"Please don't interrupt me, Isaacs."

"Dr. Hanson? Can you come look at this?" Isaacs was kneeling by the tent, staring into the ground.

Immediately, Wendell was certain it was another finger. Another pale white digit trapped beneath the ice. Or perhaps it was a whole hand. Something else lost for which there could be no reasonable explanation. Dogan approached, as did Gauthier, both alongside Dr. Hanson. Wendell remained where he was, worried about what they would find, though their faces suggested it wasn't anything as mortally frightening as a severed finger. But it was also clear no one knew if it was far worse. Wendell hesitated but approached Dr. Hanson, his heavy boots crunching the ice underfoot. When he reached the four men, any conversation between them had withered.

Something impossible was caught in the tangle of boot prints surrounding the tent: an additional set of tracks in the crushed and broken snow. They differed from the team's in size—they were smaller, hardly larger than a child's, and each long toe of the bare foot could clearly be traced.

"Is it possible some kind of animal made them?"

"No," Dr. Hanson said. "These are too close to hominid."

"They can't be, though. Can they?"

"I thought this island was deserted."

"More importantly, what was it doing standing here in front of our tent?"

"I don't like this," Isaacs said. For once, Wendell agreed with him.

"Dr. Hanson, what's going on?"

"I wish I knew, Wendell. Gauthier, what do you think?"

Gauthier looked at them over his thick beard. It was the first time Wendell had seen puzzlement in the pilot's eyes. Gauthier looked at each of them in turn as they waited for him to offer an explanation, but he had none to offer. Instead, he turned away with a furrowed brow.

"Where is everything?"

Wendell didn't initially understand what he meant, not until he walked into the center of the camp. He looked back and forth and into the distance, then pushed the insulated hood off his head.

"It's all gone. Everything."

It had happened while they slept. Someone or something had come into the camp and stolen all their food and most of their supplies.

THINGS BECAME SCRAMBLED. The men spoke all at once, worried about what had happened and what it might mean. Wendell was no different, a manic desperation for answers taking hold. Dr. Hanson did his best to calm them all, but the red rims around his eyes made it clear he too was shaken.

"I don't understand it," he repeated. "There isn't supposed to be any visitors here beyond us."

"It looks as if you were wrong. There *is* someone here. Someone who's been following us."

It sounded crazy, and Wendell fought to keep from falling down that rabbit hole. Perversely, Dogan was the one Wendell looked to for strength, and only because he could imagine nothing worse than failing apart in front of him. Isaacs on the other hand suffered no such worries. He was nearly incapacitated by terror.

"We can't stay here. Didn't you guys hear it? Last night? That muffled creaking? And the crunch—I thought it was something else. I thought it had to be. It couldn't have been footsteps, but all I see on the ground are thousands of them, and all our stuff has vanished. We can't stay. We have to go. We have to go before it's too late."

"Calm down. Nobody's going anywhere," Dr. Hanson said. "This expedition is a one-time event. It took all the grant money to send us here. If we don't bring back some-thing, we will never return to Melville Island."

"Good," Isaacs said, his whole body shaking. "We shouldn't be here. There's something wrong."

Dr. Hanson scoffed, but Wendell wasn't certain he agreed. Dogan certainly seemed as though he didn't, but said nothing. After the journey they'd taken and what they'd seen, they had to trust Dr. Hanson knew what to do.

But what he did was turn to Gauthier for an answer, only to receive none. The pilot was more interested in sizing up Isaacs. When he finally spoke, it startled all of them. Isaacs almost screamed.

"The kid is right. We can't stay here. Even if we wanted to. Our supplies and rations are gone. We wouldn't last more than a few days."

Dr. Hanson shook his head. Wendell could see he was frustrated. Scared, tired, and frustrated.

"I told you: we can't go back. This is it. There's no time to spare, not even a few days. Not if we're to complete our tasks in the window. We have to stay here."

"Do we *all* need to be here, Doctor?" Dogan asked. His voice wavered with uncertainty.

Dr. Hanson hesitated a moment. "No," he said, "I expect not. At least, not all of us."

Dogan looked directly at Wendell. Wendell swallowed, outsmarted, and prepared himself for the inevitable. Instead, Dogan surprised him.

"Send Gauthier back to replenish our supplies while we stay here and work. It's only a few days. We can hold out that long, but we can't go on forever without food."

"Maybe Isaacs should join him," Wendell added, nodding when Dogan looked over. "He sounds on the verge of cracking, and for his sake as well as ours he should be off this rock if he does."

"Yes, we should go. Can we go? Can we?" Isaacs looked ready to swallow Gauthier. His bug-eyed face was slick and pallid, and Wendell wondered if Isaacs was too sick to travel. Then he wondered if it might be worse if he stayed.

Dr. Hanson did not seem entirely convinced. None of them did. None but Isaacs. Wendell had to admit, thinking about the strange footprints in the snow outside the tent, he wasn't sure if he'd rather be the one leaving.

"Maybe we should vote?" Dogan said.

"No point," Gauthier said. "I'm leaving. The kid can come if he wants."

Isaacs looked as if he were going to dance. Hanson nodded solemnly while Dogan said nothing. Wendell wasn't sure what he felt.

They split what little food they had left among them before Gauthier and Isaacs loaded their packs and left. There were six energy bars, a bag of peanuts, and four flasks of water. The two men took only half a bar each—as little as they could to get them back to the landing strip while Wendell, Dogan, and Dr. Hanson kept the rest to help them last until the plane returned.

"I want you to get back here as soon as you can," Dr. Hanson said. "We can't afford to be down this many men for long."

"We'll be back as soon as we can," Gauthier said, then handed Dr. Hanson a small leather bag. "Take this. In case of emergency."

Dr. Hanson looked in the bag and shook his head.

The two men waved at them as they started back—Isaacs nearly bouncing on the ice, while Gauthier's gait remained resolutely determined. They passed the tall, smooth rocks without trouble, and the crunch of their boots on the icy snow faded quickly once they were out of sight. The three remaining men stood in uncomfortable silence. Wendell worried they had made a grave mistake.

"I'm sure they'll be back before we know it." Dr. Hanson tried to sound upbeat and reassuring; Wendell wondered if he was as unconvinced as he sounded. "But in the interim, we have the equipment, and we're at the primary site. I know the situation is not as fortunate as we would have liked, but let's see how much we can get done before Gauthier gets back. We are here for another three days,

so let's take the time to gather the information necessary to salvage this expedition."

The three of them trekked out from the base camp on Dr. Hanson's suggestion despite all they'd seen, right into the bleakness of Melville Island. Trapped, they needed something to occupy their minds, distract them from disturbing sights like the severed finger, like the worrying sea of bodies that had mysteriously surrounded them as they slept. The only thing the three could do was resume their search for the elusive evidence of ichthyosaurs in the Arctic Ocean. They spent what hours remained in the day scouting those locations Dr. Hanson highlighted, turning over rocks, chipping through ice and permafrost, doing their best without tools, a researcher, and a pilot. And with each hour that passed they discovered nothing, no sign of the ichthyosaurs they were certain had once swam there. Dr. Hanson grew increasingly quiet as he brimmed with frustration, and Wendell decided to stay out of his way until they finally retreated to the base camp. Dogan, however, was the braver man. Or more foolish.

"Dr. Hanson, I have to tell you, I'm concerned."

"Oh, are you? What could possibly concern you?"

Dogan didn't hesitate.

"I'm concerned for our safety. I'm concerned our emergency transportation has left, that we're undermanned, and that neither Wendell nor I truly have any idea where we are. We're just following you blindly. I'm worried about our safety."

"Well, don't be, Dogan. Let us return to the base camp. We will reassess our plans there. Perhaps you and Wendell can help determine our next course of action. There is something on Melville Island worth finding no matter what the cost. I intend to stay until we do."

But when they finally reached the base camp they discovered what that cost was. It had vanished. Along with it, any trace of their presence, including their footprints. It was as though they had never been there.

"Are you sure this is the right place?"

"Of course I'm certain. Don't you recognize the shape of rocks? Or the nook we used for shelter? This is most certainly the right place."

The three stood watching the snow for a few minutes, as though the sheer force of their collective will would make the camp rematerialize, and when that too failed to yield results Dogan sat down on the snow, spent, a heavy-browed doll whose strings had been cut.

"Maybe we should go back to the landing strip," Wendell suggested. "Gauthier and Isaacs may not have left yet."

Dr. Hanson shook his head. "We've barely begun, we can't leave."

"But, Dr. Hanson, our camp—look around us. We can't stay here. Whatever it is that's—"

"Enough!" Dogan said, struggling to his feet with a concerning wobble. "I'm not waiting to be hunted by whatever is out there. At least at the landing strip, we'll be ready to leave once Gauthier gets back. I don't give a shit about ichthyosaurs or Mesozoic migration patterns or just when the hell Melville Island formed. All I want right now is to get off this iceberg and back to civilization where it's safe. And Wendell, I'm betting you feel exactly the same. So, are you coming or not?"

Wendell liked neither solution. Dogan was right: staying seemed like idiocy—something was watching them, stealing from them, and had left them for dead. And yet, his solution made no sense. How did he know whatever was following them wouldn't track them to the landing strip? How did he know when or even if Gauthier would be back to rescue them? Wendell wasn't convinced, but to blindly ignore what he had seen so far and continue to explore Melville Island with the same willful ignorance as Dr. Hanson seemed ludicrous.

"All I know is that whatever we do, we can't stay here. We need to keep moving."

"I don't think the two of you understand the importance of what we are doing here, or the costs involved. This is not simply a trip to the shopping mall. This is not something easily aborted. We must stay and complete our expedition. We have found nothing so far to justify the cost, and without that we will never be granted the opportunity to return. My tenure at the university will shield me from losing my position, but likely I'll never complete my work. Isaacs, he'll get by on his father's wealth, but the two of you? Your careers will be irrevocably damaged. Your graduate studies will have become a waste. This is the moment. This is the place where you both have to decide your respective futures. I already know what needs to be done. I implore you both to stay with me and discover those secrets hidden long before man's eyes could witness them. Stay with me and discover the true history of the world."

But Dogan wouldn't. And Wendell reluctantly concurred.

The three men split what remained of the food and set a timeline for Dr. Hanson's research. They agreed that he would keep trying to contact Gauthier via the satellite phone the pilot had given him, and when he got through he would let Gauthier know that both Dogan and Wendell had returned to the landing strip, and what his own coordinates were so the party could return to meet him. If before then anything should occur that might suggest Dr. Hanson was still being followed, he would immediately set out for the landing strip and join the two men there. Wendell didn't like the idea of leaving him alone, especially with little more than a half an energy bar and overburdened with excavation equipment, but there was no choice. Hanson insisted on completing the expedition, no matter what the cost.

Dogan, on the other hand, was not so committed. He and Wendell took the rest of the food and began their long hike back. Clearly, it wasn't lost on Dogan that he had chosen to retreat with his worst enemy; Wendell certainly felt no better about it.

The trek across Melville Island was as quiet as it had been the first time, the two men walking single file over the uneven terrain. But Wendell's dread made the journey much worse. They had been numbered five before, not two, and they hadn't carried the suspicion they were being stalked by a predator. On the occasions the two men stopped to rest, they didn't speak, sharing an overwhelming fear of what was happening. Wendell hoped if they remained silent the entire trip would simply be a hazy dream, one from which he'd soon awake. But he didn't.

His stomach rumbled after the second hour of their journey, and the sourness on his tongue arrived after the fourth. His head ached dully, letting him know his body was winding down. Dogan, too, seemed to be having trouble concentrating on the direction they were supposed to go, and more than once he stopped to ask if Wendell wanted to take the lead while he plotted their next steps.

They took a rest after a few hours to eat a portion of their reserves. It seemed so little once Wendell saw it through the eyes of hunger, and it took immense willpower to keep from swallowing it all. He was exhausted, and Dogan looked no different, his eyes rimmed with dark circles against pale skin. His voice, too, was throated.

"Who would have thought it would be you and me, trying to keep it together?"

Wendell wanted to laugh, but just wheezed air.

"I don't think anyone would believe it if we told them."

"I'm not sure I believe it myself."

And like that, things had changed between them. Wendell didn't know how long it would last, or if it would survive their return to civilization, but at that moment they were bonded, and Wendell would have done anything to keep Dogan at his side.

It was unclear how long they sat, silently building their strength for the journey ahead, but their stupor was broken by an unsettling howl. Dogan and Wendell straightened, eyes wide and searching the landscape in all directions for its source.

"There!" Dogan shouted, and went off running toward the sound, his feet sinking into snow as he dashed, his limbs flailing for balance. Wendell followed blindly in Dogan's footsteps, hand pressed against his pack to ensure nothing was spilled. When he finally caught up, both he and Dogan were panting, barely able speak.

"What did you see?"

Dogan pointed.

There was nothing there, but that wasn't what caused Wendell to shiver uncontrollably. It was instead what *had* been there, and the evidence it left in the crusted snow—a flurry of footprints, none larger than a barefooted child's. They proceeded in a line, leading back in the same direction from which Wendell and Dogan had come, as though whoever or whatever had made them had been keeping a steady watch on the two students since they left Dr. Hanson. It was no longer possible to avoid the truth: something was following them, something that wasn't a wolf or polar bear or any other northern predator. It was something else, and they knew absolutely nothing about it.

"What are we going to do?" Wendell asked. Dogan's eyes teared from the cold.

"What else *can* we do? We get the hell out of here right now."

They didn't stop until they reached the landing strip, both afraid of what might happen if they rested too long. By Wendell's watch it was well past midnight, though the frozen sunlight still shone, lighting their way. When they arrived, they found the strip vacant. No plane, no sign of life. Just a long stretch of iced snow and an ocean off in the distance. Wendell couldn't explain why the discovery was crushing—Gauthier and Isaacs had over a day's head start, and Wendell knew they wouldn't have waited. And yet it was devastating. He and Dogan had walked so far …

"On the bright side," Dogan said, "we know they found their way back. That means they'll be returning soon. It's better than finding them stranded like us."

"True, true."

Wendell looked back at the snow and ice they had walked across. There were shadows moving out in the nooks and recesses, but none that seemed unusual. Wendell wondered what an unusual shadow would even look like, and whether he was in any condition to find out.

"We need cover. Who knows how long we'll be waiting."

There was a depression in an ice drift that shielded them from the brunt of the wind and snow. Their combined body heat warmed the air enough to diminish the chill under their jackets, and Wendell was able to peel back the farthest fringes of his hood so he might speak to Dogan without shouting. It had been so long since their last snack, simply raising his voice aggravated his headache.

"Do you think Dr. Hanson is okay?"

"If anyone would be, I'd bet on him. That old man is resilient."

"I'm not sure we should have left him, though."

"He wanted us to."

"I know, I know. I just feel it was a mistake."

Wendell closed his eyes to rest them. The brightness of the snow after being under a hood for so long was blinding. It would take some time to adjust.

"Did you get a good look at it?" Dogan asked.

"At what? The snow?"

"No, not the snow, you idiot. What was following us in the snow. What left those footprints."

"I don't want to talk about it." He didn't even want to *think* about it. Dogan wouldn't be dissuaded.

"I'm sure I was close to it, but I barely saw anything more than a blur."

"Maybe you were seeing things. Maybe your hunger—"

"Did you, or didn't you, see those footprints in the snow?"

"I—"

"Do you think I put them there?"

"No, I—"

"Did you put them there?"

"How would I—?"

"Well, they got there somehow. Just like they got inside our camp. It wasn't an accident. It was something, watching us."

Wendell took off his mitten glove and rubbed the side of his face. It made him feel better, and slightly more present. "I don't know, Dogan. It so hard to think. I'm tired and hungry and terrified of what's out there and of never getting back home. My brain feels like mush."

"How much food do you have?"

He opened his pockets and turned out what was left. An eighth of a power bar, a handful of nuts. His water supply was okay, but only because he and Dogan had been filling their flasks with snow to melt.

Dogan assessed the situation.

"Yeah, I don't have much more than that, either."

"Are you worried?"

"About being here?" He frowned. "No. I'm sure Gauthier will be back."

"How can you be so sure?"

He shrugged.

"What else do I have to do?"

WENDELL EVENTUALLY FELL ASLEEP. He and Dogan had huddled close to conserve heat, and when they both ran out of energy to talk Wendell's eyes flickered one too many times. There was the sound of the ocean, and the wind rushing past, and then nothing until Dogan shook him awake.

"Look."

The snow had accumulated since they took shelter, and the footprints they had made were buried, but Wendell could still see the wedge cut into the corridor down which they'd come, and in the distance a solitary figure staggering toward them.

"Is that Dr. Hanson?" Wendell worried he was suffering from a starved hallucination.

"I don't know."

"Is it what's been following us?"

Dogan didn't respond.

Whether from hunger or cold or exhaustion, Wendell's eyes teared as he watched the limping figure. His muscles ached, trying to tense in anticipation but too exhausted to do so. The approaching shape resolved itself first for Dogan, who made an audible noise a moment before Wendell realized what—or rather whom—he was seeing. Isaacs stumbled forward, and a few steps before meeting Dogan and Wendell he crumpled and dropped to his knees, then collapsed face-first into the frozen snow.

They scrambled to him as quickly as their tired bodies could manage. Isaacs was nearly lifeless, his left leg bent at an angle that suggested it was broken, but leaning close Wendell could hear his shallow breathing. They wasted no time dragging Isaacs back to their shielded depression, and while Wendell did his best to splint the leg, Dogan brushed the remaining snow from Isaacs's face and pulled up his hood to help protect him.

"What do you think happened?" Dogan quietly asked.

"What do you mean?"

"He looks strange. What's up with his *eyes*?"

Wendell shook his head.

"I'm more concerned about what he is doing on Melville Island at all."

Isaacs breathed heavily as he lay unconscious. They shook him and called his name, worried about what had happened, but neither Dogan nor Wendell understood what he mumbled. There was something about a plane, which did not ease Wendell's worry.

When they were finally able to rouse him, Isaacs screamed. The piercing sound overloaded Dogan's starved brain and he lashed out, striking Isaacs in the face. Then Wendell was between them, urging both to calm down. Isaacs shook, pulled the straps of his hood tighter, hid his face. All that was left were his large watery eyes.

"Isaacs, it's okay. You're okay. I'm sorry I hit you, but you're safe. Do you understand?"

He was a trapped animal, shivering uncontrollably.

"Do you understand?"

Isaacs nodded.

"What happened?" Wendell asked. "Why are you here? Where's Gauthier?"

Isaacs continued to rock, hiding behind his drawn hood.

"It's okay, Isaacs. Just tell us what happened."

"Gauthier and I made it back here to the plane," he said. Even in his semi-consciousness, he sounded terrified. "The wings were iced, he said, and we couldn't take off. He told me to go outside with a bottle of propylene glycol and spray them down after he started the plane. He said the heat and the solution would melt everything. While I was doing that the wind was blowing like crazy. I thought I heard yelling, but wasn't sure. Then out of nowhere the plane was shaking. I lost my balance, and the plane jerked and started to move. I was falling and tried to grab hold of something, but the wing was slick and I was already rolling off it. I don't remember anything after that."

Wendell tried to make sense of Isaacs's story, but couldn't wrap his mind around it. He was exhausted, hunger and the elements taking their toll, and could barely think. He looked to Dogan, who appeared just as troubled.

"Did Gauthier say anything?" Dogan asked.

Isaacs shook his head, and it carved pain in his misshapen face. He was worsening, and there was nothing Dogan or Wendell could do. Already his lips had turned a bizarre shade of red, and his eyes could not focus. He coughed violently and spit pink into the snow. Then he lay his head down. "I can't. I—I don't want to die."

Wendell put his hand on Isaacs's shoulder.

"You aren't going to die here. We won't let you."

Isaacs coughed again.

Dogan and Wendell looked at each other. Dogan shook his head.

"We have to find Dr. Hanson. We need that satellite phone."

"We can't leave Isaacs," Wendell said. "He won't last without our help. And how are we supposed to find Dr. Hanson? We'll be dead before we do. We have no idea where he is. I think we're better off waiting right here."

They spent the next few hours trying to sleep in their makeshift shelter, the three men huddled to conserve warmth. While Dogan and Isaacs slept, the wind had become a gale, and it again brought with it the overpowering stench of fish and sea, so thick Wendell could hardly keep from gagging. He tucked his face into his coat as best he could to survive it.

The men did not sleep for long, but it was long enough that when they awoke they found Isaacs had crawled away from the safety of the depression and frozen to death. It made no sense, but nothing did any longer. The arctic cold of Melville Island had upended everything. Dogan was upset and wanted to drag Isaacs back, close enough to protect his body should anything come looking for it, but he didn't have the strength left. Neither of them did. It was then they agreed, for the sake of the fallen Isaacs, that their hunger had become too severe. But when they turned out their pockets, they found them empty. Isaacs, too, had been stripped of all food and supplies. There was nothing left to sustain them. Dogan cried, certain he'd eaten all their shares unwittingly in a somnambulistic frenzy, but Wendell wasn't convinced. It didn't explain the hazy footprints that encircled them.

Dogan and Wendell paced in the subzero weather, trudging out a trail while trying to keep themselves warm. Eventually, even the effort of pacing proved beyond Dogan, and he stumbled and toppled to the ground. Wendell knelt down but didn't have strength to help. All he could do was stay nearby.

"I can't keep going," Dogan said. "I can't."

"We have to," Wendell said.

But Wendell knew they would never make it. They started talking then to keep themselves awake and alert, to remind each other not to give up. They talked about how they came to be under Dr. Hanson. They talked about Isaacs, about whether he had crawled away on purpose, or if it was due to some horrible mistake. They talked about Gauthier

and what had happened to him. But mostly they talked about themselves, their childhoods, their lives before meeting. They talked until they couldn't, until Dogan was delirious and stopped making sense. Wendell tried to rouse him, to keep him moving, but he couldn't. He didn't have the energy. So tired, he could barely keep his eyes open. They fluttered more and more until they stopped completely. Before they did, the last thing Wendell saw was something in the distance, crouching. Watching them. And then it moved.

A SLAP THAT TORE OFF HIS FACE woke him from death. He opened his stinging eyes, and only his lethargic malnourishment prevented him from screaming. The shrunken man's face hung inches from his own. It was dark brown, as though deeply tanned, with lips grey to the point of blue. He did not tremble, though he was dressed in nothing more than a cloth that covered his sex, and he was perilously thin. What startled Wendell most, however, were his eyes. They were larger than any Wendell had ever seen, and spaced so far apart they threatened to slide off his skull. He couldn't have been more than four feet tall. Wendell was certain it wasn't a dream, but if it were it was the worst dream he'd ever suffered. He tried to moisten his mouth to get his tongue working, and when he did all he could hazily croak was, "Dogan?"

The half-man grunted, then hobbled away. Wendell wanted to pull himself up, but discovered he had been swaddled with furs. He could turn his head, but only with great difficulty, and only enough to see Dogan similarly wrapped a few meters away. Dogan had two more of the dark half-men at his head, and they were trying to feed him though he was still unconscious. Isaacs lay face down a few feet further in the snow, a fourth shrunken man holding his lifeless arm to his grey lips and sniffing. Wendell nodded at no one in particular, and as the world grew dark once more he felt he was being dragged. In his delirium, the dragging went on and on forever.

◆◆◆

SOMETHING WAS WRIGGLING IN HIS MOUTH, trying to crawl down his throat. Wendell struggled awake, gagging, and managed to spit it out. A piece of unrecognizable yellow meat curled on the ice, while a short distance away those small dark half-men from his nightmare danced, their bare feet crunching on the snow. There was no longer anything binding his limbs but weakness, and he'd been left propped up next to Dogan. Both of them were awake and shaking.

Only unrecognizable pieces remained of poor Isaacs.

"I don't know what's going on, Wendell. I don't know where we are, but look." Dogan nodded his head across the ice and Wendell saw Dr. Hanson. He lay face down in the snow, unmoving, his pack beside him and torn open, equipment scattered. Wendell squinted to see if the satellite phone was still there, and in his concentration missed what Dogan was saying.

"Do you see it?" Dogan repeated.

"I think so. It's right by his hand."

"No, you idiot. Do you see *it*?"

Wendell looked up again, past Dr. Hanson and at the group of five near-naked men dancing before a shorn wall of ice. It stretched out further than the end of his sight in either direction; the break no doubt formed when tectonic plates shifted the glacier. What was uncovered was so impossible Wendell would have thought his mind had cracked had Dogan not witnessed it first.

There was a monstrous creature encased halfway in the solid ice. It had large unlidded eyes, milky white; its mouth wide and round, its scaled flesh reflecting light dully. Where its neck might have been was a ring of purplish pustules, circling the fusion of its ichthyic skull to its tendonous body. Chunked squid limbs lay outstretched, uncontrollable in its death. The air was again dominated by the overpowering odor of the sea. The shrunken men before it treated it as a god, and yet it was clear the five could not have been the ones to uncover it—with the sharpened rocks they used as tools it would

have taken generations to carve that deep and that much. They peeled strips of its flesh away and ate them raw, and when they looked back at Dogan and Wendell it was suddenly evident why their features had transformed over time, their eyes grown wider, jaws shorter, skin rougher. Their fish faces stared at Wendell, expectantly. It was true he was hungry beyond imagination, but he was not so hungry that he might eat what they presented.

The sour taste and sensation of what they had previously tried to feed him returned, and he looked down. The morsel continued to writhe slowly in the snow.

"Did you—did they make you eat any?" Wendell asked, then realized Dogan had turned the palest shade. They had. Wendell feared for his life, and his sanity.

"How do I look?" Dogan managed through his chattering teeth, and Wendell lied and told him he was fine. Was Wendell imagining the flesh had already changed him, already started prying his eyes apart? Was it even possible after so small a meal? But he realized with horror that he didn't know how much Dogan had willingly eaten, nor if either of them had been force-fed in their delirium.

"Can you move?" Wendell asked, fleetingly energized by his fear. "We need to get that phone. We need to call for help."

"How? Even if we manage to get it, we'll never escape with it. We have no idea where we are. We might not even be on Melville Island anymore."

"We have to try. Maybe Gauthier has already come back and is waiting for us at the landing strip. What else can we do? End up like Dr. Hanson and bleed out in the snow? Or worse, like Isaacs, torn to pieces?"

"We should escape."

"And what then?" Wendell whispered. "Die in the snow, waiting for them to find us?"

Dogan paled.

"Did you—did you see that?"

Wendell looked up. The five dark men sat mesmerized before their dead idol.

"It moved," Dogan said. "Did you see it move?"

"It can't move. Whatever that thing is, it's dead."

"It's not dead—look, it moved again."

Wendell looked closer at Dogan's face and saw the swelling and the subtle distortion. There was no longer time to gather strength. Whatever they fed him, Dogan had eaten more than he thought. It was transforming him. Wendell did not want to suffer the same fate.

"Stay here," he said, though when he looked over he wasn't certain he'd been heard. Dogan appeared fascinated by what was trapped in the ice.

Wendell lowered himself onto his stomach and crawled toward Dr. Hanson, keeping an eye on the gathering of disciples ahead. He moved elbow-to-knee as slowly as he dared, not willing to risk being seen. The half-men were feral, and as smart as they were, they were still animals, waiting to attack anything that moved. Wendell had only one chance to get the satellite phone and figure out a way of escaping from the nightmare he and Dogan found themselves in. His hunger had not abated, but enough strength had returned that he was able to make it to Dr. Hanson's body in under ten minutes.

The tribe of half-men had not moved from around their dead idol. They bounced on their haunches, made noises like wild animals, followed imaginary movement before them with precision. What was strange, however, was that each reacted differently to what it saw, as though they did not share the same sight. One stood while another howled, the rest looking in different directions. Wendell couldn't make sense of it, and reminded himself not to try. He had to focus on that satellite phone and getting back.

He searched the body, doing his best to forget who it had been. Dr. Hanson's face had been removed—the pale flesh frozen, tiny blood icicles reaching from the pulpy mess to the ground. Wendell turned to keep from panicking and checked the pockets of Hanson's coat and everywhere he could reach for the satellite phone. But it wasn't there. Wendell rolled on his side and tried unsuccessfully to flag Dogan for help. Dogan was staring straight ahead at the impossible giant embedded in the ice, eyes open wide and spread far apart.

Dr. Hanson's pack was ripped open in the blood-soaked snow, the items within trapped in sticky ice. Wendell heard a loud creak and froze. In his mind's eye he saw himself spotted, then swarmed by ugly bodies and ripped limb from limb. But when he raised his head he found nothing had changed. The five men remained bent in supplication. Almost by accident Wendell spotted the leather pouch Gauthier had given Dr. Hanson pinned beneath the doctor's torso. Wendell managed to pry it free of the ice, then put it into his own pocket and gently eased his way back the distance to Dogan. Or what was left of Dogan.

"Come on. Let's go," Wendell whispered, but Dogan didn't respond. Wendell grabbed his wrist and tried yanking, but Dogan had become a dead-weight, staring beatifically ahead, his face transformed. Mouth agape, eyes spread apart, staring at the dead thing as though it were alive, Dogan was unblinking as tears streamed down his sweating face. Dogan, Wendell's enemy, Wendell's friend, was gone.

There would be time for grief later. Wendell reached over and put his hand on Dogan's shoulder. "Stay strong. I'll be back as soon as I can with help." Then he attempted to stand and discovered he wasn't able. His legs had given up for good, buckling as Wendell put weight on them. He tried again and again, desperate to escape before it was too late, but he couldn't get up. After a few minutes, Wendell felt the sensation in his hands going, too, his control slipping away. Everything he saw took on a hazy glow, the edges of his vision crystalizing. The sky jittered, as did the snow.

Dogan wasn't the only one who'd had his unconscious hunger overfed with flesh. It was no wonder they had been left unbound at the edge of the camp and ignored. The creatures had no worry. All the damage had long been done. They simply needed to wait.

Wendell scrambled the small leather bag he had taken from Dr. Hanson's body out of his pocket. He prayed the satellite phone would be unharmed, that Gauthier had already returned and was waiting for them. If Wendell could only call him, it might not be too late for rescue. He could still escape the horrible things he was witnessing. That creature in the ice—Wendell thought he saw it move, thought he saw one of its giant milky eyes blink, even though so much of its flesh had already been stripped. It blinked, and the coils that sprouted free from the ice twitched and rolled, and a scream built inside him. But when it escaped it wasn't a scream at all but laughter. Laughter and joy. That terrified Wendell further, the joy, because it finally turned the five beasts his way. They rolled onto their haunches, staring at Wendell and his catatonic friend.

Wendell took off his glove and reached into the bag slowly to remove the phone, but what he found there was nothing of the sort. It was another kind of escape, the one thing a man like Gauthier would hand over when he was suggesting that someone protect himself. From out of the leather bag Wendell withdrew a handgun, and even in the cold wind he could smell the oiled metal.

Those five men looking agitated and more bestial than ever before. They snarled, while behind them a giant that Wendell refused to believe was alive illuminated like the sun pinned above. It filled the horizon with streaks of light, tendrils dancing from the old one's gargantuan head. It looked at the five half-men radiating in the glow. It looked at Dogan, kneeling and waiting for it to speak to him. Then it looked at Wendell and all Wendell's hunger was satiated; he was at one with everything.

But he knew it was a lie. It was the end of things, no matter what the disembodied voices told him. The five shrunken men approaching him stealthily on all fours would not return him to civilization, would not return him to health. Dogan and he would be something more to them—sustenance in the cold harshness of the Arctic, pieces of flesh chewed and swallowed, digits shorn until they rained on the snow. These things were much like Wendell, in a way. Much like everyone. They struggled to unearth what they worshipped most, something from a world long ago gone, and if remembered, then only barely and as a fantasy. But it was far more real than Wendell had ever wished.

Those subhuman things were closing in, and there was little else Wendell could do but surrender to them, let them take him away.

Or he could use Gauthier's gun.

He lifted the weapon and squeezed the trigger. The half-men scattered, but not before he put two of them down. The alien's appendages flailed madly, and waves of emotion and nausea washed over Wendell. He couldn't stand, but was eventually able to hit the remaining three as they scrambled for cover. It took no time at all for him to be the last man alive, surrounded by the blood and gore of everyone he knew. Everyone but the mesmerized Dogan.

It was too late for either of them. Even with the half-men dead, Wendell could feel the draw of the flickering creature in the ice, and knew he would be unable to resist much longer. In an act of charity and compassion, he raised the gun to Dogan's temple and squeezed the trigger. There was a bright flash, and a report that continued to echo over the landscape longer than in his ears. Dogan crumpled, the side of his head vaporized, his misery tangible in the air.

But it was not enough. That thing in the ice, it needed him, needed somebody's worship on which to feed, and as long as Wendell was alive it would not die.

Wendell put the gun against his own head, the hot barrel searing his flesh, but he could do nothing else. His fingers would not move, locked into place from fear or exhaustion or self-preservation. Or whatever it was that had been fed to him, pulling the flesh on his face tighter. Somehow the handgun fell from his weakened grasp, dropping onto the icy snow and sinking. He reached to reclaim it and toppled forward, collapsing in a heap that left him staring into those giant old milky eyes.

WENDELL DIDN'T KNOW HOW LONG he lay in the snow. He was no longer cold, was no longer hungry. He felt safe, as though he might sleep forever. The old one in the ice spoke to him, telling him things about the island's eonic history, and he listened and watched and waited. Existence moved so slowly Wendell saw the sun finally creep across the sky. No one came for him. No one came to interrupt his communion with the dead god.

All he had was what was forever in its milky white stare, while it ate the flesh and muscle and sinew of his body, transforming him into the first of its new earthly congregation.

"On Ice" originally appeared in Simon Strantzas' collection Burnt Black Suns, *published in 2014 by Hippocampus Press.*

Simon Strantzas is the author of Burnt Black Suns *(Hippocampus Press, 2014),* Nightingale Songs *(Dark Regions Press, 2011),* Cold to the Touch *(Tartarus Press, 2009), and* Beneath the Surface *(Humdrumming, 2008), as well as the editor of* Aickman's Heirs *(Undertow Publications, 2015), a finalist for both the World Fantasy and British Fantasy Awards, and the winner of the Shirley Jackson Award. He also edited* Shadows Edge *(Gray Friar Press, 2013), and was the guest editor of* The Year's Best Weird Fiction, *Vol. 3 (Undertow Publications, 2016). His writig has been reprinted in* Best New Horror, The Best Horror of the Year, The Year's Best Weird Fiction *and* The Year's Best Dark Fantasy & Horror, *and published in venues such as* Cemetery Dance, Postscripts, *and* Nightmare. *His short story "Pinholes in Black Muslin" was a finalist for the British Fantasy Award, and his collection,* Burnt Black Suns, *a finalist for the Shirley Jackson Award. He lives with his wife in Toronto, Canada.*

Deadly planets posed a problem for Triple-S, and there was but one solution: total destruction. That is, until ... someone spoke up.

NOISEMAKER

by Marc Vun Kannon

SUDDEN, LETHAL, AND COMPLETE.
Triple-S made that verdict, and Triple-S—*AKA* Special System Services, the closest thing to a government in the Sol system—had quarantined the planet because of it. It would be the business of their operator to confirm or rescind it, in what would be his first official act as an Operator Solo. Live or die.

That man stood before the darkened glass screen of the ready room, using it as a mirror rather than viewing the planet below, the one he was about to judge. "Hi," he said to himself, "My name is Robert Marquand, and I killed a planet today. How have you been?" *Dad and his damned 'movies'. Now he's got me quoting them.* Dad would never kill a planet, though, no matter how many people wanted him to. Hopefully it wouldn't come to that, it wasn't why he'd joined up. *Following footsteps. Heh. Filling shoes. None of that prepared you for—*

He tired of his own reflections. "Screen."

The screen lit up, replacing his own ghostly visage with that of the planet he'd come to study, to save if he could, to kill if he must. It could have been the same image from his files, except for the lack of data in the corner, the big 'SILENCE' in currently-fashionable angular lettering. Despite the name, the planet called Silence wasn't golden, just the usual blue-green of a typical class M world. A very nice class M world, like Earth at its best.

A world where none of the animal life made any kind of sound.

He found this claim a little hard to believe, but the file was right about everything else. No communications detectable from orbit, no installations either, nothing the orbiting satellites could detect. No globally dominant species. Animal samples were supposed

to be ridiculously easy to capture, since they couldn't hear you coming, but not so easy to keep alive in captivity apparently. All went into some sort of paralyzed state and died shortly thereafter. This made them hard to study.

"It ain't gonna change, you know. We're in synchronous orbit."

Ah, my day is complete. Robert kept his eyes on the screen, as if he still watched it or wanted to. He didn't even blink. "I know that, Mr. Cale. It was my request, as you recall." A System Special Services operator's request is effectively an order. *Absolute authority.* Except to the medic, his caretaker, who apparently thought himself either a babysitter or a zookeeper on alternate days. "I was merely reviewing the notes, making sure I remembered them accurately. You interrupted me before I got to the latabs and the stobor." Robert kept his face straight, wondering if the other man would ask.

He didn't. "Sorry, your worshipfulness, but your shuttle is ready."

That was quick. The company funding this was desperate for its immigration license, and the sooner he got down there the sooner they would get it, native life forms be damned. *And damned they would be.* Marquand turned. "Hmm, well, I guess I shall just have to hope that the stobor don't attack while I'm there, then."

"You could just rescind the order right now."

"For some people, 'could' is a very small word." Marquand suddenly understood the meaning of his instructor's lament, a ship's crew full of understanding. "No, Mr. Cale, I cannot. An entire outpost was apparently destroyed between one transmission and the next. We have to know what did that. For ourselves and for their families." He had to know *why* he was burning a planet to the ground.

"You could take a weapon, then."

Robert smiled. "Good Heavens, Mr. Cale, that's a splendid idea. What should I take? A tranq that might not work on their biochemistry, or a stunner that might not work on their neurophysiology? No, I think I shall rely instead on my wits."

"So you're taking nothing?"

Robert looked shocked. "Of course not. We have a saying in Triple-S, Mr. Cale. A weapon should not be seen until it is used." He tapped the side of his head suggestively.

"Yeah? Well, we got a saying where I come from, too, kid. 'Don't take a brain to a knife fight.'"

Robert smiled again, genuinely amused. "I'll keep that in mind." He went over to the screen and picked up his case, its contents known only to him. "Logout." As he brushed past his caretaker he asked, "Wish me luck?"

Mr. Cale looked at him a little sourly. "Don't worry, kid. I'll see you again, soon enough."

MARQUAND WAS ON THE SHUTTLE and buckled into his seat before he realized that the medic hadn't really said anything. He patted his case, testing its bindings. Then everything fell out from under him, the shuttle dropping into space and hurtling *planetward* at its usual breakneck speed. Pilots are like that, Triple-S or not.

Triple-S passengers have better things to do. He'd read the data before going into the pod for the trip, but a review couldn't hurt. By the time they hit atmosphere he had played through almost the entire set of transmissions from the research outpost set up to study the fauna of this world *in situ*. He'd already scanned the sidebars, analyses, and reports aplenty from every scientist on hand, it seemed, all of them apparently eager to crack the mystery, get their names into the history books for their fields.

They'd done that, for sure, but not with science, and he listened not to the science, but to the scientist. The flow of words, the meter, the rhythm, the pacing. Differing personalities, all of them in competition even while they complemented each other. So that he—not being a big fan of words like *sudden*—could try to tell when it started to go wrong. Aside from some minor medical discomforts, most likely the result of having to eat local foods after an 'elephant' stepped on their food synthesizer, nothing much seemed to be out of place. Only the last contact gave any hint of a larger problem, but that could as easily have been the result of days of chronic low-level pain talking.

What could be in the last contact plus one? Whatever prevented them from making it also stopped any alarm from being given, or sending the latest reports instantly and leaving the system primed for remote access. Which hadn't happened. Marquand looked out the port, at a silent planet gone more silent than usual, wondering what it would say in its defense when he made it speak, given what it said now.

Sudden, lethal, and complete.

◆ ◆ ◆

The fence is up, so it's probably not stobor.

A second later, his implant responded, **Why? What are stobor?**

No idea, said Marquand. **But I'm glad you asked. We stole the idea from a science fiction story, where they used it to refer to a dangerous animal that didn't always look dangerous but could be. When the attack came it was a stampede or a migration or something—**

Which would have taken out the fence.

Exactly. Marquand stopped to catch his breath and look around. His case was heavy and now he'd have to go uphill to the buildings.

What if they were small?

What?

What if they were small? Like ants or rats or something?

Hell, it would take *him* a few minutes to get up there! **Too slow. The scientists could have tripped the alarm, and probably stood on chairs to escape.**

Oh yeah. The voice in his ear paused a bit. **And anything too big would've crushed the buildings, and I'm guessing they ain't crushed since you would'a said if they were.**

Correct. Marquand saved his breath for the ascent and let the other guy do his reporting for him.

So you're expecting something man-sized, but faster and nastier than a man.

Which pretty much described latabs. 'Lions and tigers and bears, oh my!' **Stop cheering me up.**

◆ ◆ ◆

LATABS, DEFINITELY, but smaller, faster, meaner. Smarter, if the patterns of wounds meant anything. Everywhere, judging from the bullet holes. Ninja flying monkeys.

None of them lying around. Either all the bullets missed or they took their dead with them. Not good either way. *And yet very good.* Plenty of human bodies, though. No armor; they'd clearly gotten lax. Not a big surprise, just about everything shunned them, even the 'elephant' had been running *away.* He looked at his own armor. Saturn Base was also a bit lax, too accustomed to being a backwater instead of a gateway. They'd not had anything heavier or smarter when this ship came in.

His implant interrupted his muttered observations. **Take lots of blood samples, Operator. Set up the Q-Mod.**

Blood samples. Marquand opened his case. Right. Brain suck for the computer. He plugged the cable from his portable Q-Mod unit into the nearest port and started it going. This would also open the system so the ship above could copy the same data. As an afterthought he turned on the speakers, just to hear a friendly voice. Any voice. Even the wheezy-voiced anatomist with a penchant for big words.

Heh. 'Meta-sympathetic?' *What the hell does* that *mean?* Marquand listened for a minute more. *Thought so. He made it up.* Good thing Marquand had a BA in BS.

Back to the case, and ... the scanner! Record the scene for posterity. And for family. Behind him the speaking voice changed, one of the biochemists. Marquand paused to listen to the new scientist, only to discover that he sounded like the old scientist, the one he'd just listened to. *Well, no surprise that the anatomist shared his theory with someone.* Robert thought about that. *No he wouldn't. Let someone else get the glory?* Hell no.

The scanner could verify identities without him having to get too close. Well, most of the time, but it couldn't find some of the transponder chips that should have been in the bodies and he really didn't want to know where they were now. Behind him the speaking voice changed, and again Marquand paused to listen. 'Meet the new boss,' he played the lyric in his head, 'Same as the old boss.' *No.* That was completely untenable in this scenario. He'd have to see what Bergman had to say, a physicist instead of all these old bio-types. Plus she didn't agree with anyone, not without a fight. Never totally. This ... like-mindedness ... was odd, and in the Operator business odd was never good.

Bad enough he had to get close enough to scan the ID strip, backup to the transponder, or in one case, the *second* backup, an ID strip on the bottom of the shoe, which almost never gets eaten. Behind him the speaking voice changed: Bergman, thank God. He devoted more of his attention to her and less to the scene before him.

Not. Great steaming piles of Not. Logs and logs of infighting, vicious in their way, don't come to nothing overnight.

CRASH!

Marquand spun into a crouch, arm coming up, finger already squeezing the trigger as he aimed at the spot his ears had pinpointed. The great brute beast on the table where his Q-Mod had been never stood a chance as he ... scanned it. *Dammit.* Too late to go for his pistol, he'd lost the element of surprise. None of them, and he saw quite a few, even looked at him as he moved and drew, but they all perked up as he took their picture.

They bared their teeth, but he doubted they were smiling for him. He stood.

They cringed, and backed away. *What the hell?* "Are you afraid of me?" He asked, not to get an answer, but to have the question on record.

The one up on top of the table moved. Faster than Marquand could track, it flowed down off the table, across the floor, and slammed into his chest, driving its exposed claws into the light armor as it pinned him against the wall and sent the scanner flying. This one wasn't afraid, no, but it was *something.* Marquand stared his death in the eye. "I'm not like them, am I?"

It backed off.

The others advanced, forming a ring around them as the leader dropped down, claws shrieking against the armor, and stalked away. *Interesting.* Too bad there was no time to send a detailed report via implant, but station optics should give them in the ship a good show. Any good Triple-S man should be able to take it from there.

Not good enough. There would be no "there" to take it to. Them, up in the ship, would be more than happy to torch the place if he should fall, rather than leave it quarantined. By the time some other Triple-S man realized their mistake it would be far too late, for *this* world.

The latabs trembled, claws flexing against the floor. Anticipation, maybe. Or perhaps a desire to rip him to pieces at war with a desire to run away. They feared him, he knew, but the leader didn't, and they were following for now. Waiting for it to prove to them that he wasn't anything to fear, and then they'd start tearing into him too.

He'd brought his brain to a knife fight.

Of course, he'd also brought a knife, because he wasn't a total fool. Mr. Cale's knife, to be precise, plucked neatly from its concealed sheath as Marquand brushed by him that final time. His own blade was much too large, a weapon he only showed because he didn't plan to use it. He liked the feel of Cale's blade as it slid into his hand, and decided to get one for himself.

The latab leader came back into view, mounting the table where he'd first seen it, and the followers grew still.

Now would be a good time for some Boost. Marquand hated most accelerants, a few seconds of speed and strength in exchange for a few hours of feeling like total crap. He'd also seen how fast this latab could move, though, so he signaled his relatively dumb armor to dose him with the stimulant. His skin felt like it had caught fire, as he knew it would.

The gesture provoked the latab leader to attack, as he thought it might. It moved, it flowed ... ever more slowly to his senses, Boosted as they were to superhuman speeds. He could perceive almost as fast as he could see, move nearly as fast as he could perceive. Hopefully move faster than he would feel. Bodies weren't designed to move as fast as minds, and they reminded their owners of that fact as soon as they caught up.

The latab loped across the floor, and Marquand waited, letting his target come to him. Boosted reflexes could tear him up inside just walking across the room, so he meant to move as little as possible ... *Now*.

Sudden. Lethal.

Complete.

And very, very, messy. The remaining pack animals fled the room as fast as they could dig trenches in the floor for the traction. Marquand sealed the doors behind them.

Then the Boost wore off.

Oh, ow. He didn't ask for nerveblock. His armor wouldn't have allowed it anyway, Boost and painkillers don't mix. Death-dealing should have consequences.

Marquand wanted to sink into the nearest chair. He couldn't move. He didn't want to try. He had to think and he didn't want to do that either. At least it didn't *hurt*. His Q-Mod, lying useless on the floor, called to him and his sense of duty. Nothing else got him to shuffle over there, put the knife on the console, and bend all the way down to the floor and all the way up again, just to plug it back into the port. He rewarded himself by sitting down.

The room stank of dead beast. Another's sacrifice. Another consequence of a job well done. *Only fair.* Certainly the beast wasn't feeling any pain now. Marquand turned his head—slowly!—to look at it. Lots of blood samples. "All things considered," he muttered, "I'd still rather feel like me than you." He saluted the creature, he owed it that much.

Time to call in. He wasn't going to get anything else done today.

◆◆◆

"HEY KID," SAID CALE, entering the room with a vigor that made everyone else tired immediately. "Told you I'd be seeing you again."

Marquand raised a brow. "With my shield, or on it?"

"Yeah." Cale was being either obtuse or obscure, Marquand couldn't tell which. "I'd tell you what you look like, but there's children present."

They were alone in the room. *Ha-ha.* "You should see the other guy."

Cale shook his head. "Saw the vid already. Nice job. We got the body on ice till we get back, should make the suits happy."

Most of the things that made suits back home happy bothered Marquand. "Why?"

Cale looked at him funny. "This is a joke, right? You can't be that stupid. Look, kid, what good's an immigrant license gonna do 'em if they can't get immigrants? Who'd colonize a planet with 'Sudden, Lethal, and Complete' stamped all over it? People can live with 'sudden animal attacks.'" He chuckled. "So to speak. You clear up the mystery and they can start organizing safaris, for God's sake."

Hunting parties. Which would kill without sport, and then be killed without mercy. Just like the outpost, a ghastly vision. "Sorry to disappoint you."

Cale initiated another test, to see if his patient was able to take painkillers yet. "Huh? What are you talking about, you did it already."

So close, he could feel it. So close he could stare into its eyes, feel its breath on his cheek. "No, I didn't," Marquand said with a sigh. "Lethal and complete, maybe."

"What about 'sudden'?"

"Yes, what about 'sudden'?" Marquand actually waved a hand around, he was so excited. "These scientists were so ignored for so long that the guards weren't even wearing armor! The largest animals, the fiercest predators, all run away. *Ran* away. Until they didn't, and then they did again. It makes no sense." *Why* did it turn away?

Cale nodded. "You'd think they'd try to kill one of 'em first, at least one. Cut the weakest from the herd, like a pack would on Earth."

Marquand found himself nodding, and stopped. *Hmmm....*

ROBERT MARQUAND STARED at the little red dot

on the screen of the ready-room, a dot indicating the position of the now-defunct base. That dot was a major victory for him, of sorts, one that could turn into a minor black-eye if his suspicions turned out to be…um…baseless. They certainly seemed strange enough. Only his Operator's authority had kept the captain from laughing in his face and blowing the place from orbit.

His position wouldn't save him from Triple-S if they should decide against him, which is why he spent more time than usual on his report. All the time with his mentor didn't prepare him for this. His parents did him far more good, even as a photo and a set of memories. They'd been pulled off of normal cases to handle strange cases, off of strange cases to handle stranger cases. He wished he could talk to them about this one. Ironic, for a case that was all about communication.

On a silent world.

If there was a word Marquand liked less than 'sudden' it was 'telepathy', another familial prejudice. Pack behavior required some form of communication, and the scientists had been the first to dismiss body language as insufficient. Something in between, maybe, like that anatomist's 'metasympathy'. Just another sort of … sense. What must it be like, to hunt your prey by 'sense', to evade your hunter by 'sense'? What terror must have struck in the hearts of all, even the strongest latabs, when the first researchers arrived, not broadcasting anything. What hunters they must have seemed, and such prey, when they suddenly, completely, lethally started broadcasting. Or maybe it was the Q-Mod, they'd gone after that first when he went down, hadn't even noticed him until he scanned them.

Well. Whatever the cause, he'd want some solid research to back it up, and you can't do solid research if the base was blown from orbit. Research licenses were trickier than immigration licenses, but a world where eating local foods made you a target for every predator was marginal at best, not colonizable without a burn-and-reseed. Choosing between a definite cost like that and a possible bonanza that research might bring should be a no-brainer for any corporate. If they didn't have enough funding, that was *their* problem, not his. They could always sell the license.

His problems were more mundane. He had to finalize his report—Done!—and send it off to the nearest beacon—Done!—and then he could get ready for the pod. "Logoff."

The screen went dark, his own face staring back at him. "Hi," he said to himself. "My name is Robert Marquand, and I just saved a planet today. How have you been?"

☻ ☻ ☻

Marc Vun Kannon, after surviving his teen age years, entered Hofstra University. Five years later, he exited with a BA in philosophy and a wife. He still has both, but the wife is more useful. Since then he almost accumulated a PhD in philosophy and has acquired a second BA in Computer Science. After dabbling in fulfilling pursuits such as stock boy and gas station attendant, he found his spiritual home as a software support engineer, for CAMP Systems International.

Marc puts his degrees in Philosophy and Computer Science to good use writing stories about strange things that happen to ordinary people. His wife and three children think it's harmless enough, and it keeps him out of trouble. As a philosopher (his first novel, Unbinding the Stone, *demanded he write it while he was in Graduate School), his main interest is in the characters, and as a Computer geek his technique is to follow the character's and story's logic to 'grow' a story organically. His main rule when writing is to not do again what he's already seen done before, resulting in books that are hard to describe. Visit Marc at authorguy.wordpress.com*

What was the deadly truth awaiting the crew of the *Louis Leaky* ... deep within a crater on a barren alien world?

METANOIA

by Kurt Newton

MY NAME IS GARY HARDINGER, SENIOR ECOBIOLOGIST OF THE EXPLORERSHIP *ECHO.* Three of our crew are now dead: Tom Pritchard, Arnaud Jakes and Cristo Gianopolis. Sacrificed in the name of corporate exploration in the ever-widening search for living space and just plain greed. "Free" enterprise, they call it. But then, nothing is ever truly free. Everything has its price, its cost, if not monetary, then in sweat and tears, and most often, in blood.

I sit here, stranded on this alien landscape, separated from our last remaining crew member, who sits holed up inside our landing craft, the *Louis Leaky,* unwilling to let me in. He believes I am a threat. I believe him irrational, mentally broken by what has transpired. I don't blame him. But I will die out here if I don't get onto the lander before it takes off on its scheduled launch, 48 hours from now.

This is for the Investigators, for my family, but mostly for myself. I need something to occupy my mind, to fill the void that would otherwise be drowned by the terror that waits for me each night as the sun slips quietly below the horizon.

DAY 1

WE LANDED FOUR HUNDRED METERS southwest of the proposed site, on a narrow plain between a cluster of craters. The *Louis Leaky* grabbed onto the hard-packed surface with a jolt, but it was an otherwise perfect landing. We gazed out at the alien environment. The terrain was barren, nothing but rocks and dust, but air-sampling indicated this planet may once have supported vigorous plant life, a perfect candidate for class-M regeneration.

Another trophy for the shelf of the Collective.

We named her *Arroyo.*

Volcanic ranges to the north spit clouds of phosphorus and sulfur dioxide in a low-level concentration—not enough to require full breathing apparatus, but nosetubes were in order. The added sweetness of oxygen helped to color the taste of powdered egg yolk. Only Jakes, our crew chief, opted to breathe the atmosphere direct. He said the tubes were like having somebody else's finger up your nose. Jakes had seen and probably smelled much worse.

By twilight we had set up camp on a ridge overlooking our focal point—a medium-sized dust-bowl crater. If the computer was right, deep down inside, trapped in the regolith, lay the remnants of a dying world just waiting to be reborn.

As I recall, the excitement level was high that first night. Tom, Cristo and I were stretched out by the thermal generator, tired from the long day of campsite setup. Henry was clearing the debris from the evening's meal, whistling a melody from his disc of off-world show tunes. Even Jakes, whose ass was as hard as the stones we rested our heads upon, was feeling upbeat. He lit up one of his contraband cigars and blew white puffs of aromatic smoke into our faces. "Life is good," he said. He coughed then, his face turning red in the alien starlight. "Did I ever tell you guys the story of Enos Jackson?"

There was a collective groan. All except from Henry, who took every opportunity to bathe in Jakes' afterglow. "Go ahead, Chief, I'd like to hear it."

Tom turned to me and rubbed his nose. I, in turn, made a ring with my hands and pretended to stick my entire head through it. Cristo tried to keep from laughing. "Yes, Chief, go ahead, we'd love to hear it," said Tom. We sat back and listened as Jakes' voice cut into the rarified air.

"Enos Jackson was a crew member on one of the very first exploratory missions into the Alpha Systems. Enos and five others landed on what was to become New Earth, a planet still in the early stages of development. During exploration, a seismic disruption caused a rockslide, burying two of the crew and trapping three others in a cave pocket at the base of a cliff, alive but unable to free themselves. Enos had been back at the landing craft and both had been untouched. He radioed for help, but in the early days a distress signal took days to be answered, and help wouldn't arrive for months. All he needed to do was to keep his head and provide food for those trapped until help came. Enos must have panicked. When the rescue ship landed, three months later, they found Enos sealed inside the landing craft, the radio equipment destroyed. He was still alive, though hysterical. He kept saying he could hear voices. The rest of the crew was found behind the rubble at the base of the cliffside. The three trapped crew members were long dead. The official cause: starvation. It was rumored, however, that two of the three had been found with their append-

ages removed. Funny thing—physically, Enos looked no worse for the wear, he hadn't dropped a pound."

Jakes took a long pull on his cigar and let the smoke stream out of his mouth like P10 gas. "Enos was put in a government facility on Mars. They said he had shouting matches with no one anyone could see. Two names were said to be heard most often—the two former crew members who were found with their body parts missing. A few months later, Enos was found dead. Official cause: undetermined. Although, some say Enos' body looked like it had been beaten to death ... from the inside."

There was a long pause before Tom said, "That's one cheery tale, Chief."

"Yeah, I'm all warm and fuzzy inside," I added.

"Can you tell us another one?" asked Henry.

Cristo burst out laughing.

"No, Henry. That's all for tonight." Jakes gently ground out his cigar, pocketing the remainder for later. "I'll see you boys bright and early. Pleasant dreams." He headed off to his sleeper. Henry followed close behind.

Tom saluted from his prone position. "Well, I'm turning in, too. See you guys in the morning."

Cristo also got up and quietly headed off to his own sleep area.

I didn't want to move. But if I didn't slip into my sleeper, before too long, the cold would descend and turn my blood to ice crystals. I turned off the thermal generator and, after logging the day's events, I settled into my protective sheath and zipped up.

The stars overhead filled my view. I lay for moment, my eyes wide, taking in the alien pattern overhead, excited about our mission and proud that I was a part of it. I could still hear Dr. Holwitt's reverberating dialogue as we sat in the Academy's planetarium watching a holo of a rare summer downpour in the region known as the Painted Desert on Old Earth. "Now watch," his voice intoned. We watched as the dull and lifeless plain of sand and scrub brush was suddenly turned damp and dark by a brief cloudburst. Then, magically, like a Disneyesque dream, the buds of a thousand different cacti began to bloom in a kaleidoscope of color. There were close-ups of individual plants sprouting new fingers of growth in the illusion of time-lapsed holography. But it was no illusion. It was the most beautiful vision I had ever witnessed, and it lasted a mere twenty minutes. Insects swarmed, pollen was swapped, the cycle was quickly completed before the sun once again gained dominance and the land returned to its former state of desiccation and death. "Imagine if we could control the elements of Nature," Dr. Holwitt said then, "what beauties we could behold."

I thought this the loftiest of ideals. Now I could curse Holwitt and all the others like him, proselytizing the virtues of vain, ignorant God-playing, the type of God-playing that leads to mistakes and pain and even death.

But I must remind myself, we were only following orders.

DAY 2

MORNING CAME as quietly as a whisper. There was one thing about a lifeless planet. There were no animal sounds, no wind blowing through the trees, no rain, no rumble of thunder. But we were here to change all that.

Jakes, Tom, and I made the first descent into the crater. Cristo stayed topside with Henry. As the senior ecobiologist, I was in charge during this particular phase of the operation. Our goal over the next several days was to map the crater's basin, lay out a grid and determine the optimum nodes for introduction of the bacterial protoplasmic reagents—the soup starter that would set the rebirth of this planet in motion. But the planet had its own plans, it seemed, as Tom was the first to find out.

We had finished mapping the first quadrant. The sun was past its midpoint and the shadow from the crater's opposing cliff had been steadily creeping toward us. Tom was out front at the perimeter of the grid drilling

the first core sample. Jakes and I were 100 meters east, confirming coordinates. An invisible current circulated inside the bowl of the crater, a condition brought on by the temperature gradient between the sunlit portion and the encroaching shade. The air felt warm as it brushed past my face, then it turned suddenly cool. That's when I heard Tom's voice in my ear.

"What the hell?" There was surprise in his voice. There was also panic.

Tom? What is it?" asked Jakes.

"*What the hell!*" Tom repeated.

I turned to see Tom drop to the ground. We took off toward him.

When we reached him, Tom was pulling at his suit. At first we didn't know what was wrong.

"Stay calm, Pritchard," demanded Jakes. I grabbed Tom by his shoulder, but quickly let go. Jakes also stepped back.

The skin on Tom's hand began to bubble and bulge. He looked up at us. "*What the hell is it?*"

The core sample he had taken lay on its side. The sample was nothing out of the ordinary, it contained the usual striations. A hole five centimeters across had been made in the basin. It stared up at us like an empty black eye. But there was a glitter of light from down within.

"I don't know, Tom, I don't know." I was helpless to respond. My gut feeling was that it was some kind of contaminant. Tom's skin was moving underneath his suit. He pounded his fists against his body to try and stop its progress. He grabbed for my leg but I danced out of reach.

"Any suggestions, Hardinger?"

Jakes looked to me for answers, but I had none. This shouldn't be happening, I wanted to say. I looked at the sky and realized the sun was at such an angle that we were now standing in shade. Toward the opposing cliffside, which had darkened considerably, I could see a strange phosphorescence appearing along the edge of the basin. Jakes could see it, too.

"No, suggestions, sir."

"Then let's retreat. We don't know what we're dealing with here."

"But we can't just—"

"That's an order!" Jakes began a slow jog back to our climbing equipment.

Tom looked up at me, his eyes large with fear. But there was also something else in his eyes—something swarming behind them now that frightened me, something that wasn't Tom at all.

I moved. I turned and ran as my best friend's body lay convulsing on the crater floor. I didn't look back until I was halfway up the cliffside. The strange phosphorescence I had seen had now spread with the encroaching shade and had overtaken him. It swarmed around his body like vines climbing over a fallen tree. Soon the entire basin was covered with the alien luminescence.

Cristo and Henry were there to greet us when we reached the top.

"What the hell is it?" asked Henry. "Where's Tom?"

We didn't answer. We didn't want to acknowledge what had happened.

"Hey, guys, where's Tom?"

Jakes pointed. "Down there," he said angrily, and tossed off his gear.

"You left him behind?"

With the sun now sinking into the horizon, the spectacle below only grew in intensity. The luminescence appeared to be laid out in some kind pattern. There were areas that seemed to be vibrating, as if pebbles were being dropped into a neon screen, sending out ripples of light. It had a pulse. I didn't have to follow the contour of the waves to know that they converged upon the point where we had left Tom.

"How could you leave him behind?" shouted Henry.

"He's dead, Henry," Jakes grumbled.

"But how? What happened?"

"We don't know yet. It appears to be some kind of contagion."

Henry's eyes grew wide. He backed away from Jakes and me. "A contagion? Like a disease?"

"It's okay, Henry," I told him and reached out to put a hand on his shoulder, but he pulled away violently. "Henry, whatever it is, it's quick. If we had it, we'd be dead already." I wish I could have said "quick and painless," but Tom made it excruciatingly clear that it wasn't. Whatever it was it could take over a body in a matter of minutes.

Henry looked at us and pointed his finger. "You two just stay away from me." He stormed off.

"Let him go," Jakes said.

I guess it was easier for Henry to be angry than to feel the loss we all felt. Meanwhile, Cristo was on his knees, gazing over the crater's lip like a child admiring an ant farm. "Look how it glows," he whispered, "like it's alive." He fell silent, seemingly wrapped in its hypnotic spell.

There was a moment of silence then like a dead weight that seemed to confirm the impossible in everyone's brains—one of our crew was gone.

I looked down into the crater. The undulating landscape resembled a pool of black with a thousand minute runways crisscrossing its surface. "Whatever is down there seems to be staying put. As long as we're up here, I believe we're safe."

"I hope to hell you're right," Jakes said.

I hoped so, too.

IT WAS DIFFICULT TO SLEEP that night. Our thermal liners helped to keep our bodies regulated, but they did little to ease our minds. I was exhausted from the day's work and I kept telling my body it could let go now. The world always seemed a much better place when one is descending into a dream.

And I thought I *was* dreaming when I heard the clatter of stones and the soft-crunch of footsteps. It's only Cristo, I thought, getting up for a last minute ... something. Go back to sleep, I told myself. But the noise persisted, the orientation confusing. It was coming from the direction of the crater.

A sudden perspiration broke across my

skin, temporarily off-setting my thermal regulator and bathing me in an icy film. I opened my eyes and saw a figure. It was standing near the edge of the crater, its outline visible against the star-filled sky. I unsealed my liner and sat up.

"Tom?" I could hear my voice crack in the night. The figure waited a moment. Then it took one shuffling step forward. My first thought was that Tom had miraculously survived. I touched on the spotlamp and light flooded the camp.

It was Tom all right, but Tom's eyes told me he hadn't survived anything. They gazed at me with a luminescent stare that ebbed and brightened like tiny fires being fed by a draft.

I scrambled out of my liner and got to my feet. I accidentally nudged the spotlamp and plunged the outpost into darkness again. I could still see Tom's outline clear in the dark, and realized a low intensity glow was emanating from the crater behind him, resonating in concert with the light in his eyes.

"I want my things," he said, his voice a vacuous whisper, "you have my things." He took another shuffling step forward. I fumbled for the lamp and turned it back on. I stepped back.

"Tom! It's me, Gary."

"My things..." Another step. The glow behind him surged, or was it my own adrenalin boosting my night vision up a notch?

"My things ... Gar ... Gar—"

"That's right, Tom. *Gary.* Your best friend. Remember the Academy?"

"Gar-y?"

"Tom, what is it? What's down there?"

"Gar-y, I want my things..." He shuffled another step closer. By now, Cristo and Jakes had been awakened by the commotion. I could see them moving off to my left. As far as I knew, Henry was still asleep.

"Okay, Tom, I'll get your things. I'll bring them to you." Tom's liner was rolled up. I grabbed it and I felt for the handle of his personal locker. "I've got them, Tom. Over here." His eyes followed me in the night like search lights, pulsating.

I slowly circled my way around the equipment and the supplies, around the area that he and I had cleared when setting up the outpost the day before, until I brought myself to within ten feet of him, each of us still several feet from the edge of the crater.

"Tom," I said, slowly edging my way toward the glowing lip of the crater. "I've got your things." I held the bedroll out for him to see. "Come and get 'em."

"Gar-y?"

I sidestepped to within three feet of the drop-off. Tom shuffled toward me, his body obeying the direction of his eyes.

"What's down there, Tom? What does it want?"

The intensity grew below, illuminating our faces to a blinding white contrast. I gazed into the crater for only a moment, but a moment was all it took for the feeling to overtake me.

The entire basin was alive and flowing with energy. Streams of phosphor raced like blood coursing through a complex network of veins. It was gearing up, charging itself. Or was it waiting to be charged, anticipating new life, new power, new energy? I wanted to pull away, but the motion, the light—I had become entranced by it all. And, yes, the thrill, the exhilaration of coming into contact with something greater than myself, something ancient and powerful—I felt myself drawn to it.

"Gar-y..."

I was startled by the closeness of Tom's voice. My entire body felt as if it had just run a mile.

"I need you, Gar-y," he said, and his arm reached out.

In a sudden rush of fear and adrenalin, I swung the permaplast locker in a roundhouse motion and met the side of Tom's face with a sickening compression of flesh and bone. The blow knocked him sideways and he fell towards the gap of air that would have sent him back into his thousand foot-deep grave, but he collapsed instead against a crest of rock and grappled to hang on, his legs hanging over the edge. The side of his face was now split open, and there was (God help me!) *sand*—sand the color of rust emptying out, depositing on the ground in tiny cones before him.

"Come with me," he said, his voice a hideous plea.

I couldn't move. I couldn't react.

A leg appeared. It was Cristo's. Before I could stop him, Cristo placed a boot on Tom's forehead and gave him a shove.

"No, don't touch him!" I yelled, but it was too late. Tom reacted with the quickness of a rattlesnake, lunging up and grabbing Cristo's ankle and sinking his teeth into his leg. Cristo screamed.

"Nobody move," shouted Jakes, and the spring-loaded charge of a piton gun recoiled in the night. The piton hit Tom in the face and sent him backwards, scrabbling for purchase. Cristo pulled away as Tom finally lost his grip and tumbled down the cliffside into the crater below.

Cristo's leg was now afire with luminescent light. "Get it off me! Get it off!" he cried. I rushed to the equipment case and grabbed the laser cutter. As Cristo squirmed in agony, I took aim, but hesitated.

"Do it, damn it! Just do it!" ordered Jakes.

I thumbed the safety and shot. The laser cut through Cristo's leg as if it were made of clay. Cristo looked up in shock when he realized what I had done. A grin seemed to meet his lips. "Thanks, man," he said, and then he passed out.

Jakes dragged him over to his liner and began wrapping his leg.

"We're all going to die."

This came from Henry, who was curled up under one of the sample tables, shivering in the cold. His eyes were the eyes of someone who believed they had just seen a ghost.

Jakes stared at him coldly. "Henry, we're not going to die. Why don't you help, instead of sitting there cowering like a child."

Henry shook his head slowly from side to side. "It won't give up until it has us all." He

pointed. "See?"

We followed Henry's line of sight. Near the crater's edge lay Cristo's severed foot. The phosphorescent glow had consumed its surface. It also began to twitch with movement, inching its way toward us—back toward Cristo's body.

I found an empty container and let it crawl inside, and sealed it up tight.

"Okay, Gary, you've got first watch. If Cristo wakes give him a shot of ibumorphine." Jakes nodded in Henry's direction. "If he gives you any trouble ... just do what you have to do. I'll see you at 0400."

I inhaled deeply.

I want my things.

I walked over to the crater's edge and tossed Tom's locker and his liner into the void. I could hear a distant tumble of rock and rubble and then nothing more. I gazed into the lights.

I need you, Gary.

Perhaps knowing it would have to go hungry for the night, the entity below began to dim and fade, allowing the dark to regain its dominance. Soon, only the trace of a few remaining pinpoints of phosphor (moments of restless sleep?) here and there helped to fight the growing feeling that it had all been one incredibly nightmarish dream.

DAY 3

NEEDLESS TO SAY, the day that followed became a blur of second guesses and accusations. I blamed the equipment that should have detected sentience. Jakes blamed Cristo for the actions that led to his own incapacitating injury and left our mission severely undermanned. But mostly we blamed ourselves. We felt helpless in the face of the uncertainty that now surrounded us. How long before Tom returned? Was this an anomaly or did every crater contain these mysterious entities?

Most troubling of all was that it would still be another three days—and nights—before the *Echo* returned from its elliptical orbit. Three nights of trying to stay alive.

Three days of thinking about the impending nightfall.

Cristo awoke drenched in sweat. He was running a fever and I administered antibiotics, along with a healthy shot of ibumorphine. He was happy after that and rested comfortably under a makeshift awning.

Meanwhile, Jakes and I used the lab table to study the bottom portion of Cristo's leg. We used long metallic probes to peel back the clothing and remove the boot. Once exposed, the skin showed no signs of the contaminant.

Cristo mumbled in his drug-induced stupor.

"It must recede from the surface of whatever it occupies," I speculated.

Jakes poked and prodded to no effect.

Behind us, Cristo laughed and squirmed and made baby noises.

Jakes and I looked at each other, fearing the worse.

"I think we should try an experiment," Jakes suggested. "Grab the cutter."

Jakes picked up the container and set it down on the soil in the direct sunlight. The foot lay motionless.

Cristo sat upright. "Hey, guys, what are you doing? Hey, that's my foot, you know. C'mon, guys, not my foot."

We ignored Cristo's drug-induced pleas. I stood over the container, the laser in hand.

"Let's see what's inside this thing."

I set the beam to minimum width and intensity and pressed the switch. A smoldering line began to appear on the surface of the skin. I increased the intensity and it cut even deeper. The higher I turned it up, the deeper it cut and the more Cristo protested.

"You don't understand ... it means no harm ... it only wants to live, just like us. Ow, ow, owwwwwwww... that burns!"

Cristo howled as the laser cut into the bone and exposed the marrow to the sunlight. A curious thing happened then. The foot ignited, like a flash of gunpowder, and sent a cloud of pungent grey smoke into the air.

Cristo lay silent, once again passed out.

"Now we know it can be killed." Jakes pulled the unfinished cigar from his shirt. "Got a light?" he said, and allowed a grin to tug at the corner of his mouth.

WE TIED UP CRISTO as a precaution, and put Henry in charge of taking care of him. As long as Cristo was restrained, Henry didn't seem to mind. He spoon fed him his meals and even carried on conversations. Cristo protested about the restraints, but the ibumorphine kept him non-combative.

When Henry wasn't attending to Cristo's needs, he sat in the shade of the *Louis Leaky* and rocked back and forth, mumbling a long, continuous litany of God and mother and academy pledges. His usual annoying smirk and his sarcastic manner would have been welcome if it meant not having to be in the company of those death's-head eyes and the fatalistic tone that had invaded his voice. But Jakes and I had a job to do, even if it now meant planning just to stay alive.

Jakes said, "What if we went ahead and introduced the reagent? Maybe we could fight fire with fire."

I had considered it. Perhaps the entity we were dealing with was just as primitive. Perhaps the reagent would act like a virus and set off a chain-reaction that would supplant the existing life form.

"It's a possibility," I said. "But there is a chance it could also combine with the entity and encourage its growth, leading to God knows what. It would also need to be introduced directly, which means going back down there."

Jakes stroked the week-old stubble on his chin. "Gary—what do you think it is?"

"The only thing like it back on Old Earth that comes to mind—the size, the aversion to sunlight—was *armillaria ostoyae*. The honey mushroom."

"A fungus?"

"It was discovered in the late twentieth century in the northwest region of the United States and was determined to be the Earth's largest organism, covering more than twenty-two hundred acres. If something that large were left alone on a planet without natural predators ... well, you can do the math."

"A sentient fungus?"

"Why not? It only took several hundred thousand years for us to go from the trees to the moon. Its roots probably extend deep enough to tap into the geo-thermal energy of the planet."

Jakes looked past me. I turned.

Henry was leaning over Cristo. Cristo appeared to be whispering into his ear. Henry finally nodded, then turned in our direction. His haunted face bore no expression. He picked up some empty food plates and brought them over to the refuse container. He then continued on with his daily chores.

"We need to keep an eye on him," Jakes said. He pulled the unloaded piton gun from his hip and aimed it at Henry's back. Click went the firing mechanism. "First thing in the morning we do it, okay, Gary?"

At first I wasn't sure what Jakes was talking about. But then I remembered his suggestion about the reagent. "We'll give it a shot," I told him.

JAKES AND I SET UP AN EARLY WARNING SYSTEM around the camp using the surveying equipment and several remote sensing devices. Four miniature Argon lasers mapped out a diamond-shaped perimeter atop the plateau. If any of the four beams were broken, a very loud version of Wagner's *Ride of the Valkyries* would alert us.

Jakes bedded down as soon as the daylight waned. Henry retreated to the *Louis Leaky*, perhaps finding a mother-like comfort in the bosom of its shadow. Cristo floated in and out of consciousness, his blood still coursing with the injections of ibumorphine. I sat near the ridge overlooking the crater.

The lights below were faint, but they dotted the basin with an array of patterns that was both captivating and frightening. How can something so beautiful be so deadly? It was like staring into the eye of the unknown.

As the sunlight faded in the east and the long night began, I noticed a lone figure moving in the distant heat-haze. I put on my long-distance visor and saw that it was Tom dragging his contorted frame about like a partially crushed ant obeying the only message it knew: to walk, to survive, to find its way home.

That moment, I believe, was the first step, the beginning, in a long descendent climb into what could only be described as insanity.

The night passed without incident.

DAY 4

WHEN MORNING CAME, we left Henry standing at the edge watching over us as we rappelled the steep, almost vertical lip of the crater, down to the first of a series of narrow sediment plateaus that ringed the crater's inner wall. It was assumed the plateaus were formed by the erosion of soft soil that settled in the initial impact crater—the megatons of dust and debris lofted into the atmosphere eons ago that was eventually deposited, layer upon layer, gathering first at the bottom well, then mounting up the sides. We could only speculate at the kinds of erosion that were needed to create the plateaus. Whether wind or rain, neither was prevalent now.

How I wished for the feel—the wetness—of rain against my face, or the cool invigoration of a breeze, just then. Instead, as I looked up, there was only the pale blue expanse of cloudless sky, turned dull and somehow artificial by the reflective haze of the limitless dust; the pale, sun-bleached crust, rising like a sedentary wave forever breaking; and, of course, Henry's face peering over the edge, his expression unreadable.

Jakes tapped me on the shoulder. "Don't mind him. Henry will be just fine."

A thousand feet down we reached the soft slope of the pediment. We unhooked our lines and began walking. Ahead, the landscape was dotted with tiny red flags, each a marker we had placed there to denote a drill location. It was odd, but it felt as if Jakes and I were the aliens, giants trampling upon a small city, our ignorance as large as our feet.

The reagent canister knocked against my shoulder, reminding me of our mission. It also reminded me of two days earlier and Tom's needless death. Were we wasting our time—time better spent studying the alien life form, admiring its immensity, applauding its survival mechanisms, rather than simply trying to destroy it.

We approached the spot where we had left Tom behind. The soil was scored where he had drilled the first core sample. The tool still lay there beside the hole.

"Will you look at that."

Jakes stared at the area where Tom had been *consumed*. There was a faint imprint upon the soil like a flash burn in the shape of a human body.

"Like Lazarus," I said.

Jakes merely nodded. "Let's do this."

I kneeled next to the drill hole and unpacked the reagent.

"Just be damn careful, Gary," said Jakes.

I uncapped the nitrogen-cooled container. A wisp of white gas hovered over the opening. I withdrew the gel packet that held the protoplasm and, with one final look at Jakes for confirmation, dropped the packet down into the hole. It would take several minutes before the daytime temperature degraded the packet and allowed the bacteria to enter the soil, and even longer for the reagent to react with the host. Our job done, we gathered our gear and headed back.

We would be topside before noon, we thought, in time for one of Henry's specially prepared microwave lunches. As we approached the crater wall, something didn't look right. On the slope lay two coils of climbing rope. Henry had cut them free.

"I am going to kill that little BASTARD!" The word "bastard" echoed across the basin. Jakes picked up the cut end of the rope and threw it back down again, as if he couldn't believe it was no longer attached.

"Jakes, we've got to find a way out of here."

"I know that. Don't you think I know that!"

I had seen Jakes lose his temper before, but I had never seen him lose control. Perhaps he was afraid for the first time in his life.

"If Tom could find his way to the top, so can we."

Jakes sucked in a deep breath, his eyes ablaze with anger.

We headed south, traversing the first soft sediment plateau until we reached the next level. We continued climbing until we reached a point where there were no more levels to traverse. We found a crevice that opened a narrow fissure in the cliffside. It would be difficult but it was a way up. We decided to take a break.

Jakes took a drink from his water bottle. He craned his neck skyward. The sun was now past noon and we had moved far enough away from the camp side of the crater that we could no longer see our starting point with the naked eye.

"I still find it hard to believe Tom could make it out of here with the injuries I saw."

"Maybe he had help."

I looked at Jakes. "What do you mean?"

"Maybe this fungus slime-crap has a way of communicating to him. Maybe it shows him the way. How else would he find his way back to camp?"

"And Henry? Is something communicating with him? Why would he cut the ropes?"

Jakes stuffed his water bottle back into this vest. "Henry's just scared we're going to bring something back with us. He's probably huddled inside the *Louis Leaky* right now wetting his pants. Never mind Henry, it's that damn sun we should be thinking about." Jakes nodded toward the glowing white orb in the sky. I looked down and saw that the shadow-line was beginning to stretch across the basin below.

Jakes slapped me on the shoulder. "You ready?" It was good to see him back in command-mode.

It would be a race back to camp.

KEEPING OURSELVES WEDGED BETWEEN the narrowest portions of the crevice, we were able to worm our way toward daylight. Unnerving was the view beneath us. Deep in the crevice, which extended down into the basin and perhaps even deeper, the space was filled with a yellowish light. It undulated like a lava flow, hungry, eager for one misstep or slipped hand-hold.

When we reached the top, the sun was an hour from setting. We could see the *Louis Leaky* sitting like a child's toy in the distance. I remember thinking that I was going to be glad when were back on the *Echo* and this was finally over with.

We made it back to camp just as the sun sank into the horizon and the basin below came alive with light. In our fatigue, we didn't see the blue laser line at our feet. The air suddenly filled with music—*Ride of the Valkyries* blasting loud enough it would have made old Richard proud. Red warning lights bathed the site. Henry must have reset the early warning system. We were hungry and tired and Jakes was in no mood for any more crap.

"HENRY!" he shouted. But his voice was drowned out by the music.

The first thing we noticed was that Cristo was gone. Equipment had been tossed onto the ground and the thermo-generator had been broken beyond repair. A barricade of tables and cabinets surrounded the *Louis Leaky*. From inside the viewport, we could see Henry's face staring out at us.

Jakes turned to shut the music off. I gestured to Henry that it was okay to come out, we were all right and that we weren't angry with him. We understood why he was so afraid. But the expression on his face turned to stone as he receded from the glass.

The music stopped. I turned in time to see Cristo loom up behind Jakes, his eyes full of yellow light. He then sank his teeth into Jakes' shoulder. Jakes eyes went wide as he twisted to face his attacker. When he did, a chunk of his flesh and suit tore free, leaving Cristo with a piece of red muscle between his teeth, its juices running down his chin. Cristo tilted his head back and swallowed the chunk whole.

"Why you one-legged bastard!" Jakes punched Cristo in the jaw and sent him flying backwards over the thermo-generator. He grabbed Cristo by the arms and began dragging him toward the ledge.

"We should have done this first thing," Jakes yelled at Cristo, who squirmed futilely. "But we wanted to save your measly-assed life. And this is the thanks I get?"

Cristo extended his neck and tried to bite Jakes' hands, as they approached the edge. With a final tug, Jakes sent Cristo tumbling unceremoniously over the lip of the crater. "Bye-bye."

Jakes stood over the crater in silence, his body suddenly slouching. He reached up to feel his shoulder.

I didn't know what to say. I had the laser cutter in my hands. We had left the piton gun behind for Henry. Henry probably had it with him inside the module. Jakes turned. He began walking toward me. I gripped the laser cutter.

"I guess it's down to you two," Jakes said.

"Jakes, what happened to Cristo might not happen to you," I told him. "The contaminant might be small enough for your immune system to fight."

"Gary, you saw his eyes. It will happen."

"You don't know that," I shouted, tears began to sting the corners of my eyes.

"And you want to take that chance?" Jakes reached into this pocket and pulled out a fresh cigar. He put it in his mouth. "Got a light?"

I looked into his eyes. What I saw was mostly fear, but there was also a look of resignation. He was the one who didn't want to take that chance.

I thumbed the safety and aimed the cutter at the cigar. I turned the power up to full. Jakes watched me the whole time, his teeth gritted, a bitter grin on his lips. He nodded imperceptibly and I pressed the button. My eyes closed as the cutter swept across his neck. When I opened my eyes again, Jakes' body lay on the ground, his head lay several feet to one side.

I dragged Jakes to the crater's lip and it, too, went tumbling over the edge. When I went back to retrieve its head, it stared up at me, its mouth still gripping the broken stump of the cigar, eyes still open. For one lingering moment I expected it to speak to me, for its eyes to fill with yellow light and say, "*Gar-y ... I need you, Gary...*" I grabbed it by its hair and flung it as far as I could into the night, down into the crater and into the lights which were now pulsating with activity, enervated by the new life forms that were being tossed into its network like meaty tidbits thrown into the open maw of a circus lion.

As I turned away, I noticed something different on the crater's floor. There was a gap in the network of lights, a dead zone in the area where Jakes and I had introduced the reagent. It worked. The protoplasmic bacteria was chewing it up! But any excitement I could have felt was drowned by the fact that, now, more than half of our crew was gone.

I went to the *Louis Leaky*, pushed Henry's makeshift barricade aside and pounded on the viewport. "Henry? We need to talk."

It was too dark to see inside.

"Henry? It's okay, they're gone now. The reagent is working. I believe we can stop it."

Silence. No movement. The night air was growing cold and I was too tired to try and talk Henry out of his fear-grip. I reset the early warning system and settled into my liner for the night.

It was the most solitary ten hours of my life.

DAY 5

I AWOKE WITH THE SUN. It was difficult not to believe that everything that had transpired had all been the product of a bad dream. A part of me wanted to wake to see Jakes alive, always the first one up, smoking one of his lung-rot cigars, drinking his black coffee. To see young Cristo, his face full and eager, ready to experience the next new wonder. And Tom, still rubbing the sleep from his eyes, our long friendship held in the corners

of his grin.

But it was just Henry and I, and a creature that was biding its time, waiting for us to make the wrong move.

Once again, I pounded on the *Leaky*'s door. But Henry wasn't coming out. He sat with the piton gun cradled in his lap, his eyes staring with the cold black determination of a rat hiding in a cargo hole. Not only had he destroyed most of the equipment, leaving only my liner to keep me warm at night, he left no food, no water. Which left me no choice.

I spent the morning clearing the debris from the site—grabbing anything that belonged to either Jakes or Cristo and tossing it into the crater. When I picked up a damaged sleep liner, I uncovered one of the remote computer key-screens. I tapped the tiny Collective icon and, to my relief, the screen menu appeared. It was still operational.

I rested, thankfully chewing on a soy-stick I'd found in Cristo's pack, a makeshift awning screening the afternoon sun. I began making entries into this diary. It might well be the only record for the Collective investigators to rely on to piece together what really happened here. I also put my limited knowledge of programming to task and worked at cracking into the *Louis Leaky*'s entry system.

Like I said, Henry left me no choice. In a little over twenty-four hours the lander's lift-off sequence would automatically engage, and I had no intention of being left behind.

AS THE SUN DISAPPEARED below the horizon, I stood for one last time overlooking the crater, admiring its beauty. The dead zone that had appeared the night before was now completely gone; lights once again crisscrossed the area in a topographic relief. The entity had overcome its attacker and had patched its wound. The reagent wasn't strong enough. Or perhaps it had been convinced to simply change sides.

It didn't matter now. My main concern was survival.

I set the necessary trip alarms and settled into my liner for the night. My stomach was empty, my mind racing. I fell sleep wondering how long it would take for a headless man to find its way back home. It was something I didn't want to know the answer to.

THAT NIGHT I DREAMED OF HOME, my wife, Giselle, and my infant child. I was lying in the soft, womb-like comfort of my own bed, and with the foreknowledge found only in dreams, I realized Giselle was no longer by my side. I got up and searched the apartment. It was dark and I could barely see. I walked down the hallway to the baby's room. The door was closed, but a strange luminescence spilled out from beneath the door into the hall. Panic gripped my chest. I rushed into the room. My wife lay lifeless, sprawled on the carpet, a piton lodged in the center of her forehead. A figure stood leaning over my child's crib. The figure turned, its eyes alight with yellow fire, the piton gun still gripped in its hand. It was Henry. He smiled. I froze. He aimed the gun at my face and pulled the trigger—

I awoke with a start, my face slapping against the sleep liner's inner surface, my forehead slick with perspiration.

It was still dark outside, and through the smeared surface of the transparent liner, I thought I saw movement. I quickly unsealed. Cold air flooded in. I sat up and instinctively reached for the laser cutter.

It was gone.

I heard the *Louis Leaky*'s entry door seal shut with an audible hiss.

I realized I was lucky. Henry could have killed me in my sleep. Instead, he let me live. Why? If there was an investigation, I guess my death by his hand would be difficult to explain. It was best to let me fend off Tom, Jakes and Cristo by myself and let nature take its course.

Defeated, I sat in a fetal position staring into the night, cursing any god that would listen. A hundred light years of space separated me from my wife and child and I felt every inch of it.

I sat until the sun began to fuel the sky. I had a long day ahead of me.

DAY 6

BY NOON I was still several overrides away from getting past the *Louis Leaky*'s entry locks. Also, once I initiated the override, I had no way of knowing which door would open: the crew deck where Henry lay in wait, armed with deadly force; or the cargo bay; or possibly both. My only weapon would be the element of surprise. I had to hope that would be enough.

As I worked, furiously tapping in code, the reality of the entity had faded to the back of my mind. It had become secondary to my getting onto the landing craft. I had forgotten to factor into this simple survival formula the danger that my dead crew mates presented. How quickly this came to light when I looked up from my key-screen and far across the open expanse of the crater, I saw a small dust cloud moving along the rocky edge.

They were coming.

The long-distance view visor was gone, thrown into the crater below to try and minimize the lure of their returning back to camp. But anything Jakes, Cristo or Tom may have touched was a potential magnet. Including myself. I could see that it was them. And without weapons to fend them off, I now needed more than ever to find a way inside the *Louis Leaky*, take my chance that Henry wouldn't be foolish enough to try and kill me, and hope like hell I wouldn't have to do the same to him.

The clock was ticking.

TWO HOURS TILL LIFT OFF.

The final override was set. I prepared to rush the ship. I inhaled deeply. The thin air choked my lungs. I initiated the control sequence.

Nothing happened.

"INVALID COMMAND," a feminine voice chided me from the key-screen.

I tried it again. No go. I made several more attempts, each time making minor changes in the sequence.

Still nothing.

My hopes began to fade, as did the sunlight.

My eyes nervously scanned the planet's terrain.

They were clearly visible now, moving slowly, inexorably in the direction of the camp—a five-and-a-half-legged abomination returning for additional converts. They pulled and dragged themselves along the crust of the planet, the antithesis of the three wise men, on a mission not to witness the birth of their new savior but to prevent the new savior from being born.

I swallowed my nervousness, along with a gritty clot of dust, and continued working.

ONE HOUR TILL LIFT OFF.

I introduced an auto-sequencer into the programming. It was akin to trying to hit the jackpot on an old world slot machine, except I had to line up about a million cherries in a row to win. All I needed was time. Something that was now in short supply.

The sun was inching toward the horizon, saying farewell to another day. For me, it could very well be the last time I'd see it again. I stared at the white-hot ball of fiery gases until my eyes began to water. I had to do something. I just couldn't sit by and wait for death to come and claim me.

I pleaded with Henry one last time.

"Damn it, Henry! If you leave me here, it's the same as murder!"

Henry shrugged his shoulders.

"You might think you'll get away with it. You might even believe you'll receive a commendation for your bravery and your name in the history books for discovering a new sentient life form. But the investigators will never believe you, Henry. Because I've got it all here. This is what they'll find." I held up the key-screen for him to see. "Call it my epitaph, my last will and testament—testament that you, Henry Marchand, Assistant to Crew Chief Arnaud Jakes, pulled an Enos Jackson and your cowardice fatally sabotaged this mission."

For the first time Henry's expression changed. Anger boiled to the surface of his face. He grabbed the laser cutter and looked at me threateningly. But then thought better of it. A smile danced across his lips. He saluted me and retreated away from the window and began making preparations for take-off.

Daylight seeped into the horizon. Without a rich atmosphere to prolong it, darkness simply swallowed up the sunlight like waste water down an ejection tube. I stumbled over a stone as I walked away from the landing craft, and in my frustration, I picked up the fist-sized object and threw it at the command deck's portal. It bounced off the glass ineffectually. But, inside, I made Henry jump. That was satisfaction enough.

It was then that I nearly jumped out of my suit when *Ride of the Valkyries* blasted from the early warning speakers. Red lights flashed a slow swirling pulse beat. My dead crew mates had finally arrived.

FIVE MINUTES TILL LIFT OFF.

The *Leaky*'s exhaust jets began their cooling sequence. White nitrogen exited in tiny streams into the rarified air.

I let Wagner own the night; the music filled my ears with an odd sense of triumph. I had to laugh at the irony. Here I was, about to die, and it was Henry who would be the lone survivor.

I crouched near the leg of the landing craft, a small pile of stones at my feet. If I wasn't getting off the planet, I was going to make sure there wasn't enough left of me to assimilate. When the *Louis Leaky* blasted off, it would literally leave me in the dust.

A figure lurched into view. Behind it, came two others. The three of them dragged and pulled their broken bodies onto the campsite and over to my sleep area. Along the way, one of them must have snagged the speaker wire, because the night suddenly fell silent.

Two beats of my heart later, my key-screen

chimed and a voice spoke calmly: "SE-QUENCE FOUND ... ENTRANCE SECURITY WILL DISENGAGE IN TEN SECONDS... NINE... EIGHT..."

I looked up. Bathed in the red glare of the warning lights, all three figures turned in my direction.

"Gar-y..." Tom's voice bellowed in the night. His face was hideously misshapen, the piton still protruded from his forehead. His body listed to one side.

"We need you, Gary... That's an order..." Jakes cradled his head in one arm as if it were an infant child. The head still functioned, its mouth moving slightly out of synch with its voice, as if it were some kind of puppeteer's mad joke.

Cristo held onto Jakes' shoulder for balance and merely stared.

"...FIVE... FOUR..."

The trio lurched toward me, their eyes fueled with a devilish intensity.

"...TWO... ONE..."

I stood and ran for the loading bay door, but the trio's movements were surprisingly quick. Jakes and Cristo tried to block my way, while Tom lunged for my back. I put my shoulder into Cristo's chest and sent him and Jakes toppling like dominos. I felt a tug at my suit from behind but my adrenal fear-rush gave me the added boost I needed to pull away.

I charged toward the *Louis Leaky*'s loading bay. Henry appeared at the entrance, the piton gun at his side, his surprise clearly evident. He raised the gun but I was running too fast. We collided, knocking both of us to the deck. Henry was sent sprawling, the gun separated from his grip, the wind gone from his lungs. I got to my feet first and tried to run into the control area, but Henry grabbed my heel and my face hit the deck.

"I won't let you," Henry growled. "This is my ship, my moment, and you're not going to steal it away from me!"

He lunged for the piton gun, which had slid near the still-open entrance. He got to his feet and aimed the gun at my chest.

"Henry! The door! Get away from the door!"

"Shut up! I'm giving the orders now!"

"Hen-ry... you bas-tard..."

Henry turned just as the headless body of Jakes reached out with his free hand and grabbed him by the throat. Henry fired the piton gun point blank, but it buried into Jakes' chest with no effect except for a minor grimace on the face of the head cradled in the dead man's arm.

"We need you, Hen-ry..." Tom and Cristo leaned in and each grabbed one of Henry's legs. Together, the three of them pulled Henry out into the night.

I got to my feet and hit the loading bay's entrance switch. The door sealed shut. I stumbled up front and collapsed into the command chair, strapped myself in and let my mind wind down in the last thirty seconds before the *Leaky* lifted off.

I SIT HERE NOW, on the *Echo*, biding my time until my sleepvac reaches optimum, listening to my own voice in the silence of space.

I have destroyed my previous entries. I will tell the Collective that the ridge we were camped upon gave way, sending our four crew members to their death. They may believe me, they may not. By the time they investigate, the change will have already occurred.

You see, it appears I was wounded in my attempt to escape—one last parting gift from my friend Tom. The wound itches beneath my suit. The muscles in my back burn. But with the pain comes a realization, a sense of comfort, a sense of belonging. A sense of relief.

Tom, Jakes, Cristo and Henry were just men. Multitudes of their kind have spread across the galaxy like a plague, destroying whatever their fingers have touched. They must be stopped. They need to leave things alone.

But who am I to tell them? My name is Gary Hardinger. I am an ecobiologist. My job is to see that all living things survive. It is in my blood.

I also appear to be a carrier. That is in my blood, also.

My sleepvac is ready, now. It's time to rest.

I can't wait to finally return home and see my wife and child for the first time in months.

I want to hold them in my arms.

Hold them tight.

👽 👽 👽

As a child, Kurt Newton was weaned on episodes of Twilight Zone *and* The Outer Limits, *and* Chiller Theater *(which showed many of the classic sci-fi horror movies of the '50s and '60s), laying the groundwork for his fertile imagination. His short stories have appeared in numerous publications over the last twenty years, including* Weird Tales, Weirdbook, Space and Time, Dark Discoveries, Daily Science Fiction, The Arcanist *and* Hinnom Magazine. *He lives in Connecticut.*

Astute readers may notice similarities between "Metanoia" and the movie *The Last Days on Mars* (reviewed in this issue). The movie was released in 2013, more than a decade after Kurt Newton's creepy story appeared in a 2002 issue of *Burning Sky*.

FALLOUT

FALLOUT:

Next issue *Black Infinity* will feature the best letters and emails from our rabid readers. Excuse us, our *avid* readers. Pearls of praise will be cherished; nuggets of creative insight hoarded for future issues; and the caustic "coal" of criticism grudgingly tolerated. (HEY, we're sensitive!)

Address your comments to the editor, at: deadletterpress@cox.net

Or send a note to:
Tom English
Dead Letter Press
Box 134, New Kent VA 23124-0134

Todd Treichel's

HOW WEIRD IS THAT?

Wild, Weird, Deadly World

MY DAUGHTER STARTED IT. She noticed a growing internet meme, consisting of photos of staring, glaring, looming animals, with the superimposed caption, SOON.

Soon? My whole family shares a deep appreciation for nature and science, and especially for wildlife. We see and think about human impacts every day. Naturally we joke around with the idea that the animal kingdom will rebel against stunned and helpless humans.

We joke around. You see, I too have been slow to face the truth. For it is terrifying.

Everyone knows about poisonous snakes and spiders, and apex predators that can slay in moments when angered or desperate. Squadrons of mosquitoes quietly spread a plethora of diseases. Probably most readers are aware that hippopotamuses, not leopards or lions, are the most lethal animal in Africa. They may seem docile, loafing languidly in lakes and rivers, but they are prone to unexpected rage and kill thousands each year. If pestered or just paddled past, they bite, trample and drown intruders without hesitation.

But the threat is more widespread, and much weirder, than all of that.

Insects are already mobilizing. Order *Hymenoptera* brings a swarm of nasty shock troops to the order of battle. Consider the yak-killer hornet (left) of Japan. Pause to consider how such a nickname originated. These hornets are huge, they are fast, they love to behead things, and they wield a super-painful, cell-destroying venom. The fragments of cells in the bloodstream then overwhelm your kidneys.

At least the hornets only attack for understandable reasons. Africanized honeybees attack by the thousands at any possibility of a threat, pursue their quarry relentlessly over significant distances, and do not cool down for hours. Hundreds have died from this early example of an escaped genetically "modified" agricultural organism. These troops line up alongside the bullet ants' immensely painful bite, and driver ants, so called because they drive everything and anything before them in terror. At the inexorable vanguard of an army ant advance, every creature of any size that can't get out of the way is devoured. These ants serve as their own barracks, forming nests out of their own bodies. They're like the Mongol hordes, only with bigger appetites.

Many other invertebrates will report for duty, and bring weapons of more subtlety. Kissing bugs like to bite the lips of sleeping humans, and inject a serious parasite. Botflies lay eggs on a transient host, such as a tick, so that the eggs can drop off onto a human, resulting in fat, spiny larvae that wiggle and crawl around under the skin.

The assassin caterpillar of Brazil looks just like a plant or lichen, so people put their hands on it or step on it without a thought. Soon they regret it, as the massive internal and external bleeding begins, and will not stop, due to anticoagulants in the venom. Hundreds have died in this painful manner. And what's really weird, except perhaps in the context of the coming revolution, is that until recently there were no known epidemics of dozens of poisonings at once. But today, they are disturbingly common. One might guess that more people are entering this lurker's habitat now than ever before—but maybe there's more to it.

While we are busy watching our step for little threats, gliding snakes will drop onto our heads. They are only somewhat venomous, but have the advantage of total surprise. Readers will have heard of poisonous frogs of the Amazon rain forest. The golden dart frog (right) is the one to watch out for. Not only is its poison lethal upon touch, but these frogs move about in large groups. It would not take long for a big gang of them to subdue a platoon of Marines. It has to unsettle you to consider that poisonous frogs and Japanese water snakes get their venom from eating other poisonous creatures. Get outta here with your habañeros.

There are even poisonous birds. Do not be tempted to pet the next blue-capped ifrit, little strikethrush or pitohui you encounter. Their skin and feathers bear the same poison as their co-conspirators, the deadly little Amazonian frogs. And do not dine upon spur-winged goose, its flesh rendered toxic by the blister beetles it eats. Certain quail eat certain seeds and become toxic as well; they've been wreaking this vengeance since ancient times.

Should we venture into the water, cone snails will tempt collectors with their beauty, then sting them with devastating venom. The beautiful blue-ringed octopus will deliver a painless little bite that may kill before it is even noticed.

How many will surrender immediately when the candiru fish (featured on several outlandish TV doctor dramas) approaches the battle? Its mode of attack is a clandestine and little-known operation: it may swim into human genital openings and lodge there. Certain leeches may rendezvous with them up in there. (Things could get ugly if the pearlfish is recruited; it likes to enter the anus/breathing hole of a sea cucumber and hide, mate or enjoy a snack consisting of the poor echinoderm's reproductive organs.) Piranha attacks are somewhat less subtle. Who can even speculate what the supremely weird creatures of the deepest seas may bring to the fight.

Rumors of other, stranger entities, such as remnant aquatic dinosaurs, cannot be confirmed or denied at this time, unless you have the proper clearance.

While collectively this arsenal may be mostly a potential threat at this time, our reconnaissance reveals that intelligent Humboldt squids are increasingly conducting wolf-like cooperative attacks against divers, boats and fishermen in the Pacific Ocean, and have been known to destroy cameras that were watching their behavior. Their range is increasing rapidly. Chances are they will rise alongside *your* boat any minute now.

We had better start preparing. Soon.

🕸 🌐 🕸

Like every farmer on every planet, Duncan had to hunt down anything that damaged his crops—even though he was aware this was ...

THE PLANET THAT COULDN'T BE

by Clifford D. Simak

Illustrated by GAUGHAN

THE TRACKS WENT UP ONE ROW AND DOWN ANOTHER, and in those rows the *vua* plants had been sheared off an inch or two above the ground. The raider had been methodical; it had not wandered about haphazardly, but had done an efficient job of harvesting the first ten rows on the west side of the field. Then, having eaten its fill, it had angled off into the bush—and that had not been long ago, for the soil still trickled down into the great pug marks, sunk deep into the finely cultivated loam.

Somewhere a sawmill bird was whirring through a log, and down in one of the thorn-choked ravines, a choir of chatterers was clicking through a ghastly morning song. It was going to be a scorcher of a day. Already the smell of desiccated dust was rising from the ground and the glare of the newly risen sun was dancing off the bright leaves of the hula-trees, making it appear as if the bush were filled with a million flashing mirrors.

Gavin Duncan hauled a red bandanna from his pocket and mopped his face.

"No, mister," pleaded Zikkara, the native foreman of the farm. "You cannot do it, mister.

You do not hunt a Cytha."

"The hell I don't," said Duncan, but he spoke in English and not the native tongue.

He stared out across the bush, a flat expanse of sun-cured grass interspersed with thickets of hula-scrub and thorn and occasional groves of trees, criss-crossed by treacherous ravines and spotted with infrequent waterholes.

It would be murderous out there, he told himself, but it shouldn't take too long. The beast probably would lay up shortly after its pre-dawn feeding and he'd overhaul it in an hour or two. But if he failed to overhaul it, then he must keep on.

"Dangerous," Zikkara pointed out. "No one hunts the Cytha."

"I do," Duncan said, speaking now in the native language. "I hunt anything that damages my crop. A few nights more of this and there would be nothing left."

Jamming the bandanna back into his pocket, he tilted his hat lower across his eyes against the sun.

"It might be a long chase, mister. It is the *skun* season now. If you were caught out there...."

"Now listen," Duncan told it sharply. "Before I came, you'd feast one day, then starve for days on end; but now you eat each day. And you like the doctoring. Before, when you got sick, you died. Now you get sick, I doctor you, and you live. You like staying in one place, instead of wandering all around."

"Mister, we like all this," said Zikkara, "but we do not hunt the Cytha."

"If we do not hunt the Cytha, we lose all this," Duncan pointed out. "If I don't make a crop, I'm licked. I'll have to go away. Then what happens to you?"

"We will grow the corn ourselves."

"That's a laugh," said Duncan, "and you know it is. If I didn't kick your backsides all day long, you wouldn't do a lick of work. If I leave, you go back to the bush. Now let's go and get that Cytha."

"But it is such a little one, mister! It is such a young one! It is scarcely worth the trouble. It would be a shame to kill it."

Probably just slightly smaller than a horse, thought Duncan, watching the native closely. It's scared, he told himself. It's scared dry and spitless.

"Besides, it must have been most hungry. Surely, mister, even a Cytha has the right to eat."

"Not from my crop," said Duncan savagely. "You know why we grow the *vua*, don't you? You know it is great medicine. The berries that it grows cures those who are sick inside their heads. My people need that medicine—need it very badly. And what is more,

out there—" he swept his arm toward the sky "—out there they pay very much for it."

"But, mister...."

"I tell you this," said Duncan gently, "you either dig me up a bush-runner to do the tracking for me or you can all get out, the kit and caboodle of you. I can get other tribes to work the farm."

"No, mister!" Zikkara screamed in desperation.

"You have your choice," Duncan told it coldly.

HE PLODDED BACK ACROSS THE FIELD toward the house. Not much of a house as yet. Not a great deal better than a native shack. But someday it would be, he told himself. Let him sell a crop or two and he'd build a house that would really be a house. It would have a bar and swimming pool and a garden filled with flowers, and at last, after years of wandering, he'd have a home and broad acres and everyone, not just one lousy tribe, would call him mister.

Gavin Duncan, planter, he said to himself, and liked the sound of it. Planter on the planet Layard. But not if the Cytha came back night after night and ate the *vua* plants.

He glanced over his shoulder and saw that Zikkara was racing for the native village.

Called their bluff, Duncan informed himself with satisfaction.

He came out of the field and walked across the yard, heading for the house. One of Shotwell's shirts was hanging on the clothes-line, limp in the breathless morning.

Damn the man, thought Duncan. Out here mucking around with those stupid natives, always asking questions, always under foot. Although, to be fair about it, that was Shotwell's job. That was what the Sociology people had sent him out to do.

Duncan came up to the shack, pushed the door open and entered. Shotwell, stripped to the waist, was at the wash bench.

Breakfast was cooking on the stove, with an elderly native acting as cook.

Duncan strode across the room and took

down the heavy rifle from its peg. He slapped the action open, slapped it shut again.

Shotwell reached for a towel.

"What's going on?" he asked.

"Cytha got into the field."

"Cytha?"

"A kind of animal," said Duncan. "It ate ten rows of *vua*."

"Big? Little? What are its characteristics?"

The native began putting breakfast on the table. Duncan walked to the table, laid the rifle across one corner of it and sat down. He poured a brackish liquid out of a big stew pan into their cups.

God, he thought, what I would give for a cup of coffee.

Shotwell pulled up his chair. "You didn't answer me. What is a Cytha like?"

"I wouldn't know," said Duncan.

"Don't know? But you're going after it, looks like, and how can you hunt it if you don't know—"

"Track it. The thing tied to the other end of the trail is sure to be the Cytha. We'll find out what it's like once we catch up to it."

"We?"

"The natives will send up someone to do the tracking for me. Some of them are better than a dog."

"Look, Gavin. I've put you to a lot of trouble and you've been decent with me. If I can be any help, I would like to go."

"Two make better time than three. And we have to catch this Cytha fast or it might settle down to an endurance contest."

"All right, then. Tell me about the Cytha."

Duncan poured porridge gruel into his bowl, handed the pan to Shotwell. "It's a sort of special thing. The natives are scared to death of it. You hear a lot of stories about it. Said to be unkillable. It's always capitalized, always a proper noun. It has been reported at different times from widely scattered places."

"No one's ever bagged one?"

"Not that I ever heard of." Duncan patted the rifle. "Let me get a bead on it."

He started eating, spooning the porridge into his mouth, munching on the stale corn bread left from the night before. He drank some of the brackish beverage and shuddered.

"Someday," he said, "I'm going to scrape together enough money to buy a pound of coffee. You'd think—"

"It's the freight rates," Shotwell said. "I'll send you a pound when I go back."

"Not at the price they'd charge to ship it out," said Duncan. "I wouldn't hear of it."

They ate in silence for a time. Finally Shotwell said: "I'm getting nowhere, Gavin. The natives are willing to talk, but it all adds up to nothing."

"I tried to tell you that. You could have saved your time."

Shotwell shook his head stubbornly. "There's an answer, a logical explanation. It's easy enough to say you cannot rule out the sexual factor, but that's exactly what has happened here on Layard. It's easy to exclaim that a sexless animal, a sexless race, a sexless planet is impossible, but that is what we have. Somewhere there is an answer and I have to find it."

"Now hold up a minute," Duncan protested. "There's no use blowing a gasket. I haven't got the time this morning to listen to your lecture."

"But it's not the lack of sex that worries me entirely," Shotwell said, "although it's the central factor. There are subsidiary situations deriving from that central fact which are most intriguing."

"I have no doubt of it," said Duncan, "but if you please—"

"Without sex, there is no basis for the family, and without the family there is no basis for a tribe, and yet the natives have an elaborate tribal setup, with taboos by way of regulation. Somewhere there must exist some underlying, basic unifying factor, some common loyalty, some strange relationship which spells out to brotherhood."

"Not brotherhood," said Duncan, chuckling. "Not even sisterhood. You must watch your terminology. The word you want is *ithood*."

The door pushed open and a native walked

in timidly.

"Zikkara said that mister want me," the native told them. "I am Sipar. I can track anything but screamers, stilt-birds, long-horns and donovans. Those are my taboos."

"I am glad to hear that," Duncan replied. "You have no Cytha taboo, then."

"Cytha!" yipped the native. "Zikkara did not tell me Cytha!"

Duncan paid no attention. He got up from the table and went to the heavy chest that stood against one wall. He rummaged in it and came out with a pair of binoculars, a hunting knife and an extra drum of ammunition. At the kitchen cupboard, he rummaged once again, filling a small leather sack with a gritty powder from a can he found.

"Rockahominy," he explained to Shotwell. "Emergency rations thought up by the primitive North American Indians. Parched corn, ground fine. It's no feast exactly, but it keeps a man going."

"You figure you'll be gone that long?"

"Maybe overnight. I don't know. Won't stop until I get it. Can't afford to. It could wipe me out in a few days."

"Good hunting," Shotwell said. "I'll hold the fort."

Duncan said to Sipar: "Quit sniveling and come on."

He picked up the rifle, settled it in the crook of his arm. He kicked open the door and strode out.

Sipar followed meekly.

II

Duncan got his first shot late in the afternoon of that first day.

In the middle of the morning, two hours after they had left the farm, they had flushed the Cytha out of its bed in a thick ravine. But there had been no chance for a shot. Duncan saw no more than a huge black blur fade into the bush.

Through the bake-oven afternoon, they had followed its trail, Sipar tracking and Duncan bringing up the rear, scanning every piece of cover, with the sun-hot rifle always held at ready.

Once they had been held up for fifteen minutes while a massive donovan tramped back and forth, screaming, trying to work up its courage for attack. But after a quarter hour of showing off, it decided to behave itself and went off at a shuffling gallop.

Duncan watched it go with a lot of thankfulness. It could soak up a lot of lead, and for all its awkwardness, it was handy with its feet once it set itself in motion. Donovans had killed a lot of men in the twenty years since Earthmen had come to Layard.

With the beast gone, Duncan looked around for Sipar. He found it fast asleep beneath a hula-shrub. He kicked the native awake with something less than gentleness and they went on again.

The bush swarmed with other animals, but they had no trouble with them.

Sipar, despite its initial reluctance, had worked well at the trailing. A misplaced bunch of grass, a twig bent to one side, a displaced stone, the faintest pug mark were Sipar's stock in trade. It worked like a lithe, well-trained hound. This bush country was its special province; here it was at home.

With the sun dropping toward the west, they had climbed a long, steep hill and as they neared the top of it, Duncan hissed at Sipar. The native looked back over its shoulder in surprise. Duncan made motions for it to stop tracking.

The native crouched and as Duncan went past it, he saw that a look of agony was twisting its face. And in the look of agony he thought he saw as well a touch of pleading and a trace of hatred. It's scared, just like the rest of them, Duncan told himself. But what the native thought or felt had no significance; what counted was the beast ahead.

Duncan went the last few yards on his belly, pushing the gun ahead of him, the binoculars bumping on his back. Swift, vicious insects ran out of the grass and swarmed across his hands and arms and one got on his face and bit him.

He made it to the hilltop and lay there,

looking at the sweep of land beyond. It was more of the same, more of the blistering, dusty slogging, more of thorn and tangled ravine and awful emptiness.

He lay motionless, watching for a hint of motion, for the fitful shadow, for any wrongness in the terrain that might be the Cytha.

But there was nothing. The land lay quiet under the declining sun. Far on the horizon, a herd of some sort of animals was grazing, but there was nothing else.

Then he saw the motion, just a flicker, on the knoll ahead—about halfway up.

He laid the rifle carefully on the ground and hitched the binoculars around. He raised them to his eyes and moved them slowly back and forth. The animal was there where he had seen the motion.

It was resting, looking back along the way that it had come, watching for the first sign of its trailers. Duncan tried to make out the size and shape, but it blended with the grass and the dun soil and he could not be sure exactly what it looked like.

He let the glasses down and now that he had located it, he could distinguish its outline with the naked eye.

His hand reached out and slid the rifle to him. He fitted it to his shoulder and wriggled his body for closer contact with the ground. The cross-hairs centered on the faint outline on the knoll and then the beast stood up.

It was not as large as he had thought it might be—perhaps a little larger than Earth lion-size, but it certainly was no lion. It was a square-set thing and black and inclined to lumpiness and it had an awkward look about it, but there were strength and ferociousness as well.

Duncan tilted the muzzle of the rifle so that the cross-hairs centered on the massive neck. He drew in a breath and held it and began the trigger squeeze.

The rifle bucked hard against his shoulder and the report hammered in his head and the beast went down. It did not lurch or fall; it simply melted down and disappeared, hidden in the grass.

"Dead center," Duncan assured himself.

He worked the mechanism and the spent cartridge case flew out. The feeding mechanism snicked and the fresh shell clicked as it slid into the breech.

He lay for a moment, watching. And on the knoll where the thing had fallen, the grass was twitching as if the wind were blowing, only there was no wind. But despite the twitching of the grass, there was no sign of the Cytha. It did not struggle up again. It stayed where it had fallen.

Duncan got to his feet, dug out the bandanna and mopped at his face. He heard the soft thud of the step behind him and turned his head. It was the tracker.

"It's all right, Sipar," he said. "You can quit worrying. I got it. We can go home now."

IT HAD BEEN A LONG, HARD CHASE, longer than he had thought it might be. But it had been successful and that was what counted. For the moment, the *vua* crop was safe.

He tucked the bandanna back into his pocket, went down the slope and started up the knoll. He reached the place where the Cytha had fallen. There were three small gouts of torn, mangled fur and flesh lying on the ground and there was nothing else.

He spun around and jerked his rifle up. Every nerve was screamingly alert. He swung his head, searching for the slightest movement, for some shape or color that was not the shape or color of the bush or grass or ground. But there was nothing. The heat droned in the hush of afternoon. There was not a breath of moving air. But there was danger—a saw-toothed sense of danger close behind his neck.

"Sipar!" he called in a tense whisper, "Watch out!"

The native stood motionless, unheeding, its eyeballs rolling up until there was only white, while the muscles stood out along its throat like straining ropes of steel.

Duncan slowly swiveled, rifle held almost at arm's length, elbows crooked a little, ready to bring the weapon into play in a fraction of a second.

Nothing stirred. There was no more than emptiness—the emptiness of sun and molten sky, of grass and scraggy bush, of a brown-and-yellow land stretching into foreverness.

Step by step, Duncan covered the hillside and finally came back to the place where the native squatted on its heels and moaned, rocking back and forth, arms locked tightly across its chest, as if it tried to cradle itself in a sort of illusory comfort.

The Earthman walked to the place where the Cytha had fallen and picked up, one by one, the bits of bleeding flesh. They had been mangled by his bullet. They were limp and had no shape. And it was queer, he thought. In all his years of hunting, over many planets, he had never known a bullet to rip out hunks of flesh.

He dropped the bloody pieces back into the grass and wiped his hand upon his thighs. He got up a little stiffly.

He'd found no trail of blood leading through the grass, and surely an animal with a hole of that size would leave a trail.

And as he stood there upon the hillside, with his bloody fingerprints still wet and glistening upon the fabric of his trousers, he felt the first cold touch of fear, as if the fingertips of fear might momentarily, almost casually, have trailed across his heart.

HE TURNED AROUND and walked back to the native, reached down and shook it.

"Snap out of it," he ordered.

He expected pleading, cowering, terror, but there was none.

Sipar got swiftly to its feet and stood looking at him and there was, he thought, an odd glitter in its eyes.

"Get going," Duncan said. "We still have a little time. Start circling and pick up the trail. I will cover you."

He glanced at the sun. An hour and a half still left—maybe as much as two. There might still be time to get this buttoned up before the fall of night.

A half mile beyond the knoll, Sipar picked up the trail again and they went ahead, but now they traveled more cautiously, for any bush, any rock, any clump of grass might conceal the wounded beast.

Duncan found himself on edge and cursed himself savagely for it. He'd been in tight spots before. This was nothing new to him. There was no reason to get himself tensed up. It was a deadly business, sure, but he had faced others calmly and walked away from them. It was those frontier tales he'd heard about the Cytha—the kind of superstitious chatter that one always heard on the edge of unknown land.

He gripped the rifle tighter and went on.

No animal, he told himself, was unkillable.

HALF AN HOUR BEFORE SUNSET, he called a halt when they reached a brackish waterhole. The light soon would be getting bad for shooting. In the morning, they'd take up the trail again, and by that time the Cytha would be at an even greater disadvantage. It would be stiff and slow and weak. It might be even dead.

Duncan gathered wood and built a fire in the lee of a thorn-bush thicket. Sipar waded out with the canteens and thrust them at arm's length beneath the surface to fill them. The water still was warm and evil-tasting, but it was fairly free of scum and a thirsty man could drink it.

The sun went down and darkness fell quickly. They dragged more wood out of the thicket and piled it carefully close at hand.

Duncan reached into his pocket and brought out the little bag of rockahominy.

"Here," he said to Sipar. "Supper."

The native held one hand cupped and Duncan poured a little mound into its palm.

"Thank you, mister," Sipar said. "Food-giver."

"Huh?" asked Duncan, then caught what the native meant. "Dive into it," he said, almost kindly. "It isn't much, but it gives you strength. We'll need strength tomorrow."

Food-giver, eh? Trying to butter him up, perhaps. In a little while, Sipar would start whining for him to knock off the hunt and head back for the farm.

Although, come to think of it, he really was the food-giver to this bunch of sexless wonders. Corn, thank God, grew well on the red and stubborn soil of Layard—good old corn from North America. Fed to hogs, made into corn-pone for breakfast back on Earth, and here, on Layard, the staple food crop for a gang of shiftless varmints who still regarded, with some good solid skepticism and round-eyed wonder, this unorthodox idea that one should take the trouble to grow plants to eat rather than go out and scrounge for them.

Corn from North America, he thought, growing side by side with the *vua* of Layard. And that was the way it went. Something from one planet and something from another and still something further from a third and so was built up through the wide social confederacy of space a truly cosmic culture which in the end, in another ten thousand years or so, might spell out some way of life with more sanity and understanding than was evident today.

He poured a mound of rockahominy into his own hand and put the bag back into his pocket.

"Sipar."

"Yes, mister?"

"You were not scared today when the donovan threatened to attack us."

"No, mister. The donovan would not hurt me."

"I see. You said the donovan was taboo to you. Could it be that you, likewise, are taboo to the donovan?"

"Yes, mister. The donovan and I grew up together."

"Oh, so that's it," said Duncan.

He put a pinch of the parched and powdered corn into his mouth and took a sip of brackish water. He chewed reflectively on the resultant mash.

He might go ahead, he knew, and ask why and how and where Sipar and the donovan had grown up together, but there was no point to it. This was exactly the kind of tangle that Shotwell was forever getting into.

Half the time, he told himself, I'm convinced the little stinkers are doing no more than pulling our legs.

What a fantastic bunch of jerks! Not men, not women, just things. And while there were never babies, there were children, although never less than eight or nine years old. And if there were no babies, where did the eight-and nine-year-olds come from?

"I suppose," he said, "that these other things that are your taboos, the stilt-birds and the screamers and the like, also grew up with you."

"That is right, mister."

"Some playground that must have been," said Duncan.

He went on chewing, staring out into the darkness beyond the ring of firelight.

"There's something in the thorn bush, mister."

"I didn't hear a thing."

"Little pattering. Something is running there."

Duncan listened closely. What Sipar said was true. A lot of little things were running in the thicket.

"More than likely mice," he said.

He finished his rockahominy and took an extra swig of water, gagging on it slightly.

"Get your rest," he told Sipar. "I'll wake you later so I can catch a wink or two."

"Mister," Sipar said, "I will stay with you to the end."

"Well," said Duncan, somewhat startled, "that is decent of you."

"I will stay to the death," Sipar promised earnestly.

"Don't strain yourself," said Duncan.

He picked up the rifle and walked down to the waterhole.

The night was quiet and the land continued to have that empty feeling. Empty except for the fire and the waterhole and the little mice-like animals running in the thicket.

And Sipar—Sipar lying by the fire, curled up and sound asleep already. Naked, with not a weapon to its hand—just the naked animal, the basic humanoid, and yet with underlying purpose that at times was baffling. Scared and shivering this morning at mere mention of the Cytha, yet never faltering on the trail; in pure funk back there on the knoll where they had lost the Cytha, but now ready to go on to the death.

Duncan went back to the fire and prodded Sipar with his toe. The native came straight up out of sleep.

"Whose death?" asked Duncan. "Whose death were you talking of?"

"Why, ours, of course," said Sipar, and went back to sleep.

III

Duncan did not see the arrow coming. He heard the swishing whistle and felt the wind of it on the right side of his throat and then it thunked into a tree behind him.

He leaped aside and dived for the cover of a tumbled mound of boulders and almost instinctively his thumb pushed the fire control of the rifle up to automatic.

He crouched behind the jumbled rocks and peered ahead. There was not a thing to see. The hula-trees shimmered in the blaze of sun and the thorn-bush was gray and lifeless and the only things astir were three stilt-birds walking gravely a quarter of a mile away.

"Sipar!" he whispered.

"Here, mister."

"Keep low. It's still out there."

Whatever it might be. Still out there and waiting for another shot. Duncan shivered, remembering the feel of the arrow flying past his throat. A hell of a way for a man to die— out at the tail-end of nowhere with an arrow in his throat and a scared-stiff native heading back for home as fast as it could go.

He flicked the control on the rifle back to single fire, crawled around the rock pile and sprinted for a grove of trees that stood on higher ground. He reached them and there he flanked the spot from which the arrow must have come.

He unlimbered the binoculars and glassed the area. He still saw no sign. Whatever had taken the pot shot at them had made its get-

away.

He walked back to the tree where the arrow still stood out, its point driven deep into the bark. He grasped the shaft and wrenched the arrow free.

"You can come out now," he called to Sipar. "There's no one around."

The arrow was unbelievably crude. The unfeathered shaft looked as if it had been battered off to the proper length with a jagged stone. The arrowhead was unflaked flint picked up from some outcropping or dry creek bed, and it was awkwardly bound to the shaft with the tough but pliant inner bark of the hula-tree.

"You recognize this?" he asked Sipar.

The native took the arrow and examined it. "Not my tribe."

"Of course not your tribe. Yours wouldn't take a shot at us. Some other tribe, perhaps?"

"Very poor arrow."

"I know that. But it could kill you just as dead as if it were a good one. Do you recognize it?"

"No tribe made this arrow," Sipar declared.

"Child, maybe?"

"What would child do way out here?"

"That's what I thought, too," said Duncan.

He took the arrow back, held it between his thumbs and forefingers and twirled it slowly, with a terrifying thought nibbling at his brain. It couldn't be. It was too fantastic. He wondered if the sun was finally getting him that he had thought of it at all.

He squatted down and dug at the ground with the makeshift arrow point. "Sipar, what do you actually know about the Cytha?"

"Nothing, mister. Scared of it is all."

"We aren't turning back. If there's something that you know—something that would help us...."

It was as close as he could come to begging aid. It was further than he had meant to go. He should not have asked at all, he thought angrily.

"I do not know," the native said.

Duncan cast the arrow to one side and rose to his feet. He cradled the rifle in his arm. "Let's go."

He watched Sipar trot ahead. Crafty little stinker, he told himself. It knows more than it's telling.

THEY TOILED INTO THE AFTERNOON. It was, if possible, hotter and drier than the day before. There was a sense of tension in the air—no, that was rot. And even if there were, a man must act as if it were not there. If he let himself fall prey to every mood out in this empty land, he only had himself to blame for whatever happened to him.

The tracking was harder now. The day before, the Cytha had only run away, straight-line fleeing to keep ahead of them, to stay out of their reach. Now it was becoming tricky. It backtracked often in an attempt to throw them off. Twice in the afternoon, the trail blanked out entirely and it was only after long searching that Sipar picked it up

again—in one instance, a mile away from where it had vanished in thin air.

That vanishing bothered Duncan more than he would admit. Trails do not disappear entirely, not when the terrain remains the same, not when the weather is unchanged. Something was going on, something, perhaps, that Sipar knew far more about than it was willing to divulge.

He watched the native closely and there seemed nothing suspicious. It continued at its work. It was, for all to see, the good and faithful hound.

LATE IN THE AFTERNOON, the plain on which they had been traveling suddenly dropped away. They stood poised on the brink of a great escarpment and looked far out to great tangled forests and a flowing river. It was like suddenly coming into another and beautiful room that one had not expected.

This was new land, never seen before by any Earthman. For no one had ever mentioned that somewhere to the west a forest lay beyond the bush. Men coming in from space had seen it, probably, but only as a different color-marking on the planet. To them, it made no difference.

But to the men who lived on Layard, to the planter and the trader, the prospector and the hunter, it was important. And I, thought Duncan with a sense of triumph, am the man who found it.

"Mister!"

"Now what?"

"Out there. *Skun!*"

"I don't—"

"Out there, mister. Across the river."

Duncan saw it then—a haze in the blueness of the rift—a puff of copper moving very fast, and as he watched, he heard the far-off keening of the storm, a shiver in the air rather than a sound.

He watched in fascination as it moved along the river and saw the boiling fury it made out of the forest. It struck and crossed the river, and the river for a moment seemed to stand on end, with a sheet of silvery water splashed toward the sky.

Then it was gone as quickly as it had happened, but there was a tumbled slash across the forest where the churning winds had traveled.

Back at the farm, Zikkara had warned him of the *skun*. This was the season for them, it had said, and a man caught in one wouldn't have a chance.

Duncan let his breath out slowly.

"Bad," said Sipar.

"Yes, very bad."

"Hit fast. No warning."

"What about the trail?" asked Duncan. "Did the Cytha—"

Sipar nodded downward.

"Can we make it before nightfall?"

"I think so," Sipar answered.

It was rougher than they had thought. Twice they went down blind trails that pinched off, with sheer rock faces opening out into drops of hundreds of feet, and were forced to climb again and find another way.

They reached the bottom of the escarpment as the brief twilight closed in and they hurried to gather firewood. There was no water, but a little was still left in their canteens and they made do with that.

AFTER THEIR SCANT MEAL of rockahominy, Sipar rolled himself into a ball and went to sleep immediately.

Duncan sat with his back against a boulder which one day, long ago, had fallen from the slope above them, but was now half buried in the soil that through the ages had kept sifting down.

Two days gone, he told himself.

Was there, after all, some truth in the whispered tales that made the rounds back at the settlements—that no one should waste his time in tracking down a Cytha, since a Cytha was unkillable?

Nonsense, he told himself. And yet the hunt had toughened, the trail become more difficult, the Cytha a much more cunning and elusive quarry. Where it had run from them the day before, now it fought to shake them

off. And if it did that the second day, why had it not tried to throw them off the first? And what about the third day—tomorrow?

He shook his head. It seemed incredible that an animal would become more formidable as the hunt progressed. But that seemed to be exactly what had happened. More spooked, perhaps, more frightened—only the Cytha did not act like a frightened beast. It was acting like an animal that was gaining savvy and determination, and that was somehow frightening.

From far off to the west, toward the forest and the river, came the laughter and the howling of a pack of screamers. Duncan leaned his rifle against the boulder and got up to pile more wood on the fire. He stared out into the western darkness, listening to the racket. He made a wry face and pushed a hand absentmindedly through his hair. He put out a silent hope that the screamers would decide to keep their distance. They were something a man could do without.

Behind him, a pebble came bumping down the slope. It thudded to a rest just short of the fire.

Duncan spun around. Foolish thing to do, he thought, to camp so near the slope. If something big should start to move, they'd be out of luck.

He stood and listened. The night was quiet. Even the screamers had shut up for the moment. Just one rolling rock and he had his hackles up. He'd have to get himself in hand.

He went back to the boulder, and as he stooped to pick up the rifle, he heard the faint beginning of a rumble. He straightened swiftly to face the scarp that blotted out the star-strewn sky—and the rumble grew!

In one leap, he was at Sipar's side. He reached down and grasped the native by an arm, jerked it erect, held it on its feet. Sipar's eyes snapped open, blinking in the firelight.

The rumble had grown to a roar and there were thumping noises, as of heavy boulders bouncing, and beneath the roar the silky, ominous rustle of sliding soil and rock.

Sipar jerked its arm free of Duncan's grip and plunged into the darkness. Duncan whirled and followed.

They ran, stumbling in the dark, and behind them the roar of the sliding, bouncing rock became a throaty roll of thunder that filled the night from brim to brim. As he ran, Duncan could feel, in dread anticipation, the gusty breath of hurtling debris blowing on his neck, the crushing impact of a boulder smashing into him, the engulfing flood of tumbling talus snatching at his legs.

A puff of billowing dust came out and caught them and they ran choking as well as stumbling. Off to the left of them, a mighty chunk of rock chugged along the ground in jerky, almost reluctant fashion.

Then the thunder stopped and all one could hear was the small slitherings of the lesser debris as it trickled down the slope.

Duncan stopped running and slowly turned around. The campfire was gone, buried, no doubt, beneath tons of overlay, and the stars had paled because of the great cloud of dust which still billowed up into the sky.

He heard Sipar moving near him and reached out a hand, searching for the tracker, not knowing exactly where it was. He found the native, grasped it by the shoulder and pulled it up beside him.

Sipar was shivering.

"It's all right," said Duncan.

And it *was* all right, he reassured himself. He still had the rifle. The extra drum of ammunition and the knife were on his belt, the bag of rockahominy in his pocket. The canteens were all they had lost—the canteens and the fire.

"We'll have to hole up somewhere for the night," Duncan said. "There are screamers on the loose."

HE DIDN'T LIKE WHAT HE WAS THINKING, nor the sharp edge of fear that was beginning to crowd in upon him. He tried to shrug it off, but it still stayed with him, just out of reach.

Sipar plucked at his elbow.

"Thorn thicket, mister. Over there. We could crawl inside. We would be safe from screamers."

It was torture, but they made it.

"Screamers and you are taboo," said Duncan, suddenly remembering. "How come you are afraid of them?"

"Afraid for you, mister, mostly. Afraid for myself just a little. Screamers could forget. They might not recognize me until too late. Safer here."

"I agree with you," said Duncan.

The screamers came and padded all about the thicket. The beasts sniffed and clawed at the thorns to reach them, but finally went away.

When morning came, Duncan and Sipar climbed the scarp, clambering over the boulders and the tons of soil and rock that covered their camping place. Following the gash cut by the slide, they clambered up the slope and finally reached the point of the slide's beginning.

There they found the depression in which the poised slab of rock had rested and where the supporting soil had been dug away so that it could be started, with a push, down the slope above the campfire.

And all about were the deeply sunken pug marks of the Cytha!

IV

Now it was more than just a hunt. It was knife against the throat, kill or be killed. Now there was no stopping, when before there might have been. It was no longer sport and there was no mercy.

"And that's the way I like it," Duncan told himself.

He rubbed his hand along the rifle barrel and saw the metallic glints shine in the noonday sun. One more shot, he prayed. Just give me one more shot at it. This time there will be no slip-up. This time there will be more than three sodden hunks of flesh and fur lying in the grass to mock me.

He squinted his eyes against the heat shimmer rising from the river, watching Sipar hunkered beside the water's edge.

The native rose to its feet and trotted back to him.

"It crossed," said Sipar. "It walked out as far as it could go and it must have swum."

"Are you sure? It might have waded out to make us think it crossed, then doubled back again."

He stared at the purple-green of the trees across the river. Inside that forest, it would be hellish going.

"We can look," said Sipar.

"Good. You go downstream. I'll go up."

An hour later, they were back. They had found no tracks. There seemed little doubt the Cytha had really crossed the river.

They stood side by side, looking at the forest.

"Mister, we have come far. You are brave to hunt the Cytha. You have no fear of death."

"The fear of death," Duncan said, "is entirely infantile. And it's beside the point as well. I do not intend to die."

They waded out into the stream. The bottom shelved gradually and they had to swim no more than a hundred yards or so.

They reached the forest bank and threw themselves flat to rest.

Duncan looked back the way that they had come. To the east, the escarpment was a dark-blue smudge against the pale-blue burnished sky. And two days back of that lay the farm and the *vua* field, but they seemed much farther off than that. They were lost in time and distance; they belonged to another existence and another world.

All his life, it seemed to him, had faded and become inconsequential and forgotten, as if this moment in his life were the only one that counted; as if all the minutes and the hours, all the breaths and heartbeats, wake and sleep, had pointed toward this certain hour upon this certain stream, with the rifle molded to his hand and the cool, calculated bloodlust of a killer riding in his brain.

SIPAR FINALLY GOT UP and began to range along the stream. Duncan sat up and watched.

Scared to death, he thought, and yet it stayed with me. At the campfire that first night, it had said it would stick to the death and apparently it had meant exactly what it said. It's hard, he thought, to figure out these jokers, hard to know what kind of mental operation, what seethings of emotion, what brand of ethics and what variety of belief and faith go to make them and their way of life.

It would have been so easy for Sipar to have missed the trail and swear it could not find it. Even from the start, it could have refused to go. Yet, fearing, it had gone. Reluctant, it had trailed. Without any need for faithfulness and loyalty, it had been loyal and faithful. But loyal to what, Duncan wondered, to *him*, the outlander and intruder? Loyal to itself? Or perhaps, although that seemed impossible, faithful to the Cytha?

What does Sipar think of me, he asked himself, and maybe more to the point, what do I think of Sipar? Is there a common meeting ground? Or are we, despite our humanoid forms, condemned forever to be alien and apart?

He held the rifle across his knees and stroked it, polishing it, petting it, making it even more closely a part of him, an instrument of his deadliness, an expression of his determination to track and kill the Cytha.

Just another chance, he begged. Just one second, or even less, to draw a steady bead. That is all I want, all I need, all I'll ask.

Then he could go back across the days that he had left behind him, back to the farm and field, back into that misty other life from which he had been so mysteriously divorced, but which in time undoubtedly would become real and meaningful again.

Sipar came back. "I found the trail."

Duncan heaved himself to his feet. "Good."

They left the river and plunged into the forest and there the heat closed in more mercilessly than ever—humid, stifling heat that felt like a soggy blanket wrapped tightly round the body.

The trail lay plain and clear. The Cytha now, it seemed, was intent upon piling up a lead without recourse to evasive tactics. Perhaps it had reasoned that its pursuers would lose some time at the river and it may have been trying to stretch out that margin even further. Perhaps it needed that extra time, he speculated, to set up the necessary machinery for another dirty trick.

Sipar stopped and waited for Duncan to catch up. "Your knife, mister?"

Duncan hesitated. "What for?"

"I have a thorn in my foot," the native said. "I have to get it out."

Duncan pulled the knife from his belt and tossed it. Sipar caught it deftly.

Looking straight at Duncan, with the flicker of a smile upon its lips, the native cut its throat.

V

HE SHOULD GO BACK, he knew. Without the tracker, he didn't have a chance. The odds were now with the Cytha—if, indeed, they had not been with it from the very start.

Unkillable? Unkillable because it grew in intelligence to meet emergencies? Unkillable because, pressed, it could fashion a bow and arrow, however crude? Unkillable because it had a sense of tactics, like rolling rocks at night upon its enemy? Unkillable because a native tracker would cheerfully kill itself to protect the Cytha?

A sort of crisis-beast, perhaps? One able to develop intelligence and abilities to meet each new situation and then lapsing back to the level of non-intelligent contentment? That, thought Duncan, would be a sensible way for anything to live. It would do away with the inconvenience and the irritability and the discontentment of intelligence when intelligence was unneeded. But the intelligence, and the abilities which went with it, would be there, safely tucked away where one could reach in and get them, like a necklace or a gun—something to be used or to be put away as the case might be.

Duncan hunched forward and with a stick of wood pushed the fire together. The flames blazed up anew and sent sparks flying up into the whispering darkness of the trees. The night had cooled off a little, but the humidity still hung on and a man felt uncomfortable—a little frightened, too.

Duncan lifted his head and stared up into the fire-flecked darkness. There were no stars because the heavy foliage shut them out. He missed the stars. He'd feel better if he could look up and see them.

When morning came, he should go back. He should quit this hunt which now had become impossible and even slightly foolish.

But he knew he wouldn't. Somewhere along the three-day trail, he had become committed to a purpose and a challenge, and he knew that when morning came, he would go on again. It was not hatred that drove him, nor vengeance, nor even the trophy-urge—the hunter-lust that prodded men to kill something strange or harder to kill or bigger than any man had ever killed before. It was something more than that, some weird entangling of the Cytha's meaning with his own.

He reached out and picked up the rifle and laid it in his lap. Its barrel gleamed dully in the flickering campfire light and he rubbed his hand along the stock as another man might stroke a woman's throat.

"Mister," said a voice.

IT DID NOT STARTLE HIM, for the word was softly spoken and for a moment he had forgotten that Sipar was dead—dead with a half-smile fixed upon its face and with its throat laid wide open.

"Mister?"

Duncan stiffened.

Sipar was dead and there was no one else—and yet someone had spoken to him, and there could be only one thing in all this wilderness that might speak to him.

"Yes," he said.

He did not move. He simply sat there, with the rifle in his lap.

"You know who I am?"

"I suppose you are the Cytha."

"You have done well," the Cytha said. "You've made a splendid hunt. There is no dishonor if you should decide to quit. Why don't you go back? I promise you no harm."

It was over there, somewhere in front of him, somewhere in the brush beyond the fire, almost straight across the fire from him, Duncan told himself. If he could keep it talking, perhaps even lure it out—

"Why should I?" he asked. "The hunt is never done until one gets the thing one is after."

"I can kill you," the Cytha told him. "But I do not want to kill. It hurts to kill."

"That's right," said Duncan. "You are most perceptive."

He had it pegged now. He knew exactly where it was. He could afford a little mockery.

His thumb slid up the metal and nudged the fire control to automatic and he flexed his legs beneath him so that he could rise and fire in one single motion.

"Why did you hunt me?" the Cytha asked. "You are a stranger on my world and you had no right to hunt me. Not that I mind, of course. In fact, I found it stimulating. We must do it again. When I am ready to be hunted, I shall come and tell you and we can spend a day or two at it."

"Sure we can," said Duncan, rising. And as he rose into his crouch, he held the trigger down and the gun danced in insane fury, the muzzle flare a flicking tongue of hatred and the hail of death hissing spitefully in the underbrush.

"Anytime you want to," yelled Duncan gleefully, "I'll come and hunt you! You just say the word and I'll be on your tail. I might even kill you. How do you like it, chump!"

And he held the trigger tight and kept his crouch so the slugs would not fly high, but would cut their swath just above the ground, and he moved the muzzle back and forth a lot so that he covered extra ground to compensate for any miscalculations he might have made.

THE MAGAZINE RAN OUT and the gun clicked empty and the vicious chatter stopped. Powder smoke drifted softly in the campfire light and the smell of it was perfume in the nostrils and in the underbrush many little feet were running, as if a thousand frightened mice were scurrying from catastrophe.

Duncan unhooked the extra magazine from where it hung upon his belt and replaced the empty one. Then he snatched a burning length of wood from the fire and waved it frantically until it burst into a blaze and became a torch. Rifle grasped in one hand and the torch in the other, he plunged into the underbrush. Little chittering things fled to escape him.

He did not find the Cytha. He found chewed-up bushes and soil churned by flying metal, and he found five lumps of flesh and fur, and these he brought back to the fire.

Now the fear that had been stalking him, keeping just beyond his reach, walked out from the shadows and hunkered by the campfire with him.

He placed the rifle within easy reach and arranged the five bloody chunks on the ground close to the fire and he tried with trembling fingers to restore them to the shape they'd been before the bullets struck them. And that was a good one, he thought with grim irony, because they had no shape. They had been part of the Cytha and you killed a Cytha inch by inch, not with a single shot. You knocked a pound of meat off it the first time, and the next time you shot off another pound or two, and if you got enough shots at it, you finally carved it down to size and maybe you could kill it then, although he wasn't sure.

He was afraid. He admitted that he was, and he squatted there and watched his fingers shake and he kept his jaws clamped tight to stop the chatter of his teeth.

The fear had been getting closer all the time; he knew it had moved in by a step or two when Sipar cut its throat, and why in the name of God had the damn fool done it? It made no sense at all. He had wondered about Sipar's loyalties, and the very loyalties that he had dismissed as a sheer impossibility had been the answer, after all. In the end, for some obscure reason—obscure to humans, that is—Sipar's loyalty had been to the Cytha.

But then what was the use of searching for any reason in it? Nothing that had happened made any sense. It made no sense that a beast one was pursuing should up and talk to one—although it did fit in with the theory of the crisis-beast he had fashioned in his mind.

PROGRESSIVE ADAPTATION, he told himself. Carry adaptation far enough and you'd reach communication. But might not the Cytha's power of adaptation be running down? Had the Cytha gone about as far as it could force itself to go? Maybe so, he thought. It might be worth a gamble. Sipar's suicide, for all its casualness, bore the overtones of last-notch desperation. And the Cytha's speaking to Duncan, its attempt to parley with him, contained a note of weakness.

The arrow had failed and the rockslide had failed and so had Sipar's death. What next would the Cytha try? Had it anything to try?

Tomorrow he'd find out. Tomorrow he'd go on. He couldn't turn back now.

He was too deeply involved. He'd always wonder, if he turned back now, whether another hour or two might not have seen the end of it. There were too many questions, too much mystery—there was now far more at stake than ten rows of *vua*.

Another day might make some sense of it, might banish the dread walker that trod upon his heels, might bring some peace of mind.

As it stood right at the moment, none of it made sense. But even as he thought it, suddenly one of the bits of bloody flesh and mangled fur made sense.

Beneath the punching and prodding of his fingers, it had assumed a shape.

Breathlessly, Duncan bent above it, not believing, not even wanting to believe, hoping frantically that it should prove completely wrong.

But there was nothing wrong with it. The shape was there and could not be denied. It had somehow fitted back into its natural shape and it was a baby screamer—well, maybe not a baby, but at least a tiny screamer.

Duncan sat back on his heels and sweated. He wiped his bloody hands upon the ground. He wondered what other shapes he'd find if he put back into proper place the other hunks of limpness that lay beside the fire.

He tried and failed. They were too smashed and torn.

He picked them up and tossed them in the fire. He took up his rifle and walked around the fire, sat down with his back against a tree, cradling the gun across his knees.

THOSE LITTLE SCURRYING FEET, he wondered—like the scampering of a thousand busy mice. He had heard them twice, that first night in the thicket by the waterhole and again tonight.

And what could the Cytha be? Certainly not the simple, uncomplicated, marauding animal he had thought to start with.

A hive-beast? A host animal? A thing masquerading in many different forms?

Shotwell, trained in such deductions, might make a fairly accurate guess, but Shotwell was not here. He was at the farm, fretting, more than likely, over Duncan's failure to return.

Finally the first light of morning began to filter through the forest and it was not the glaring, clean white light of the open plain and bush, but a softened, diluted, fuzzy green light to match the smothering vegetation.

The night noises died away and the noises of the day took up—the sawings of unseen insects, the screechings of hidden birds and something far away began to make a noise that sounded like an empty barrel falling slowly down a stairway.

What little coolness the night had brought dissipated swiftly and the heat clamped down, a breathless, relentless heat that quivered in the air.

Circling, Duncan picked up the Cytha trail

not more than a hundred yards from camp.

The beast had been traveling fast. The pug marks were deeply sunk and widely spaced. Duncan followed as rapidly as he dared. It was a temptation to follow at a run, to match the Cytha's speed, for the trail was plain and fresh and it fairly beckoned.

And that was wrong, Duncan told himself. It was too fresh, too plain—almost as if the animal had gone to endless trouble so that the human could not miss the trail.

He stopped his trailing and crouched beside a tree and studied the tracks ahead. His hands were too tense upon the gun, his body keyed too high and fine. He forced himself to take slow, deep breaths. He had to calm himself. He had to loosen up.

He studied the tracks ahead—four bunched pug marks, then a long leap interval, then four more bunched tracks, and between the sets of marks the forest floor was innocent and smooth.

Too smooth, perhaps. Especially the third one from him. Too smooth and somehow artificial, as if someone had patted it with gentle hands to make it unsuspicious.

Duncan sucked his breath in slowly.

Trap? Or was his imagination playing tricks on him?

And if it were a trap, he would have fallen into it if he had kept on following as he had started out.

Now there was something else, a strange uneasiness, and he stirred uncomfortably, casting frantically for some clue to what it was.

He rose and stepped out from the tree, with the gun at ready. What a perfect place to set a trap, he thought. One would be looking at the pug marks, never at the space between them, for the space between would be neutral ground, safe to stride out upon.

Oh, clever Cytha, he said to himself. Oh, clever, clever Cytha!

And now he knew what the other trouble was—the great uneasiness. It was the sense of being watched.

Somewhere up ahead, the Cytha was crouched, watching and waiting—anxious or exultant, maybe even with laughter rumbling in its throat.

He walked slowly forward until he reached the third set of tracks and he saw that he had been right. The little area ahead was smoother than it should be.

"Cytha!" he called.

His voice was far louder than he had meant it to be and he stood astonished and a bit abashed.

Then he realized why it was so loud.

It was the only sound there was!

The forest suddenly had fallen silent. The insects and birds were quiet and the thing in the distance had quit falling down the stairs. Even the leaves were silent. There was no rustle in them and they hung limp upon their stems.

There was a feeling of doom and the green light had changed to a copper light and everything was still.

And the light was *copper!*

Duncan spun around in panic. There was no place for him to hide.

Before he could take another step, the *skun* came and the winds rushed out of nowhere. The air was clogged with flying leaves and debris. Trees snapped and popped and tumbled in the air.

The wind hurled Duncan to his knees, and as he fought to regain his feet, he remembered, in a blinding flash of total recall, how it had looked from atop the escarpment—the boiling fury of the winds and the mad swirling of the coppery mist and how the trees had whipped in whirlpool fashion.

He came half erect and stumbled, clawing at the ground in an attempt to get up again, while inside his brain an insistent, clicking voice cried out for him to run, and somewhere another voice said to lie flat upon the ground, to dig in as best he could.

Something struck him from behind and he went down, pinned flat, with his rifle wedged beneath him. He cracked his head upon the ground and the world whirled sickeningly and plastered his face with a handful of mud and tattered leaves.

He tried to crawl and couldn't, for something had grabbed him by the ankle and was hanging on.

With a frantic hand, he clawed the mess out of his eyes, spat it from his mouth.

Across the spinning ground, something black and angular tumbled rapidly. It was coming straight toward him and he saw it was the Cytha and that in another second it would be on top of him.

He threw up an arm across his face, with the elbow crooked, to take the impact of the wind-blown Cytha and to ward it off.

But it never reached him. Less than a yard away, the ground opened up to take the Cytha and it was no longer there.

Suddenly the wind cut off and the leaves once more hung motionless and the heat clamped down again and that was the end of it. The *skun* had come and struck and gone.

Minutes, Duncan wondered, or perhaps no more than seconds. But in those seconds, the forest had been flattened and the trees lay in shattered heaps.

He raised himself on an elbow and looked to see what was the matter with his foot and he saw that a fallen tree had trapped his foot beneath it.

He tugged a few times experimentally. It was no use. Two close-set limbs, branching almost at right angles from the hole, had been driven deep into the ground and his foot, he saw, had been caught at the ankle in the fork of the buried branches.

The foot didn't hurt—not yet. It didn't seem to be there at all. He tried wiggling his toes and felt none.

He wiped the sweat off his face with a shirt sleeve and fought to force down the panic that was rising in him. Getting panicky was the worst thing a man could do in a spot like this. The thing to do was to take stock of the situation, figure out the best approach, then go ahead and try it.

The tree looked heavy, but perhaps he could handle it if he had to, although there was the danger that if he shifted it, the bole might settle more solidly and crush his foot beneath it. At the moment, the two heavy branches, thrust into the ground on either side of his ankle, were holding most of the tree's weight off his foot.

The best thing to do, he decided, was to dig the ground away beneath his foot until he could pull it out.

He twisted around and started digging with the fingers of one hand. Beneath the thin covering of humus, he struck a solid surface and his fingers slid along it.

With mounting alarm, he explored the ground, scratching at the humus. There was nothing but rock—some long-buried boulder, the top of which lay just beneath the ground.

His foot was trapped beneath a heavy tree and a massive boulder, held securely in place by forked branches that had forced their splintering way down along the boulder's sides.

HE LAY BACK, propped on an elbow. It was evident that he could do nothing about the buried boulder. If he was going to do anything, his problem was the tree.

To move the tree, he would need a lever and he had a good, stout lever in his rifle. It would be a shame, he thought a little wryly, to use a gun for such a purpose, but he had no choice.

He worked for an hour and it was no good. Even with the

rifle as a pry, he could not budge the tree.

He lay back, defeated, breathing hard, wringing wet with perspiration.

He grimaced at the sky.

All right, Cytha, he thought, you won out in the end. But it took a *skun* to do it. With all your tricks, you couldn't do the job until....

Then he remembered.

He sat up hurriedly.

"Cytha!" he called.

The Cytha had fallen into a hole that had opened in the ground. The hole was less than an arm's length away from him, with a little debris around its edges still trickling into it.

Duncan stretched out his body, lying flat upon the ground, and looked into the hole. There, at the bottom of it, was the Cytha.

It was the first time he'd gotten a good look at the Cytha and it was a crazily put-together thing. It seemed to have nothing functional about it and it looked more like a heap of something, just thrown on the ground, than it did an animal.

The hole, he saw, was more than an ordinary hole. It was a pit and very cleverly constructed. The mouth was about four feet in diameter and it widened to roughly twice that at the bottom. It was, in general, bottle-shaped, with an incurving shoulder at the top so that anything that fell in could not climb out. Anything falling into that pit was in to stay.

This, Duncan knew, was what had lain beneath that too-smooth interval between the two sets of Cytha tracks. The Cytha had worked all night to dig it, then had carried away the dirt dug out of the pit and had built a flimsy camouflage cover over it. Then it had gone back and made the trail that was so loud and clear, so easy to make out and follow. And having done all that, having labored hard and stealthily, the Cytha had settled down to watch, to make sure the following human had fallen in the pit.

"HI, PAL," SAID DUNCAN. "How are you making out?"

The Cytha did not answer.

"Classy pit," said Duncan. "Do you always den up in luxury like this?"

But the Cytha didn't answer.

Something queer was happening to the Cytha. It was coming all apart.

Duncan watched with fascinated horror as the Cytha broke down into a thousand lumps of motion that scurried in the pit and tried to scramble up its sides, only to fall back in tiny showers of sand.

Amid the scurrying lumps, one thing remained intact, a fragile object that resembled nothing quite so much as the stripped skeleton of a Thanksgiving turkey. But it was a most extraordinary Thanksgiving skeleton, for it throbbed with pulsing life and glowed with a steady violet light.

Chitterings and squeakings came out of the pit and the soft patter of tiny running feet, and as Duncan's eyes became accustomed to the darkness of the pit, he began to make out the forms of some of the scurrying shapes. There were tiny screamers and some donovans and sawmill birds and a bevy of kill-devils and something else as well.

Duncan raised a hand and pressed it against his eyes, then took it quickly away. The little faces still were there, looking up as if beseeching him, with the white shine of their teeth and the white rolling of their eyes.

He felt horror wrenching at his stomach and the sour, bitter taste of revulsion welled into his throat, but he fought it down, harking back to that day at the farm before they had started on the hunt.

"I can track down anything but screamers, stilt-birds, longhorns and donovans," Sipar had told him solemnly. "These are my taboos."

And Sipar was also *their* taboo, for he had not feared the donovan. Sipar had been, however, somewhat fearful of the screamers in the dead of night because, the native had told him reasonably, screamers were forgetful.

Forgetful of what!

Forgetful of the Cytha-mother? Forgetful

of the motley brood in which they had spent their childhood?

For that was the only answer to what was running in the pit and the whole, unsuspected answer to the enigma against which men like Shotwell had frustratedly banged their heads for years.

STRANGE, HE TOLD HIMSELF. All right, it might be strange, but if it worked, what difference did it make? So the planet's denizens were sexless because there was no need of sex—what was wrong with that? It might, in fact, Duncan admitted to himself, head off a lot of trouble. No family spats, no triangle trouble, no fighting over mates. While it might be unexciting, it did seem downright peaceful.

And since there was no sex, the Cytha species was the planetary mother—but more than just a mother. The Cytha, more than likely, was mother-father, incubator, nursery, teacher and perhaps many other things besides, all rolled into one.

In many ways, he thought, it might make a lot of sense. Here natural selection would be ruled out and ecology could be controlled in considerable degree, and mutation might even be a matter of deliberate choice rather than random happenstance.

And it would make for a potential planetary unity such as no other world had ever known. Everything here was kin to everything else. Here was a planet where Man, or any other alien, must learn to tread most softly. For it was not inconceivable that, in a crisis or a clash of interests, one might find himself faced suddenly with a unified and cooperating planet, with every form of life making common cause against the interloper.

The little scurrying things had given up; they'd gone back to their places, clustered around the pulsing violet of the Thanksgiving skeleton, each one fitting into place until the Cytha had taken shape again. As if, Duncan told himself, blood and nerve and muscle had come back from a brief vacation to form the beast anew.

"Mister," asked the Cytha, "what do we do now?"

"You should know," Duncan told it. "You were the one who dug the pit."

"I split myself," the Cytha said. "A part of me dug the pit and the other part that stayed on the surface got me out when the job was done."

"Convenient," grunted Duncan.

And it *was* convenient. That was what had happened to the Cytha when he had shot at it—it had split into all its component parts and had got away. And that night beside the waterhole, it had spied on him, again in the form of all its separate parts, from the safety of the thicket.

"You are caught and so am I," the Cytha said. "Both of us will die here. It seems a fitting end to our association. Do you not agree with me?"

"I'll get you out," said Duncan wearily. "I have no quarrel with children."

He dragged the rifle toward him and unhooked the sling from the stock. Carefully he lowered the gun by the sling, still attached to the barrel, down into the pit.

The Cytha reared up and grasped it with its forepaws.

"Easy now," Duncan cautioned. "You're heavy. I don't know if I can hold you."

But he needn't have worried. The little ones were detaching themselves and scrambling up the rifle and the sling. They reached his extended arms and ran up them with scrabbling claws. Little sneering screamers and the comic stilt-birds and the mouse-size kill-devils that snarled at him as they climbed. And the little grinning natives—not babies, scarcely children, but small editions of full-grown humanoids. And the weird donovans scampering happily.

They came climbing up his arms and across his shoulders and milled about on the ground beside him, waiting for the others.

And finally the Cytha, not skinned down to the bare bones of its Thanksgiving-turkey-size, but far smaller than it had been, climbed awkwardly up the rifle and the sling to safety.

Duncan hauled the rifle up and twisted himself into a sitting position.

The Cytha, he saw, was reassembling.

He watched in fascination as the restless miniatures of the planet's life swarmed and seethed like a hive of bees, each one clicking into place to form the entire beast.

And now the Cytha was complete. Yet small—still small—no more than lion-size.

"But it is such a little one," Zikkara had argued with him that morning at the farm. "It is such a young one."

Just a young brood, no more than suckling infants—if suckling was the word, or even some kind of wild approximation. And through the months and years, the Cytha would grow, with the growing of its diverse children, until it became a monstrous thing.

It stood there looking at Duncan and the tree.

"Now," said Duncan, "if you'll push on the tree, I think that between the two of us—"

"It is too bad," the Cytha said, and wheeled itself about.

He watched it go loping off.

"Hey!" he yelled.

But it didn't stop.

He grabbed up the rifle and had it halfway to his shoulder before he remembered how absolutely futile it was to shoot at the Cytha.

He let the rifle down.

"The dirty, ungrateful, double-crossing—"

He stopped himself. There was no profit in rage. When you were in a jam, you did the best you could. You figured out the problem and you picked the course that seemed best and you didn't panic at the odds.

He laid the rifle in his lap and started to hook up the sling and it was not till then that he saw the barrel was packed with sand and dirt.

He sat numbly for a moment, thinking back to how close he had been to firing at the Cytha, and if that barrel was packed hard enough or deep enough, he might have had an exploding weapon in his hands.

He had used the rifle as a crowbar, which was no way to use a gun. That was one way, he told himself, that was guaranteed to ruin it.

DUNCAN HUNTED AROUND and found a twig and dug at the clogged muzzle, but the dirt was jammed too firmly in it and he made little progress.

He dropped the twig and was hunting for another stronger one when he caught the motion in a nearby clump of brush.

He watched closely for a moment and there was nothing, so he resumed the hunt for a stronger twig. He found one and started poking at the muzzle and there was another flash of motion.

He twisted around. Not more than twenty feet away, a screamer sat easily on its haunches. Its tongue was lolling out and it had what looked like a grin upon its face.

And there was another, just at the edge of the clump of brush where he had caught the motion first.

There were others as well, he knew. He could hear them sliding through the tangle of fallen trees, could sense the soft padding of their feet.

The executioners, he thought.

The Cytha certainly had not wasted any time.

He raised the rifle and rapped the barrel smartly on the fallen tree, trying to dislodge the obstruction in the bore. But it didn't budge; the barrel still was packed with sand.

But no matter—he'd have to fire anyhow and take whatever chance there was.

He shoved the control to automatic, and tilted up the muzzle.

There were six of them now, sitting in a ragged row, grinning at him, not in any hurry. They were sure of him and there was no hurry. He'd still be there when they decided to move in.

And there were others—on all sides of him.

Once it started, he wouldn't have a chance.

"It'll be expensive, gents," he told them.

And he was astonished at how calm, how coldly objective he could be, now that the chips were down. But that was the way it was, he realized.

He'd thought, a while ago, how a man might suddenly find himself face to face with an aroused and cooperating planet. Maybe this was it in miniature.

The Cytha had obviously passed the word along: *Man back there needs killing. Go and get him.*

Just like that, for a Cytha would be the power here. A life force, the giver of life, the decider of life, the repository of all animal life on the entire planet.

There was more than one of them, of course. Probably they had home districts, spheres of influence and responsibility mapped out. And each one would be a power supreme in its own district.

Momism, he thought with a sour grin. Momism at its absolute peak.

Nevertheless, he told himself, it wasn't too bad a system if you wanted to consider it objectively. But he was in a poor position to be objective about that or anything else.

THE SCREAMERS WERE INCHING CLOSER, hitching themselves forward slowly on their bottoms.

"I'm going to set up a deadline for you critters," Duncan called out. "Just two feet farther, up to that rock, and I let you have it."

He'd get all six of them, of course, but the shots would be the signal for the general rush by all those other animals slinking in the brush.

If he were free, if he were on his feet, possibly he could beat them off. But pinned as he was, he didn't have a chance. It would be all over less than a minute after he opened fire. He might, he figured, last as long as that.

The six inched closer and he raised the rifle.

But they stopped and moved no farther. Their ears lifted just a little, as if they might be listening, and the grins dropped from their faces. They squirmed uneasily and assumed a look of guilt and, like shadows, they were gone, melting away so swiftly that he scarcely saw them go.

Duncan sat quietly, listening, but he could hear no sound.

Reprieve, he thought. But for how long? Something had scared them off, but in a while they might be back. He had to get out of here and he had to make it fast.

If he could find a longer lever, he could move the tree. There was a branch slanting up from the topside of the fallen tree. It was almost four inches at the butt and it carried its diameter well.

He slid the knife from his belt and looked at it. Too small, too thin, he thought, to chisel through a four-inch branch, but it was all he had. When a man was desperate enough, though, when his very life depended on it, he would do anything.

He hitched himself along, sliding toward the point where the branch protruded from the tree. His pinned leg protested with stabs of pain as his body wrenched it around. He gritted his teeth and pushed himself closer. Pain slashed through his leg again and he was still long inches from the branch.

He tried once more, then gave up. He lay panting on the ground.

There was just one thing left.

He'd have to try to hack out a notch in the trunk just above his leg. No, that would be next to impossible, for he'd be cutting into the whorled and twisted grain at the base of the supporting fork.

Either that or cut off his foot, and that was even more impossible. A man would faint before he got the job done.

It was useless, he knew. He could do neither one. There was nothing he could do.

FOR THE FIRST TIME, he admitted to himself: He would stay here and die. Shotwell, back at the farm, in a day or two might set out hunting for him. But Shotwell would never find him. And anyhow, by nightfall, if not sooner, the screamers would be back.

He laughed gruffly in his throat—laughing at himself.

The Cytha had won the hunt hands down.

It had used a human weakness to win and then had used that same human weakness to achieve a viciously poetic vengeance.

After all, what could one expect? One could not equate human ethics with the ethics of the Cytha. Might not human ethics, in certain cases, seem as weird and illogical, as infamous and ungrateful, to an alien?

He hunted for a twig and began working again to clean the rifle bore.

A crashing behind him twisted him around and he saw the Cytha. Behind the Cytha stalked a donovan.

He tossed away the twig and raised the gun.

"No," said the Cytha sharply.

The donovan tramped purposefully forward and Duncan felt the prickling of the skin along his back. It was a frightful thing. Nothing could stand before a donovan. The screamers had turned tail and run when they had heard it a couple of miles or more away.

The donovan was named for the first known human to be killed by one. That first was only one of many. The roll of donovan-victims ran long, and no wonder, Duncan thought. It was the closest he had ever been to one of the beasts and he felt a coldness creeping over him. It was like an elephant and a tiger and a grizzly bear wrapped in the selfsame hide. It was the most vicious fighting machine that ever had been spawned.

He lowered the rifle. There would be no point in shooting. In two quick strides, the beast could be upon him.

The donovan almost stepped on him and he flinched away. Then the great head lowered and gave the fallen tree a butt and the tree bounced for a yard or two. The donovan kept on walking. Its powerfully muscled stern moved into the brush and out of sight.

"Now we are even," said the Cytha. "I had to get some help."

Duncan grunted. He flexed the leg that had been trapped and he could not feel the foot. Using his rifle as a cane, he pulled himself erect. He tried putting weight on the in-jured foot and it screamed with pain.

He braced himself with the rifle and rotated so that he faced the Cytha.

"Thanks, pal," he said. "I didn't think you'd do it."

"You will not hunt me now?"

Duncan shook his head. "I'm in no shape for hunting. I am heading home."

"It was the *vua*, wasn't it? That was why you hunted me?"

"The *vua* is my livelihood," said Duncan. "I cannot let you eat it."

The Cytha stood silently and Duncan watched it for a moment. Then he wheeled. Using the rifle for a crutch, he started hobbling away.

The Cytha hurried to catch up with him.

"Let us make a bargain, mister. I will not eat the *vua* and you will not hunt me. Is that fair enough?"

"That is fine with me," said Duncan. "Let us shake on it."

He put down a hand and the Cytha lifted up a paw. They shook, somewhat awkwardly, but very solemnly.

"Now," the Cytha said, "I will see you home. The screamers would have you before you got out of the woods."

VI

They halted on a knoll. Below them lay the farm, with the *vua* rows straight and green in the red soil of the fields.

"You can make it from here," the Cytha said. "I am wearing thin. It is an awful effort to keep on being smart. I want to go back to ignorance and comfort."

"It was nice knowing you," Duncan told it politely. "And thanks for sticking with me."

He started down the hill, leaning heavily on the rifle-crutch. Then he frowned troubledly and turned back.

"Look," he said, "you'll go back to animal again. Then you will forget. One of these days, you'll see all that nice, tender *vua* and—"

"Very simple," said the Cytha. "If you find me in the *vua*, just begin hunting me. With you after me, I will quickly get smart and remember once again, and it will be all right."

"Sure," agreed Duncan. "I guess that will work."

The Cytha watched him go stumping down the hill. Admirable, it thought. Next time I have a brood, I think I'll raise a dozen like him.

It turned around and headed for the deeper brush.

It felt intelligence slipping from it, felt the old, uncaring comfort coming back again. But it glowed with anticipation, seethed with happiness at the big surprise it had in store for its new-found friend.

Won't he be happy and surprised when I drop them at his door, it thought.

Will he be ever pleased!

👽 👽 👽

A rare gem indeed, "The Planet that Couldn't Be" first appeared in the January 1958 issue of Galaxy Science Fiction.

American writer Clifford D. Simak began his career in the early 1930s by publishing a handful of super science tales in Wonder Stories, *a magazine founded by Hugo ("The Father of Science Fiction") Gernsback. Over the next few years Simak continued to delve into SF sporadically, while producing numerous western and war stories for the adventure pulps of the day. Once Simak finally settled down to strange worlds and sensational ideas, he proved himself both thoughtful and prolific. Clifford's prose is always profound, but never preachy, and fans and professionals acknowledged his genius with three Hugo Awards, a Nebula, a Jupiter and a Bram Stoker Award for Lifetime Achievement.*

Simak writes, "I have been happily married to the same woman for thirty-three years (...without whom I'd never have written a line) and have two children. My favorite recreation is fishing (the lazy way, lying in a boat and letting them come to me). Hobbies: Chess, stamp collecting, growing roses."

The Green Slime are coming!

BLACK INFINITY #2 (early 2018): Blobs, Globs, Slime & Spores

The Builders had constructed a self-contained world—safe, secure and, above all, familiar. But like most worlds, it held its own unique perils, such as ...

GOING HARVEY IN THE BIG HOUSE

by Douglas Smith

BIG G's FIRST THOUGHT EACH WAKE TIME was how much he missed his drawer in his old sector of the House. His new cube was too big.

Rubbing his eyes with a beefy hand, he sat up on his sleep shelf, ducking his head needlessly from habit born of years of waking in a drawer. Triggered by his movement, the ceiling tiles glowed to full brightness.

Big G looked around his cube. Dull green walls. A floor covered with a gray coarse carpet. His private in-chute and dis-chute in the opposite wall, with a hidden compartment big enough to make his few personal items seem lonely lying inside. He shook his head. All of this luxury still made him uneasy.

But what bothered him most was the size of the cube. Six and a half feet long, and five feet wide, with a ceiling so far overhead that he had to stand to touch it.

He sighed. Too much space. It wasn't right.

Sometimes now, he'd wake in sleep time, reach out, and feel nothing. He'd panic then, flinging out his arms and legs, snapping his neck back, only to thump his head and crack his knuckles on the walls beside him.

Falling reflex. That's what Tapper, his partner, called it. From when our ancestors built the House generations ago to shelter us from the poisons of the Outside. The Builders would fall sometimes, Tapper said, and they'd throw out their arms and legs, trying to catch a girder or a beam to save themselves.

Tapper used to work in Archives, so he had lots of stories of Outside and the Builders and the House. Big G didn't know about those things. He just knew his new cube

made him nervous.

But the Inners had made him a Smoother, and the Inners were the direct descendants of the Builders. *The House protects the People, and the Inners protect the House.* And Smoothers were the arms and legs of that protection. Smoothers needed to be respected and feared, so the Inners gave them cubes. Big cubes.

His ID chip pulsed in his head, signaling an incoming call. Grabbing his specs from where they hung above his sleep shelf, he slipped them over his eyes. The word "Dispatch" flashed in red on the left lens. He touched a finger—the one with his Smoother chip imbedded in the tip—to a stud on the temple of the specs.

"Yeah?" he answered, sounding groggy even to himself.

"What 'yeah'?" snapped the voice in his ear. It was Marker. Marker was an asshole, even for Dispatch.

Big G bit back a retort, glad that ID chips could only transmit basic biometrics, and not thoughts. Still, it wouldn't do for his readings to show him getting angry. He swallowed hard. "I mean, Smoother on shift, sir."

"Better be. Got a Harvey for you and Tapper. Here're the cords." The coordinates for the Harvey's location in the House flashed on his lens as they stored themselves in his specs: Sector E7-S8, Block D32-W26-S33, Cube U19-N7-W28.

The com light winked out, as Marker ended the call without another word. Big G sighed. He'd pissed off a Dispatcher. "Got off on the wrong floor with 'im," Tapper would say. Plus he'd been stuck with a Harvey. Great start to the shift.

Beside his sleep shelf stood the flush. Despite protests from his bladder, he just stared at the facility with distaste. His own flush. Before, he'd shared one with his whole block, lining up to use it or to dump his bag. He even missed the smell. Now he only had to bag up for time outside his cube.

Tossing the specs back onto their hook, Big G got up to use the flush. The sleep shelf folded up into the wall, making the room seem even larger.

A soft "hiss-plop" signaled his tube of glop arriving in his in-chute, prompted by his use of the flush. He squeezed the glop into his mouth, enjoying its familiar chalky taste. After his promotion, he'd tried other flavors available to Smoothers, but had quickly gone back to the standard citizen issue.

Glop should taste like glop, he'd told Tapper. Tapper had laughed. "Think it's standard issue? The citizens get No-aggra in *their* glop. We don't. The Inners *want* us aggressive," he'd said. "And happy," he'd added, making a gesture at his crotch.

Big G finished his tube and dropped it into the dis-chute, reminding himself to request a conjugal visit for his next off-shift. Another benefit of being a Smoother.

After wiping depil cream on and off his face and head, he took a quick buzz bath, passing the electrostatic wand over himself. He bagged up and shrugged into his red one-piece. Yeah, his cube was too big, but he still grinned when he put on his reds. Red said Smoother. Red said, "Don't mess with me."

He retrieved his specs and stepped onto the flow disk in front of his door. Calling up the Harvey's cords on his specs, he spoke the "Go" command. As the disk received the destination from the specs, the door to his cube "shooshed" open, and the smells and sounds of the House assailed him.

A RHYTHMIC PULSE on her chip awakened Laryn. One slow, two fast. She sat up on her sleep shelf, fully alert. Her illegal trojan programs were warning her of a status change for one of her people. Brushing long dark hair out of her eyes with thin fingers, Laryn donned her specs and spoke the display command.

And swore. Another recent recruit for the Movement had gone Harvey. A Smoother team was already on its way.

After ensuring that her trojans had given the call to the right team, she flagged the file for tracking. She would watch the progress of this one until she went on-shift in an hour.

Laryn sat back, biting her lip, no longer able to ignore the pattern. This Harvey pushed the regression rate in new recruits to over thirty percent. *Has humanity lost so much*, she thought? *Is it already too late for us?*

Or were the Movement's selection criteria flawed? Laryn herself had programmed the trojan that searched for recruits. The trojan constantly scanned the terabytes of data on citizens flowing through the House, searching for a specific mix of intellect, initiative, and motivation, expressed via complex psychological patterning algorithms. She'd based her trojan on software her fellow Inners used to find their own new initiates.

And she was living proof of the flaws in *that* process.

The citizens believed the Inners to be direct descendants of the Builders themselves, believing it because the Inners told them to. But the family social structure that could have supported that myth had died soon after the birth of the House.

In reality, the Inners *chose* who would enter their circle, selecting candidates at a young age after careful screening and then subjecting them to intensive indoctrination.

Not for the first time, Laryn wondered how she'd slipped through. How *she* had become an Inner. *If the Inners can choose so badly, then so can we,* she thought. *Are we doomed already?*

To restore her resolve, she opened a hidden compartment and removed the object that had become her touchstone. She sat back on her sleep shelf, telling herself yet again that she held the power to free the people in her hand.

The object she held was simple enough: an image of a thing, a thing her fellow Inners told the people no longer existed.

In her hand, she held the *truth*.

Staring at the image, Laryn realized that perhaps the Inners had *not* erred in choosing her those twenty years ago.

They'd chosen her to be a leader.

And a leader she would be.

She imagined again that she could see it all happen. In her mind, cracks appeared in the walls, in all the thousands, millions, billions of walls of the House. Next, the ceilings began to sag under the weight of the truth they hid, struggling not to fall, straining not to reveal the thing waiting above.

But she knew that they would fall. They would all fall. The House would fall.

As the people rose up.

IN THE HALL OUTSIDE Big G's open door, a river of humanity flowed by him in both directions at a steady twenty miles per hour. Each person stood on their own flow disk, each disk moving over the magnetic flow fields below, programmed for a wake or sleep time destination.

Big G's cube sat on the east side of an EW-hall. The hall, like most in the House, was twelve feet across with two main central flows running in opposite directions. On each side, short merge paths led from the cube doors lining the hall to the central flow for that side.

Before he was a Smoother, Big G had been in Flow, assigned to Block U7-W23-N14, Sector W3-S8. He'd been in Flow since being certified Clean—no retro traits—at nine calendars of age. But Big G had grown, into his name and out of a job. He could no longer squeeze his bulk through the access doors in the floors and along the maintenance tunnels that ran two feet high below the flow tracks that moved the citizens through the House.

As Big G's flow disk accelerated smoothly forward from his doorway into the merge path, he weight-shifted by habit, not even holding the balance bar that formed a half-circle at waist height. The east-flow adjusted, creating a space between two white-garbed Techs into which Big G's disk slipped with no noticeable change in speed for the other east-side travelers. Big G thought of his years in Flow and felt a stab of pride at his small part in how the House worked, how the Flow kept flowing, moving the people to where they had to be.

The ever-present buzz-hum of the Flow that was the song of the House washed over him. He breathed in the people smells he missed in his new cube, thick and pungent, and tinged here with a sting of ozone. He watched the travelers passing in the west-flow, mostly white Techs and blue Makers in this sector, some gray Crats, a black Recycler. Each person looked away, avoiding eye contact with a Smoother. He had their respect, their fear.

After ten minutes, his disk entered the flow circle in the intersection with a NS-hall. It orbited, queuing for the down-side of the UD-tube at the circle center. He checked the Harvey's cords. Down sixty-two levels. Flush it, he thought. He hated big drops.

His turn came, and his disk slid onto the next empty slot on the down-side of the tube. Big G swallowed and forced his face to relax as the slot clamps stabilized his disk. Not good to let the people see a Smoother sweat over something as common as a drop. But he still counted every level as they flashed by.

He knew that Tapper would be on his way to the same cords. Tapper was his partner, and Dispatch always sent two Smoothers to a Harvey. Never knew how bad these calls would be. He hoped the Harvey would already be dead. That happened a lot.

He'd asked Tapper once why they called them Harveys. Tapper had said that it came from an alcool drink the Builders had made—Harvey Wallbanger, they'd called it. *Wallbanger*, get it? Then he'd laughed. Even Tapper didn't believe that one.

Well, Harveys did generally start with banging the walls of their drawers. Frowning, he checked the Harvey's cords again. This one was in a cube. Harveys were usually in drawers.

His disk reached the Harvey's level and slid out of the down-tube into another traffic circle. It looped around to the north-flow, rode that for ten blocks, then demerged and slipped into the small, dimly lit access lane for the cubes on the inside of that block. Six cubes along, it slowed and stopped.

Tapper was waiting, his small thin frame leaning on the wall, bony fingers drumming a rhythm on his thigh like a mech-claw in a loop. That's how he got his name. But the Inners didn't name him. Inners knew you by your ID and called you by your job. People you worked with, they gave you your name.

"Took ya enough," Tapper said with a sharp-featured grin. "Whadya do? Try to find a route with no drop?" The grin disappeared as he dodged a cuff from Big G.

"So why didn't you clean it up yourself, shorty, you in so much of a hurry?" Big G growled.

Tapper sniffed, faking all serious. "Against the regs. Going solo on a Harvey."

Big G laughed. "When'd you ever stick to regs?"

Tapper's grin returned. "When I'm first at a Harvey call."

Snorting, Big G touched his Smoother finger to a small indentation beside the door of the Harvey's cube. The snoop spot irised open, and he bent down to peer in. He moved his head back and forth, and then straightened. "Can't see a thing."

"Dispatch thinks he covered the lens with glop."

"That's a new one."

"Guess he got sick of that one flavor you like so much."

Big G chuckled, relaxing a bit when he heard that it wasn't a woman. Female Harveys were the worst, at least for him. He didn't like having to hurt them.

"You activate his camera?" Big G asked.

All cubes, except for Inners, contained cameras, as did all intersections, supposedly capturing each citizen's every action. As a Smoother, Big G now knew that it would be impossible to monitor such displays or even store an hour's activity in the House. The ID chips were far more efficient, tracking movements and restricting access to areas as needed. But cameras *could* be activated for a specified ID chip at the request of a Smoother.

Tapper shook his head. "Covered that lens too."

"So how do we know he's in there?"

Tapper touched a stud on his specs. "Central says his chip's inside. So unless he's carved it out of his head—"

"Been done before."

"In which case, he's bleeding to death somewhere else."

"At least that wouldn't be our call," Big G muttered.

Tapper's face went all smooth, calm. He reached up and squeezed Big G's shoulder. "S'okay. Just our job. Harveys, well, they're already gone once they get to this stage. Nothin' we can do. Nothin' anybody can do. Just gotta finish the job."

"Just our job," Big G repeated, trying to believe it.

"That's right."

"Nothing else to do."

"Nothin'."

Big G sighed and glanced at Tapper. "Ready?"

Nodding, Tapper moved to the door, taser

in hand. Big G didn't use a taser, preferring his size and strength in Harvey calls. Besides, Tapper said a taser in Big G's hand was like a warning sign on a hallway riot cannon. Redundant, he called it.

Big G touched his Smoother finger to the cube's door lock. The door slid open, and Tapper dove inside first, Big G shouldering through behind him.

The stench of the room hit him almost as hard as the Harvey. He had just enough time to see Tapper slump to the floor before a naked whirlwind of flesh slammed Big G into the wall beside the door. Something metallic bright, metallic sharp glinted in the hand that flashed up at his throat.

Big G shot out his left arm, blocking the thrust, and drove the heel of his right palm up and hard into the Harvey's nose. He felt the bone give under the blow. The man's head snapped back, long dirty hair flying, and he crumpled to the floor. A foot-long piece of jagged plasteel, which Big G recognized as part of a sleep shelf support, dropped from the man's hand.

Big G hauled Tapper to his feet with one hand and started checking for blood. Tapper slapped his hands away.

"I'm okay. I blocked him with my taser arm," he muttered.

Big G felt relieved. Partners looked out for each other. It wouldn't look good to have your partner go down. Besides, Tapper was his only friend.

"So why'd you...?" Big G frowned, and then started to laugh. "You zapped yourself!"

"He knocked my arm," Tapper said reddening, and Big G laughed harder.

"Shaddup," Tapper said, but he was grinning. He knelt to touch the Harvey's neck as they'd been taught. His grin disappeared. He stood, shaking his head. Pressing a stud on his specs, he spoke, "One unit for recycling, these cords."

Big G turned away, wanting to throw up but not from the smell. He'd used a killing blow by reflex, from training. It had been self-defense, but that didn't make him feel any better.

Tapper spoke finally, low and quiet. "Y'okay?"

"Yeah," Big G replied, just as quietly.

Pause. "Nothing else you could do."

"Yeah." Big G wanted to talk about something else. He looked around the room. "Most Harveys are in drawers," he said, cursing the quaver in his voice.

Tapper nodded. "Some're in cubes, but never this big."

"Even bigger than the ones we get."

Tapper grinned, then spread his arms out to each side and spun around, doing a little dance, oblivious now to the body at his feet. "Yeah. Ain't it great? All this space?"

Big G stared at Tapper as if he'd just gone Harvey himself. "You *like* big cubes?"

"Sure do. Ya don't feel like the walls are closin' in." He shivered, but then grinned. "Hey! Maybe *we'll* get one of these if we do good."

Big G just shook his head. He knew that he wouldn't like an even bigger cube. His walls were already too far away. He continued to survey the room.

To avoid looking at the body, he looked up. Glop covered the ceiling as well, except for a clean circle about a foot across with a small square of color stuck in its center. He reached up and tugged at the square. It came away easily, leaving behind a dab of dried glop.

The square was a pictab, a piece of plasper with an image encoded into its surface. Big G blinked, trying to make the image come into focus, to make sense. It seemed to be a mass of white swirls and curls and curves hanging in a blue nothingness. He'd never seen anything like it. It fascinated him.

"What do you think it is?" Big G asked.

Tapper started to shrug, but then his eyes locked on the image. "Dunno. Let's see," he said, reaching for the pictab.

But Big G pulled his hand back to stare at the image again. "Think it had something to do with him going Harvey?"

"It's a flushin' pictab. Toss it in the dis-chute, and let's get out of this stink before I puke," Tapper snapped.

But Big G continued to study the image, struggling to make sense of it. Tapper sighed. "Okay, tell you what. Give it to me, and I'll check with Archives to see if they know what it is." He held out his hand to take it.

Big G hesitated, reluctant to part with the strange vision. "You'll give it back after?"

"Yeah, sure." Tapper plucked the square from Big G's fingers and slipped it inside his reds. Big G watched it disappear. "Now let's go," Tapper said, stepping out the door.

Big G looked down at the body, then around the cube, and finally up at the ceiling. "Wonder why he put it up there?"

Tapper didn't answer. Tapper was gone.

STILL IN HER CUBE, Laryn cut her illegal link to Central. Nothing more to discover there. The situation was controlled—the Smoother team had killed her recruit. After sending a coded update to her cell members, she sat back, biting her lip, this time aware of the habit from the pain it caused.

She'd found no trace of interest in her direction, but how long would it take them to see a pattern? To find a connection?

To find her?

She needed to scrub the Harvey's file of any links to her or the Movement. But her spec display was counting down to her work shift. The scrub would have to wait.

THAT SLEEP TIME, Big G didn't dream of falling. Instead, he floated in white swirls and curls and curves hanging in a blue nothingness. The image in the pictab. No straight, sharp, hard lines of floors meeting walls meeting ceilings running on and on and on forever. He felt scared but also excited.

His first call next wake time was a flow break. An easy shift. A sector had lost east-west flow, and he and Tapper had to lead stranded travelers along dim Smoother corridors to the next hall. When he saw Tapper, Big G asked about the pictab.

Tapper looked away as they walked. "Archives had nothin'."

Big G waited for more, but Tapper just kept walking, staring ahead, grumbling about how small the corridors were.

"So where is it?" Big G asked finally.

"Where's what?" Tapper asked.

"The pictab! You said you'd bring it back. It's mine."

Tapper glanced up at Big G, but then quickly looked away again. "They kept it. Gonna add it to the Harvey's file."

Big G stopped walking, and somebody bumped into him. He turned and glared, and the line of faces behind him, Crats mostly, cowered back. He started walking again.

"It's mine," he repeated.

Tapper swallowed and kept glancing up at him, but Big G ignored him. He was thinking of what Tapper had said, about the Harvey having a file.

THINGS WERE NOT GOING WELL for Laryn. She'd drawn a double shift, delaying her scrub of the Harvey's file. Now back in her cube, she sat at her secure link and called up the file. Her breath caught as the status flag flashed on her specs.

Someone else was accessing the same file.

Forcing calm on herself, she quickly spoke the command to start the scrub, praying that she wasn't too late.

OFF-SHIFT, BIG G sat in his cube searching the Harvey's file on his specs. New to being a Smoother and the power it brought, he'd expected an "access denied" message. But after a delay of a heartbeat, the data began to scroll down his lens.

The Harvey had been a mid-level Crat, with a clean work record, no flags anywhere on his file. Big G kept scanning, not even sure what he was looking for.

Until he found it: a repeat visitor, irregular but at least once per seven-shift for the past cycle. A woman. Conjugal visits? But the Recycling autopsy showed that he'd been taking his No-aggra, so it hadn't been sex. Work relationship maybe.

He spoke the command to link the woman's ID to her file. The screen flashed "Link Error." He scrolled back through the Harvey's file to pick up the ID code and enter it directly. No luck. He did a search command then scrolled from beginning to end and back again before he accepted what had happened.

All evidence of the woman's visits had disappeared.

Big G never thought he might have imagined it—he didn't credit himself with having imagination. Shrugging mentally, he spoke the cords of the woman's cube that he'd seen on the file: Sector E8-S8, Block D13-W25-S30, Cube U6-N2-W23/24. Few people could have recalled one of the cords, let alone all eight, but Big G had worked in Flow for fifteen years before Smoothing. Both jobs meant memorizing cords several times a shift.

Storing the cords, he scheduled a visit to the woman for his next shift. An official visit as a Smoother investigating a Harvey, he thought. But then an image of white on blue swirled behind his eyes, and he knew he was lying to himself.

LARYN SIGHED IN RELIEF as the scrub completed. But her respite was short-lived. The incom light flashed on her specs. She swore as she read the message. A Smoother was requesting a meeting. An unknown Smoother, not the one she expected.

She cross-linked the Smoother's ID to the recent Harvey call. And got a match. No coincidence then.

Fighting down the panic that tried to rise in her, she sat back, frowning. If her fellow Inners had discovered her role in the Movement, they'd move immediately with no warning. But this Smoother was simply requesting a meeting, a full shift away. No sign of urgency. So there was no need for any rash action by her. No need for what had first flashed through her mind.

To run.

In a way, she felt disappointed. For a heartbeat, her fear of capture had overwhelmed another, much older fear.

A fear of the only place to which she *could* run. A place of legends, legends from childhood and childhood's nightmares.

Laryn sighed. No need for escape yet. Or to wonder how she would lead the people to a place she still feared herself.

BEFORE HIS VISIT, Big G tried to discover more about the woman. To no avail. The system refused to provide any details concerning the occupant of the cords that he'd memorized.

What the cords themselves told him did not sink in until the time for his visit arrived. Standing on his flow disk, he called them up on his specs. And froze. He stepped off his disk and sat heavily on his sleep shelf.

The woman's cube was U6-N2-W23/24. He stared at the last portion. W23/24. Not just W23 or W24. She had a double cube.

She was an Inner.

Big G sat thinking, already over the shock. Things didn't throw him for long—one of the reasons he'd been picked as a Smoother. "If you met a two-headed citizen," Tapper had once said, "first thing you'd do is check if both heads had a chip."

This explained why he had found nothing on her. He ran a big hand over the smooth skin of his head. He probably should cancel. An Inner's business with a Harvey was none of his.

No. He'd better make the call, if only to explain his mistake. He stepped onto his disk and spoke the "Go" command.

LARYN SAT WATCHING the big Smoother as he *apologized* rather than accused. He spoke in short nervous sentences, looking around her cube, not meeting her gaze. He'd have been amazed to know how much she'd learned of him since he first contacted her.

She'd run her trojan that profiled possible recruits against Big G, and found him suitable for the movement—not as a leader, but as a follower. He fell below the desired level of intelligence. But he was fiercely loyal to a cause that tied to his belief system—a key trait for the Movement.

Some of his indicators were ambiguous, especially those reflecting his views on personal freedom versus authority. Still, she could only believe that anyone, once they knew the truth of the House, would rank the right to freedom for billions above maintaining the status quo.

Her last concerns gone, her mind focused on the man. He wanted something and was about to tell her what it was. There was opportunity here. She smiled at him. He seemed to like that. She smiled again. Yes, definitely opportunity.

Big G wanted to be anywhere but sitting in front of this beautiful woman in her far too large cube as she played with her long dark hair and smiled at him. Any Inner he'd ever met had been stern and frightening. To his surprise, she had told him to call her by her name, Laryn. She wasn't even wearing her Inner golds, just off-shift stripes like a normal citizen. Her golds hung by the door like any other garment, and somehow the casualness of their display made him even more nervous.

But as he explained his visit, he realized that he'd come here not to apologize, but to learn. Knowing then that all his discomfort would be for nothing unless he found the courage to ask his question, he stumbled on.

"...since you knew this Harvey, I mean, this man ... that is ... see, I found this thing in his room—" Big G stopped.

Laryn had straightened slightly, her smile freezing like a seized servo-lock. "What kind of thing?" she asked.

He swallowed. "A pictab. It was ... it..." He struggled to describe what still haunted him every time he closed his eyes.

But before he could find words, she produced a pictab from somewhere he didn't catch and placed it on the small table between them. "Was it like this?"

He stared down at the image, different but the same. More blue in this one, but still the swirls of white, still the feeling of floating in something, the absence of the straight hard lines of the House. He swallowed. "Yes," he whispered.

"What do you see?" she asked.

"I don't know. Something blue covered by something white. Or the other way around."

She smiled at him. Big G felt his face burning. He'd made her smile. He wanted to do that again.

"White on blue," she said.

Big G nodded, praying she'd say more. She seemed to be studying him, judging whether he was worthy of a great secret. For he was sure the pictab involved a great secret.

Finally she spoke. "Enough for now. But I'd like to meet with you again, here in my cube. Every off-shift for the next two cycles. To *prepare* you to receive the answer you seek."

Big G swallowed. That meant committing his free time for over fifty off-shifts. But he nodded his agreement.

"You will make no further inquiries into the Harvey that you killed..." She paused as he flinched, then continued, "or regarding this." Here she pointed at the pictab. "You will do nothing out of the ordinary, nothing to attract attention to yourself. Is that understood?"

He nodded again. And their first fateful meeting ended.

Over the following cycles, Big G complied with Laryn's instructions to the letter, driven to learn the pictab's secret. But soon his compliance owed itself as much to another reason.

As a Smoother, he could request a conjugal partner any off-shift. But this was different. No woman had ever initiated sex with him or made him feel desired. Her interest in him excited him as much as her body. He thought of her even while on-shift. And off-shift, instead of watching a *realee* on his specs, he'd lay there thinking of her, waiting for their next time together.

Strange and new to him, his feelings for her confused him.

But not as much as the true history of the House confused him, as Laryn slowly taught him during their sessions together.

"It was the greatest undertaking in history," Laryn began his first lesson. "To build a safe haven for billions from an environment that had finally lost the war we'd waged on it for centuries. An environment of deadly toxins, depleted ozone, and mutating retroviruses spread by multiplying parasites."

The House began, Laryn said, as a "military" "project" by the "government" of the "country" that first conceived the idea.

Big G struggled with these strange concepts, especially with people *choosing* their leaders. Laryn said that, before the House, the people used to have freedom to make most decisions in their lives—their jobs, where to live, what to eat, how to dress, how to spend their time. Big G didn't see how such a world could even function. It seemed so disordered.

In a later session, Laryn explained how the environment's death led also to the death of something called the "economy."

"Industries failed. International money markets and trade collapsed. Free market capitalism fell," she said. "Relations between nations died as each fought its own internal battles."

Laryn spent several sessions explaining these ideas. Big G pretended to understand, but all he could really grasp was that more and more people had come to work on the House project, even from other "countries," as their old jobs disappeared.

"The House paid only in shelter, food and protection," Laryn explained, "but these people had no other options."

What else, Big G thought later, would you want?

"When industries necessary for the House failed—food, high tech, steel—the government took them over, absorbing those workers too, until they controlled all sources of production for the House. The government itself shrank, lopping off branches no longer needed or not essential to the project."

Laryn had paused then, sighing. "And so, a once great country reduced itself to one single purpose: build the House."

Something new was puzzling Big G. In recent sessions, as the strange, disturbing world Laryn had first described grew closer to the one he knew, he had become more excited. Here was the true story of the Builders! Yet Laryn seemed more concerned, even *sad*, over the strangeness that had been lost.

But he forgot about it as he learned more each session.

"Hundreds of millions of people now worked on the House," Laryn explained, "all under a strict project hierarchy, each with a specific role on sub-teams under teams under team leaders under project managers, all reporting up to a small program committee that was the remnant of the once-elected government."

Big G nodded. The words were strange, but it sounded very much like the House today. Tidy, orderly, efficient. Laryn's next comment echoed that thought.

"We had *become* the House," she said.

Again, he sensed her sadness.

"Elections were postponed so as not to disrupt progress. Dissent was minimal—the need to complete the House was too great." She stared at him intently. "Can you guess what happened next? What *had* to happen?"

Big G's heart jumped. Was *this* his test? If he failed, would the secret of the pictab be lost to him? To his relief, Laryn answered herself.

"All talk of elections, of democracy, gradually died away. The very project structure that had given a small group the power to direct millions of people to *build* the House was used by that same group to *keep* that power. To *rule* those millions."

Laryn paused. "Billions now," she whispered, her eyes no longer on him, unfocused, seeing something he could not. Then she seemed to come to herself and fixed him with a stare. "Do you know *who* that small group was? Who they are *still*?"

Big G swallowed. "The Inners?" he said. Laryn nodded, and he relaxed.

"Should a few have the right to direct the lives of billions?" she asked quietly, her eyes not leaving him.

Big G squirmed his bulk on his seat. To even ask that question seemed ... wrong. But Laryn was an Inner. Surely the Inners were allowed to question themselves. Perhaps that was how the House stayed strong. Still he struggled for an answer.

"*The House protects the People*—" he began to recite.

Laryn sighed. "*And the Inners protect the House. Yes, yes. But what if the world has changed*? From when the House was first built? Wouldn't the House need to change too?"

What did she mean? The House *was* the world. Big G wished this lesson were over. "How would it change?" he asked.

She leaned forward, taking one of his large hands in both of hers. "To a world where people are free again."

The world before the House that she had told him of, he thought. That strange world of chaos and disorder.

Then the pictab flashed in his mind, with its random white and blue soft swirls, its own chaos and disorder contrasting with the clean predictable lines of the House.

For the first time, Big G felt a twinge of fear of the secret he chased.

THE END OF THE TWO CYCLES of teaching Big G was nearing, and Laryn was crying.

She cried a lot lately. At first, she had cried because she was using him. But she'd used others in the past and had used sex as a means before. So why did it bother her this time?

Part of it was Big G himself. To her surprise, she'd grown to care for him over their time together. He was a clumsy lover but gentle, simple but honest, with none of the cynicism of the others in the Movement. Trusting and malleable, he was a child, believing what he was told, believing the lies the Inners fed him, just as *she* had believed as a child.

He *was* the people, embodying all that humanity had become.

But soon, he would be ready for the great truth. And that was why she cried. When she told him, that child in him would die, and with it, the last remnant of the child *she* had once been. But it was too late. Whatever he felt for her—and she was still unsure if he felt more than lust—she knew the blue and white vision still burned in him. He would not stop until he found the secret. She had seen this before.

Better, she thought, *to have him with us when he finds out.*

THE NEXT SESSION, Big G arrived at Laryn's cube to find her dressed in her Inner golds.

"It's time," she said, once they were safely inside.

Big G's heart jumped. "You're going to tell me the secret?" he asked, his voice barely a whisper.

"Better than that. I'm going to take you to it," she said.

He opened his mouth but then just nodded, afraid to say the wrong thing and prove himself unworthy after all.

"First," Laryn said, "we must ensure that our movements don't attract attention." She handed him a pair of specs. "Put these on. They block the signal in your ID chip, replacing it with one that says you're still right here in my cube. You won't be able to be tracked, and you won't trip any cameras."

After a moment's hesitation, he took the specs from her. It bothered him to glimpse a system inside a system, one designed to hide. Who did Laryn fear? Surely not the Inners? Laryn was an Inner. But then who?

Laryn knelt and popped the cover off his disk. "I must also program your disk, so that it leaves no record of this trip. Notice anything unusual about these cords?" she asked.

Peeking over her shoulder, he watched her punch coordinates directly into his disk. "Only that I've never been that high."

"Right first time," she said. She smiled at him, and his face grew hot. "In fact, you can't go higher. Not in the House." She stood, wiping her hands on her golds as if they were just the whites of a Tech. Motioning him onto his disk, she stepped on hers and spoke the "go" command. The door to Laryn's cube slid open, and their disks slipped into the Flow.

Their route confused Big G. It looped and crossed itself and even dropped levels. But always it rose again, higher each time. They rode in silence, Laryn in front, an Inner with a Smoother escort. As they rode, Big G struggled to make sense of what she had said: *You can't go any higher. Not in the House.* That seemed to mean that you could go higher if...

He stopped that thought, shying back from it, from an idea so impossible, so forbidden that it froze him with fear. If...

...if you went *outside* the House. But the Outside was poisoned. No one could live Outside. That's why the Builders made the House. The Inners said so. But Laryn was an Inner...

He had no more time to ponder. They reached the upper level of the cords and began moving along an empty EW corridor. He checked NS halls at every intersection, but never saw another person. He realized then that he heard only the sound of their own disks. The normal background buzz of the Flow was missing.

As if reading his mind, she spoke. "This level is accessible only to Inners. No one lives or works here."

But as they neared the cords, Big G saw a thin, red-clad figure leaning on a wall. A block away, he knew who it was.

"Pull up that chin of yours 'fore ya trip over it," Tapper said as they stopped in front of him. He grinned but kept kicking the floor with a toe. He did that when he was nervous.

Big G looked at Laryn. She nodded. "Tapper's been with us for some time now. That's why it will be so wonderful to have you join us. We'd have a complete Smoother team."

Big G turned to Tapper. "You kept my pictab."

Tapper jerked his head in Laryn's direction. "Orders."

"Sorry," she said. "We don't want that in circulation. Now, are you ready?"

Big G was still trying to understand Tapper being here, and what Laryn meant about "joining" and "a complete Smoother team." He and Tapper *were* a team. But he said nothing and just nodded.

Tapper turned to the wall and touched his Smoother finger to what must have been a hidden security spot. A door slid open to reveal a small closet-sized space with a series of metal rungs attached to the facing wall.

Laryn stepped forward, grabbed a rung, and began to climb. "Let's go," she called. Tapper clambered up behind her.

Big G followed, barely able to squeeze his way up the narrow chute, but finding the closeness comforting after the strange emptiness of the corridors below. He'd never seen that much open space before, and it had frightened him.

His comfort didn't last. The rungs ended near the top of the chute, which was just a square hole cut in the floor above. Tapper scrambled out. Big G grabbed the side of the opening and hauled his bulk over the edge onto the floor.

And gasped.

There were no walls. Slender columns marched in east-west and north-south processions into the dimness of distance, supporting a ceiling covered in crisscrossing jumbles of pipes, ducts, and glow tubes—a ceiling that hung far too high above.

Tapper was jumping up and down, skipping and laughing. "Isn't this great?" he cried. "Lookit all this space. No walls. Nothin' to close you in."

Big G was well aware of the lack of walls. He was still lying on the floor, afraid to get up, ashamed of being afraid, especially in front of Laryn. Groaning, he crawled to the nearest pillar and wrapped an arm around it, clutching its closeness to him as he clamped his eyes shut against the space.

"Big G," Laryn said softly, her voice close to his ear.

He forced his eyes open. Laryn knelt beside him. She was biting her lip. He knew she did that when she was nervous, like Tapper kicking the floor.

"We're almost there," she said, pointing to a pillar with another set of rungs leading up to what appeared to be a trap door in the ceiling, almost hidden by ducts and cables.

"Is it … like this?" he gasped.

She bit her lip again. "It's what you saw in the pictab." She knelt beside him. "It's the secret I promised."

Her closeness helped him push the terror of the open space from his mind. Locking his eyes on the nearness of the floor, he stood on shaking legs and let her lead him to the ladder.

The climb seemed endless. Finally, he bumped into Tapper's feet. Above, he heard a screech of metal grating on metal. He hung there, eyes shut, surrounded by more emptiness than he had ever known, gripping a rung, hugging the pillar, until he heard the thud of something heavy falling on the ceiling overhead.

At first, he thought that they'd opened the cube of some gigantic Harvey. A roar, as from a great mouth, erupted above. The air came alive. It clawed at him with cold fingers. It choked him with strange smells, thin and sharp and cutting, none of the thick muskiness of the House. The shock snapped his eyes open, then his fear of the space around him overcame his fear of what lay above, propelling him up and through the opening…

And into a light brighter than any he'd ever seen. Eyes scrunched tight again, he crawled from the hole to fall panting on his back. Finally, his eyes adjusted, and he opened them.

He lay under a great bowl of blue in which billows of white swirled above him. The image from the pictab. But the white shapes in the pictab hadn't been alive, hadn't writhed like mouths ready to devour him. The air tore at him as if it had claws and wished to pluck him from the House and feed him to the mouths above. The blueness and its twisting white monsters surrounded him in all directions, dropping finally to meet the distant edges of this strange highest floor of the House, a floor that curved down to disappear at those edges as if they now sat on some impossibly huge ball.

"It's called the sky, and those are clouds," Laryn said, but her voice seemed stripped of its usual power. Up here, it was a tiny thing, swallowed by the vastness engulfing them. She named other things—wind, roof, horizon. "And that is the sun."

He looked to where she pointed. A cloud, chasing others across the blue, glowed as with some hidden light. The glow grew along one edge, and then a ball of indescribable brightness burst forth, burning his eyes with light and his skin with heat.

He cried out like a child and hid his face from the thing. Blinded, panicking, he flailed about for the trap door as the wind kept clawing at him. Grabbing an edge, he hauled himself head-first through the opening, catching the ladder at the last moment. He half-climbed, half-fell, first to the floor below, then down the other ladder to collapse on the empty House floor with its familiar halls, the comforting solidity of a wall at his back and a ceiling above him that didn't move as if alive.

After a time, he felt a touch on his arm. Laryn sat down beside him. "*That* is what the Inners hide from the people," she said. "The old legends of the Outside may have been true once, but no more. There's a *world* out there again—with air we can breathe and water we can drink—a world to which we can finally return. We're not ready yet, but we will be."

She talked on. Big G listened but didn't hear, unable to grasp what he'd seen. Despite all of her teaching, he had never believed until now that there *was* an Outside. The only world he knew was here, in the House. He lay drinking in the comforting closeness of the dimly lit ceiling, tracing where it met each wall in clean, straight, hard lines, feeling his breathing slow, trying to forget what he'd seen, just happy to be home.

Being back in the House was having a different effect on Tapper. The smaller man sat huddled on the floor, shivering, his eyes darting around the corridor. He mumbled something.

"What?" Big G said, grabbing at something else to focus on.

"Get up, Tapper," Laryn said, rising herself.

Tapper got up, but he just stood there hugging himself, shoulders hunched, head tucked down as if the ceiling was too low and he didn't want to bump his head. "Small," he whispered.

"Let's go," Laryn snapped, stepping onto her disk.

"What's wrong, Tap?" Big G asked, putting a hand on Tapper.

Tapper shivered again. "Too small. In here. Too small." Tapper turned to him. Something familiar but out of place peeked from behind Tapper's eyes. Big G had seen that look before, but he couldn't remember where. Head lowered, Tapper stepped on his disk and moved down the corridor after Laryn.

Big G looked around. It didn't feel too small to him. The walls, the ceiling—especially the ceiling—all felt wonderfully close.

LARYN KNEW that it hadn't gone well, that she'd pushed Big G too fast. He'd barely slept since the trip to the roof four shifts ago. He lay beside her each sleep time, staring up at the ceiling. He said whenever he closed his eyes, *it* was always there—the *sky*, writhing like a thing alive.

And she worried about Tapper, who was showing much different signs. Different but familiar.

Big G left her to start his shift. Just then, her trojans warned her of activity concerning one of her people.

The news was bad. Very bad.

Feeling ill, she stopped the display, wishing she could stop what would happen next as easily. And she found, to her surprise, that it was for him that she was afraid, not herself.

What had she done to his world?

TO START HIS NEXT ON-SHIFT, Big G was ordered to another Harvey call. He rode the Flow, his thoughts still on the sky, aware of, yet oblivious to, the call's familiar cords. Until he arrived. Until he saw another Smoother team outside Tapper's cube, saw the black-garbed Recyclers carrying out his body.

A gold-clad Inner, a small man with eyes as cold as scan cams, turned and locked those eyes on him. The Inner mouthed a command, and Big G knew that he was scanning Big G's ID chip. The man walked over, looking up but making Big G feel like he was looking down on him.

"Your partner's dead," the man said.

Big G blinked, still trying to make sense of the scene, aware of the Inner's eyes on him. "How?" he asked, ashamed at how normal his first words were. As if this was no big deal. As if you lost your best friend every shift.

The Inner shrugged. "He went Harvey. Notice any unusual behavior recently?" he asked, burning Big G with those eyes.

Big G remembered Tapper huddled inside on the floor after seeing the sky. Guilt swept over him. He'd known something was wrong. Now he recognized the look he'd seen in Tapper's eyes. He should have understood. He should have been able to stop this. He should have done something. Instead, he'd done...

"Nothing," he whispered.

Taking that as an answer, the Inner

nodded. But those eyes still burned into him. Big G just stood there, more in grief over Tapper than in fear of the Inner, a small voice whispering to him that right now grief was good, that safety lay in grief.

The Inner reached into his golds and withdrew a pictab. "Do you know what this is?" the man asked.

Big G knew what it would be before he looked down at the blue and white swirls. He took the pictab, because he knew he should, even though he wanted nothing more to do with it. He turned it over, and on the back was the remnant of dried glop. He handed it back.

"We found it in a Harvey's cube. Tapper took it."

"But do you know what it is?" the Inner repeated.

Big G looked at the Inner. "No, sir," he said, and that was true. He really didn't know what the thing called *sky* was.

The Inner stared at him, but Big G felt no fear, only an emptiness, as he thought of doing his next shift without Tapper.

"You can return to your shift now, Smoother," the Inner said finally. "You've been assigned a new partner."

Big G asked who it was, but the Inner just shrugged, so Big G stored the cords for his next call and left.

That night, he dreamed again of falling. Not down a drop tube, not as a Builder falling from the still-being-born House, but of falling through a swirling blue and white void that went on and on. He fell and fell, a blue-white, white-blue mist hiding what he fell towards. And then he knew, in the way one knows in dreams, that the House was gone as Laryn had planned, that he was falling towards nothing, that the blue-white, white-blue was all there was, and he would fall through it forever.

He woke up screaming.

When his next shift started, he turned Laryn in.

LARYN WAITED FOR HIM in her cube, waited well past the end of his shift, well into his sleep time when he should have been there with her. She knew then, as she lay awake staring at the ceiling so close above her in the dark. She knew it was over.

She rose, blinking as the lights came up. Taking a pictab of blue and white swirls from its hidden place, she inserted it in a device and spoke the words she wished written on its back.

"I forgive you. Remember me. Remember the sky." She paused, then added, "I love you." Placing the pictab in a mail pellet, she coded a destination and dropped it in her out-chute.

They were outside her cube now. She activated her illegal security measures, knowing that it would only slow them down.

She wondered if he was with them.

WHEN BIG G had scanned on-shift that wake time, the call was on the board at Dispatch, a red "X" beside her name. A kill mark. And his name assigned to it, his name beside hers.

But Squat was on Dispatch, so Big G had asked him to give it to another Smoother. If it'd been Marker, he wouldn't have asked. Marker would've made him do it, made him be the one.

Squat had stared at him, and Big G had wondered if his name being there wasn't a random thing, if the Inners wanted him to do it. But then Squat had nodded. Said he was sorry about Tapper. Told Big G to scan off-shift and cube down.

So that's what he'd done. Back to his cube, to walls and floor and ceiling that had once been hard and strong and sure, but now seemed so fragile, ready to be blown away by a thought.

Or by a vision.

A vision on a pictab that appeared in the tray of his in-chute. A vision of white swirls and curls and curves hung in a blue nothingness. No straight, sharp, hard lines of floors meeting walls meeting ceilings running on and on and on.

Big G took the pictab from the tray and

held it in his large hands. He read her message on the back. He stared at it for several labored breaths and then, with great and careful precision, he tore it slowly in half. Covering the face of one half with that of the other so that the image was hidden, he again tore the pieces in two. One final time he tore them.

He did not even need to move to reach the dis-chute. So efficient a design, he thought, so practical and proper. He opened the chute door gently, as if removing a garment of a lover. Letting the fragments slip from his hand into the blackness, he held the chute open for a moment, listening for the small "poof" that the pieces made as they vaporized.

He closed the chute again and for a time just stood there, running his hand over the wall, stroking it, taking comfort in its coldness, its solidity. He turned finally to his tiny sleep shelf. Lying on his back, he pressed the top of his head against the wall above his pillow, then stretched out his legs until his feet touched the opposite wall. He placed his left hand on the third wall to which the bed attached.

The humming of the block, of the entire House, sang through the skin of his hand, up his arm, into his chest. It filled his skull and echoed in his mind. This was as it should be. Here lay solace from the void, from unending blue emptiness.

He closed his eyes, and for a moment, the thing called sky hung above him once more, impossibly distant, untouchable.

Shuddering, he opened his eyes to the closeness of the ceiling before him and slowly, slowly reached out a trembling right hand to feel for the last wall.

"Going Harvey in the Big House" was a 2005 finalist for Canada's prestigious Aurora Award for best speculative fiction short story.

Douglas Smith is an award-winning Canadian author described by Library Journal as "one of Canada's most original writers of speculative fiction." His fiction has been published in twenty-six languages and thirty-two countries. His work includes the urban fantasy novel, The Wolf at the End of the World, and the collections Chimerascope, Impossibilia, and La Danse des Esprits. His non-fiction guide for writers, Playing the Short Game: How to Market & Sell Short Fiction, is a must read for any short story writer.

Doug is a three-time winner of Canada's Aurora Award, and has been a finalist for the John W. Campbell Award, CBC's Bookies Award, Canada's juried Sunburst Award, and France's juried Prix Masterton and Prix Bob Morane. A short film based on Doug's story "By Her Hand, She Draws You Down" won several awards at film festivals around the world.

Spiritual
BOOT
CAMP
for
Creators
& Dreamers

ENCOURAGEMENT, INSPIRATION &
BASIC TRAINING TO HELP YOU ACHIEVE YOUR DREAMS

TOM ENGLISH
★ ★ ★ ★ & ★ ★ ★ ★
WILMA ESPAILLAT ENGLISH

A Ravens' Read!

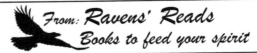

From: Ravens' Reads
Books to feed your spirit

In the time of the Pharaohs, an Egyptian *femme fatale* was tried for perverse crimes against her people. She was sentenced to be buried alive in a specially sealed tomb, hidden beneath the desert floor. She has slept undisturbed for thousands of years beneath an ocean of sun-parched sand—waiting to be freed; waiting for three American archaeologists who will ignore the inscription above the portal of her tomb:

WHOSO COMETH,
NOW OR HEREAFTER,
WAKE NOT THE SOUL THAT
SLEEPS WITHIN.

C. Bryson Taylor's "lost" 1904 novel featuring a vampiric female mummy!

IN THE *DWELLINGS* OF THE *WILDERNESS*

C. BRYSON TAYLOR

From the novel: *"He must have wanted to sleep sound, whoever he was,"* Holloway observed with flippancy. *"...If the old man's still here, I'd like to collect him before it gets too dark."*

Soon a force of men was at work, a swarm of ants prying around the edges of the walled-up door, where, above, the ancient message gave its warning. From this inscription Deane found himself unaccountably unable to keep his eyes. He and Holloway discussed it in low tones, to the accompaniment of the thud of falling pick and spade. Holloway wavered between the seductive idea of bur-ied treasure, whose owner had perhaps sought to guard it with a theatrical warning, and the bejewelled mummy of the king he wished to collect. Deane hoped there would be tablets to decipher; Merritt said nothing. When Holloway questioned, wishing his theories on the subject, Merritt answered short-ly: "I'm not expecting anything.... It's the unexpected that turns up and floors you, no matter what you think you'll get."

Trade edition: $7.00   ISBN-13: 978-097963359

DEAD LETTER PRESS
WWW.DEADLETTERPRESS.COM

Script & pencils: Jack Kirby ◆ Inks: Al Williamson
Harvey Comics: Race to the Moon #3, November 1958

SHE READS MINDS, BOYS! PICKED THE LANGUAGE OUT OF MY THOUGHTS IN NOTHING FLAT!

I ALSO KNOW THAT THE CAPTAIN FEARS ME-- FEARS THIS PLACE!

BUT THERE IS NOTHING HERE TO HARM YOU! YOU ARE THE FIRST LIVING CREATURES TO EVER COME FROM THE GREAT DARKNESS. I WANT YOU TO STAY--THERE IS SO MUCH TO TALK ABOUT!

YOUR EVERY COMFORT HAS BEEN ARRANGED FOR! I'M SURE YOU SHALL BE HAPPY HERE!

CAPTAIN! WHAT A LAYOUT!

THERE WERE SOFT CHAIRS, GOOD FOOD, LUXURIOUS SURROUNDINGS--EVERYTHING OUR LITTLE HEARTS DESIRED. YOU CAN'T IMAGINE HOW GREAT IT FELT AFTER BEING CONFINED IN A ROCKET FOR MONTHS IN SPACE!

BOY! THIS SURE IS THE LIFE!

THIS IS DELICIOUS! BEST I'VE EVER TASTED!

WE ATE AND WE RESTED AND SWAM IN A POOL WHOSE CRYSTAL WATERS SHIMMERED IN THE PLEASING RAYS OF THE PLANET'S SUN.

COME ON IN, CAPTAIN JAMES! THE WATER'S FINE!

YOU ENJOY YOURSELF, KIP! I'LL JUST WATCH!

THE CAPTAIN WAS WATCHING ALL RIGHT! HE WAS LIKE A MAN CONSTANTLY ON GUARD--WAITING FOR SOMETHING TO MATERIALIZE--ALTHOUGH, FOR THE LIFE OF ME, I COULDN'T SEE WHAT! THIS PLACE WAS PERFECT--AN ENTIRE PLANET LIKE A GARDEN OF EDEN. THEN ONE DAY...

VACATION IS OVER, BOYS! GET YOUR GEAR! WE'RE SHOVING OFF!

WHAT?

GOSH, CAPTAIN! YOU KNOW THAT SURVEY MEN CAN STAY ON A PLANET UNTIL THE RESEARCH ROCKETS SHOW UP TO TAKE OVER!

YES! WHY THE BIG RUSH, CAPTAIN? THEY'RE NOT DUE FOR TWO MONTHS YET!

THEY'RE NOT COMING! I'M GOING TO WARN THEM --THAT THIS PLACE IS A TRAP!

CAPTAIN, YOU SOUND SPACE-HAPPY! THIS PLACE IS PERFECT!

YOU'VE BEEN HAVING TOO GOOD A TIME TO ASK YOURSELF SOME QUESTIONS, KIP! IT'S TOO LATE FOR THAT NOW! LET'S GO!

SUDDENLY, IT HAPPENED! ANIZAAR SHOWED UP-- BUT NOT AS WE'D EVER SEEN HER!

NO! YOU MUST STAY! ANIZAAR WISHES TO LEARN MORE ABOUT YOUR SPECIES!

ONE QUESTION, FIRST! *WHO IS ANIZAAR?*

THE GROUND SUDDENLY ERUPTED IN FLAME! THEN, THINGS BEGAN TO HAPPEN FAST!

I AM ANIZAAR!

THE GARDEN OF EDEN WAS GONE AND THE VERY LAND ITSELF BECAME AN UGLY, HOSTILE ENEMY THAT TURNED ON US WITH HARMFUL INTENT!!

I AM ANIZAAR!

THE VEGETATION, NO LONGER THINGS OF BEAUTY, LASHED OUT AT US LIKE ANGRY BRUTES!

CAPTAIN! WHAT IS ALL THIS? THE WHOLE PLANET SEEMS TO HAVE GONE HAYWIRE!

IT IS THE PLANET! DON'T YOU SEE? IT'S BEEN THE PLANET ALL ALONG!

THE GROUND SEEMED TO RECOIL LIKE A LIVING THING AS THE CAPTAIN BLASTED HIMSELF LOOSE FROM AN AREA THAT SOFTENED UNDER HIM AND ALMOST DREW HIM IN!

I DON'T GET YOU, CAPTAIN! HEY! IT'S RAINING COTTON-BALLS!

GAS-SPHERES WOULD HAVE BEEN A BETTER NAME FOR THEM! THEY RELEASED AN ETHER-LIKE VAPOR WHEN THEY EXPLODED! WE JUST ABOUT STAGGERED THROUGH ON OUR FEET IN THAT DANGEROUS HAIL!

I WAS THE FIRST TO REACH THE SHIP--AND I DIDN'T REALLY THINK I'D MAKE IT!

INSIDE, QUICK! IF WE CAN BLAST OFF BEFORE THE PLANET DECIDES TO WRECK THE SHIP--

THE CAPTAIN'S MEANING BEGAN TO DAWN ON ME WHEN WE WERE ALL INSIDE AND READY TO LEAP FOR THE SKY!

CAPTAIN, DO YOU MEAN THAT THE PLANET ITSELF IS ATTACKING US?

EXACTLY!

WE WERE HARDLY OFF THE SURFACE WHEN AN IMMENSE WALL OF WATER SWEPT TOWARD US!

ANIZAAR IS A LIVING, INTELLIGENT ORGANISM OF PLANETARY SIZE! THE GIRL WAS JUST AN ILLUSION!

HE MOLDED HER FROM HIS OWN ATOMIC STRUCTURE IN ORDER TO COMMUNICATE WITH US! HE TURNED HIS ENTIRE PLANETARY SURFACE INTO A GARDEN OF EDEN TO KEEP US CONTENT!

AND WHEN WE DECIDED TO TAKE OFF HE GREW ANGRY AND SHOWED US HIS TRUE SELF!

THE WHOLE SETUP MADE ME SUSPICIOUS! IT WAS TOO PERFECT-- AS IF NATURE ITSELF WAS TRYING TO PLEASE US! AND THAT ISN'T NATURE'S WAY!

IMAGINE! A PLANET THAT'S ACTUALLY ALIVE! WHAT A DISCOVERY, CAPTAIN!

IMAGINE HOW ANIZAAR FELT WHEN WE ARRIVED! MICROBES THAT FLEW ABOUT IN SPACE SHIPS!-- HE WANTED TO STUDY US-- FIND OUT EVERYTHING ABOUT US! I COULDN'T LET HIM DO THAT!--

--NOT UNTIL WE LEARN MORE ABOUT HIM-- AND HIS POWERS! WHEN THE RESEARCH BOYS HEAR ABOUT THIS, ANIZAAR WILL HAVE MORE COMPANY THAN HE CAN HANDLE!

In 1966 Kirby returned to his idea of a deadly **living planet**, when he created the Marvel Comics character **Ego**, recently featured in *Guardians of the Galaxy Vol. 2.*

THE END